The Winner Takes It All

MELISSA McCLONE

ALISON ROBERTS

MARIE DONOVAN

MILLS & BOON

First Published in Great Britain 2018
by Mills & Boon, an imprint of HarperCollins*Publishers*
1 London Bridge Street, London, SE1 9GF

THE WINNER TAKES IT ALL © 2018 Harlequin Books S. A.

Winning Back His Wife © 2013 Melissa Martinez McClone
In Her Rival's Arms © 2014 Alison Roberts
Royally Seduced © 2011 Marie Donovan

ISBN: 978-0-263-26800-3

05-0618

MIX
Paper from
responsible sources
FSC™ C007454

This book is produced from independently certified FSC™ paper to ensure responsible forest management.

For more information visit: www.harpercollins.co.uk/green

Printed and bound in Spain
by CPI, Barcelona

WINNING BACK HIS WIFE

MELISSA McCLONE

For Elizabeth Brooks

Special thanks to: Dave Tucker, John Scurlock,
Terri Reed and Jennifer Shirk.

CHAPTER ONE

DR. CULLEN GRAY trudged through the Wy'East Day Lodge, his sore feet entombed in climbing boots he couldn't wait to remove. His muscles ached after two grueling days on Mount Hood. But whatever he'd been through was worth it.

A climber had been rescued.

That trumped a night spent in a warm, comfy bed, a hot shower in the morning and a homemade breakfast complete with scrambled eggs, chicken-apple sausage and buttermilk pancakes with huckleberry syrup.

The smell of coffee wafted in the air, the aroma tickling Cullen's cold nose and teasing his hungry, grumbling stomach. A jolt of caffeine would keep him going long enough to survive the rescue debriefing and the short drive home to Hood Hamlet.

Twenty feet in front of him, members of Oregon Mountain Search and Rescue, OMSAR, sat at a long cafeteria table with coffee cups in front of them. Backpacks, helmets and jackets were scattered on the floor.

Almost there.

Cullen was looking forward to taking off his backpack and sitting, if only for the length of the debriefing.

He passed a group of teenagers, students at the Hood Hamlet Snowboarding Academy, who laughed while they took a break from riding. A little girl, around six years old and dressed in pink from her helmet to her ski boots, wobbled away from the hot-chocolate machine holding a cup with both hands.

A few hours ago, a life had hung in the balance, cocooned

inside a rescue litter attached by cables to a hovering helicopter. But down here, lower on the mountain, everything had continued as usual, as if what run to take on the slopes was the most important decision of the day. He much preferred being up there, though not because of any element of danger or adrenaline rush. He took only calculated risks to help others and save lives.

Cullen lived simply in the quaint, Alpine-inspired village of Hood Hamlet. Work and the mountain comprised his life. Sometimes it was enough, other times not even close. But days like today reminded him why he did what he did, both as a doctor and as a volunteer mountain rescuer. Satisfaction flowed through his veins.

A successful mission.

It didn't get much better than that. Well, unless the climber hadn't fallen into the Bergschrund crevasse to begin with. But given the distance of the fall, the climber's serious injuries and the technical nature of the rescue, Cullen thought Christmas magic—something Hood Hamlet was famous for—had been in play even though it was May, not December.

Either that or plain old dumb luck.

Cullen preferred thinking Christmas magic had been involved. Luck seemed too…random. He might be a doctor, but living here for almost a year had opened his mind. Not everything could be explained and proven scientifically. Sometimes patients defied their diagnosis and survived with no logical explanation.

As soon as he reached the table, he shrugged off his backpack. Gear rattled inside. Carabiners clinked on the outside. When the straps left his shoulders, relief shot straight to his toes.

The pack thudded against the floor. The sound echoed through the cafeteria and drew a few glances from the skiers, riders and tourists.

Let them look. Complain even. Nothing, not even his tight muscles or tiredness, could ruin this day.

He removed his black parka with the white block letters spelling RESCUE on the sleeve, tucked it under one of the outside straps of his pack, then sat. His feet felt as if they were sighing in delight at not having to support any weight.

"Nice work up there, Doc." Bill Paulson, another volunteer with OMSAR, sat on the opposite side of the table. He passed Cullen a cup of coffee from the extras sitting between them. "What you did in the Bergschrund to save that guy's life…"

Cullen bent over to loosen his boots. He didn't like anyone fussing over what he did, let alone another mountain rescuer. He didn't want the praise. The result—a life saved—was payback enough. "All in a day's work."

"Maybe in the emergency department, but not down inside a crevasse." Paulson raised his cup. "I'm buying the first round at the brewpub tonight."

A beer was in order after this mission. "You're on."

Zoe Hughes, the pretty wife of OMSAR team leader Sean Hughes and an associate member herself, stood behind Cullen. "Want anything?"

Heat from the coffee cup warmed his cold fingers. "This is all I need right now."

"Let me know when you want a refill." Her wide smile reached all the way to her blue eyes. "Rumor has it you were a real hero up there today."

He shifted in his seat. Some considered mountain rescue a reckless pursuit, but nothing could be further from the truth. Rescuer safety was the priority, no matter what the mission. "Just doing my job."

She touched his shoulder. "Sean doesn't think he's a hero, either. But you're all heroes. What you guys do, who you are, is the very definition of the word."

"Damn straight. That's why we always get the girls." Paulson winked. "You're going to be my wingman tonight, Gray. We're going to get so many numbers we'll need more memory for our cell phones."

Paulson, a firefighter with Hood Hamlet Fire and Rescue, had a reputation of being a player. No one would accuse Cullen of being one. He had never expected to be living like a monk, but he had a good reason. One that would end soon enough. Until then...

He stared into his coffee, black and strong, fighting memories and resentment.

Going out and doing anything other than drinking a beer and eating a burger didn't appeal to Cullen in the slightest. The one woman he wanted didn't want him. Time to move on. He understood that. He'd come to terms with it. But he saw no reason to frustrate or tempt himself with something he couldn't have right now. He lifted his cup. "You'll get those phone numbers whether I'm there or not."

"True that," Paulson agreed. "But think of the fun we'll have together. Just so you know, I'm partial to blondes. Though I don't mind brunettes or redheads."

Zoe shook her head, her long hair swaying back and forth. "One of these days you're going to have to grow up and realize women weren't put on this planet solely for your enjoyment."

Paulson flashed her a charming grin. "Not going to happen."

Zoe grimaced. "Too bad, because love does conquer all."

"Love sucks," Paulson countered before Cullen could echo the sentiment.

"Sometimes." A sigh seemed poised to float away from her lips at any moment. "But other times it's pure magic."

Yeah, right. Cullen sipped his coffee. Love caused nothing but heartache and pain. He'd stick with Christmas magic.

Zoe went to refill someone else's cup. The din of conversation increased, and so did the number of people in the cafeteria. More rescue-team members arrived. A photographer snapped pictures. Someone placed a plate of cookies on the table. It had to be getting closer to briefing time.

He checked his watch. "What's taking so long?"

Paulson grabbed a chocolate chip cookie from the plate. "Hughes must still be outside talking to reporters."

Cullen wasn't a big fan of the media when it came to the way they covered and dramatized rescue missions on Mount Hood. Whenever anything went down on the mountain, reporters and news trucks raced to the rescue operation's base at Timberline

Lodge, eager to capitalize on some poor soul's misfortune to increase ratings, web-page hits or circulation.

His stomach growled. He reached for an oatmeal raisin cookie. "Better Hughes than me. I want no part of that feeding frenzy."

Paulson snickered. "Once the press finds out who was lowered into the Bergschrund…"

"How about we say it was you?" Cullen bit into his cookie.

"I'm game," Paulson said. "Especially if the hot blond reporter from Channel Nine wants to talk to me again."

Cullen took another bite. Tasted like one of Carly Porter's cookies. Her husband had been on the mission, too. Jake owned the local brewing company and brewpub. A pint of Porter's Wy'East Lager, with Paulson buying, would hit the spot tonight.

Sheriff's Deputy Will Townsend approached the table with Sean Hughes at his side. Concern clouded their gazes. Worry was etched in their features.

Cullen wrapped his hands around his coffee cup. He hoped the climber hadn't taken a turn for the worse on the helicopter ride or at the hospital. The guy was married with two young kids.

"Hey, Doc." Will tipped his deputy's hat. "Cell phone turned off?"

"Battery died." Cullen wondered what his cell phone had to do with anything. He placed his cup on the table. "Not a lot of places to recharge up there."

Will's eyes darkened. "We've been trying to reach you."

The deputy's words tightened Cullen's throat. He recognized the serious tone and steady cadence. He'd used both when delivering bad news at the hospital. "What's going on?"

"You're listed as Sarah Purcell's emergency contact."

Hearing the name startled Cullen. His coffee spilled, spreading across the table. "Damn."

Paulson grabbed napkins. "No worries, Doc. I've got it."

Cullen stood and faced the deputy. "What about Sarah?"

The deputy's prominent Adam's apple bobbed up and down. "There was an accident on Mount Baker."

"Accident?" Cullen asked.

A muscle twitched at Will's jaw. "The details are sketchy, but it appears Sarah was at the crater rim when a steam blast occurred. She was hit by rock and fell a significant distance."

Shock reverberated through Cullen's body. His vision blurred. The world tilted sideways.

A hand tightened around his arm. "Steady, Doc."

Hughes.

"Deep breaths," another voice said.

Paulson.

Cullen felt himself being seated.

Sarah. Please, God, not her.

His emotions swirled like a whirlpool. Fear and dread spiraled, one on top of the other. Nightmares from another time joined in. Images of his twin brother, Blaine, flashed with strobe-light intensity until Cullen thought his head would explode. He forced himself to breathe. "Is she…?"

What was happening? He was a doctor. Death was something he saw almost every time he worked a shift at the hospital. But he couldn't bring himself to say the word.

Will leaned forward. "Sarah's at a hospital in Seattle."

Not dead. A hundred pounds of anxiety melted away from each of Cullen's bone-weary shoulders. Tears of relief pricked his eyes. He hadn't seen Sarah in months. Cullen had wanted her out of his life, but he hadn't wanted anything bad to happen to her.

Will named one of the top trauma centers in the Pacific Northwest.

Cullen blinked, gaining control in an instant. He'd done his residency there. Sarah would receive top-notch treatment, but he needed to make sure it was the right care. A good thing Seattle was only a four-hour drive away.

He stood, nearly toppling over before he could catch his balance. Tired. He was tired from the mission. "I've got to go."

Hughes steadied him. "Not so fast."

"We've been getting updates," Will explained. "Sarah is in surgery again."

Again. Not good. Cullen's hands fisted. Surgery could mean anything from pinning a fracture to relieving pressure on the brain. Volcanoes weren't safe places. Being a volcanologist had put Sarah in danger, but no serious injuries had resulted. Bumps, bruises, a few stitches. But this…

Cullen dragged his hand through his hair. He was a doctor. He could handle this. "Any prognosis yet?"

Hughes touched Cullen's shoulder with the strength of a rescue leader and the compassion of a friend. "She's in critical condition."

A snowball-size lump burned in his throat. While he'd been on the mountain saving a life, Sarah had been fighting for hers. Bitter-tasting regret coated his mouth. Oh-so-familiar guilt, too. He hadn't been able to help Blaine. Cullen had to help Sarah.

He couldn't waste any more time. Sarah needed someone with her, and he was all she had.

Cullen grabbed his pack. "I've got to get to Seattle."

Hughes touched his shoulder again. "Johnny Gearhart has a plane. Porter's making arrangements. I'm going to drive you home in your truck so you can change and pack a bag, then we'll get you there. ASAP. I promise."

A protest sat on the tip of Cullen's tongue. He hadn't lived in Hood Hamlet long, unlike several of these guys who'd grown up on the mountain. He'd climbed and drunk beer and watched sports on television with them, but he relied on himself and didn't ask for help. He didn't need help. But Sarah did. He swallowed the words he normally would have said and tried a new one instead. "Thanks."

"That's what friends are for," Hughes said. "Let's go."

Cullen nodded once.

"I'm in." Paulson, carrying his gear, fell into step with them. "So Sarah… Is she family? Your sister?"

"No," Cullen said. "Sarah's my wife."

Where am I?

Sarah Purcell wanted to open her eyes, but her eyelids felt as if they'd been glued shut. No matter how hard she tried, she couldn't open them.

What was going on?

Something pounded. It took her a minute—maybe longer—to realize the pounding was coming from her head. Maybe she shouldn't try opening her eyes again.

Her head wasn't the only thing hurting. Even her toenails throbbed. But the pain was a dull ache as if it were far off in the distance. Much better than being up close and personal like a battering ram of pain pummeling her.

She'd been hurting more. A whole lot more. This was…better.

White. She'd been surrounded by white.

Cold. She'd been so cold, but now she was warm. And dry. Hadn't she been wet? And the air… It smelled different.

Strange, but it felt as if something were sticking out of her nose.

Beep. Beep. Beep.

She didn't recognize the noise, the frequency of the tone or the rhythm. But the consistent beat made her think of counting sheep. No reason to try opening her eyes again. Not when she could drift off to sleep.

"Sarah."

The man's voice sliced through the thick fog clouding her brain. His voice sounded familiar, but she couldn't quite place him. Not surprising, given she had no idea where she was or why it was so dark or what the beeping might be.

So many questions.

She parted her lips to speak, to ask what was going on, but no words came out. Only a strangled, unnatural sound escaped her sandpaper-dry throat.

Water. She needed water.

"It's okay, Sarah," he said in a reassuring tone. "You're going to be okay."

Glad he thought so. Whoever he might be.

She wasn't sure of anything. Something told her she should care more than she did, but her brain seemed to be taking a sabbatical.

What had happened?

Clouds had been moving in. A horrible noise had filled the air. Swooshing. Exploding. Cracking. The memory of the teeth-grinding sound, worse than two cars colliding on the freeway, sent a shudder through her.

A large hand covered hers. The warmth of the calloused, rough skin felt as familiar to Sarah as the voice had sounded. Was it the same person? She had no idea, but the touch comforted and soothed. Maybe now she could go back to sleep.

"Her pulse increased." Concern filled his voice. He seemed to be talking to someone else. "Her lips parted. She's waking up."

Not her. He couldn't mean her.

Sarah wanted to sleep, not wake up.

Someone touched her forehead. Not the same person still holding her hand. This one had smooth, cold skin. Clammy skin.

"I don't see a change," another man said, a voice she didn't recognize. "You've been here a long time. Take a break. Eat a decent meal. Sleep in a real bed. We'll call if her condition changes."

The warm hand remained on hers. Squeezed. "I'm not leaving my wife."

Wife.

The word seeped through her foggy mind until an image formed and sharpened. His eyes, as blue as the sky over Glacier Peak on a clear day, had made her feel like the only woman in the world. His smile, rare to appear but generous when it did, had warmed her heart and made her want to believe happy endings might be possible, even if she'd known deep in her heart of hearts they didn't exist. His handsome face, with its high forehead, sculpted cheekbones, straight nose and dimpled chin, had haunted her dreams for the past year.

Memories rushed forward, colliding and overlapping with each other, until one came into focus.

Cullen.

He was here.

Warmth flowed through her like butter melting on a fresh-from-the-oven biscuit.

He'd come for her. Finally.

Urgency gripped Sarah. She wanted—no, needed—to see him to make sure she wasn't dreaming.

But the heavy curtain, aka her eyelids, didn't want to open. She struggled to move her fingers beneath his hand. It had to be Cullen's hand, right? Nothing happened.

A different machine beeped at a lower frequency. Another machine buzzed.

Cullen.

Sarah tried to speak again, but couldn't. Whatever was stuck in her nose seemed to be down her throat, too. No matter. She was so thankful he was with her. She needed to tell him that. She wanted him to know how much…

Wait a minute.

Common sense sliced through the cotton clogging her brain.

Cullen shouldn't be here. He'd agreed divorce was the best option. He no longer lived in the same town, the same state as she did.

So why was he here?

Sarah forced her lips apart to ask, but no sound emerged. Her frustration grew.

"See," Cullen said. "Something's going on."

"I stand corrected, Dr. Gray," the other person said. "This is a very good sign."

"Sarah."

The anxiety in Cullen's voice surprised her as much as the concern. She tried to reconcile what she was hearing. Tried and failed. She wanted to believe he cared about her and that even if they'd both given up on marriage, their time together hadn't been so bad he'd wanted to forget about everything.

Maybe if she could open her eyes a little she could let him know that.

Sarah used every bit of strength she could muster.

A slit of light appeared. So bright. Too bright. She squeezed her eyes shut.

The light disappeared as darkness reclaimed her, but the pounding in her head increased. No longer far away, the pain was in her face, as if someone were playing Whac-A-Mole on her forehead.

She gritted her teeth, unsure if the awful growling sound

she'd heard came from her. Everything felt surreal, as if she were a part of some avant-garde indie film. She wanted out. Now.

"It's okay, Sarah. I'm right here." Cullen's rich, warm voice covered her like one of his grandmother's hand-sewn quilts. "I'm not leaving you."

Not true. He had left her.

As soon as she'd mentioned divorce, he'd moved out of their apartment in Seattle, taking everything of his except the bed. After completing his residency, he'd taken off to Hood Hamlet, Oregon. She'd finished her PhD at the University of Washington, then accepted a postdoctorate position with MBVI—Mount Baker Volcano Institute—in Bellingham, a town in northwest Washington.

Another memory crystalized.

Sarah had been developing a program to deploy additional seismometers on Mount Baker. She'd been trying to determine if magma was moving upward. She'd needed more data. Proof one way or the other. Getting the information meant climbing the volcano and digging out seismometers to retrieve data. Putting in expensive probes that provided telemetered data didn't make sense with their limited funding and the volatile conditions near the crater.

The crater.

She'd been at the crater rim to download data to a laptop and rebury the seismometer. She'd done that. At least, she thought so. Everything was sort of fuzzy.

Apprehension rose. Anxiety escalated.

The rotten-egg scent of sulfur had been thick and heavy in the air. Had she retrieved the data or not? Why couldn't she remember?

Machines beeped, the noise coming faster with each passing second.

She tried to recall what had happened to her, but her mind was blank. Pain intensified, as if someone had turned up the volume to full blast on a television set, then hidden the remote control.

"Sarah." His voice, sharp-edged like fractured obsidian, cut through the hurting. "Try to relax."

If only she could. Questions rammed into her brain. The jack-hammering in her head increased tenfold.

"You're in pain," Cullen said.

She nodded.

The slight movement sent a jagged pain ripping through her.

Her throat burned. Her eyes stung. The air in her lungs disappeared when she exhaled. Inhaling, she could hardly take a breath. A giant boulder seemed to be pressing down on her chest.

"Dr. Marshall."

Cullen's harsh tone added to her discomfort, to her fear. Air, she needed air.

"On it, Dr. Gray."

Something buzzed. Footsteps sounded. Running. Wheels clattered against the floor. More voices. She couldn't hear what they were saying, nor did she care.

She gasped for a breath, sucking in a minuscule amount of air. The oxygen helped. Too bad the hurting more than doubled.

Make it stop. Please, Cullen. Make it...

The fear dissipated. The pain dulled. The boulder was lifted off her. By Cullen? He used to take such good care of her, whether she wanted him to or not. If only he could have loved her....

Floating. Sarah felt as if she were a helium-filled balloon let loose and allowed to float away in the sky. Up, up toward the fluffy white clouds. But she didn't want to go yet. Not until...

"Cull..."

"I'm right here, Sarah." His warm breath fanned her cheek. "I'm not going anywhere. I promise."

Promise.

The word echoed through her fuzzy brain.

Promise.

They'd promised to love, honor and cherish each other until death do them part. But Cullen had withdrawn from her, putting his heart into his all-consuming work and nothing into her. He'd seemed so stable and supportive, but he wasn't as open as she'd originally thought, and he'd held back emotionally. Still, they'd shared some wonderful times and adventures together. A year living in Seattle. Climbing, laughing, loving.

But none of that had mattered in the end. She'd brought up divorce, expecting at least to discuss their marriage. Instead, he'd said okay to a divorce, confirming her fear that he regretted his hasty decision to marry her. Not only had he been willing to let her go without a fight, but he'd been the first one to leave.

That was why she couldn't believe Cullen was promising to stay now. Maybe not today, but tomorrow or the next day or the day after he would be gone, leaving her with only memories and a gold wedding band.

The knowledge hurt, a deep, heart-wrenching pain, worse than any physical pain she'd endured.

I'm not going anywhere.

A part of her wished Cullen would remain at her side. A part of her wished marriage vows were more than words exchanged in front of an Elvis impersonator. A part of her wished love…lasted.

But Sarah knew better. She knew the truth.

Nothing ever lasted. No one ever stayed. Even when they promised they would.

CHAPTER TWO

Cullen lost track of time sitting in Sarah's hospital room. His friends returned to Hood Hamlet after driving his truck to Seattle so he'd have transportation. They supported him via text and phone calls. His family offered to come, but he told them no. They didn't need more grief in their lives, and that was all they would find here, in spite of Sarah's progress.

This small room, four walls with an attached bathroom, had become his world except for trips to the cafeteria and a few hours spent each night at a hotel. And his world revolved around the woman asleep in the hospital bed.

He rubbed his chin. Stubble raked his fingertips.

Maybe that was why this felt so strange. He was married to Sarah, but she'd stopped being his wife nearly a year ago. In Hood Hamlet she hadn't existed. At least not to anyone he knew. Not until her accident.

He rose from his chair, wishing he could be anywhere but here. Not even the familiar artificial lighting and antiseptic smells brought him comfort. He'd spent more time at hospitals than anywhere else the past six years—longer if he counted his four years at medical school. But nothing could quiet the unease tying his stomach in figure-eight knots.

His anxiety made no sense.

Sarah's condition wasn't as serious as her initial prognosis had indicated. Antibiotics had cured an unexpected infection and fever. The nasogastric tube had been removed from her nose. Her cuts had scabbed over. The incisions from her surgeries were healing. Even her closed-head injury had been relatively minor, with no swelling or bleeding.

Surely that had to mean…something. Time to settle matters between them? Cullen wanted to close this chapter in his life.

The woman lying in the hospital bed looked nothing like the beautiful, vibrant climber he'd met at the Red Rock Rendezvous—an annual rock-climbing festival near Las Vegas—and married two days later. He wanted this injured Sarah to replace the image he carried in his heart—make that his head. Her long chestnut-colored hair, clear green eyes, dazzling smile and infectious laughter had been imprinted on his brain along with memories of hot kisses and passionate nights. She was like one of those adrenaline-rushing, stomach-in-your-throat, let-me-off-now carnival rides. The kind of ride that looked exciting and fun from a distance, but once on, made you wonder what you'd been thinking when you handed over your ticket.

That had been his problem with Sarah. He hadn't been thinking. She'd overwhelmed him. Too bad he couldn't blame eloping on being drunk. Oh, he'd been intoxicated at the time—by her, not alcohol.

Cullen crossed the room to the side of her bed.

He'd been trying to forget Sarah. He wanted to forget her. But thoughts of her entered his mind at the strangest of times—on the mountain, at the hospital, in bed. But he knew what would stop that from happening—divorce.

After the divorce things will be better.

These past months the words had become his mantra when he was frustrated or lonely.

Sarah's left hand slipped off the edge of the bed. That didn't look comfortable. He placed her arm back on the mattress. Her skin felt cold.

Cullen didn't want her to catch a chill. He pulled up the blanket and tucked it under her chin.

Sarah didn't stir. So peaceful and quiet. Words he would never have used in the past to describe her. She'd been fiery and passionate, driven and always up for a challenge or adventure. Nothing, not even the flu, had slowed her down much.

The silence in the room prodded him into action. Staring at Sarah wasn't what the doctor ordered. Her doctor, that was. Dr. Marshall hadn't wanted her to sleep the day away—not that Sarah could with nurses coming in and out. But she hadn't been too coherent when she woke up, and then she'd drifted back to sleep like a newborn kitten.

Might as well get on with it, Cullen thought. If she followed the same pattern, she wouldn't be awake for long. "Rise and shine, Lavagirl."

Saying her nickname jolted him. He used to tease her about being a volcanologist until he realized she loved the piles of molten rocks more than she loved him.

He would try again. "Wake up."

Sarah didn't move. Not surprising, given her medications. If he kept talking she would wake up.

"So I…" Cullen had tried hard not to miss her. After what she'd done to him, he shouldn't miss her. He'd missed the sex, though. A lot. But he was only human—emphasis on the *man* part of the word. "I've been thinking about you."

He'd told families that talking to patients was important. Now the advice sounded stupid. But when it came to Sarah, he'd never been very smart.

Keep talking, Doc.

He struggled for something to say. His resentment toward her ran deep. Maybe if he started at the beginning of their relationship when things had been better this wouldn't feel so awkward. "Remember that first night in Las Vegas, you wanted our picture taken in front of the slot machines? We got the photo, but we also got thrown out of the casino."

The two of them had stood on the sidewalk laughing, unsure of the time because of the neon lights. Her laughter had rejuvenated his soul. She was so full of light and love he couldn't get enough of her.

"You looked up at me. Mischief gleamed in your pretty green eyes."

He'd been enchanted, transported back to the time when freedom and fun reigned supreme, when he and Blaine had been impulsive and reckless, goading each other into daredevil challenges and stunts, believing they were untouchable.

"Then you kissed me."

Changing all the plans he'd had for his life in an instant. He hadn't been able to think straight from that moment on. He hadn't cared. Being with her was a total rush. An adventure. Perfect. Nothing else mattered.

"The next night we strolled past the Happily Ever After Wedding Chapel on the strip. You joked about going inside and making things official."

She'd said if they eloped now he couldn't forget about her when they returned to Seattle or leave her standing at the altar after she wasted years of dating him and planning their big wedding. He'd promised he would never leave her like that.

The affection in her eyes had wiped out whatever brain cells remained in his head. For the first time since Blaine's descent into drugs, Cullen had felt whole, as if the missing piece of him that had died with his twin brother had been found in Sarah.

"I couldn't let you get away."

Cullen had pulled her through the chapel's double glass doors. Forgetting about his vow to take only calculated risks in the future, he'd dived in headfirst without doing his due diligence and performing a cost-benefit analysis. He hadn't weighed the odds or considered the consequences of marrying a woman he knew nothing about.

Common sense couldn't override his heart. She'd made him feel complete in a way he'd never thought he'd feel again. He'd been downright giddy when she'd accepted his impromptu proposal. Thirty minutes and $99 later, they walked out wearing matching plain gold bands and holding a marriage certificate.

A whim? A mistake?

More like a regret.

He'd remembered back in December, when everyone was kissing under the mistletoe in Hood Hamlet and he was alone. That was when it hit him. He'd wished he'd never been introduced to Sarah Purcell.

But Cullen had. He'd married her. That was why he was here

now. They were husband and wife until a judge declared otherwise. But he couldn't wait to be free, to get his life in order and put his plan back in place. He was scratching one thing off the list, though. He sure as hell wasn't getting married again. Been there, done that—no need to repeat that particular disaster.

At least he would have Paulson to hang with. The guy was a confirmed bachelor, if there ever was one.

But until Cullen's divorce was final he was stuck with a wife who'd wanted to talk, to fight, to slice open one of his veins and have him bleed out every single thought and feeling he'd ever had.

After the divorce things will be better.

Cullen sat on the edge of Sarah's bed. He wanted to hate her, but seeing her like this, he couldn't. "Your lips are dry."

He picked up a tube from the bed tray, removed the cap and ran the balm over Sarah's chapped lips. She didn't stir. "Better now?"

As he returned the tube to the table, a movement in his peripheral vision caught his attention. The blanket had slipped. She'd moved her left arm again. "Sarah."

She blinked. Once. Twice. Her eyes opened, looking clear and focused. Her mouth formed a perfect O. "You're still here."

Sarah sounded surprised, but relieved. Her reaction offended him. "I told you I wasn't going anywhere."

She grabbed his hand and squeezed. "You did."

Heat emanated from the point of contact, shooting out to the tips of his fingernails and sparking up his arm. He expected her to let go. Instead she stared at him with wide eyes. The corners of her lips curved upward in a hesitant smile.

O-kay. It was a simple touch. Out of gratitude for his being here. No big deal. Except the heat tingled. It felt good. Too good. Cullen pulled his arm away. "Thirsty?"

She nodded. "Water, please."

He pushed a button on the control device that raised the head of her bed, reached for the cup sitting on the bed tray and then brought the glass to her mouth. He positioned the straw against her lower lip. Even after the balm, her lips were dry and peeling. He remembered how they used to be so soft and moist and taste so sweet.

Don't think about that. There weren't going to be any more kisses, no matter how much he'd enjoyed them in the past.

"Sip slowly," he cautioned.

Sarah did. She released the straw. "Where am I? What happened?"

The roughness in her voice scratched his heart. He held on to the glass of water. That would keep at bay the temptation to brush the hair off her face. "You're at a hospital in Seattle. There was a steam blast on Baker. You got hit by falling rock and fell."

Her mouth quirked. "Did the steam blast continue?"

"No," he said. "But Tucker Samson—he introduced himself as your boss and the head of MBVI—said this could be a sign of an impending event."

Her eyebrows slanted. Beneath the bandage on her forehead, lines formed as if she were deep in thought. "I…don't remember much."

Sarah had a mind like a steel trap and never forgot anything. He didn't blame her for sounding worried. "It's okay. You have a concussion, but it's a closed-head injury. No traumatic brain injury."

His words didn't ease her concern. Panic flickered in her eyes. "I wasn't up there by myself."

"Two others were injured, but they've been released from the hospital. You took the brunt of it. Fell quite a distance."

The words were easy to say now, but the image of Sarah when he'd first arrived at the hospital haunted him. His uselessness then reminded him of trying to help Blaine—who had wanted only to blame Cullen for his drug addiction—and of trying to revive his brother later, after he'd overdosed. Being forced to watch from the sidelines as others took care of Sarah was like having his heart ripped from his chest. He'd felt the same after being pushed away from his unconscious brother when the paramedics had arrived at their parents' house. But Sarah didn't need to know any of that.

A corner of her mouth rose into a more certain smile. "Guess that's why I feel like I've gone nine rounds in a boxing match."

"Mixed Martial Arts seems more your style."

"Yeah, now that you mention it, this does feel more like MMA than a few punches, hooks and jabs."

She hadn't lost her sense of humor. That and her intelligence had been two of Sarah's most appealing traits. She'd had a hot body, too. The hospital gown and blanket covered much of her, but she'd lost weight. Her cheekbones appeared more prominent and she looked smaller, almost fragile, a word he would never have associated with her before.

He pushed the straw toward her lips again. "Drink more."

Sarah took another sip. "I've had enough. Thanks."

"Ice chips will soothe your throat. It has to be sore from the tube." He placed the cup on the bed tray. "Hungry?"

"No." A question formed in her eyes. "Should I be?"

She sounded nothing like the strong, independent woman he'd married. The vulnerability in her gaze and voice tugged at his heart, twisting him inside out. He wanted to hold her until she felt better and her uncertainty disappeared. But touching her, even out of compassion, wasn't a smart idea. "Your appetite will return soon enough."

"Maybe my appetite doesn't want hospital food."

That was more like his Sarah. Not his, he corrected. "Then your appetite is one smart cookie."

She smiled.

He smiled back.

This conversation was going better than he'd imagined. Maybe the bump on her head had shaken some sense into Sarah. Not that it changed anything between them. "I'll sneak in some decent food."

"I should eat even if I don't feel like it. I need to get back to the institute to look at data."

Her words made him bristle. Sarah was a scientist, first and foremost. Studying volcanoes wasn't a job for her, but a passion. The need to be where the action was happening was as natural an instinct as breathing to Sarah. Her work was for the greater good of science and mankind. If only she cared to put as much effort into her personal relationships.

Into him.

"Other scientists can analyze the data," he said. "You need to recover first."

"I'm the institute's specialist. They need me. Those are my seismometers up there."

"Yours?"

Her lips pursed, but not in the kiss-me-now way she had perfected. "A grant paid for them, but the data… Was the equipment damaged?"

"Tucker said the equipment was recovered. The data from the laptop is being analyzed."

"Thank goodness." She glanced around the room until her gaze landed on the door. "How soon until I can get out of here?"

He held up his hands, palms facing her. "Not so fast."

"We may be able to use the data to figure out what's going to happen on Baker. If we predict an eruption successfully, we can use the same process with other volcanoes and save lives."

Her passion cascaded out. Cullen understood why she was so adamant about her work. He felt the same about his. But he had to play devil's advocate, even if he wanted nothing more than to send her on her merry way to Bellingham. "A concussion is only one of your injuries."

Sarah looked down at herself, as if finally realizing she was more than a talking head. Her eyes narrowed at the cast on her arm. "I can slog up Baker with a sling."

As ridiculous as the image of her doing that was, he could see her attempting it. She would hurt herself more, given the pain medication she was on, if she even survived another fall. "How will you self-arrest if you slip? It's hard enough to dig in an ice ax to stop yourself with two usable hands and arms."

She moistened her lips and lifted her chin with a look of defiance. "I won't need to stop myself if I don't slip."

A smile threatened to appear at her bravado. He pressed his lips together. The last thing he wanted to do was encourage her.

"You suffered internal injuries, a collapsed lung, broken ribs and an arm fracture. Not to mention you've had two surgeries."

"Surgeries?"

"You have a pin in your right arm, and you no longer have a spleen. Due to the trauma and bleeding, they had to remove it with an open procedure rather than using laparoscopic techniques."

"Oh." Sarah looked as if he'd told her she'd overslept her alarm, not had an internal organ removed through a four-inch incision. "You don't really need a spleen, right?"

A groan of frustration welled up inside him. Why couldn't she be one of those ivory-tower-type scientists who worked in a lab and never cared if they breathed fresh air or saw sunlight? Then again, he wouldn't have been attracted to someone like that. "You can survive without one."

"That's a relief." She touched her cast. "How soon before I can get back to the institute? Next week?"

Try four to six weeks, if everything went well with her recovery. Most likely six to eight with the surgery. But he reminded himself he wasn't in charge of her medical care. "You'll have to ask your doctor."

Her gaze pinned him. "You're a doctor."

"I'm not *your* doctor."

"You have to have some idea."

Cullen had more than an idea. But he wasn't here as a medical professional. He was here to support her, even if he wasn't part of her life anymore.

He'd been surprised to find out he was her only emergency contact. She'd mentioned her parents to him once, saying they were no longer a part of her life. He supposed the blank line on the employment form had needed a name, any name. No one ever thought the person listed would be contacted. "More than a couple of weeks."

She rubbed her lips together. "Guess I'd better talk to my doctor and find out."

"Once you know—"

"You'll go home," she finished for him.

She wanted him out of her life. He would be happy to accommodate her. "Yes, but not until you're out of the hospital."

Leaving her alone until then wouldn't be right.

"Thank you." Her voice dropped to a mere whisper. "Thanks for being here. This had to have messed up your schedule."

Sarah's unexpected sincerity curled around his heart and squeezed tight, like a hug. He shifted his weight between his feet. "My schedule doesn't matter."

Her gaze met his with an intensity he knew well. She might look bruised and battered, even broken, but intelligence and strength shone in the depths of her eyes. Her eyes were what he'd noticed first about her when they'd met over morning coffee at a campfire. He wanted to look away, but couldn't.

"Your schedule matters," she countered. "It always has before."

"I don't want you to be alone." That much was true. "You're still my wife."

Her face paled. "My fault. I've been so busy at the institute I never followed through on my end with the divorce. I'm sorry. I'll have to get on that."

After bringing up a divorce, she'd been too busy slogging up and down Mount Baker in the name of research to file the marriage-dissolution paperwork. He'd contacted an attorney. He rubbed the back of his neck. "No need."

Her eyes widened. Her lips parted. "What do you mean?"

A part of him wanted to get back at Sarah, to hurt her the way she'd hurt him.

You're a great guy. You'll make some woman a fantastic husband. But our eloping was impulsive. I acted rashly and didn't think about what I was doing. Or what would be best for you. I'm not it. You deserve a wife who can give you the things you want. Things I can't give you.

Correction. Things she didn't want to give him.

Regret rose like bile in his throat. "I knew you were busy, so once I established residency in Oregon I got things started there."

"Oh." Her gaze never wavered from his. "Okay."

It felt anything but okay to him. The knots in his stomach

tightened. His throat constricted. He'd had their entire future planned out. A house, pets, kids. And now...

Putting Mount Rainier, Mount St. Helens, Mount Adams and Mount Hood between Sarah and him had never appealed to Cullen more. "I'll go see if your doctor is around so we...you...can find out when you might be discharged."

He strode toward the door without waiting for her reply.

"Is it okay to get out of bed and use the bathroom?" Sarah asked.

Cullen stopped, cursing under his breath. He needed to help Sarah. But the last thing he wanted was to touch her, to hold her. What if he didn't want to let go?

With a calming breath, he glanced over his shoulder. "Yes, but not on your own. I'll grab a nurse and be right back."

Cullen exited the room. He could have hit the button to call the nurse, but he needed some distance, if only for as long as it took him to reach the nurses' station.

He would let the nurse determine the best way to get Sarah on her feet. If he was pressed into service, so be it. But he hoped the nurse was one of the practical types who would handle things herself.

The less he had to do with Sarah until her release, the better.

Sarah washed her hands in the bathroom sink.

A blond nurse named Natalie hovered nearby. The woman wore blue scrubs, and never stopped talking or smiling. "After surgery and pain meds, it takes a while for your system to get back to normal. But you're doing great already!"

Heat rose in Sarah's cheeks. She wasn't used to being congratulated for using the toilet. Maybe when she was a kid, but knowing her parents, she doubted it. At least Natalie had given her *some* privacy. And it sure beat having Cullen help her, even though he was stationed outside the door.

Don't think about him.

She dried her hands, wishing every movement didn't take so much effort or hurt so much. "Um, thanks. I'm not used to going to the bathroom being a community event."

"Don't be embarrassed. This is nothing compared to labor and delivery," Natalie said. "There's no room for modesty there."

Sarah couldn't imagine. Nor did she want to. Given she had no desire to marry again, she doubted she would ever set foot into labor and delivery. Unlike Cullen. If ever a man was meant to be a father...

An ache deep in her belly grabbed hold of her, like a red-tailed hawk's talons around his prey, and wouldn't let go. She struggled to breathe.

Her incision. Maybe her ribs. She leaned against the sink to allow the pain to pass.

Natalie placed a hand on Sarah's shoulder. "Sit on the toilet."

A knock sounded. "Need help?"

Cullen's voice stopped whatever had been hurting. Sarah straightened. "I'm fine."

Natalie adjusted the back of the gown. "Let's get you back before Dr. Gray gets on me for keeping you away too long. Doctor hubbies are the worst, since they're sure they know what's best for their wives."

Maybe some doctors, not Cullen. He'd looked as if he wanted to bolt earlier. She didn't blame him. This was the height of awkwardness for both of them.

Natalie opened the bathroom door. "Here she is, Dr. Gray."

Sarah shuffled out of the bathroom. She felt each step. An ache. A pain. A squeezing sensation. Nausea, too.

Cullen held his arms out slightly, but he wasn't spotting her as closely as before. Dark circles under his eyes and stubble on his face made her wonder how much sleep he'd been getting. Not much, by the looks of it. But he was still the most handsome man she'd ever seen. That bothered her. She shouldn't be thinking about her future ex-husband that way. Maybe it was the pain medication.

"You're walking better." He sounded pleased.

A burst of pride shot through her. "Just needed to find my legs."

"It's awful when they go missing," Natalie joked. "The two

of you should take a short walk down the hall and back. Sarah needs exercise."

Excitement spurted through Sarah. She would love to get out of this room.

Cullen's lips narrowed. He didn't look as if he wanted to go anywhere with her.

Disappointment shot straight to the tips of her toes, even though she knew he had every right to feel that way. Why would he want to spend more time with her than he absolutely had to? She'd hurt his pride by bringing up a divorce. As if shutting her out of every part of his life outside the bedroom hadn't hurt her. But she'd had to do something. It was only a matter of time before he left her. She'd saved them from suffering more hurt in the future.

"You should be walking a few times each day," Cullen said.

Of course he had to say that. He was a doctor. But he'd done enough. She wasn't about to force him into escorting her.

Sarah padded toward the window. "I'll parade around the room. This gown isn't made for walking in public unless I want to flash the entire floor."

"I doubt anyone would complain." Cullen's lighthearted tone surprised her. "Especially not Elmer, the eighty-four-year-old patient two doors down."

Natalie laughed. "Elmer would appreciate it. He's such a dirty old man. But I'm sure you wouldn't mind too much yourself, Dr. Gray."

Cullen winked at the nurse. "Well, Sarah *is* my wife."

Sarah stared at him dumbfounded. Legally she was his wife. But he wanted the divorce as much as she did. Why was he joking around as though they were still together?

He strode to the cupboard resembling a built-in armoire with a drawer on the bottom. "And since I'd rather not have any men leering at her, it's a good thing I bought this."

Sarah had no idea what he was talking about. "What?"

Cullen opened one of the cupboard doors and pulled out something orange and fuzzy. "This is for you."

She stared in disbelief at a robe. "I…"

"I hope orange is still your favorite color," he said.

She was touched he remembered. "It is."

Natalie clapped her hands together. "How sweet!"

His gesture sent a burst of warmth rushing through Sarah. This was so…unexpected. She cleared her throat. "Th-thanks."

"Now your backside will be covered, and I won't have to get into any territorial pissing matches." He held up the robe so she could stick her left arm through the sleeve. "Let's drape this over your right shoulder and not bother your cast."

Sarah nodded, not trusting her voice. She appreciated Cullen staying with her at the hospital, but his company was enough. She didn't want him buying her anything, especially something as lovely and as thoughtful as this robe.

He tied the belt around her waist. "Now you're set."

She didn't feel set. She felt light-headed. Chills ran up and down her arms. Neither had anything to do with her injuries, but everything to do with the man standing next to her.

"Ready?" he asked.

No, she wasn't.

"Go on," Natalie encouraged. "You can do this."

No, Sarah didn't think she could.

Cullen extended his arm toward her. She reached for his hand, unsure if touching him would hurt or not.

He laced his fingers with hers, sending tingles shooting up her arm. "It'll be okay."

Chills and tingles were not okay.

"I won't let you fall," he said confidently.

Sarah had no doubt he would catch her if her body gave out and gravity took over. But who would stop her heart from falling for him? Or catch her if it did?

CHAPTER THREE

THE LAST THING Cullen had expected to become was Sarah's walking buddy, but that was what happened over the next three days. His reluctance gave way to anticipation for the after-meal strolls through the hospital corridors. He'd wanted to be here and help her. This offered him the perfect opportunity to do both.

They didn't discuss the past. They barely mentioned the future unless it related to her recovery. Sometimes they didn't say much at all. It was enough to be with her, supporting her. Enough, he realized, for now.

As they walked through the hospital's atrium full of tall trees and flowering plants, Cullen held Sarah's hand. A satisfied smile settled on his lips. "You did have the energy to make it down here."

"Told you so. This is much better than walking the hallways upstairs." Sarah glanced up at the skylights. The ends of her long chestnut hair swung like a pendulum. Her bruises were fading, more yellow and brown than blue. "I can't wait until I can go outside."

"It won't be long." Sarah looked better, healthier. He squeezed her hand. "You're getting stronger every day."

Her green eyes sparkled. "It's all this exercise."

He wished it was because of him.

Yeah, right. He wasn't foolish enough to think this time together meant anything. These walks were about her health, nothing else. "Exercise can be as important as medication in a patient's recovery. So can laughter."

She grinned wryly. "That's why you wanted to watch the comedy show last night."

"You laughed."

"I did. And I'm smiling now."

"You have a very nice smile."

"Thanks." She glanced at their linked hands. "Do you think I could try walking on my own?"

Cullen had gotten so used to being her living, breathing walker, holding her hand had become second nature. But it wasn't something he should get used to, even if it was…nice. He released her hand. "Go ahead."

Sarah took a careful, measured step. And another.

He flexed his fingers, missing the feel of her warm skin against his. "Tomorrow you'll want to hop on a bike instead."

Her lips curved downward in a half frown, half pout. "I like our walks."

"Me, too."

Her smile, as bright as a summer day at Smith Rock, took his breath away. He rubbed his face. Stubble pricked his hand. He'd been in a rush to get to the hospital and forgotten to shave again.

"But I have to be honest." She looked around, as if seeing who might be listening. "I'm ready to escape this joint."

"I don't blame you." Except once she left, everything would go back to the way it had been. They would live separate lives, in separate states. The realization unsettled him. "You should be released soon."

"Has Dr. Marshall mentioned a discharge date?"

The anticipation in her voice made Cullen feel foolish for enjoying this time together. She wanted a divorce. He wanted one, too. "No. But given your progress, Dr. Marshall might have one in mind. Ask him when he makes his rounds."

Hope danced in her eyes. "I will."

Sarah took another step, swaying. She stumbled forward.

"Whoa." Cullen wrapped his right arm around her waist and grabbed her left hand. "Careful."

She clutched his hand. "I lost my balance."

If that was the case, why was she leaning against him with

her fingers digging into his hand? But he liked the way she clung to him. "This is the longest walk we've taken. Let's head back to your room."

He expected an argument. Instead she nodded.

Sarah loosened her grip and flexed her hand. "I can make it on my own."

He laced his fingers with hers. "I know, but humor me anyway."

She held on to his hand. "I suppose that's the least I can do after all you've done for me."

A list of what he'd done for her the past two years scrolled through his mind. "I suppose it is."

Sarah owed him, and he would gladly take this as payback. He wasn't about to let go of her. And that had nothing to do with how good having her close felt. He caught a whiff of her floral-scented shampoo. Or how good she smelled. Nothing at all.

That afternoon, Sarah gripped the edge of the hospital blanket. She stared at Dr. Marshall, wondering if she'd misunderstood him. She sure hoped so. "Don't you mean an independent discharge?"

"An independent discharge is not going to happen." Dr. Marshall looked like a grandfather, rather than one of Seattle's top surgeons, with his silver-wire-frame glasses and thinning gray hair, but the man was turning out to be the devil in disguise. "You are unable to care for yourself. Your discharge planner and orthopedist agree."

She hadn't been waiting all afternoon full of hope only to hear this. "That's…silly."

Cullen, who leaned against the far wall near the window, gave a blink-and-you'd-miss-it shake of his head.

Her fingers tightened on the fabric, nearly poking through the thin material. She didn't like being so aware of Cullen's every movement. Her senses had become heightened where he was concerned. She'd wondered if he felt the same way. Now she knew.

No!

Frustration tensed her muscles, making her abdomen hurt more. Disappointment ping-ponged through her. They'd shared lovely walks though the hospital, holding hands like high-school sweethearts. She'd assumed Cullen would support her independent-discharge request, but he hadn't. He didn't want her returning to her apartment in Bellingham to stay by herself.

"Nothing about this is silly," Dr. Marshall said. "You are lucky to be alive."

"Damn lucky," Cullen murmured.

She didn't feel that way. Nothing but bad luck could have put her at the crater rim when a steam blast occurred, something that hadn't happened on Mount Baker in nearly four decades. Now she was stuck in the hospital with only her soon-to-be ex-husband for company when she needed to be at the institute figuring out if the event was a precursor to an eruption or just the volcano letting off steam as it had done in 1975. "*Silly* was the wrong word to use, but I'm not an invalid. I'm getting around better."

Dr. Marshall gave her the once-over. "There's a big difference between walking the hallways and being capable of caring for yourself."

"You overdid it this morning," Cullen added, as if dumping a carton of salt onto her wounds helped matters.

"I know I have a way to go in my recovery." She would be doing fine once the pain of her incision and ribs lessened. The throbbing in her head, too. "But I don't need a nursemaid."

A knowing glance passed between Dr. Marshall and Cullen. Sarah bit the inside of her cheek.

"No one is suggesting a nursemaid. But I agree with Dr. Marshall. You're right-handed." Cullen's gaze dropped to her cast. "Dressing yourself, doing anything with your left hand, is going to take some adjustment. Not to mention your sutures and ribs. You'll need assistance doing most everyday things. There will also be limitations on lifting and driving."

Maybe she shouldn't have expected Cullen to take her side. But even with his lack of support now, she had no regrets. Bringing up a divorce was better than waiting around for him to do it. And he would have. People always walked away. He would walk away from her once she was out of the hospital, leaving her alone. Again.

The sinking feeling in her stomach turned into a black hole, sucking her hope down into it.

No, she couldn't give in and admit defeat. The institute relied upon her expertise. Others had been looking at the data since the steam blast, but volcanic seismology was her specialty. She couldn't let people down. It wasn't as if she had anything else in her life but her work. She glanced at Cullen, then looked away. "I don't care if it hurts. I'll figure out a way. I need to get back to the institute. I have a job to do."

"Is your current health and your long-term health outlook worth risking for your job?" Dr. Marshall asked.

Sarah raised her chin. "If it means determining how to predict a volcanic eruption, then yes. It's worth it."

A muscle ticked at Cullen's jaw. "If you return to the institute too soon, you won't be doing them or yourself any favors."

She saw his point, even if she didn't like it. "I'll be careful."

"What does your job entail, Sarah?" Dr. Marshall asked.

"Analyzing data."

"After she climbs Mount Baker to gather it," Cullen added. "Or am I wrong about that, Dr. Purcell?"

Of course he wasn't wrong. From his smug grin he knew it, too. That was why he'd used her title. "I can send a team up to download the data."

Maybe that would appease him—rather, Dr. Marshall.

"Are you able to work remotely from home?" Dr. Marshall asked.

Sarah would rather be at the institute, but she would take what she could get. "Telecommuting is an option. I have internet access in my apartment."

Dr. Marshall looked her straight in the eyes. "Is there someone who can stay at your apartment and care for you?"

Sarah's heart slammed against her chest so loudly she was sure the entire floor of the hospital could hear the boom-boom-boom. Even though she knew the answer to his question, she mentally ran through the list of coworkers at the institute. Most would be happy to drop off food or pick up her mail, but asking one to stay with her would be too much. She couldn't impose on any of them like that.

She'd never had a close friend, a bestie or BFF she could count on no matter what. Her life had been too transitory, shuttled between her parents and moving frequently, to develop that kind of bond with anyone. Not unless you counted Cullen. She couldn't. It wouldn't be fair to either one of them.

She chewed on her lower lip. "I could hire someone."

"Home care is a possibility," Dr. Marshall said.

Fantastic. Except her studio apartment was tiny. The floor was the only extra place to sleep, the bathroom the only privacy. She hated to admit it, but home care wouldn't work.

"If Sarah's in Bellingham, nothing will keep her from going to the institute or heading up the mountain if she feels it's necessary," Cullen said matter-of-factly.

She opened her mouth to contradict him, but stopped herself. What he said was true.

"You know I'm right," he said.

It annoyed her that he knew her so well.

"Is that true?" Dr. Marshall asked her.

She tried to shrug, but a pain shot through her. "Possibly."

Cullen laughed. The rich sound pierced her heart. One of Cupid's arrows had turned traitorous. "A one-hundred-percent possibility."

No sense denying it. He'd had her number a long time ago.

Dr. Marshall gave her a patronizing smile, as if she were a five-year-old patient who would appreciate princess stickers rather than a grown adult who wanted him to work out her discharge. "My first choice in cases involving a head injury, however minor, is home care by family members, but Dr. Gray has explained your situation."

Sarah assumed Dr. Marshall meant their marriage, since Cullen was the closest thing to family she had. She wasn't an orphan. Her parents were alive, but they'd chosen their spouses over her years ago. "I'm on my own."

"That leaves a sniff. A skilled nursing facility," Dr. Marshall explained. "We call them SNFs. There are several in the Seattle area."

Cullen's smile crinkled the corners of his eyes, making her heart dance a jig. So not the reaction she wanted to have when she was fighting for her freedom. Independence. Work.

"That sounds like a perfect solution," Cullen said.

Maybe for him. In Bellingham she had access to the institute and her own place to live. Down here in Seattle, she had… nothing. But what choice did she have? Sarah swallowed her disappointment. "I suppose. As long as I have my laptop and access to data."

Dr. Marshall adjusted his wire-framed glasses. "Many SNFs have Wi-Fi."

Might as well look on the bright side. "That's better than dial-up."

"Your concussion will make it difficult for you to concentrate for any length of time." Cullen sounded so doctorlike. Totally different from the man who had helped her back to her room this morning. "If you push too hard, you may experience vision problems and headaches."

"I'll use a timer to limit my computer usage," she offered.

"No symptom is a one-hundred-percent certainty, but Dr. Gray is correct. You don't want to do too much too soon," Dr. Marshall said.

Something about his tone and eye movement raised the hair on her arms. "What exactly am I going to be allowed to do?"

"Rest and recuperate," Dr. Marshall said, as if those two things would appeal to her.

R & R was something a person did when they were old. Not when the second-most-active volcano in the Cascades might erupt. "The SNF sounds like my only option, but you might as well put me out of my misery now, because—"

"You'll die of boredom," Cullen finished for her.

In their one-plus year of marriage—over two if you counted the time they'd been separated—he'd figured her out better than anyone else in her life. That unnerved Sarah.

Dr. Marshall adjusted his glasses. "A few weeks of boredom is a small price to pay."

Small price? The SNF sounded like an institutional cage. She'd be locked away and forced to sleep or "rest." She stared at the cast on her arm.

Lucky to be alive. Maybe if she kept repeating the words she would believe them. Because right now life pretty much sucked.

"There is another option," Cullen said.

Her gaze jerked to his. The room tilted to her left as if she were standing in a mirrored fun house. She closed her eyes. She must have walked too far earlier. When she opened them everything was back where it belonged, and Cullen was staring at her with his intense gaze.

She swallowed the lump of desperation lodged in her throat. Anything would be better than a nursing facility. "What other option?"

"Come home with me to Hood Hamlet."

Her mouth gaped. The air rushed from her lungs.

"I have Wi-Fi," Cullen continued, as if that made all the difference in the world. "I promise you won't be bored."

No, she wouldn't be bored. She would be struggling to survive and keep her heart safe.

Here at the hospital, people came in and out of her room. She and Cullen were never alone for long. He left each night to go to his hotel. What would it be like if it were only the two of them?

Dangerous.

Sarah tried to speak, but her tongue felt ten sizes too big for her mouth, as if she'd been given a shot of Novocain at the dentist's office. But she knew one thing....

Going home with Cullen was a bad idea. So bad she would rather move into the SNF and die of boredom or stay in the hospital and die of starvation or go live in a cave somewhere with nothing but spiders and other creepy-crawly things for company.

Having him here made her feel warm and fuzzy. Taking walks reminded her of how comfortable they'd once been together. But she couldn't rely on him to be her caretaker. She'd been vulnerable before they'd separated. She would be totally at his mercy in his care. If she found herself getting attached to him, or worse, falling in love with him all over again…

He would have the power not only to break her heart, but shatter it. She couldn't allow that to happen.

Cullen wore a digital watch, but he swore he heard the seconds ticking by. He braced himself for Sarah's rejection. He'd offered her a place to recover, but she'd reacted with wide-eyed panic, as if she was about to be sentenced to life in prison.

Stupid. Cullen balled his hands with a mix of frustration and resentment. He should never have made the suggestion. But she'd looked so damn miserable over the idea of the SNF, he'd had to do something. A good attitude was important in a patient's recovery. He didn't want her to experience any setbacks. Skilled nursing facilities had their role in patient recovery, but Sarah was better off elsewhere. He knew that as a trained physician. He knew that in his gut.

But no one was going to step up and offer Sarah an alternative. No one except him.

And she hadn't even cared. At least not according to her anything-but-that reaction.

Might as well get the word *sucker* tattooed on him. He'd let their pleasant walks and hand-holding soften him up.

A buzzing sound disturbed the silence.

Dr. Marshall checked his pager. "I have to go. Tell the nurse your decision and have her relay it to me and the discharge planner."

The surgeon strode out of the room without a glance back.

The minute the door shut, the tension in the air quadrupled. Cullen had faced challenges working as a doctor and as a mountain rescuer, but he'd never felt more out of his element than standing here with his wife, a wife who didn't want him for a husband. Not that he wanted her, either, he reminded himself.

Sarah toyed with the edge of her blanket. Her hands worked fast and furiously, as if she were making origami out of cloth.

The silence intensified. Her gaze bounced from her cast to

the colorful bouquet of wildflowers from MBVI to everything else in the room. Everything except him.

Hard to believe that at one time they were so crazy about one another they couldn't keep their hands or lips off each other. Now she couldn't bear to look at him.

He hated the way that gnawed at him. Time to face the music, even if a requiem played. "I'm only trying to help. Give you another choice."

"I'm surprised you'd want me around."

Her words cut through the tension with the precision of a scalpel. He was about to remind her she had been the one to ask for the divorce, but held his tongue because she was right. He didn't want her around because she messed with his thoughts and his emotions, but he had to do the right thing here, whether he liked it or not. "I want you to recover. Get you feeling better and back on your feet in the shortest amount of time possible. That's all."

She studied him as if she were trying to determine what type of volcanic rock he might be. "That's nice of you."

Her wariness bugged him. "We've been getting along."

Her lips parted. She pressed them together, then opened them again. "It's just…"

He hated the hurt lying over his heart. "Would it be that awful for a few weeks?"

"No, not awful," she admitted. "Not at all."

Her words brought a rush of relief, but added to his confusion. "Then what's the problem?"

"I don't want to be a burden."

A burden was the last label he'd use for her. "You're not."

"You've put your life on hold this past week."

"I won't have to do that when I'm in Hood Hamlet. I can get back to work and my mountain-rescue unit."

Sarah moistened her lips. "I didn't think I was supposed to be alone."

"Friends have offered to help."

Her gaze narrowed. "So you won't be around that much?"

"I work twelve-hour shifts at the hospital. The rescue unit keeps ready teams stationed on the mountain in May and June."

"Oh."

That single word didn't tell him much. He rocked back on his heels. "So what do you think?"

"I appreciate the offer."

"But—?"

Sarah squinted. "I…I don't know."

Her uncertainty sounded genuine. He had expected to hear a flat-out *no*.

She sank into her pillow. "Is it something I need to decide right now?"

"Dr. Marshall wants you to tell the nurse your decision. Arrangements have to be made if you choose a SNF."

She rubbed her thumb against her fingertips.

"Attitude plays a role in healing," he continued. "Hood Hamlet will be better for you in that regard."

"Give me a minute to think about it."

Cullen didn't know why she needed more time or why he was trying so hard to convince her. Yes, he wanted to do the right thing, but her decision changed nothing. If she refused his offer, the next time they saw each other… They wouldn't be seeing each other unless she challenged the divorce terms. The way it would have been if she hadn't had her accident.

The bed dwarfed her body, making her look small and helpless. Strange, given she was the strongest women he knew next to Leanne Thomas, a paramedic and member of OMSAR.

Sarah grimaced.

Two long strides put him at the side of her bed. "Your head."

She gave an almost imperceptible nod. "I may have overdone the walking today."

His concern ratcheted. "Does anything else hurt?"

"Not any more than usual."

Using the back of his hand, he touched her face. She wasn't flushed, but a temperature could mean another infection. "You don't feel warm."

She closed her eyes. "My brain might be rebelling from having to work again. Think I probably need another nap."

"Probably."

But Cullen preferred to err on the side of caution. He checked the circulation of each finger sticking out from her cast. He wanted to blame his anxiousness on the Hippocratic oath, but he knew there was more to it than that. The *more* part revolved around Sarah. He wished it weren't so. In time he hoped—expected—not to care or to be so concerned about her. Time healed all wounds, right?

She opened her eyes. "You always had a nice bedside manner."

He didn't want her words to mean anything. He hated that they did. "It's easier with some patients."

"With me?" she asked, sounding hopeful.

"Yes."

Sarah's lips curved into a slight, almost shy smile. "Thanks."

He brushed hair off her face. "You're welcome."

Her eyelids fluttered like a pair of butterfly wings.

He remembered when she'd slept against him and her eyelashes had brushed his cheek. The urge to scoop her up in his arms and hold her close was strong, but he couldn't give in to temptation. This woman had trounced his heart once. Whatever else he did, he couldn't let himself fall in love with her again.

"I'm not trying to be difficult," she said softly.

"You're being yourself. I wouldn't expect any less."

But he expected more from himself.

Seeing Sarah injured and hurting brought out his protective instincts, but he had to be careful. He had to be smart about this, about her.

She'd claimed to love him right up to the day she brought up divorce. She'd lied about her feelings and let him down in the worst possible way.

He didn't trust her. He couldn't. No matter what she might do or say.

Memories and feelings he'd thought he'd buried deep kept surfacing. He liked keeping his emotions under wraps, but he found it much too easy to lose control around Sarah. He couldn't wait for her to turn down his offer so he could be done with her.

She stared at him. "I don't need any more time to decide. My goal is to recover as soon as possible. My apartment is too small for a caretaker to stay with me. A SNF would be too impersonal."

The implication of her words set him on edge. "So that means…?"

"I'll go to Hood Hamlet with you. If that's still okay?"

It wasn't okay, not with the way Cullen was feeling right now. His heart pounded and his pulse raced, as if he'd run to the summit of Hood post-holing through four feet of fresh snow. An adrenaline rush from physical activity, no problem. Adventures with calculated risks, fine. The way he was reacting to Sarah? Unacceptable.

Still, Cullen had made the offer. He wouldn't go back on his word. But he would have to keep a tight rein on his emotions and remain in control. He clenched his teeth. "It's fine."

CHAPTER FOUR

GET SARAH HOME. Get her well. Get her back where she belonged.

Driving to Hood Hamlet on Highway 26, Cullen focused on the road and tried to ignore the woman seated next to him. Not an easy thing to do with the scent of her sweet, floral shampoo tickling his nostrils. He grasped the leather-covered steering wheel with his hands in the ten and two o'clock positions, exactly as he'd been taught in driver's ed.

He'd rarely driven this way as a teenager. "Hell on Wheels" best described his brother's and his driving styles back then. But after Blaine had overdosed, Cullen prided himself on doing things, including driving, the right way, the correct way, to make things easier on his grieving parents. He'd made some stupid mistakes in the past, but he hoped he wouldn't make any more where Sarah was involved.

As he pressed harder on the accelerator to pass a semitruck, he fought the urge to sneak a peek at her. He'd done that too many times since leaving Seattle. Concentrating on the road in front of him was better. Safer. He flicked on the blinker to return to his own lane.

"You haven't touched your milk shake," Sarah said.

The meaningless, polite conversation of the past four hours made him wish for a high-tech transporter beam that could carry them to the cabin in less than a nanosecond. He'd settle for silence, even the uncomfortable kind of quiet that made you squirm while you struggled to think of something to say.

He stretched his neck to one side, then the other. "I'm not that thirsty."

Cullen hadn't had much of an appetite since last night. He hadn't slept much, either, tossing and turning until the sheets strangled him like a boa constrictor. He rolled his shoulders to loosen the bunched muscles.

"You're missing out. My chocolate milk shake is delicious."

Sarah sounded as though she was smiling. A quick glance her way—he couldn't help himself—showed she wasn't. Her lips were tight.

She stirred her drink with the straw. "Thanks for suggesting we stop."

Making stops along the way had allowed her to walk around and change positions, but had added time to the drive. "You needed to stretch your legs."

Their final stop hadn't been all about Sarah. The truck had felt cramped. Confined. He'd needed some fresh air and space.

"If you'd rather have chocolate, we can trade." She held out her cup to him. "I like vanilla."

Memories of other road trips to rock climb flashed through his mind. Stopping to buy two different kinds of milk shakes had become the routine. Sharing them during the drive had been the norm. Pulling over to have sex had been his favorite break. Hers, too.

Whoa. Don't go there. He tightened his grip on the steering wheel. "Thanks, but I'm good."

"Suit yourself, but I'm willing to share."

Her lips closed over the end of the straw sticking out of the cup. She sipped. Swallowed.

His groin twinged. Blood boiled. Sweat coated his palms.

Damn. He needed to cool off. Quickly. "I'm happy with mine."

Cullen snagged his milk shake from the cup holder and sucked a mouthful through the straw. The cold vanilla drink hit the spot. A few more sips and his temperature might return to normal.

He was much too aware of her—from the way she glanced

sideward at him to the crooked part in her hair. Things he shouldn't notice or care about.

And he didn't. Care, that is.

But now that she was an arm's distance away, her feminine warmth and softness called to him like a PLB, personal locator beacon, beckoning in the night. Only, no one was lost. Nothing was lost except the impulsive, reckless side of who he used to be. The side Sarah brought out in him. The side he had buried alongside his brother.

Sure, Cullen missed the sex. What man wouldn't? But he'd been surviving without it. Without her. Celibacy was the better choice for now. Blaine had lost himself in drugs. Cullen had seen what losing control did to a man, to his brother. He wouldn't lose himself in Sarah.

He returned his drink to the cup holder. Maybe if he didn't say anything to her, she wouldn't talk to him.

"Is Hood Hamlet much farther?" Sarah asked.

So much for that tactic. He gritted his teeth. "Twenty-five minutes if we don't hit any traffic."

"That sounds pretty exact."

He'd been checking the clock on the dashboard every five minutes for the past two hours. "I drive this way to the hospital."

"You work in Portland, right?" she asked.

Great, more small talk. "Gresham. Northeast of the city."

"A long commute."

"Twelve-hour shifts help."

"Still a lot of driving," she said. "Why do you live so far away?"

He tapped his left foot. "I like Hood Hamlet."

"There have to be closer places."

"Yes, but I prefer the mountain."

"Why?"

"It's…"

"What?"

"Charming."

"You've never been one for charming," she said. "You thought

Leavenworth was, and I quote, 'a Bavarian-inspired tourist trap on steroids.'"

He had said that of the small town on the eastern side of the Cascade Mountains. "I liked climbing there."

"Nothing else."

He'd liked spending time with her in Leavenworth. A glance at the speedometer made him ease up on the gas pedal. "Hood Hamlet is different."

"Different, how?"

"There's something special about it."

"Special?"

He nodded. "Almost…magical."

She half laughed as if the joke was on him. "When did you start believing in magic?"

He understood her incredulous tone. A year ago he would have laughed at such a thought himself. After Blaine died, Cullen's belief in any kind of "magic" had died, too. He hadn't believed in anything that wasn't quantifiable—whether it was a diagnosis or a cure. Everything had to have an explanation. The one thing in his life that defied reason—his relationship with Sarah—had blown up in his face. "It's hard not to believe when you're there. A lot of people feel the same way."

"Must be something in the water," she joked.

A trained scientist like Sarah wouldn't understand. He'd been the same way until three things had changed his mind—the rescue of two climbers trapped in a snow cave last November, the town pulling off its Christmas Magic celebration in mid-December and Leanne Thomas getting engaged on Christmas Day. The three events had defied logic, but had happened anyway. "Maybe."

"The mountain air, perhaps," she teased.

"You never know." But he knew it was neither of those things.

"Whatever it is, I hope it's not contagious."

"I have no doubt you're immune as long as Mount Hood remains dormant."

He expected her to contradict him, if only to argue with him. She didn't.

"What else does the town have beside magic?" Sarah asked.

"The people. It's a great community." He'd realized how supportive they truly were with the numerous offers of help following Sarah's accident. "Very welcoming to strangers. That's how I ended up moving there. I'd driven up to Mount Hood on a day off. I had lunch at the local brewpub and met the owner, Jake Porter. When he found out I was involved with mountain rescue in Seattle, he told me about their local unit, OMSAR. He invited me to go climbing, and we did. I met a few more people. One told me about a cabin for rent. Next thing I knew, I was signing my name on a year lease."

"That's serendipity, not magic."

"Semantics," he countered.

"A year lease is a commitment."

"It's worked out fine."

"That's great, but I prefer a month-to-month lease."

Of course she would. A month-to-month marriage would have been her first choice if that had been allowed. "You've always liked to give yourself an out with everything you do."

Sarah stiffened. "I know better than to back myself into a corner."

She'd always been independent, but she sounded defensive, as if the world were against her. He hadn't meant to attack her. "Someone might be there to help you escape."

"I'd rather not deal with the consequences if they're not."

So jaded. He hoped their separation hadn't done this to her. "People can surprise you."

"They usually do, but not in the way I expect."

Cullen wasn't sure what she meant, but the tip of a knife seemed to be pressing against his heart. He wasn't sure he wanted to know the answer, but curiosity compelled him to ask the question. "Does that include me?"

"Yes."

The knife pierced his heart. Her answer shouldn't have surprised him. She was impulsive and impatient with a tendency to erupt like the volcanoes she loved so much. He'd tried to take care of her when they were married, but she'd pushed him away. He'd tried to make her happy, but she never seemed happy enough. A lot like Blaine. Cullen's jaw tightened to the point of aching. "Care to elaborate?"

"You've been great about my accident." Gratitude shone in her eyes. "I wasn't expecting that."

He felt the tension in his jaw ease. "Couples in our situation can be friendly to each other."

She nodded. "Especially when divorce is what we both want."

The knife dug a little deeper into his heart. "It is."

A cheery love song played on the radio. The upbeat tempo was the antithesis of how he felt. He fought the urge to press the power switch so the music would stop.

"I'm glad you found the place you belong," Sarah said.

"Hood Hamlet is the best thing that's happened to me in a long time." He remembered the list he'd put together of places they could live after he finished his residency. Portland had been near the top because of the Cascades Volcano Observatory in nearby Vancouver, Washington, but he'd never considered Mount Hood. And wouldn't have if they'd stayed together. "The only drawback is everyone wants to know everybody's business."

She clucked her tongue. "Typical small town."

"I sometimes forget how small."

"Does that mean people are going to be talking about us?"

He took a deep breath and exhaled slowly. "They already are."

"Why is that?"

Cullen shouldn't have said anything. His stomach roiled.

"Why?" Her voice rose.

His palms sweated. He wiped one on his jeans. "No one in Hood Hamlet knew I was married until your accident."

Her mouth gaped. She closed it. "Why didn't you tell them?"

He didn't want to admit he'd been nursing a wound so deep when he arrived in town he wasn't sure he would recover. But he had. And he was doing fine until she'd crashed back into his world. "You were no longer a part of my life. I could start over in Hood Hamlet with a clean slate once the divorce was finalized."

The color drained from her face. Hurt clouded her eyes. "You pretended to be single."

Her tone and stiff posture put him on the defensive. "Not intentionally."

She turned toward the window.

"Hey, I'm not the bad guy here." He lowered his voice. "Don't forget you're the one who brought up a divorce."

"True, but you agreed," she countered. "And I didn't move to a new town and act like I was single."

"I didn't act that way, either," he explained.

She stared at her cast with a downtrodden gaze. "Sure you didn't."

"I didn't." Her reaction surprised him. They'd been separated and hadn't seen each other for almost a year. Divorce was a mere formality. "What were people supposed to think? I moved to Hood Hamlet alone. I wasn't wearing a wedding band. No one asked if I'd been married, so I saw no a reason to tell them."

Sarah had grasped her milk shake so hard she'd put a dent in the cup. "If they had asked?"

Not carrying around the baggage of a failed marriage had helped him move on. He'd never expected anyone, including Sarah, to find out. But by trying to make things easier on himself over this past year, he'd made them harder now. For Sarah, too. "I would have told the truth."

She bit her lower lip. "No wonder people are talking."

"Friends were with me when you were in ICU. They had questions."

She lifted her chin. "What do your friends know about our situation?"

"Not much."

"Cullen…"

She sounded more annoyed than hurt. But he wouldn't call that progress. "They know we've been separated for almost a year but are together now."

She drew back with alarm. "Together?"

"For now."

Her mouth twisted.

"While you recover," he clarified.

"Well, I hope it won't take me long to get better so you can make your fresh start in Hood Hamlet and I can get back to Mount Baker."

At least they agreed on something. "Me, too. Except you can't rush through your recovery. If you focus on one day at a time, you'll get to where you're supposed to be."

And so would he.

Then they could both get on with their lives separately.

Cullen couldn't wait for that to happen.

Sarah couldn't wait to arrive in Hood Hamlet. The drive had been uncomfortable and painful to her injuries, but also to her heart. She couldn't change what had happened with Cullen. She could only learn from her mistakes and move forward with her life. That was what she needed to do. He already seemed to have done that. She hated that knowing he'd moved on twisted up her insides.

She stared out the truck's window. The highway snaked up Mount Hood, giving panoramic views of the tree-covered mountainside. The dark green of the pines contrasted with the cornflower-blue sky. Breathtaking. She couldn't get Cullen's image out of her head.

He'd shaved, removing the sexy stubble from his face. But he still looked totally hot, with the strong profile she knew by heart, warm blue eyes fringed by thick dark lashes that danced with laughter and lush lips perfect for kisses.

Had been perfect. Past tense.

A ballad played on the radio. The lyrics spoke of heartbreak and loneliness, two things she was familiar with.

But Sarah knew she and Cullen were better off apart. He'd found the place he belonged—Hood Hamlet. She'd never had that, not even when they'd lived together. Once she finished her postdoc she would keep looking until she found the haven she'd been searching for her whole life.

After a childhood of being shuttled between parents and stepparents as if she were a smelly dog no one wanted, she didn't need much. Nothing big and fancy, just a place where she belonged and mattered. Where she was loved.

She'd thought she found that with Cullen, but she'd been wrong. After a few months of marriage she'd seen the familiar signs. But she was older and wiser and knew what was going to happen. Only, this time she didn't have to wait to be shuffled off and abandoned. She could be the one to leave before that happened.

Cullen touched her forearm. "Sarah…"

She jumped. The seat belt kept her in place, but her cast hit the door with a thud.

"You okay?" he asked.

Anxiety rose like the pressure building inside Yellowstone's Old Faithful. But Sarah couldn't afford to erupt. She swallowed around the caldera-size lump in her throat. The stronger she appeared, the more in control, the sooner she could return to Bellingham and work. She nodded, afraid her voice might quiver like her insides.

"We're coming into Hood Hamlet," he said.

He flicked on the left-hand blinker. The traffic heading west slowed. He turned onto a wide street. A gas station and convenience store sat on one corner, and trees lined the left side of the road, the treetops glistening in the sun. A short distance away she saw the peaks of roofs.

She didn't believe in magic, but anticipation built over seeing this town Cullen called home.

The truck rounded a curve. Hood Hamlet came into view. Surprise washed over her. It was lovely. Picture-book perfect. Sarah could almost imagine herself in the Swiss Alps, not the Cascades, due to the architecture of the buildings.

"Welcome to Hood Hamlet." Cullen's voice held a note of reverence she understood now. No wonder he wanted to live here.

An Alpine-looking inn resembled a life-size four-story gingerbread house. A vacancy sign out front swayed from a wood post. Flowers bloomed in planters hung beneath each of the wood-framed windows and from baskets fastened on wood rafters. "It's so quaint."

They approached a busier part of the street. He slowed down. "This is Main Street."

A row of shops and restaurants had a covered wooden sidewalk. People popped in and out of stores. A woman with three children waved at Cullen.

He returned the gesture with a smile. "That's Hannah Willingham with her kids, Kendall, Austin and Tyler. Her husband, Garrett, is a CPA and OMSAR's treasurer."

A feeling of warmth settled at the center of Sarah's chest. "*Charming* is the perfect way to describe Hood Hamlet."

"You should see the place at Christmastime. The town goes all out."

Hood Hamlet was made for Christmas, with its mountain setting, ample snow and pine trees. She would love to see it in person. Too bad she would be long gone by then. "It must be wonderful."

"A winter wonderland." His eyes brightened. "There's an annual tree-lighting ceremony after Thanksgiving. The entire town turns out no matter the weather. Wreaths and garland are hung across Main Street. Every streetlight is strung with red and white lights to look like candy canes."

It sounded so inviting and special. Her Christmases had never been like that. No holiday had been. "Is Easter a big deal in Hood Hamlet, too?"

"The town holds an annual egg hunt. It's pretty low-key. Nothing like the shindig my mom and sisters put on. They could teach the Easter Bunny a thing or two," he joked.

She'd found nothing humorous about it. Her hands balled. "Easter at your parents' house was like stepping into the middle of a magazine spread or home-decorating show."

"Holidays are big deals to my family."

No kidding. "Your mom and sisters put Martha Stewart to shame. It was exhausting watching them do so much." Easter with Cullen and his family had shown Sarah how different their childhoods and lives had been. Her parents didn't do much for the holidays. Meals, special occasion or not, were eaten in front of the television or in the car, or they were skipped. She'd planned a wedding that had never happened, but she didn't know how to cook for a huge crowd or be a proper hostess. No way could she be the kind of wife Cullen and his family expected. "I tried to help, but I only slowed them down."

"Yeah, they go all out," he agreed. "I love it."

Cullen's words confirmed what Sarah had realized back then. She would never be able to pass muster with the Grays. Her shoulders sagged. The pain shooting down her right arm matched the hurt in her heart. She forced herself to sit straight.

"Holidays are more down-to-earth in Hood Hamlet, but nice, too. Lots of town traditions," he continued. "Santa and the Easter Bunny have been known to show up on Main Street to have their picture taken with kids and pets."

Pets? He'd never talked about animals before. "Do you have a pet?"

"No, but if I wasn't gone for so long when I work, I might consider getting one."

"I thought you didn't like dogs and cats."

"I like them, but my mom's allergic," he said. "One of the guys on the rescue unit has a Siberian husky named Denali. She's a cool dog."

"Get a cat. They're independent. A good pet for someone who is away a lot. Especially if you have two. That's what my boss Tucker says."

"I don't know if I'm a cat person. I'd like to know a pet cares if I'm around or not."

She knew the feeling. "Cats care, but they don't show it."

"Then what's the use of having one?"

Sarah could have asked him the same question about having a husband. His serious nature and stability had appealed to her when they'd first met. He'd been the exact opposite of the other men in her life, the same men who had disappointed and hurt her. But after they'd married she realized the traits that initially appealed to her kept him from being spontaneous or showing a lot of emotion, leaving her feeling isolated and alone, like when she'd been a kid.

The one emotion he'd had no difficulty expressing was desire. No issues in that department. A heated flush rushed through her, along with more memories she'd rather forget. "You're better off without a pet."

Cullen made a left-hand turn onto a narrow street that wound its way through trees. Homes and cabins were interspersed among the pines.

"This is convenient to Main Street," she said.

"Especially to the brewpub."

Cullen's former mountain-rescue unit in Seattle went out for beers after missions, but call outs hadn't been weekly occurrences. She couldn't imagine rescues were that frequent on Mount Hood. He must like to go out with his friends.

No doubt women were involved. Her left hand balled into a fist. She flexed her fingers. "That must come in handy on Friday and Saturday nights."

"Very handy."

The thought of Cullen with another woman sent a shudder through Sarah. "Who do you go to the brewpub with?"

"Mostly OMSAR members and a few firefighters."

"Nice guys?"

"Yes, but not all are men."

Her shoulders tensed. This was none of her business. Some people dated before a divorce was finalized. She shouldn't care or be upset over what Cullen did.

A quarter mile down the road, he turned the truck onto a short driveway and parked in front of a small, single-story cabin. "This is it."

Sarah stared in disbelief. She'd been expecting an A-frame, not something that belonged in a storybook. The log cabin was delightful, with wood beams and small-paned windows. A planter containing colorful flowers sat next to the front door. "It's adorable. I half expect to see Snow White walk out the front door, followed by the seven dwarfs."

He stopped the truck and set the parking brake. "It was used as a vacation rental so has curb appeal, but I wouldn't go that far."

"You have to admit it's cute."

He pulled the keys out of the ignition. "It suits my purpose."

She opened the passenger door. "I can't wait to see the inside."

"Stay there." Cullen exited, crossed in front of the truck and stood next to her. He extended his arm. "I'll help you inside."

She'd noticed his manners the first time they met. She'd appreciated the gentlemanly behavior. It wasn't something she was used to and it made her feel special. Too bad she hadn't felt as special after they married. Ignoring her soreness, she reached for his hand. "Thanks."

"Go slowly." He wrapped his hand around her waist. "I'll get the luggage once you're settled."

She wasn't about to argue. Not when the warmth of his skin sent heat rushing through her veins. All she had to do was make it to the front door and inside the cabin. Then she could let go and catch her breath.

Cullen escorted her toward the cabin as if she was as delicate as a snowflake. She took cautious steps, fighting the urge to hurry so she could let go of him. The scent of him embraced her. Every point of contact was sweet torture. Relief nearly knocked her over when she reached the porch step.

He squeezed her hand. "Careful."

Yes, she needed to be careful around Cullen. Reactions to him could bring disaster down on her already hurting head.

Reaching around her with his other hand, he unlocked the door. A feeling of déjà vu washed over her. When they'd arrived in Seattle after eloping, Cullen had taken her to his apartment. He'd swept her up into his arms and carried her over the threshold. The romantic gesture had sent her heart singing and told her she hadn't made a mistake eloping.

"It's a good thing Snow White and her crew aren't here, or this place would be too crowded." He pushed open the door with his foot. "Go on in."

No romance today. Sarah hated the twinge of disappointment arcing through her. She released his hand and stepped through the doorway.

The decor was comfortable and inviting. The kitchen was small but functional, with stainless-steel appliances and a tiled island with a breakfast bar. The bar stools matched the pine table and six chairs in the dining room that separated the kitchen from the living room. "Nice place."

A river-rock fireplace with a wood mantel on the far wall drew her attention. She imagined a crackling fire would be nice when the temperature dropped. A large television was tucked into the space above the fireplace. A three-cushion, overstuffed leather couch was positioned in front of the fireplace/TV to the left. The perfect place to relax after a long day. Log-pole coffee- and end tables, as well as photographs and artwork, added a touch of the outdoors to the rustic yet welcoming decor. "You got new furniture."

He closed the door behind him. "I rented this place furnished."

"Did you put your stuff in storage?"

"I sold it."

She glanced around. Nothing looked familiar. "Everything?"

"Most of it was castoffs from friends and family anyway. No sense dragging all that old stuff here with me."

Sarah ignored a flash of hurt. She'd given him a framed photograph from Red Rocks on their first wedding anniversary. And then she remembered. "A fresh start."

"Yes."

"Nice cabin." Much nicer than any place she'd ever lived, including the apartment they'd shared. "I can see why you signed a year lease."

"I'm comfortable here."

If she'd ever wondered if Cullen needed her, Sarah had her answer today. He didn't need her. He had a nice place to live, friends and a good job. His life was complete without her.

Too bad she couldn't say the same thing about her life without him.

CHAPTER FIVE

"SOMETHING SMELLS GOOD."

The sound of Sarah's voice sent a thunderbolt of awareness through Cullen, jolting him back to reality. For the past two hours he'd relished the solitude of the cabin, pretending she wasn't asleep in the guest bedroom. He placed the hot pad on the counter, then turned away from the stove. "Dinner."

She stood where the hallway ended and the living room began with bare feet, tangled hair, looking sleep-rumpled sexy. A half smile formed on her lips. "I didn't expect to wake up to dinner cooking."

He glimpsed ivory skin where the hem of her T-shirt rode up over her waistband. The top button on her jeans was undone, making him think of her shimmying out of them.

Appealing idea, yes. Appropriate, no.

Cullen focused on her face. Still a bit roughed-up after the accident, but pretty nonetheless. "You took a long nap."

"The bed makes the mattress back at the hospital seem like a slab of granite. I felt like I was sleeping on a cloud."

She'd tended toward the devilish in the past, making it difficult to imagine her as an angel now. "I told you this place would be better than a SNF."

"Yes, you did."

Having her around wasn't turning out to be the best thing for him, though. His gaze strayed to the enticing band of bare skin. The hint of flesh tantalized, reminding him of what had been kept from him. And would never be his again.

He jammed a spoon into the pot of refried beans and stirred.

"I'm glad I listened," she said.

He realized she was wearing the same clothes as earlier. "You can't be comfortable in those jeans. Put on pajamas or sweats."

Shrugging her left shoulder, she studied a photograph of Illumination Rock hanging on the wall.

His stomach dropped. "You can't undress yourself."

Damn. The thought of helping her had never crossed his mind. He'd been thinking about his needs, not hers.

"I probably could if I tried. Natalie told me to leave the button on my jeans undone," Sarah said. "But I didn't think about changing when we arrived. I hit the mattress and was out."

Cullen felt like a jerk. He should have checked on her more carefully. But he hadn't wanted to get too close after the drive.

Good work, Dr. Gray.

The sound of Blaine's voice mocking Cullen, blaming him with a growing list of transgressions, was almost too much for him to take. He lowered the temperature on the beans, then checked the Spanish rice.

He should have done more for Sarah. But he'd needed a break. He might be a physician, but he was still a man. One who hadn't kissed or touched a woman in almost a year. In spite of their marriage falling apart and the hard feelings that brought with it, undressing Sarah would have meant his needing a cold shower.

Cullen would have to get past that. He was responsible for her well-being. "I'll help you after…"

Sarah's face paled.

His stomach roiled. *What the—*

She swayed unsteadily.

Adrenaline surged. Cullen ran.

She slumped against the wall.

He wrapped his arms around her before she crumpled to the ground like a house of cards. "I've got you."

Her warmth, softness and smell were like sweet ambrosia. His groin tightened. He recalled parts of the anatomy…in Latin.

"Thanks." Her breath caressed his neck, sending pleasurable sensations through him. "I was dizzy. I must have gotten out of bed too fast."

He would gladly take her back to bed. And join her.

Bad idea. "You've had a long day. It's been a while since you ate."

"The milk shake—"

"Food."

She straightened. "I feel better now."

"Good, but let's not take any chances." He swept her up into his arms, ignoring her sharp inhalation and how good it felt to hold her. "I don't want you to fall."

As if concern explained the acceleration of his pulse or his breathlessness.

Wariness clouded her eyes. "I don't want you to strain your back."

"Thanks for the concern, but you hardly weigh anything." Sarah had always been fit, but never this thin. He carried her to the couch. "We'll have to put some meat on you."

Sarah's gaze narrowed. "That's not what a woman wants to hear."

As he walked, her breasts jiggled.

Desire slammed into him, hard and fast like a line drive to third base. A fire ignited low in his gut.

Forget the Latin. Organic chemistry equations might work better. "Men like women with curves. Gives them something to hold on to."

Awareness flickered in her eyes. Sarah parted her lips.

All he had to do was lower his mouth to hers and...

"Some men," she said.

If he'd had a thermometer under his tongue, the mercury would have shot out the end and made a real mess. "This man."

Tension sizzled in the air. The physical chemistry between them remained strong, and, if the past sixty seconds were anything to go by, highly combustible.

Fighting the urge to get the hell away from her before his control slipped any further, he placed her gently on the couch. "Rest while I finish getting dinner ready."

He strode to the kitchen with one purpose in mind—put distance between him and Sarah, even if it was less than twelve feet. Attraction or not, this had disaster written all over it. She was injured. She was his soon-to-be ex-wife. Thinking of her as anything other than a patient would be…wrong.

Cullen checked the beans and the rice. He glanced at the clock on the microwave. "Time for your meds."

"I'd rather not take them." The back of the couch hid all but the top of her head. "They make me loopy."

"Staying ahead of the pain is important."

"I'm ahead of it."

Not for long. Her voice sounded strained. He filled a glass with water and dispensed her pills. "This isn't up for negotiation."

She poked her head up. "Whatever you're cooking smells so good."

"Enchiladas."

"One of my favorites."

Changing the subject wasn't like Sarah. She must not feel well. He carried the water and medicine to her. "Here you go."

She stared at the pills as if they were poison. "Your patients must call you Dr. Hardnose."

He handed her the pills. "They might, but not to my face. Well, except you."

"I'm not your patient." She shot him a chilly look, popped the pills into her mouth and drank the water. "Satisfied?"

"Very. It's not often you do what you're told."

"I only took the pills because you made dinner."

"Then it's a good thing I didn't tell you someone else made the meal."

"Who?"

"Carly Porter." He placed Sarah's water glass on the coffee table. "She stopped by while you were sleeping."

A thoughtful expression crossed Sarah's face. "That sure is nice of Carly."

Sarah's voice sounded tight, almost on edge. A good thing

she'd taken her pills. "Carly and her husband are good people. Jake's the one who owns the brewpub."

A corner of Sarah's mouth curved upward in a lopsided smile. "Oh, you mentioned him earlier."

The timer on the oven dinged.

"Dinner's ready," Cullen said. "You can eat on the couch."

"I've been eating in bed. I'd rather sit at the table, if that's okay?"

His stomach twisted. This would be their first meal together since she'd brought up divorce.

She touched her cast. "If you'd rather I eat here—"

"The table works." He was being stupid. Just because the last time had ended badly didn't mean this time would. Hell, he'd wanted to kiss her a few minutes ago. No matter how he looked at this situation, an epic fail seemed imminent. "Give me a sec."

Cullen set the table. Utensils clattered against the plates. His hands shook. He wasn't sure what had gotten into him, but he felt clumsy, a way he wasn't used to feeling.

He placed the hot casserole dish, bowls of rice and refried beans and a bottle of sparkling apple cider on the table. He left the six-pack of Wy'East Brewing Company's Hogsback Ale, courtesy of Jake, in the refrigerator. Cullen needed his wits about him with Sarah here. "Dinner's ready."

He helped her up from the couch, conscious of her every movement and aware of each brush of his skin sparking against hers.

She squeezed his hand. "Thanks."

A lump formed in his throat. He grumbled, "You're welcome," then escorted her to the table. He kept his arm around her in case she became light-headed—yeah, that was the reason, all right—pulled out a chair and helped her sit. His hand lingered on her back.

"Everything looks delicious," she said.

Her lips sure did. What was he doing? Sarah had an excuse for acting loopy. Cullen didn't. He looked away and dropped his hand to his side.

"I can't believe someone made you dinner." She sounded amazed.

He sat across from her, then dished up chicken enchiladas smothered in a green tomatillo sauce. "Carly and Jake did this for you, too."

"No one's ever done something like this for me."

He dropped a spoonful of refried beans onto her plate and then his. "People are helpful in Hood Hamlet."

She motioned to the serving spoon in his hand. "You included."

Cullen added a scoop of the rice. "You'll serve yourself soon enough."

Sarah's shoulders drooped as if someone had let the air out of her. "I'd make a big mess right now, and you'd have to clean up after me."

That was what she'd done with the divorce. Left him to deal with it. He took a sip of the sparkling cider. The sweetness did nothing to alter the bitter taste in his mouth. Maybe a beer wasn't such a bad idea. Just one. He never had any more than that.

"You're smart for serving tonight," she continued.

A smart man would never have allowed his heart to overrule logic so that he ended up marrying a total stranger in Las Vegas. "Just trying to be helpful."

"I…appreciate it."

As they ate, Cullen wondered if she did. She hadn't appreciated what he'd done when they were together.

Bubbles rose in his glass, making him think of champagne. Marriage was like champagne bubbles, first rising in pairs, then groups of three, then individually. He was thankful he and Sarah had skipped the middle part by not having a baby right away. A divorce was bad enough without having to deal with a custody battle. "It's a practical decision. I don't have time for extra chores tonight. I have to work the graveyard shift at the hospital tomorrow night and need to get back into my routine."

Maybe sleeping in his bed at home would give him a restful night of sleep. He hoped so.

She studied him over the rim of her glass. "Who will be my nursemaid?"

"I found the perfect babysitter."

Sarah stuck her tongue out at him.

That was more like it. He grinned. "We could go with *nanny* if you prefer."

She waved her cast in the air. "I bet this thing could do some damage."

"To yourself most definitely."

"Very funny." She feigned annoyance, but laughter danced in her eyes. "So who's stuck here with me first?"

"Leanne Thomas," Cullen said. "I know her from OMSAR. She's also a paramedic."

"Sounds capable."

"I'd trust her with my life. In fact, I have," he admitted. "You'll be in good hands.

"I'm in good hands now."

He appreciated the words, but he'd fallen down on the job this afternoon. "I'm trying to do my best."

"You are," she agreed. "I'm not sure how I'll ever repay you."

"You don't have to." That was the truth. He didn't want anything from her. Well, except to finalize their divorce. Soon… "I remember what it was like."

Wrinkles formed on her forehead. "Remember what what was like?"

"To have a broken arm."

She leaned over the table. "When did you break your arm?"

"I was eleven." He took another enchilada from the pan. "Want more?"

"No, thanks." Sarah stared at him. "I had no idea about your arm. How did you break it?"

"A soccer tournament. This big kid shoved me out of bounds after I scored a goal. I landed wrong and fractured my arm in two places."

"Ouch."

"That's all I could say in between grimacing and crying."

She drew back, as if horror. "You cry?"

"Past tense. I was eleven."

"I'm teasing," she said. "Nothing wrong with crying, no matter what your age."

"Only if you're an emotional, overwrought sissy man."

"Wouldn't want someone to take away your man card."

"Damn straight."

She sipped her cider. "Tell me more about your broken arm."

He patted his mouth with a napkin. "Not much more to tell. It happened in early July, so I spent the rest of my summer in a cast. It sucked."

"You do know how I feel."

He nodded. "I couldn't swim or go in the sprinklers. I wasn't allowed to ride my bike or skateboard. No going on rides at the county fair, either. Casts weren't allowed."

"That must have been the worst summer of your life."

Nope. That was a toss-up between last summer when he was trying to get over her and the summer after his brother died. But her rejection had hurt lots more than his arm fracture. He was relieved he'd moved past that. "It wasn't fun, but I survived. So will you."

His tone came out harsh, without an ounce of sympathy or compassion. He needed to try harder. Apologize. Being with Sarah brought out strong feelings and emotions, ones he would rather forget existed. He'd seen what losing control had done to Blaine. Cullen wouldn't allow the same thing to happen to him.

Forks scraped against plates. Glasses were raised and returned to the table. The lack of conversation was awkward. But Cullen didn't know what to do about it. He'd never known what to do with Sarah except kiss her and take her to bed.

Not an option. Even if a part of him wished it were.

As Cullen loaded the dishwasher, Sarah sat at the table with a plate of cookies within arm's reach. Medication dulled the pain, but made her feel as if she'd drunk one beer too many. Maybe that was why dinner with Cullen had seemed so weird. Forget walking on eggshells—the floor was covered in shattered glass and she kept stepping on the shards.

An uncomfortable silence had enveloped them during the meal. The same unsettling quiet had consumed their marriage. If Sarah could have made it to the guest bedroom on her own, she would have bolted after she'd finished eating. But, since she couldn't, death by chocolate chips sounded like the best alternative.

She bit into a cookie. The sweet flavor exploded in her mouth. "Great cookie."

Cullen glanced over his shoulder. "Carly is known for her baking skills."

"I can see why." Sarah had been surprised about Cullen's broken arm. She wondered what else she didn't know about him. Sex had been the way they'd been able to communicate best. But even that hadn't been enough after a while. Uh-oh. Thinking about sex and Cullen wasn't going to help matters. "I think I'll have another cookie."

"Save me one."

She held her left hand above the plate. "There are over a dozen."

Cullen glanced over his shoulder. Amusement—at least that was what she hoped it was—flashed in his eyes. "I know how much you love cookies."

"You gave me a cookie bouquet for my birthday." That had been five months into their marriage. He'd also covered their bed with rose petals. A romantic gesture when romance had been nonexistent. "They were tasty."

"I never got one."

"That's because you left for your shift at the hospital and I didn't hear from you for two days."

Cullen gave her one of those you-have-to-be-kidding looks. "I had to work."

By the time he'd returned, the cookies had been eaten and the rose petals had wilted. "You never called or texted. Not even during breaks."

He tugged at his collar. "I need to concentrate when I'm at the hospital."

He had never owned up to his behavior in the past. Why had

she expected anything different now? Best to forget everything that had happened between them. Good or bad. She pushed the plate of cookies away. "Help yourself. You'll have to roll me back to my room if I eat any more."

"Roll you, carry you." He bent to put something in the dishwasher. "Not much difference."

Maybe not for him.

A wave of helplessness washed over her, threatening to drown her. She hated not being able to do anything on her own. She hated being at someone else's mercy. She hated relying on anybody. Oh-so-familiar disappointment pressed down on her. She had finally been getting everything on track when life threw a rock at her. She didn't want to have to depend on Cullen. She didn't want to end up needing him.

The tight ball of emotion in her belly unraveled like yarn, sending pent-up feelings rolling through her.

She couldn't unsnap her bra or button her jeans or be the kind of wife a man would love forever.

Tears stung her eyes.

Oh, no. Sarah didn't want him to see her like this. She was independent and strong, not needy and emotional. Except, the only thing she felt like doing right now was crying.

She blinked. She looked up. Drops still fell. She dabbed her eyes with the napkin.

Time to get out of here.

Without Cullen's help.

Using her left hand, she pushed against the table. Mantling had always been a favorite climbing move, but this took more effort than she was used to exerting. Her muscles protested. Her abdomen ached. Still she managed to stand, scooting the chair back in the process.

Cullen looked at her. Forks clattered into the sink. He rushed to her side. "What are you doing?"

"I don't need to be rolled or carried." Her voice cracked. "I can do it myself."

Except she couldn't. All she wanted to do was sit. Pride kept her standing.

"I was kidding." He didn't sound amused. His dark eyes looked annoyed. "Like old times."

She raised her chin, but that didn't make up the difference in height. The top of her head came to his nose. She reminded herself that in every other way they were equals. And an underground city of elves lived inside Mount Shasta, too. "The old times weren't that great."

He flinched. "They weren't that bad."

She shrugged, hoping the gesture hid the hurt she was feeling. "I'm used to taking care of myself. I can do this."

But if she didn't get moving she would be flat on her butt in about ten seconds.

"Tomorrow—" he scooped her into his arms "—not tonight. Time to get you into your jammies and into bed."

Cradled against his strong, wide chest, she struggled to breathe. Her muscles tensed. Her senses reeled.

What was happening to her?

Sarah wanted to be strong, but she also wanted to collapse against him and forget everything in the past and what would happen in the future. But she couldn't. Not when the feel of his heartbeat sent hers into a frenetic rhythm. Or when the musky scent of him made her want to take another sniff.

"You don't have to do this." She tried to keep the panic out of her voice. "I'm okay."

Or would be once she was out of his arms and into bed.

Alone.

With the door locked.

Sarah's gaze locked on his lips. Heat exploded inside her. She looked away.

"You're not okay." He carried her down the hallway. "It doesn't take a medical degree to see you're exhausted."

She opened her mouth to deny it, but couldn't. "I'll feel better in the morning."

"I'd rather you feel better now."

Maybe if she had a good cry or if he kissed her...

He kicked open the bathroom door with his foot and flipped

on the light with his elbow. He set her on her feet in the bathroom, keeping his hands on her. "Let's get you ready for bed."

Her heart beat a rapid tattoo. She leaned against the sink counter for support. "My toiletry kit is in my suitcase."

A coworker had packed a bag for Sarah and driven it to the hospital yesterday.

Cullen opened a drawer and pulled out a new toothbrush. He unwrapped the plastic covering. "Use this."

"You have spare toothbrushes?"

"People sack out here if they don't want to drive home."

People? Or women? Sarah didn't want to know.

He squirted toothpaste on it. "Here you go."

She took the toothbrush. One minute he seemed upset at her, the next he was concerned. The flip-flopping made her dizzy. Or maybe it was the pain medication. That could explain her crying.

"I'll brush your teeth for you," he said.

She shoved the toothbrush into her mouth. "Got it."

"Be right back."

Sarah took advantage of the moment of privacy. Then after brushing her teeth, she washed her face and combed the tangles out of her hair. The effort wiped her out. She released a frustrated breath.

Cullen stood in the doorway. "Finished?"

Sarah nodded. He followed her to the guest room.

A queen-size bed with a headboard made of twigs dominated the room. He'd straightened the bedding and pulled back the covers for her, something he'd done for her when he worked graveyard shifts. Her chest tightened with memories and regrets.

A full glass of water sat on the knotty-pine nightstand. A cookie lay on a paper towel. Tears returned to her eyes. "I don't deserve—"

He placed his finger at her lips. "Shhh."

The slight touch sent chills down her spine. She couldn't have said anything if she'd wanted to.

Cullen tucked a strand of hair behind her ear. "I didn't take good care of you earlier."

Her heart stilled. She knew he meant today, but a part of her wished he'd meant during their marriage.

"I'm making up for this afternoon," he continued.

Sarah released the breath she hadn't realized she was holding. Her disappointment was a not-so-subtle reminder of how stupid she became around Cullen. "You're not my manservant."

Mischief did the tango in his eyes. "I could be if that's what you want."

She wanted…him.

No, that was the pain medication talking. More tears filled her eyes. She wiped her face with the back of her hand.

He embraced her. "It's going to be okay."

Not with her breasts pressed against his broad, muscular chest and her heart thudding in her chest. "I'm sorry. I'm all loopy."

"You're cute when you're all loopy."

He pulled her closer and she sank against him, too tired to keep fighting herself. He felt so good. Warm. And strong. "You're cute when I'm all loopy."

Cullen laughed. The deep sound was the best medicine of all. "Where are your pajamas?"

"In my suitcase."

"Sit."

She sat on the bed while he opened her suitcase.

He removed a floral-print nightshirt. "This work?"

"Yes."

Cullen placed the nightie on the bed. He pulled on her bra band through her T-shirt. The strap unhooked.

Heat rushed up her neck. "You've, um, always been good at that."

"A little rusty, but it's like riding a bike."

Her pulse quickened. "I haven't ridden in a while."

Too long. She missed it. Missed him. No, she missed the idea of him, of what they could have had together if fairy tales existed. This—what was happening right now—wasn't real.

He brushed his hand over her hair. "You can always hop back on."

Sarah's mouth went dry. She opened her mouth to speak, but no words came out.

"Let's get your shirt off you."

Let's not. She crossed her arm and her cast in front of her chest. "I want to see if I can do it."

"Sure."

She waited for him to turn around. He didn't. Frustration grew. "Maybe you could face the other way."

He turned to the wall.

Self-preservation helped her undress and put on the night-shirt. Thank goodness she'd taken the pain pills, or she'd be really hurting. "You can turn around."

"I'm impressed."

She was about to fall asleep. "Thanks."

"Time for bed."

Before Sarah could blink, she was horizontal with her head against the pillow. She had no idea how he'd managed to get her in this position so effortlessly, but she was beyond the point of caring.

Cullen arranged the sheet and comforter over her.

"You don't have to do this," she said quietly.

He brushed his lips across her forehead with a kiss as light as a feather. "It's been a long day, an even longer week. The least I can do is tuck you in."

Emotion overflowed from her heart. She felt so special.

"Sweet dreams, Lavagirl," he said.

Who needed dreams? Reality was pretty sweet right now. Sarah wanted him to stay, to hold her, until she fell asleep.

"Thank you, Dr. Gray." She felt dreamy and a tad wistful. "For everything."

"I'm right across the hall if you need anything."

He turned off the light, walked out of the room and closed the door behind him.

And then it hit her.

She and Cullen had never spent a night in the same place without sleeping in the same bed. Not until tonight. Her heart panged.

A door closed out in the hallway. She heard water. The shower.

Well, there was always a first time. Sarah touched the empty space next to her. But she had to admit she'd rather there wasn't.

Even if she knew better.

CHAPTER SIX

SOMEONE COUGHED. CULLEN bolted upright from a dead sleep. He blinked, not quite sure what was going on. Rays of sunlight peeked into the room around the edges of the window blinds. The digital clock on his nightstand read 6:45 a.m. Another cough.

Sarah.

Pulse pounding, he jumped out of bed, ran to her room and flung open the door. She lay in bed. Her hair was a tangled mess. Her face, what he could see through her hair, was pale. "Sarah?"

"I coughed." Her voice sounded hoarse. "It hurt."

"I'm sure it did." He sat next to her. "Let me check your incision."

Her eyes widened with a hint of panic. "It was the cough."

He brushed the hair away from her face. His fingers touched her cheek. She didn't feel warm. "I want to make sure."

She pulled the blanket to her neck. "You don't have to go to all this trouble."

"It's no trouble." He understood Sarah's leeriness. In spite of being a little out of it last night, she must have realized he'd been turned on. Even after a cold shower, he'd wanted to sleep in here, to hold her, to breathe in her scent. Loneliness did strange things to a man. "If you were in a SNF, someone would check you."

"Yes, but not…"

"Me."

She nodded. "I'm sorry."

"Don't apologize."

Her fingers rubbed the edge of the blanket. She wouldn't meet his eyes. "It's the situation. I'm not sure how to feel around you. Parts of last night were nice, then awkward, then nice again. So nice I hated sleeping alone."

A combination of relief and satisfaction radiated through him. He'd thought the same thing. He touched her shoulder.

Her muscles tensed beneath his hand.

"I get it," he admitted. "Having you here is…"

"Weird."

"Different," he said at the same time. "A little weird, too."

She blew out a puff of air. "Good. I mean, not that things are weird, but that I'm not alone or imagining things."

"You're not alone." He'd been imagining things about her all night. Unfortunately. Because those fantasies would never become reality. "We're adults. We can handle this."

"It's not like we have another choice."

If only… "It is what it is until you're ready to go back to Bellingham."

"If things get too weird we can talk it out."

She had wanted to talk about everything. He hated doing that. He'd been talked out after his parents had the family attend counseling and grief sessions following Blaine's death. The intense sessions helped, but they also frustrated Cullen because no amount of counseling or rehab had been able to help his brother kick his drug addiction.

Sarah looked expectantly at him.

"Sure, we can talk." He relented. "May I check your incision?"

She lowered the blanket. "It's not like you haven't seen this before."

He slowly raised the hem of her nightshirt over her thighs. The bruises were fading. He lifted the material higher, past her orange polka-dotted bikini panties that showed off the curve of her hip. He willed his hand not to tremble. He continued to the large incision on her abdomen from her emergency splenectomy.

Cullen might have seen her body before, but he liked seeing all that creamy skin again. His gaze strayed back to her panties. He swallowed.

Focus.

The skin around the sutures wasn't any more red then it had been at the hospital. No drainage, either. He placed his fingertips on her stomach. The skin wasn't hot, but boy did she feel nice. Soft, smooth, silky.

He dragged his hand away. "No drainage or rash. Are you hungry?"

She nodded.

"That's a good sign." He pulled down the hem of her nightshirt before he became more unprofessional. "Has the pain lessened since the surgery?"

"Yes, until I coughed."

"Next time you have to cough place a pillow over your incision." He stood. "Let's get you up and moving. That should ease some of the pain."

She scrunched her nose. "It's too early for you to be up if you have to work tonight."

Her concern brought a smile to his face. "I'll take a nap later."

"You're sure?"

"Positive." He cupped her elbow and helped her out of bed. "Is it hard to breathe?"

"Nope."

"Let's see how you feel walking."

She moved slowly and carefully, the way she should to make sure she didn't fall. "It helps."

He noticed her long legs, liked the curve of her calf, the slender slope of her ankles. "You're doing great."

She walked out of the bedroom. "I must look pretty frightening."

"Not frightening." He followed her down the hall. "You look pretty good for someone recovering from a bad fall, broken bones and surgery."

She glanced over her shoulder, her green eyes hopeful. "Any chance I could shower?"

An image of him taking off her panties flashed in his mind. He gave his head a mental shake. "Uh, sure. I'll have to wrap your cast."

"That's what the nurse did at the hospital," Sarah said with a relieved smile. "I may need you to pour the shampoo into my left hand."

Or he could join her in the shower and wash her hair for her. He wouldn't mind lathering her up.

Strike that. Cullen pushed the idea from his head. He found it too easy to think about her as his wife, not his soon-to-be ex-wife. She'd wanted out of the marriage. No reason to assume she wanted back in. Not that he wanted her back. He didn't. At least most of the time, he didn't. "Let's get you fed, then cleaned up."

Sarah stood in the bathroom wearing her orange robe and nothing underneath. She stared at the tile floor, not wanting to meet Cullen's watchful eyes. She tightened the belt around her waist as best she could with one hand so the robe wouldn't slip open.

His height and wide shoulders made the space feel cramped even though the bathroom was larger than the one at the hospital. He checked the plastic around her cast. "It should stay dry."

"I don't think any water is going to come close to my cast."

He turned on the shower. Water splashed against the tub and curtain. "That's the plan."

Cullen had always been a planner. Too bad he hadn't stuck to his plans instead of letting her derail them. That would have saved them both a lot of heartache. Well, at least her. "Have your life figured out again?"

His gaze met hers. "Pretty much. I made a few changes."

Like removing her from his future plans. She pinched the bridge of her nose, ignoring the hollow feeling inside her.

He checked the water temperature. "Ready?"

Not really. "Sure."

He pulled back the shower curtain. "There's a mat on the bottom of the tub, so you shouldn't slip, but be careful."

"Okay."

She waited for him to leave. He didn't.

"Aren't you getting in?" he asked.

Cullen stared at her as if she had something on her face. Leftover French toast, perhaps? She rubbed the back of her hand over her mouth. "Are you staying in here?"

"Yes."

It was as simple and as complicated as that.

"I need to hand you shampoo," he reminded her.

Oh, yeah. She'd forgotten about that. But still she hesitated. "This is kind of awkward."

"Only if we make it awkward."

"I'm not trying to."

"Neither am I."

"But I'm the one who is naked under my robe."

"I can undress."

She gave him a look.

He grinned, then faced the door. "Better?"

"Yes, thank you." Mustering her courage with a deep breath wasn't going to work, with her incision and ribs. She settled for a slight intake of air, untied the belt, dropped her robe and stepped inside the tub. She closed the shower curtain. "You can turn around now."

"Is the water the right temperature?"

Hot water poured over her. Steam rose toward the ceiling. She picked up a bar of soap. "Perfect."

"I remember you like it hot."

She remembered the showers they'd taken together. Hot water pulsating down on them. Washing each other. Kissing. Touching.

The soap slipped out of her hand and clattered to the tub.

"Sarah—"

"I dropped the soap," she said at the same time.

"Can you reach it?" he asked.

Bending hurt. But she wasn't about to ask him to get it for her. That would be too awkward. Too...tempting. "No, but it's okay. I really just wanted to wash my hair."

"I've got the shampoo," he said. "Stick out your hand when you want some."

Once her hair was wet enough, she extended her left arm. The cooler air temperature made her shiver. Goose bumps covered her exposed skin.

He poured a dollop of shampoo onto her palm. "Is that enough?"

"Yes."

Washing her hair was easier this time. "I'm getting the hang of using one hand."

"Just takes time."

Time she didn't have. For the past twenty-four hours, Cullen had occupied the majority of her thoughts. Not Mount Baker. Once she had work to distract her everything would return to normal. She couldn't wait for that to happen. She rinsed the shampoo from her hair.

"Need more?" he asked.

Yes, but not from him. He hadn't been able to give her what she needed. She couldn't be the wife he wanted. That was why they were better off apart. Still, the thought made her heart hurt. Not a want-to-throw-herself-a-pity-party aching, but a too-bad-this-couldn't-have-worked pining. "I'm good."

At least when it came to shampoo.

After she returned to the institute with her marriage and Cullen behind her, everything in her life would be good, too. Given how bad things had been, it sure couldn't get any worse.

Later that evening, the doorbell rang. Sarah remained on the couch while Cullen answered the door. Her babysitter for the night, Leanne Thomas, must have arrived.

Sarah was looking forward to Cullen going to work. A physical separation from him would be a relief, even though she'd spent most of her day in bed while he caught up on things around the cabin. But she'd been thinking about him constantly. On her mind was the last place he belonged. Well, actually her heart was the last place, but that wasn't going to happen again.

A pretty woman with long, shiny brown hair, an easy smile and wearing a huge diamond engagement ring carried in a platter of mini red velvet cupcakes. She placed the dessert on the kitchen table, then removed a green tote bag from her shoulder. "Hi, I'm Leanne."

"I'm Sarah." Cullen had called the by-the-book paramedic

and mountain-rescue volunteer tough as nails, but Sarah didn't get that impression at all. "Nice to meet you."

"The pleasure is mine." Leanne glanced at Cullen, who was sticking a water bottle into his backpack. "Hope I'm not late."

"Right on time." He swung a backpack strap over his right shoulder. "Thanks for taking the overnight shift. I left a list of instructions on the breakfast bar. Sarah's meds are on the kitchen counter. She should rest as much as possible. Short walks are okay, but not outside."

"Bummer. I thought I could take her on a midnight stroll around Mirror Lake," Leanne teased.

His gaze hardened. "You're kidding."

Sarah shook her head. He needed to lighten up and not take things so seriously.

Leanne's mouth quirked. "Give me a little credit."

"Just making sure," he said. "Call me if you have any questions."

What? Sarah bit her lower lip. He hadn't wanted her to call him at work no matter what was going on. If she did contact him, he never got back to her. Most of the times she'd tried calling had been because she missed him and wanted to hear his voice.

"I'm sure Sarah will be able to answer any questions I might have," Leanne said.

"Definitely." Sarah liked how direct Leanne was. "I don't know what instructions Cullen left, but my doctor's orders are to take my medication. Sleep. Rest. Sleep some more. Rest some more."

Leanne frowned. "Sounds boring."

"It is," Sarah agreed. "I fear I'm turning into a couch potato."

Cullen's lip curled. "Resting is important if you want to recover."

"True, but you can still do stuff while you take it easy," Leanne said. "I'll have to see what I can come up with."

"Thomas," Cullen said, his voice containing a clear warning.

"Relax," Leanne countered in a stern voice that made Sarah bite back a giggle. "Sarah will be fine. Get going before we throw you out."

He raised his hands in mock surrender. "I'm going."

As soon as the door closed, Leanne sat on the couch. "I'm sorry about your fall."

"Thanks. I was at the wrong place, wrong time."

"Well, you're in the right place now. Hood Hamlet will be good for you. It won't be long until you're exploring Main Street."

"I can't wait."

Colorful prisms of light reflected off Leanne's diamond ring and danced around the living room. She stared lovingly at her ring.

"Congrats on your engagement," Sarah said.

Leanne beamed. "Thanks. I still can't believe I'm getting married."

"Have you set a wedding date?"

She nodded. "The Saturday before Christmas. We hadn't been together long when my fiancé, Christian, proposed on Christmas Day so we thought a year engagement sounded good."

Very good. A year was long enough to get know someone, but not so long you would feel you'd wasted a lot of time if it didn't work out. "Cullen said you're a member of OMSAR. Does Christian belong, too?"

"No. He climbs and thought about joining, but he thinks I need something of my own, since we work together."

"Smart guy."

A dreamy expression filled Leanne's brown eyes. "Very smart and smokin' hot. Ever since we got together I feel like I won the lottery."

"I know that feeling."

"With Doc?"

Cullen had treated her with such respect from the moment they met. No other man in her life had ever done that. The cascade of memories made it hard to breathe. How had it gone so wrong? She nodded.

"How did you meet?" Leanne asked.

"I was attending the Red Rocks Rendezvous. We both lived in Seattle at the time and a mutual climbing acquaintance introduced us. A few hours later we ended up in the same self-rescue clinic."

"Sounds like fate."

"Only if fate has a really bad sense of humor."

Leanne's brow wrinkled. "Doc mentioned you're getting a divorce."

Sarah ignored the pang in her heart. "Yes."

"I've gotten to know Doc pretty well the past few months," Leanne said. "At first I thought he took himself way too seriously and had a stick up his butt. But he's a good guy."

"Cullen is a great guy. Not many men would bring their future ex-wives home to care for them."

"This is none of my business, but I'm still going to ask." Warmth and concern sounded in Leanne's voice. "Is there a possibility the two of you will reconcile?

Sarah's heart thudded. Her biggest fear was allowing him to get close to her again. "No chance. We eloped in Las Vegas two days after we met. It was impulsive and romantic. The first few months were like living in paradise. But we shouldn't have jumped into marriage without getting to know each other better."

Oh, no. She touched her mouth. She'd said way too much.

Compassion filled Leanne's eyes. "Love knows no logic."

Neither does lust. Sarah kept telling herself what she'd felt for Cullen was lust not love. She'd been too afraid to let him fully inside her heart, afraid he would leave her like everyone else in her life had. But what they'd shared had been nice—at times, wonderful—while it lasted. She only wished it could have lasted a little while longer.

Like forever.

The next morning Cullen unlocked the cabin's front door. He yawned wide enough for a hummingbird to fit inside. His restless nights had caught up with him. He had one thought on his brain—sleep. He'd considered pulling off the road and taking a catnap, but he didn't want to keep Leanne. He also wanted to see how Sarah was doing. He'd pulled out his cell phone more than once during his shift, but he hadn't wanted to wake them.

He stepped into the cabin. The scent of freshly brewed coffee and something baking made his mouth water. He wasn't used to coming home to such pleasant smells. Caffeine would mess with his sleep, but his stomach growled for whatever was cooking.

Feminine laughter filled the air—something Cullen had missed hearing. Sarah's laugh seeped into him, filling up all the empty places inside with soothing warmth. He might have a great place to live in a wonderful town with a supportive community, but something was missing from his life—a woman.

After the divorce things will be better.

His mantra didn't make him feel quite as good as it had a couple of weeks ago.

In the living room he saw the backs of Sarah's and Leanne's heads. They sat on the couch.

"Good morning, ladies," he said.

Leanne turned and greeted him with a wide smile. "Hey, Doc. Just in time. The muffins will be ready in a few minutes."

Sarah looked at him. No smile. No excitement in her eyes. Nothing.

He would have appreciated some reaction from her. Maybe she was tired. Or hurting. But he hoped not.

"Busy shift?" Sarah asked.

Cardiac arrests, fractures, appendicitis, a gunshot victim and two car accidents. Not to mention earaches, asthma attacks, fevers and cuts. "Typical."

"That'll change next week," Leanne said. "Full moon."

"Thanks for the warning." He noticed the two were looking at a magazine. "How did things go?"

"Fine," Sarah said. "I went to bed a half hour after Leanne arrived and woke up an hour ago."

"Easiest gig I've ever had. Sarah is the perfect patient." Leanne held up a thick bridal magazine full of glossy photographs. "She also has great wedding-planning advice."

"Wedding planning, huh?" That surprised Cullen. "I suppose Sarah knows all about being married by an Elvis impersonator."

Leanne's mouth formed a perfect O. She looked at Sarah. "You didn't tell me that."

She shrugged. "I figured getting married in Vegas implied an Elvis impersonator."

"He had that jiggling-leg thing going on." Cullen demonstrated. "'Darlin', do you take this man…'"

Leanne laughed. "Where is my cell phone? No one will believe this. You *sound* like Elvis."

Sarah nodded. "We bought a wedding package that included a video of the ceremony. Each time I watch it, I'm amazed how well Cullen has nailed the voice."

His heart kicked in his chest. "You still watch the video?"

Sarah's gaze flew to the magazine. "I used to. It's packed away in a box somewhere."

Cullen hadn't expected she'd kept the video. He was sure she'd destroyed all evidence of their wedding. He wouldn't have been surprised if she'd gone so far as to toss her wedding ring into the garbage. He'd thought about getting rid of his, but he'd decided to wait for the divorce to be finalized.

The oven timer buzzed.

Leanne stood, walked to the kitchen and removed a muffin tin from the oven. "I hope you like blueberry."

A tight smiled formed on Sarah's lips. "I love them. So does Cullen."

He remembered lazy mornings when he wasn't working. Sleeping in, having sex, taking long showers together, going to the corner coffee shop to pick up coffee and muffins.

Leanne put the muffins on a dinner plate and carried them to the living room with salad plates, napkins, a butter knife and butter.

"If you don't mind, I'm going to take off." She placed everything on the coffee table. "Christian is finished with his shift. We only have one day off the same since the chief put us on different squads."

"Go have fun," Sarah said. "Thanks for staying with me and making muffins."

"Happy to help out. I'll be back when it's my turn." Leanne grabbed her tote bag. "Be sure to go through the magazine and see what else you come up with."

"Will do," Sarah said.

"I'll walk you out," Cullen said.

Leanne fell in step next to him. "Ever the gentleman."

He opened the door and followed her outside.

"I'd been wondering why you haven't been dating," Leanne said.

"I figured it would be better to wait until the divorce was official."

"When will that be?" she asked.

"My attorney knows Sarah is staying with me. He thinks everything can be settled shortly."

"Sarah's great." Leanne pursed her lips. "You're sure a divorce is what you want?"

"Positive. Sarah wants one, too, so don't get any ideas. Half the town has tried setting me up on blind dates. I don't need them interfering in my estranged marriage."

Leanne held up her hands. "Just asking. And since Sarah's staying with you, you're not quite as estranged as you were."

"Thomas."

A knowing grin lit up her face. "What?"

Cullen let it go. He knew she was only trying to help. "Thanks for staying with Sarah."

"You're welcome," she said. "See you soon."

He went back inside to find Sarah looking at the bridal magazine. The muffins sat untouched. "Aren't you going to eat?"

She closed the magazine. "I was waiting for you."

That was polite. He sat next to her. "Do you want me to butter yours?"

"Thanks, but I've got it." Sarah placed a muffin on a plate. She awkwardly sliced the top then added a pat of butter. "These smell so good."

Cullen took one. "Leanne's got a thing for muffins and chocolate."

Sarah rested her plate on her lap. "She's nice. I like her."

"I thought you might," he said. "Leanne reminds me of you."

"I'm nothing like her."

"You both work in male-dominated environments. You're competent and intelligent. You ski and climb."

"Okay, I see the commonality." Sarah bit into the muffin. "But I wish I cooked as well as she does."

"Yeah, that would be nice."

She swatted his arm. "I'm not that bad."

"I'm joking. You're a good cook." He noticed the bridal magazine on her lap. "I'm curious how you know so much about wedding planning, when we eloped."

She wiped her mouth with a napkin. "I told you I was engaged."

"I assumed it was a short engagement."

"Two and a half years."

He drew back. "That's a long time."

"Longer when you add in the years we dated."

"When was this?"

"Four years before I met you."

He did a quick calculation. "You must have been really young when you met him."

"Too young. And stupid," she admitted. "But I thought I knew better."

"Why didn't you tell me?" he asked.

"You and I got married two days after we met. I figured it didn't matter."

He set his half-eaten muffin on his plate. "What happened?"

She stared at the magazine. "Dylan entered my life at a time I felt very alone. I thought I was so lucky he wanted to be with me. There were some red flags, but I charged ahead with wedding plans. That morning…"

Cullen leaned toward her, feeling as if a cornice of snow had collapsed on top of him. "The morning of your wedding day?"

She nodded. "I was in a small room at the back of the church. I'd worked two jobs to buy my wedding gown and pay for the reception. I was fixing my veil when Dylan entered. He said he'd been up all night thinking about things, about us, and had come to a conclusion. He couldn't marry me. The wedding was off."

Anger surged at how badly Sarah must have been hurt. Cullen balled his hands. "What a loser."

She shrugged. "He said I wasn't anything special. I would have held him back. I don't blame him for not wanting to marry me."

"Don't say that. The guy had some serious issues if he thought any of those things about you."

"Yeah, issues with me." If Sarah was trying to sound light-hearted, she hadn't succeeded and that bothered Cullen even more. "But I got over him. Moved on. Met you."

The conversation they'd had outside the wedding chapel in Las Vegas rushed back.

Why don't we go inside and make things official? If we elope, you won't forget about me when we get back to Seattle or leave me standing at the altar after we've dated for years and I've planned a spectacular wedding for us.

Cullen remembered his reply.

I would never leave you like that.

Guilt lodged in his throat. He *had* left her. The minute she mentioned divorce he'd hightailed it out of the apartment. Had mentioning divorce been a test? To see how committed he was? Part of him wanted to be angry if she'd been testing without his knowing it, yet…even if she hadn't been doing that, he'd failed. He'd run the second he had a chance. No wonder she'd freaked out on him whenever he tried to contact her about the divorce. "I'm sorry."

"No apologies needed. Getting jilted happened way before you."

"I know, but I left you, too. If I'd known…"

"Would it have changed anything?" she asked.

He thought long and hard. Things hadn't been going well between them. She'd been pulling away from him. He hadn't like how out of control he felt around her. "Probably not."

Sarah's lip quivered. "I appreciate your honesty."

"I appreciate your telling me about this."

A marble statue had a warmer smile than hers. "Better late than never."

Except it was too late to do anything about it now. Or was it?

CHAPTER SEVEN

WOULD IT HAVE changed anything?

Probably not.

Cullen's two words reaffirmed Sarah's actions of a year ago. He'd even apologized. Something she'd never expected him to do. She should feel relieved she'd been spot-on about their relationship. Marriage had never tied them to each other as a couple, as husband and wife. Instead of relief, a heavy sadness bore down on her. She leaned back on the couch, looking at the wood-beamed ceiling.

"Need a refill?" Cullen asked from the kitchen.

"No, thanks." She flexed her left hand to stop it from shaking. "My cup is full."

She'd known things were over between them. She was used to the heartache and resentment over her failed marriage, so she wasn't sure why what Cullen had said bothered her so much.

Face it. Some people weren't cut out for marriage. Like her. Her parents. Must be something in the DNA.

She glanced at the cover of the bridal magazine. The beautiful model dressed in a couture gown with perfectly applied makeup and coiffed hair glowed with a radiance Sarah envied. The woman wasn't a bride, but more thought had gone into the carefully executed photo shoot than into their eloping.

Her appetite disappeared.

Cullen returned to the living room with a steaming cup of coffee. "You look better today."

"I'm getting there." Physically, at least. Emotionally was another story. She rubbed her thumb against her fingertips. "You must be tired after working all night. Go to bed. I'll be fine while you sleep."

He raised his cup of coffee. "I got my second wind."

Maybe she should take a nap and give them a break from each other. She nearly laughed. Running off was Cullen's typical avoidance tactic, not hers.

"What's so funny?" he asked.

He'd been honest before. It was her turn. She met his gaze. "I'm surprised you're still here."

He sipped his coffee. "Where would I go?"

"Anywhere I'm not."

"That's—"

"What you used to do," she interrupted. "Whenever things were really good between us or when we'd disagree, you always disappeared to the hospital, some mountain-rescue thing, wherever else you could go."

He tugged at his polo-shirt collar. "I only did what I needed to do."

"Exactly."

She had never entered into the equation. It was almost as if he were different people. The Doctor. The Mountain Rescuer. The Lover. The Husband was the one role he hadn't seemed to embrace.

"I don't want to argue," he said.

"We're not arguing," she countered. "We're having a discussion."

He took a sip of his coffee. "Let's take a short walk outside instead."

She drummed her fingers on the sofa arm. "You're doing it again."

"Doing what?"

"Running away."

"I invited you on a walk."

"You're trying to change the subject because you don't want to talk."

"All you want to do is talk, even when there's nothing to discuss."

Ouch. His words stung. "I'll shut up, then."

"That's not…" He dragged his hand through his hair. "Let's go for a walk. I don't want us to fight."

"This isn't anywhere close to fighting," she explained. "Sometimes when my parents fought, the police got involved. One of my stepfathers burned our clothes in the front yard. And my ex-fiancé…"

"Did he hurt you?"

"Not physically. But Dylan's words could be as powerful as a fist."

Cullen reached for her.

She moved away from him. His compassion and tenderness were not what she needed right now. "I'm not proud I allowed it to happen for as long as it did or wasn't the one to break up, but at least I knew where I stood with him."

"You know how I feel…felt about you. There's no reason to bring this up now." He stood. "I'm going for a walk. If you'd rather stay inside…"

"No." The word spewed from her mouth like lava out of Mount Etna. "I want to go outside."

"Then let's go."

Five minutes later she found herself standing on Cullen's driveway in her boots and wearing a jacket. The sharp scent of pine wafted on the breeze. Sunlight kissed her cheeks. She breathed in, filling her lungs with the crisp mountain air.

"Isn't this better than arguing inside?" Cullen asked.

"It's nice, but the inside wasn't so bad," she said. "The best part of disagreeing is making up."

"I don't think so."

"That's because you never stuck around for the make-up sex."

Cullen started to speak, then pressed his lips together.

Humming a little tune, Sarah walked away from him. For the first time in a long while, she had the upper hand. She wanted to savor the moment.

Leaves and twigs crunched under her feet. She walked along the edge of the road.

He caught up to her. "So, is there a statute of limitation on make-up sex?"

Sarah froze. That was…unexpected. She looked over at him.

Wicked laughter lit his eyes. "Seems I missed out."

She raised her chin. "Your loss."

His charming smile unleashed a colony of bats in her stomach. "Yours, too."

Darn him. This was what he always did. Turn off the serious side. Get all sexy and fun and flirty. Make her insides hot and gooey. He hadn't changed one bit.

She casually lifted one shoulder, but her heart pounded like a jackhammer. "You win some. You lose some."

He stepped closer to her. Too close for anything other than kissing her.

He wouldn't, would he? She gulped, not sure what she wanted the answer to be. Okay, she knew. But *yes* wasn't the correct response if she wanted to play it safe.

He cocked a brow. "So the statute…"

It was up to her. Temptation flared, only to be tempered by common sense. What she wanted warred with what she needed, but self-preservation reigned supreme.

Her fingernails dug into her palms. "Expired."

Sarah marched down the road as if her life depended on putting distance between them. Her abdomen ached. She kept going. She didn't know where she was going. She didn't care.

Cullen grabbed her hand. "Slow down. You'll hurt yourself."

"I'm fine."

"No, you're not. You're mad at me. Even madder than you were inside."

She pursed her lips. She wasn't about to give him the satisfaction of being right.

"I know this because you have a crease between your eyebrows."

Sarah touched the spot.

He moved her finger. "Right here."

She felt the line, but still wasn't going to admit it.

Cullen glanced to his right. His eyes widened. "Look."

Sarah had no idea what he wanted her to see. "What?"

"Shhh." Cullen touched her lips with his finger, then positioned himself behind her. His chest pressed against her back. He brought his left arm around her and pointed. "A doe and two fawns."

Awareness hummed through Sarah. He emanated heat and strength. Her pulse raced.

She couldn't focus. Bigfoot could have been standing in front of her and she wouldn't have noticed him.

Her reaction made zero sense. She was still angry, resentful and hurt over their breakup. Their marriage was over. Yet her body didn't seem to understand that.

"See them?" he whispered.

The warmth of his breath against her neck gave her chills. Her gaze followed the length of his arm until she saw the deer. A momma and her two babies, munching on a bush. Her breath stilled. "So cute."

"I've seen these three around the cabin," he said quietly.

The deer ate without glancing at them. The fawns were more interested in keeping an eye on their mother, who paid close attention to both of them.

Sarah wished her mom had cared as much for her. Wished Cullen had, too. She shoved her left hand into her jacket pocket. "I haven't noticed them or any others."

"You will. You haven't been here long."

It felt as if she'd been here forever. "I'll be on the lookout."

The doe stiffened. She looked in their direction, then past them, as if she sensed something.

A car drove down the road. The sound of the engine splintered the silence.

The deer bounded into the trees, her two fawns following.

If only Sarah could go back to Bellingham. She wanted to pretend none of this had happened—her accident and her injuries and her reaction to Cullen. She wanted it to all go away.

He faced her. "They'll be back."

What she and Cullen had shared once would never return. A sigh welled up inside her. She parted her lips.

He lowered his head to hers and kissed her.

Sarah's heart stalled.

His kiss was gentle and sweet. He didn't touch her except with his lips. But that was enough.

Her nerve endings stirred to life as if awakened from a deep slumber. Pleasurable sensations pulsed through her. She'd forgotten how wonderful his kiss was.

He backed away from her.

Sarah took a step back herself. Swallowed. "Why did you do that?"

"Make-up kiss."

She laughed.

"The statute of limitations for a make-up kiss has to be longer than for make-up sex," he said.

"If it isn't, I doubt I'll press charges."

He grinned wryly. "That's generous of you, Lavagirl."

Her lips tingled. "Only repaying your generosity, Dr. Gray."

His smile spread, matching the heat spreading inside her. He tucked a strand of hair behind her ear.

If she weren't careful, he could overwhelm her. "But we shouldn't make kisses a habit."

"You're probably right about that," Cullen agreed. "As long as we don't argue, we should be fine."

Probably. Should be. He'd left a lot of wiggle room.

That meant it would be up to her to make sure nothing more happened. And even though Sarah knew better, she was kind of hoping there would be more kisses.

Cullen couldn't believe he'd kissed Sarah.

A momentary lapse? If that had been the case he would have kissed her with more passion. He'd been careful to keep things under control. Not easy with the images of make-up sex shuffling through his mind. But he had still enjoyed the kiss.

Had he run away, as she said?

Cullen had left a few times whenever he felt his control slipping or was too overwhelmed by her. But she had to be exaggerating the number of times, caught up in some revised history of their marriage to make her feel better, less guilty for bringing up the topic of divorce.

He peeked into her room. She was sound asleep.

Good. Cullen needed sleep himself. Caffeine was keeping him going at the moment. But he wanted to do something first. He entered his room, closed the door and made a call on his cell phone.

"Hey, Doc," OMSAR rescue leader Sean Hughes said. "How's Sarah?"

"Napping. She's looking better."

"Good to hear."

Cullen adjusted the phone at his ear. "I'm signed up for your ready team tomorrow, but I want to stay home with Sarah."

"No worries," Sean said. "We'll get it covered."

"Thanks, and I'm sorry."

"No apology necessary. Do what you have to do."

That's what Cullen was trying to do. Even though he wasn't sure why he was doing it.

A week later sunlight streamed through Sarah's bedroom window. The snow must have stopped overnight. Not that good weather would change her agenda for the day. Physical therapy and a walk were as exciting as things got. She could work on her laptop for a few minutes, but headaches and her arm limited her productivity. Still, she forced herself out of bed and into the hallway.

The scent of freshly brewed coffee and something baking filled the air. Sarah's mouth watered at the tantalizing aromas. Her tummy grumbled.

She wondered who would be staying with her today. The delicious smells wafting in the air told her it wasn't Zoe Hughes, who was scheduled to be here. The former socialite was beautiful and friendly, but she couldn't cook. Hannah had been here yesterday, so that left Carly or Leanne.

Unless it was…Cullen.

The thought gave Sarah an unexpected boost of energy. She quickened her pace.

She hadn't seen him in days. He'd been working his shifts and covering for other doctors. He'd explained he was doing this because of being up in Seattle with her, not to get away from her now. He'd even called to say hello, something he'd never done, which Sarah appreciated.

But his absences reminded her of how she'd always been so desperate to see him when they lived together. She wasn't desperate now. She was…eager. The logic behind her eagerness couldn't readily be explained, but her frustration could be.

Sarah's slow recovery gave her insight into how magma must feel as it rose out of the earth's mantle and moved into the crust. She wasn't a mix of solids, melt and gases, but the physics behind making progress with her injuries was similar and taking way too much time.

In the hallway, Sarah noticed someone in the kitchen. Someone with brown hair. Someone female with two braids.

Not Cullen. Leanne.

Sarah stumbled, but regained her balance before she fell. She'd experienced a lifetime of disappointments, everything from forgotten birthdays to having her marriage disintegrate. Not seeing Cullen was nothing in the grand scheme of things.

Leanne greeted Sarah with a smile. "You're up early today."

"I went to bed around eight." Sarah hadn't been that tired, but she'd wanted Hannah to go home and say good-night to her three children. Being tucked in meant a lot to kids. It would have meant a lot to Sarah if her parents had done that.

Cullen must have come and gone while she was sleeping. If he'd returned home at all. A few times this week he hadn't, and not knowing where he was bugged her.

Sarah leaned against the breakfast bar. "I thought Zoe was going to be here."

"She had to run to Portland, so two of us are tag-teaming it." Leanne picked up the coffeepot. "You're stuck with me until lunchtime."

"You're the one who's stuck." These women were so kind and friendly. "I appreciate what you've been doing for me."

"It's our pleasure." The sincerity in Leanne's voice touched Sarah's heart. "This is what friends do for each other."

Cullen was so lucky. Hood Hamlet was a very special place. A perfect place for a family. Not that she would ever have one...

As Leanne poured coffee into two cups, light glimmered off her diamond engagement ring. The pretty paramedic had found her one true love at the fire station. A younger man who adored her, according to Zoe.

Sarah felt a pang. Maybe happy-ever-afters were possible for some people. She hoped so for her new friend's sake.

"Sit." Leanne placed the steaming mugs on the table. "I baked banana-nut muffins."

Sarah sat. "I like those as much as blueberry ones."

People in Hood Hamlet took care of each other and strangers like her, too. Home-cooked, healthy meals were either made or arrived each day. Though Cullen had been away so much, he'd ended up with leftovers. When he came home...

Her throat tightened. Cullen hadn't fallen right back into the same pattern of their marriage, but the longer he stayed away, the more she worried he might.

Leanne returned to the table with a platter of muffins. "Dig in."

"Thanks." Sarah bit into one. The flavors and warmth filled her mouth. "Delicious. I like the walnuts."

"Me, too."

She took another bite, but couldn't stop thinking about Cullen. Thoughts of him more than made up for his physical absence. That added to her growing frustrations over her injuries and inability to get much work done. She tore off a piece of the muffin and shoved it into her mouth.

Concern clouded Leanne's brown eyes. "Taking it easy is hard for you."

Sarah stared into her coffee cup. "It's downright aggravating."

"Cullen told me you're improving every day."

Hurt sliced through her. He hadn't told her that. She shouldn't take it personally. She wasn't his friend or a climbing and ski partner like Leanne.

So what if he'd kissed Sarah? Or spent two whole days and night taking care of her before he'd returned to a marathon of shift coverage? She was a temporary roommate and no longer a permanent part of his life—a life she was beginning to envy after a week and a half in Hood Hamlet.

Being envious was silly.

Everything she wanted and cared about was in Bellingham. Mount Baker. The institute. Her postdoc.

Leanne studied her. "Since you're doing better, maybe it's time you do something in town."

Anticipation made Sarah sit straighter. "I would love that."

"Zoe wants us to go to Taco Night at the brewpub this evening. Join us."

Sarah's stomach fluttered. "Sounds like fun, but I don't know if Cullen will agree. He can't turn off the doctor switch."

Leanne grinned. "I'll talk to him. Convince him going out will be good for you."

"He still might say no."

"Then I'll ask Paulson to help me kidnap you. He's been my best friend since I was nine. He's up for anything."

"Even kidnapping?"

"Pretty much," Leanne said. "He might draw the line at disposing of a body, but with Paulson you never know, especially if a pretty woman is involved."

A smile tugged at the corners of Sarah's lips. "Sounds like an interesting guy."

Leanne sipped her coffee. "He's a real-life Peter Pan who will never grow up, but he's also a total sweetheart. You'll meet him after lunch. He's staying with you until Cullen gets home."

Sarah perked up. "Cullen will be home tonight?"

"This afternoon. That's why tonight is perfect for you to get out."

"I'd like that." Especially if she could be with Cullen.

"It'll happen." Leanne sounded so confident.

"And if not, you and Bill can kidnap me."

A fake kidnapping sounded fun, given Sarah had been lying around since she'd arrived. Now, if she'd been lying around with Cullen…

Heat rocketed through her. Uh-oh. Better stick to how she was going to get to Taco Night. Mexican food was as spicy as she could handle right now.

Cullen sat in the hospital cafeteria. A few crumbs from his fish and chips remained on his plate. He sipped his coffee. The caffeine would get him through the next two hours.

A good thing he needed to cover only eight hours today. He'd spent the past five days covering shifts for others and working his own. He'd ended up staying at an anesthesiologist's house rather than drive all the way home only to return a few hours later.

He missed Sarah, but enjoyed this reprieve. Being with her messed with his head. He didn't want her getting anywhere close to his heart.

But this time away from her had intensified his guilt. Not only for leaving her the way he had a year ago, but also for running away from her when they'd been living together as husband and wife. He hated admitting the truth, even to himself, but the more he thought about it, the more he realized Sarah had been correct about what he'd been doing. No wonder she'd been unhappy. After what her jerk of an ex-fiancé had done to her, Cullen must have made her feel like crap.

He never wanted to hurt her that way again. That was why he'd made it clear to her that he had shifts to make up. He had no ulterior motives in working so much this week.

And even though he wasn't with her, he thought about Sarah every day. More like several times each day. Wondered how her recovery was going; was she missing him as much as he missed her?

Curious, he called Leanne. She'd texted him this morning saying she was with Sarah instead of Zoe.

"Hey," Leanne answered. "I was going to call you."

His shoulder muscles tensed. "Sarah okay?"

"She looks better than I've seen her look all week. Stronger, too."

Relief washed over him. "Good."

"Sarah is doing so well you should bring her to Taco Night."

He hadn't been to the brewpub in three weeks. "She's not up for it."

"She wants to go," Leanne said to his surprise. "She needs to get out of the cabin."

"Sarah isn't a social butterfly. She's a scientist who would rather be on a volcano than anywhere else."

"It's not some fancy soiree. It's tacos at the brewpub."

Everyone he knew would be there. There would be more questions. "She'll get too tired."

"I don't know how she's managed this long." Disapproval rang clear in Leanne's voice. "Just sitting around the cabin and taking short walks isn't good for her morale or her recovery."

But it was safe. He didn't have to worry about Sarah when that was all she was doing. "She does need to get out more. Next week will be better."

"Maybe for you, but not Sarah. You can stay home tonight. Paulson will bring her."

Cullen laughed. "You want Paulson to take my wife to Taco Night?"

"It's not a problem," she said. "He's with Sarah right now. The two hit it off."

Cullen's heart went splat against the cafeteria floor.

"What?" His voice rose. He lowered it. "You texted you were with her."

"This morning. I had to attend a Christmas Magic festival meeting after lunch. No worries. Paulson will take good care of Sarah."

That was what Cullen was afraid of.

CHAPTER EIGHT

BILL PAULSON SAT next to Sarah on the couch with an impish grin on his lips and a suggestive gleam in his eyes. "So what do you want to do now?"

Charming might describe Hood Hamlet, but it didn't come close to describing the friendly, easy-on-the-eyes firefighter in well-worn jeans and a faded T-shirt. Sarah enjoyed being with him. He made her feel feminine and pretty even when she looked like a boxer, albeit one who'd been out of the ring for a couple of weeks.

"I have no idea," she admitted.

The guy had a great sense of humor. He could give any pop-star pretty boy a run for the money in the looks department and kick their butts with his athletic build. He was fun to hang out with, albeit a little immature with some of his not-so-subtle, yet humorous innuendos.

"You've kept me entertained all afternoon. I'm not sure what's left for us to do," she added.

Mischief twinkled in his eyes. "I'm sure I can think of a few things."

Bill Paulson would be considered a catch, except for two things—the guy knew he was good-looking and he was an incorrigible flirt. No way would she encourage him.

He rubbed his chin. "I could paint your toenails. That has to be tough to do with your dominant hand in a cast."

Okay, the guy was a good listener. He'd taken their earlier discussion on being right-handed and come up with this. But however tempting that might sound, she could survive without nail polish. The only man who should be doing any toenail painting on her was Cullen. Not that he would. Or that she would ask him. "Thanks, but I think a nap would be better."

He scrambled off the couch. "I'll fluff your pillows. Be right back."

Sarah bit back a laugh at his eagerness to help. Bill was half player, half Boy Scout rolled into one. Adorable, but a handful if you were a single woman who happened to be attracted to him. Neither of which she was.

The front door opened. Leanne must be back.

Sarah turned to say hello, but the word died on her lips.

Cullen stormed inside, wearing his scrubs. His gaze was intense and focused on her. Lines bracketed his mouth.

"The bed's ready," Bill announced from the hallway.

Cullen's face reddened. A muscle pulsed at his jaw.

Bill grinned. "Hey, Doc. I've been taking good care of Sarah."

Cullen balled his fingers. He looked as if he wanted to punch someone. "I'll bet you have."

Sarah had never seen him act like this. She didn't like it. "Cullen?"

He glared at Bill. "What's this about a bed being ready?"

Bill held up his hands in front of him, as if to surrender. "Dude, I don't know what's got into you, but if you're thinking I'd put the moves on your pretty wife you're way off. I just fluffed her pillows."

Cullen's dark gaze bounced from Bill to her. "You fluffed her what?"

"Her pillows," Bill said.

"The pillows on my bed," Sarah clarified. "I wanted to nap."

"A nap," Cullen repeated.

"A nap," Bill reaffirmed.

Cullen seemed to be digesting the information. She didn't know what his problem was. She looked up at Bill. "You've been a big help this afternoon."

"Anytime." He smiled. "If you need a ride to Taco Night…"

"I'm taking her," Cullen said. "After her nap."

Bill pulled out his car keys from his jeans pocket. A grin twitched at his lips. "Looks like my work here is done."

"Thanks for the brownies," she said.

"You made her brownies?" Cullen asked incredulously.

"I made both of you brownies. Well, my mom did." Bill had explained how his mom cooked his meals, cleaned his house and did his washing. No wonder the guy hadn't grown up yet. He didn't need to. "She dropped them off at my place this morning."

Sarah stood. "Thank your mom for us. And thanks for keeping me company."

"My pleasure." Bill looked at Cullen. "Your wife is quite the card shark. She kicked my butt at Texas hold 'em. A good thing we weren't playing strip poker, or I'd have been buck naked in no time."

A confused expression formed on Cullen's face.

Bill didn't seem to care. Or maybe he didn't notice, since he was looking at her. "See you at the brewpub. If Doc changes his mind about going, give me a call."

With that, Bill left.

Cullen stood next to the breakfast bar. His lips narrowed. "Please tell me you know better than to get involved with a guy like Paulson."

Defensiveness rose. "Get involved? What are you talking about?"

"A lot of women like him."

Sarah didn't like Cullen's tone. "Bill's a nice guy."

"He's a total player who will never grow up."

She saw that. She didn't need Cullen pointing it out. "You're jealous."

"No, I'm not," he said with a dismissive air.

"Then why did you storm into the house like a bull from the streets of Pamplona looking for a fight?"

He took a deep breath and another, as if reining himself in yet again. "I was worried."

"Worried."

"I like Paulson," Cullen admitted. "But he'll hit on any female with a pretty smile."

"You thought he would hit on me."

He clenched his teeth. "You deserve better."

Sarah had deserved better from him, too. She raised her chin. "Yes, I do. Bill is a big flirt, but it was innocent, all in fun."

"He didn't—"

"He was a perfect gentleman."

Cullen's brow furrowed. "*Gentleman* and *Paulson* don't belong in the same sentence."

"Maybe you don't know him as well as you think you do," she said. "Bill made me laugh and feel better than I've felt in a while. Since long before the accident." Cullen opened his mouth to speak, but she continued. "But even if I swallowed a 'stupid' pill and threw caution to the wind, I would never get involved with Bill...with any man...because you and I are still married."

Relief washed over Cullen's face. "Good."

His response angered and confused her. Why would he care, if he wanted a divorce? "That's all you have to say?"

"What more do you want?"

"An apology," she said. "You charged in here assuming the worst without considering that Bill is your friend and I'm your wife."

"I haven't been thinking straight. I've...been working a lot."

"What's new?" She didn't need to explain, but she didn't want him thinking the worst of her. "Just so you know. I have been good. Very good. Doing everything you and Dr. Marshall told me to do. Which is more than I can say for you."

Lines creased Cullen's forehead. "I have no idea what you're talking about."

"You told me you had shifts to make up, but you haven't been here at all. Heaven only knows where you've been spending your nights."

A devilish grin lit up his face. "You're the jealous one."

"Am not." Okay, maybe a little. But no way would she admit that to him. "I was...worried."

"Worried."

More than she wanted to admit. More than he would ever know. "Yes."

His eyes softened. He grinned sheepishly. "The way I was worried about you and Bill."

Busted. Darn it. She nodded once, feeling stupid and petty and pathetic.

His gaze met hers. "No need for you to worry. I stayed at a friend's place near the hospital so I could sleep more between shifts."

"Makes sense to stay with a friend."

But she didn't know if his "friend" was male or a buxom blonde named Bambi. And she wanted to know. Badly.

Cullen strode toward the couch. "I'm learning how important it is to have friends. I realize I've been taking them for granted."

The way he'd taken her for granted. But he'd never considered her a friend. Her throat tightened.

She should say something, but she hadn't a clue what. "You shouldn't get a pet if you're gone so much."

His eyes widened. "I don't always work this many shifts. A cat might work. As you said, they're independent."

"Even cats need to feel wanted and loved."

Not that he wanted and loved her, but once he had. At least, that was what he'd told her.

Cullen stood next to her.

Sarah's pulse skittered. Tension simmered between them. She shouldn't want him to kiss her. But she did. Badly.

Look away. Move away. But she couldn't—okay, didn't want to. Instead she was mesmerized by his blue eyes and full lips.

Once again she was reminded of magma rising. Only this time moving closer to the surface, where the gas pressure increased, accelerating faster and faster until erupting.

She wet her lips.

"In case you're still worried, the friend I stayed with—he's an anesthesiologist from the hospital," he said.

The surge of relief did nothing to douse the flame building inside her, threatening to explode. "Thanks."

The blue of his eyes deepened. "Thank you."

"For what?"

"This." Cullen lowered his mouth to hers and kissed her. Hard.

Heaven. His kiss made Sarah feel like she had died and gone to heaven. Best to enjoy every second, every minute if she was that lucky. She had a feeling this might be as close as she ever got to the pearly gates while her heart still beat. And beating it was.

In triple time.

His lips moved over hers with skill and familiarity. The kiss brought her home, back to where she'd longed to be for months now…in his arms. She'd thought about him, dreamed about him, missed him, even though she should have been getting over him. And now she realized why she was having so much trouble getting over him. He tasted warm and inviting. This was a yummy, comfy place she never wanted to leave. Each touch of his mouth, of his hands, made her tingle inside.

Forget pain medication—this was all she needed to feel better. Her blood simmered, rushing through her veins. It had been so long, too long, since she'd felt wanted. She didn't want the feeling to end.

His hand ran up her back, caressing her, until her hair was running through his fingers.

More. She wanted more.

Sarah parted her lips. He accepted the invitation and deepened the kiss, pressing harder against her mouth.

He'd followed her lead. It was time to follow his.

Her tongue reacquainted itself with him, exploring the recesses of his mouth. She remembered all the times they'd kissed before. Remembered the good times in their marriage when she had believed it would last forever. Maybe her memories were hazy because of the concussion, but this kiss felt different. Better, somehow.

She didn't want to analyze it too deeply. She wanted to… enjoy.

Heat pooled deep inside her. Need ached. Grew.

A moan escaped her lips.

More. Please.

Cullen drew her closer. She arched into him, only to come to an abrupt stop. She crashed into something hard, sending a jagged pain through her sore and healing abdomen. Her lips slipped off his. Spots appeared before her eyes.

Pain weakened her knees. It hurt, almost burned, so badly, but she didn't fall. Cullen held on to her.

He groaned, but didn't let go.

Sarah forced herself to breathe. A knife seemed to be slicing through her midsection. She straightened, intensifying the pain more. She looked down.

Stupid cast.

With the permanent bend in her elbow, her arm was stuck in position, a barrier between them.

In spite of her stomach hurting, she couldn't deny her reaction to Cullen's kisses. Her swollen and bruised lips throbbed. Her heart beat wildly. Her pulse hadn't settled.

She wanted to rewind time and relieve each second of his kisses.

Stupid. Dumb.

Forget about the cast getting in the way—she should have known better than to kiss him back the way she had. "I'm so sorry."

Cullen bent over, gasping for air. "Give me a sec."

The rasp in his voice made Sarah look at her cast. "More dangerous than I imagined."

He glanced up at her. "You have no idea."

Sarah reached toward him, then thought better of it. If she touched him, she would kiss him again. She pressed her left hand against her side. Pain made her want to sit. She leaned against the couch. "You okay?"

He straightened. "I can breathe now. How about you?"

Her senses reeled. Her heart screamed for more kisses. Her incisions hurt. "I've been better. But the pain's subsiding quicker than it usually does."

Cullen's mouth twisted. He looked so serious. As if the fate of the world rested on his shoulders and he'd screwed things up. "This was…"

"A mistake." Better for her to admit it before him. She should never have kissed him back. "If you're worried I'm thinking this changes things between us, don't be. The other kiss didn't. This one won't, either."

He didn't say a word, but his dark gaze remained on her.

"Kisses are an old habit for us. The opportunity arose again. I wanted to be kissed. It was bound to happen," she rambled, trying to justify what had occurred. "Someday we'll look back at this and laugh."

He raised a brow. "You think?"

She had no idea, but laughing this off was better than analyzing it to death and not liking her conclusion. "Sure."

"Most kisses aim for romance, not humor."

Was he aiming for romance by kissing her? Her pulse accelerated. No more kisses. "True, but romantic kisses are a dime a dozen. This one…"

A grin tugged at his lips. He rubbed his stomach. "I won't be forgetting this one anytime soon."

Her neither. But for different reasons than his.

Warning bells sounded in her head. Who was she kidding? She was past the warning stage. Alarms blared.

Best not to travel this road again. Giving in to desire would lead to disappointment and heartache. She couldn't do that to herself, to her heart. "But it won't happen again."

"Definitely not."

That was fast. Almost too fast. And he had said *probably* before, but *definitely* this time. Disappointment spiraled to the tips of her toes. At least they agreed, right?

She pressed her lips together, unsure what to say or do next. That seemed to be standard operating procedure whenever she was around Cullen. So why had she been so eager to see him when she woke up this morning?

He walked into the kitchen. "You mentioned taking a nap. While you sleep, I'll figure out dinner. I'm sure we have enough leftovers."

"It's Taco Night at the brewpub."

"You're in pain."

She didn't want to stay inside, with him so close and her aching with surprise need. "I want to go out."

His gaze raked over her, assessing her like one of his patients. "It'll be too much for you after such a long day."

"I've done nothing but lie or sit around, except for a walk outside with Bill."

Cullen's eyes narrowed. "There's snow on the ground. You could have slipped."

"We didn't go far, and Bill never let go of my arm."

"How gentlemanly of him."

Sarah didn't appreciate Cullen's sarcastic tone, but maybe she could use this to her advantage. "Do you want to go to the brewpub tonight or not?"

"I like Taco Night, but I'm happy to stay home tonight. It's been a long week."

She empathized with that. "You must be exhausted."

He opened the refrigerator. "Let's go next week."

"You can go then." She straightened. "I'm going tonight. I'll call Bill."

Cullen slammed the fridge door. "Why do you want to go so badly?"

"I'm desperate to get out of the house."

He arched a brow. "Desperate?"

Sarah nodded. "I've been doing everything I'm supposed to do, but enough is enough. I need to get out and do something. Have…"

"Fun," he finished for her.

It would be fun to kiss him again. She didn't dare admit that. "Lying around all day resting is the antithesis of fun. I can sit at the brewpub as easily as I can here."

"You won't be here alone."

That was the problem tonight. She was alone with him. "I've enjoyed having people around. Everyone is nice and we're getting to know each other. But I need to get out, have a change of environment, scenery, whatever you want to call it, or I'm going to lose my mind."

Or burn with unspent desire.

Kissing Cullen again would send her over the edge completely.

Going to the brewpub made the most sense. The other option—spending the evening at home with Cullen—didn't seem like a smart idea. Sure, they'd agreed not to kiss again, but they'd also agreed to divorce. Who knew what could happen with the two of them here alone tonight? She didn't want to take any chances. She couldn't afford more kisses. She couldn't lose her heart to him. That would destroy her.

"Leanne told me about the soft pretzels with the house dipping sauce," Sarah explained. "I love pretzels."

"I didn't know that."

She wished he had made more time for her so they could have gotten to know each other better.

"I didn't know about your broken arm." Sarah waited for him to respond. She didn't understand his hesitation. "If you'd rather stay home, that's fine. Bill will drive me if you're not up for it."

Cullen's nostrils flared. "I'm up for it."

"But you said—"

"I changed my mind, okay?"

More than okay. She didn't care if jealousy was the reason or not, even if it gave her an unexpected rush of feminine power. "It's great. Thanks."

"Take a short nap first," he ordered in that oh-so-strict doctor's voice of his.

Such a change from the way he'd been kissing and touching her a few minutes ago. She gave a mock salute. "Aye, aye, Captain. Pillows are fluffed and the sheet turned down ready for nap, sir."

If only he'd join her…

Playful images flitted through her mind. Her temperature rose.

On second thought, napping by herself was better. Safer. Even if she would be…lonelier.

CHAPTER NINE

TACO NIGHT AT the Hood Hamlet Brewpub always put a smile on Cullen's face. Nothing beat good food, great beer and hanging with friends, but it was the last place he wanted to be tonight. He gripped the steering wheel and turned onto Main Street, trying to ignore the floral scent of Sarah's shampoo drifting his way.

She peered out the window. "It's crowded for a Thursday."

Her kisses had sent him to the brink. He'd been on the verge of losing all control until she'd taken him out with her cast. He'd never been so relieved to be punched in the gut. It hurt, but he could have been hurt a lot more if he'd continued kissing her. "Fresh snowfall brings skiers and riders to the mountain."

Sarah turned toward him. "What about climbers?"

His gaze lingered on her lips. He jerked his attention back to the road. She was the one with the concussion, but he needed to have his head examined. Imagining her with Paulson during the drive home had done crazy things to Cullen.

His self-control had been nonexistent. Whenever Sarah was involved, his feelings overrode common sense. But he hadn't withdrawn or run away from her. This time he'd done something worse. He'd kissed her.

Talk about reckless behavior.

Finding out *she* was jealous about who he was with had been a real turn-on. Kissing her had seemed the most natural thing in the world. But he couldn't allow himself to be taken in by her again. "If they're smart, they'll wait for a better weather window and an avalanche report."

"If not?"

"You hope they get lucky. Otherwise OMSAR pings us with a mission call out."

"Some people think they can conquer the mountain."

He parked across the street from the brewpub. "Yeah, but the mountain always wins."

"Mother Nature gets a shot in once in a while."

"Leanne's fiancé, Christian, can tell you all about that."

"She mentioned how OMSAR rescued his cousin and him."

Cullen turned off the ignition. "They got caught in a wicked storm, but it ended well."

Sarah unfastened her seat belt. "It's too bad there aren't more happy endings like that."

Her wistful tone surprised him. Sarah could be impulsive, but she didn't give in to flights of fancy or fairy tales. She must be talking about her rescue. "Yours has a happy ending."

Her gaze narrowed. "What are you talking about?"

"Mount Baker. Your accident," he explained. "Your data could have been destroyed. Your injuries could have been worse. You could have died. But none of those things happened. Happy ending."

"It will be happy once I'm back at the institute."

Away from him.

The words were unspoken, but implied. They stung, given how passionately she'd kissed him back this afternoon.

She reached across her chest and fumbled with the door handle.

He leaned over to help. His arm brushed her breast, sending a burst of heat rushing through him. He pulled back. "Sorry."

"I've got it." On the third try she opened the door.

She exited as if a bomb were about to blow. He hurried around the truck, then held her hand. "Be careful."

Annoyance burned in the depths of Sarah's eyes. She tugged her hand out of his. "I know to be careful."

"Just watching out for you."

"It's not as if I did something stupid to make myself fall. If the steam blast hadn't happened…"

She wouldn't be here. The thought brought a strange mix of relief and regret.

"I can cross the street by myself," she continued.

"There could be ice," he cautioned. She must be hungry. Hunger would explain her short fuse. "I'd say the same thing to anyone else who was with me, so don't get your panties in a twist."

She pursed her lips. "That would be hard to do, since I'm not wearing panties."

Cullen's mouth went dry. His gaze dropped to her hips. All he saw were jeans, but the thoughts running through his head raised his temperature twenty degrees.

"Trust me, I'd know if my thong was twisted," she added.

A thong. He remembered her thongs. His temperature spiraled. He needed to take off his jacket.

He realized a moment too late she was crossing the street without him. "Wait up, Lavagirl."

Sarah stood on the sidewalk, tapping her toe.

"You're hungry," he said.

Her foot stopped moving. She nodded with a contrite expression.

"The taco bar is all-you-can-eat," he said.

She bit her lip.

He motioned her toward the entrance, but she didn't move.

Her gaze filled with uncertainty. "Is there anything I should know before we go inside?"

"About the taco bar?"

"About the people I'm going to meet."

Not only hungry. Nervous. "You've met Carly, Zoe, Hannah and Leanne."

"And Bill."

Unfortunately. Cullen wasn't too happy with Paulsen right now. "Jake Porter, Sean Hughes and Christian Welton, if he's not on duty, will be here. I'm not sure about Hannah and Garrett Willingham or Rita and Tim Moreno, since they need babysitters. You never know who will show up. But no worries. Everybody will make you feel right at home."

An older couple holding hands exited the brewpub. Sarah stepped aside to let them pass. Cullen did the same.

Sarah glanced at the door to the brewpub as if it were a black hole. "I'll make sure I don't embarrass you in front of your friends."

"You've never embarrassed me."

"That time I danced on the bar at the hole-in-the-wall dive near Joshua Tree."

The taste of tequila shots with lemon and salt rushed back. He remembered the way she'd moved to the pulse-pounding music. "I was turned on, not embarrassed. I would have preferred a private performance without the other men leering at you. Then you could have taken it all off and not just undone only a couple of buttons."

"Well, then—" she flipped her hair behind her shoulder in a seamless, sexy move that nearly cut him to his knees "—I guess I have nothing to worry about tonight."

She might not, but Cullen couldn't say the same thing. He had a feeling he would be worrying for as long as Sarah was in town. Maybe even after she left.

Being out should have perked up Sarah's spirits and energized her like a toy bunny with brand-new batteries. But as soon as she stepped inside the brewpub, the smells of hops and grease assaulted her. Her stomach churned, not with hunger, but a severe case of nerves.

Rock music played, but the din of conversation drowned out the lyrics. Servers dressed in jeans and black T-shirts carried pitchers of beers, pint glasses and sodas.

"They're in the back," Cullen said.

She had no idea how he'd found his friends among all the people, but she followed him, weaving around crowded tables and past jam-packed booths. She ignored the strong impulse to grab his hand.

That would be a bad move. Just like kissing him back and coming here. Sarah should have stayed at the cabin, locked away in her bedroom, where she wouldn't be so hypersensitive. She didn't know if it was aftereffects of his kiss or the anticipation of meeting more of his friends or…

Yours is a happy ending.

Yeah, that was what had gotten her panties—make that thong—in a twist and turned her insides into a quivering mess.

Sarah wanted a happily-ever-after of her own. Once upon a time she thought she'd found hers with Cullen. But she should have known it wasn't meant to be. As a child, she might have dreamed of living a storybook-type life, but she'd learned the chances of happily ever after were slim to none. She accepted that reality, though she hated it.

You were no longer a part of my life. I could start over in Hood Hamlet with a clean slate once the divorce was finalized.

She'd thought the same thing about living without him before her accident. Now she wasn't so sure.

Cullen had found the perfect place to spend the rest of his life, to fall in love, get married again and raise a family. She would return to the institute, work until her grant was over then find another job at a volcano somewhere else in the world. That adventurous way of life had always appealed to her.

Until now.

What was she thinking? She loved what she did. Work fulfilled her. It was her life.

The confusion, envy and dissatisfaction had to be from the concussion and her injuries, tiredness and hunger. Once she ate, she would feel better.

Cullen motioned to a long table with attractive men sitting on one end and beautiful women on the other. "Looks like most of the crew made it."

Bill sat with two men Sarah hadn't seen before. Cullen fit right in with that bunch of eye candy.

Zoe Hughes waved. She wore a colorful sleeveless shirt with ruffles on the front. A sparkly clip held up her hair with stylish, artfully placed tendrils around her face. "Leanne said we might see you tonight. I'm so glad you came."

Sarah wasn't used to people being so happy to see her. It felt good. "It took some convincing, but the good doctor finally relented."

Cullen raised his hands. "I know when to surrender."

Zoe's blue eyes twinkled. "Proud of you, Doc."

Introductions were made and a pitcher of Jake's handcrafted root beer ordered for Sarah.

Leanne shooed him away. "Go sit with the guys, Doc, so us girls can chat."

Cullen pulled a chair out for Sarah. "Let me know when you're ready to eat. I'll go with you to the taco bar. It'll be hard for you with one hand."

With a nod, she sat.

He pushed in her chair, then joined his friends a few feet away.

Carly pushed her long blond hair behind her ears. "Cullen is so overprotective of you."

Leanne nodded. "I always knew there was more to him than met the eye."

"It's so sweet." Zoe sighed. "I can't imagine what Sean would be like if I was injured in an accident. I doubt he'd let me out of his sight or want me to do anything, either."

As if Cullen loved Sarah that much. A lead weight settled in the bottom of her stomach. He might care, he might be concerned, but not the way a devoted husband would be if something happened to his beloved wife.

Sarah glanced his way.

Tenderness filled his gaze.

Her heart bumped. Flustered, she looked away.

"You have more color than this morning," Leanne said. "Feeling better?"

Sarah might still be flushed after being kissed so thoroughly. Or it could be embarrassment. She cleared her throat. "I went for a walk today with Bill. Got some fresh air."

"And now the brewpub," Carly said. "That's more excitement than you're used to."

Especially when you added in Cullen's kisses. Sarah nodded.

The server placed a pitcher of root beer and a glass on the

table. Cullen already had a beer in his hand. Carly filled the glass and gave it to Sarah.

"Thanks." She took a sip. Thick and rich with the right amount of sweetness. "This is great."

Carly grinned. "Jake makes the best root beer in Oregon."

Leanne grinned. "The two of you are so cute. You act like newlyweds, even with a baby."

"Nicki is officially a toddler now," Carly said.

Sarah noticed how Jake and Carly smiled at each other a lot. The same with Sean and Zoe.

A diamond-engagement-ring-size lump lodged in Sarah's throat. These happy couples gave her hope some marriages could succeed. They also were a harsh reminder of how hers had failed.

How did some people get so lucky? That was what she wanted to know.

A plate with two large pretzels and a small bowl of mustard dipping sauce appeared in front of her. She looked over her shoulder to see Cullen standing there.

He smiled. "You wanted to try a pretzel."

His gesture touched her. If only they could have been one of the lucky couples. "I do."

"The pretzels are almost as good as the root beer," Carly said.

Zoe flipped her hair. "The pretzels are better."

"Try one," Cullen urged.

"Listen to the good doctor," Leanne said. "He would never lead you astray."

No, he had only turned Sarah's world inside out by making her believe happy endings were possible. But they weren't for her. She took another sip of her root beer.

Cullen held a piece of pretzel in front of her face. Mustard covered an end. "Open up."

The lump in her throat doubled. She looked up at him.

A devilish smile curved his lips. "You know you want it."

Her heart slammed against her chest. What was he doing? This felt like…flirting.

As he brought the pretzel closer, wicked laughter lit his eyes. She parted her lips and cautiously bit off the end of the pretzel. The bread, salt and mustard sauce complemented each other perfectly. But she was more interested in the way Cullen looked at her—as though he wanted to taste her.

"How is the pretzel?" Jake asked.

The pretzel. Right. She focused on the men at the far end of the table. "Delicious. Like the root beer."

But not quite as yummy as Cullen. Her pulse picked up speed, accelerating as if she were tumbling downhill. Which was what she'd be doing if she didn't stop acting like a lovesick teenager. She looked away to find Zoe, Leanne and Carly staring at her with rapt interest.

Sarah sipped her root beer. She understood their curiosity. Cullen feeding her made them seem like a couple. She had no idea what was going on and wasn't sure she had the strength to find out. Kissing him had been bad enough. Getting her hopes up and then discovering this was another fantasy would hurt worse than being hit by another steam blast.

No, thank you.

On the drive home from the brewpub, Sarah closed her eyes. The evening had taken its toll, physically as well as emotionally. If anything, seeing Carly and Jake Porter and Zoe and Sean Hughes together had made Sarah realize how far apart she and Cullen really were. And always had been. She sighed, not a sigh of frustration but of resignation for what would never be.

The truck's engine stopped. She opened her eyes. The porch light illuminated the path to the cabin's front door through the darkness. The night was playing tricks on her vision. The distance appeared longer than it really was. Too bad that wasn't the case with the separation between her and Cullen and their dreams.

"Tired?" Cullen sounded concerned.

Through the shadows in the truck's cab, she saw his worried gaze upon her. Their situation would be easier to handle if he didn't act as though he cared what happened to her.

Cullen is so overprotective of you.

Too bad he was the same way with everyone he knew. Strangers, too. "I'm a little tired."

That gave her a good excuse to go straight to her room. No reason to linger and wish for what might have been or a goodnight kiss.

Not. Going. To. Happen.

Sarah climbed out of the truck and hurried to the front door. Cullen followed at her heels. "Slow down."

Sarah didn't. She couldn't. All the happy couples tonight were an in-her-face reminder. She wasn't like the women she'd been with tonight. She would never have the perfect kind of wedded and domestic bliss the others had achieved. She could never be a perfect, proper wife. She wasn't made that way.

He unlocked and opened the door.

Sarah stepped inside ready to retreat to her room, but a hand touched her left shoulder. She nearly jumped.

"Let's sit for a minute," Cullen said, so close she could smell him, musky and warm and inviting.

The ache in her stomach increased. "Can't this wait until morning?"

"No." He led her to the sofa. "It won't take long."

Of course it wouldn't. Cullen never liked to talk. Sarah remembered all the times she'd needed to talk to him, but he'd retreated and left her more upset. She didn't want to do the same thing to him. She took a seat.

He sat next to her. "You looked like you were having fun tonight."

She nodded. "Your friends are very nice."

"They like you," he said. "Especially Paulson."

Sarah blew out a breath. "Bill's harmless."

"As harmless as a howitzer tank and about as subtle."

That made her smile.

"I'm glad you talked me into going," Cullen said. "Seeing you with everyone tonight. Laughing and joking. It's like you've been a part of the group forever."

Sarah stiffened. "What do you mean? I'm nothing like your friends. They're so...domestic."

"Paulson isn't."

"*Domestic* isn't the right word." She backtracked. "What I mean is they're caretakers. They look out for each other. All for one. I'm more of an…adventurer."

"Your research will save lives in the future. I don't know how much more of a caretaker you could be."

Cullen was wrong. She could never be the kind of wife he wanted. "I'm a loner, not the family type. Nothing like Carly, Zoe and Hannah. Or your mother and sisters…"

"What about my mom and sisters?" he asked.

Oops. Sarah hadn't meant to say that aloud. "It's nothing."

"Let me be the judge of that."

"It's just…" Sarah rubbed her mouth. "Well, it was pretty obvious your family didn't like me much."

Cullen flinched as if she'd slapped him. "That's not true."

Sarah raised her left shoulder, but she knew her gut instincts were 100 percent correct. She wasn't proper wife material. "It is. The way your family acted that Easter. I've never felt so inadequate in my life."

He made a face. "Come on."

The disbelief in his voice set her nerves even more on edge. She hadn't fitted into his family's out-of-this world holiday at all. "I wanted to help with dinner. I tried to help. But I only got in their way. They kicked me out of the kitchen and told me to go find you."

"That's because they didn't want to put you to work. You were a guest."

"A guest." The word tasted like ash in her mouth. "I was your wife. I thought I was family."

She'd wanted to be family. More than anything. But that hadn't happened. She could never be the kind of wife he would want. That was when she'd realized his family would never accept her and Cullen wouldn't want her.

Tears welled in her eyes. She blinked them away.

He started to speak, then stopped himself.

Sarah wasn't surprised he had nothing more to say. She picked at the cast's padding around her fingers.

Cullen leaned toward her. "I should have told you. Warned you."

The regret, thick and heavy, in his voice shocked her. "About what?"

His clouded gaze met hers. "Easter. My family. Blaine."

"What does your twin brother have to do with this?" she asked.

"Everything."

The one word sent a chill down Sarah's spine. Cullen's grief and sadness were as clear as they'd been that afternoon at Red Rocks when he'd mentioned his twin brother who had died. That was the one and only time he'd spoken of Blaine. She'd asked a few questions, but he'd never answered them.

She reached for his hand. His skin felt cold, not warm as usual. "You told me Blaine died when you were in college."

"He died on Easter."

Surprise washed over her. Cullen had never told her any details. "On Easter Sunday?"

Cullen nodded. His hand wrapped around hers. Squeezed. "Blaine used to love Easter. He always wanted more decorations and food. There were never enough eggs and candy for him. Because of what happened, my family goes all out on the holiday. Overcompensates."

She sat back, stunned and angry he hadn't shared this information with her. Not telling her about breaking his arm as a kid was one thing, but this...

Easter weekend with the Grays had been the tipping point for her to bring up divorce. She'd realized then it was only a matter of time before Cullen checked out of their marriage for good.

"I..." A million thoughts swirled through her mind, but she didn't know where to begin. "I had no idea."

Cullen scooted closer. His thigh pressed against hers. Self-preservation urged her to move away from him, but she hated that he was hurting.

His gaze locked on hers. "It's not just Easter. Putting on over-the-top holidays and birthdays, especially mine, is my family's way of dealing with grief and the empty place at the table."

Easter hadn't been as perfect as she'd imagined—far from it actually. The realization left her off-kilter. With this new information she tried to relate how she'd felt then.

His family sure had put on a good act. She'd never sensed what was going on beneath the surface. She'd been so focused on her own insecurities she hadn't thought what the holidays would mean to them after losing a son and a brother. But she wasn't about to give Cullen a free pass over this. "You should have talked to me about this. You realize I don't even know how Blaine died?"

"My brother was a drug addict." Cullen's voice cracked, but his gaze never wavered from hers. "Blaine died of an overdose. I like to think it was accidental, but who knows? I found him unconscious when I went to get him for Easter dinner."

Horror flooded her. She gripped his hand, ignoring the urge to hold him. "Oh, Cullen. I'm so sorry."

"Me, too." Self-recriminations twisted his lips. "I failed Blaine. Interventions. Rehab. Tough love. I tried everything I could and I still couldn't save him."

Her heart ached for him, for all the Grays. "Addiction doesn't work that way."

"I know, but when it's your twin brother…"

"It's a horrible, impossible situation." Even knowing that, she couldn't begin to comprehend what Cullen had gone through, both when his brother was alive and afterward. Still, she wondered what else she might have misunderstood about him and his life. "If I'd known…"

It might have made a difference in their marriage. She could have understood why his family acted the way they had. She could have helped Cullen.

"I didn't want to burden you." He stroked her hand with his thumb. "I hadn't thought about how not knowing might affect you. I should have discussed this with you so you would understand."

"That would have helped. But I'm glad you told me now." Sarah waited for him to pull his hand away from hers. He didn't. Until he did, she would hold tight. She didn't want to break the connection with him. This was the most open Cullen had been with her, and she feared he would shut down or run away from her again. She didn't want that to happen. "I'm sorry for not asking about Blaine before and not trying to understand your family's behavior."

"We both kept secrets from each other."

Sarah nodded. She hadn't told him about her ex-fiancé.

Cullen had hidden his pain the same way she'd hidden hers. She'd protected herself and her heart, never trusting he'd stay in the relationship to fully open up to him. No doubt he'd felt the same way about her by not telling her about Blaine. Regrets grew exponentially until she struggled to breathe.

"We're quite the pair." Distrusting and afraid to let anyone in. Their marriage had never stood a chance without that kind of openness—the kind of openness that would have allowed him to tell her the truth about his brother and family. The kind of openness that wouldn't have blinded her to Cullen's and his family's grief. "Holding back didn't help our marriage."

"No, but it feels good to let it all out finally."

Seeing him like this reminded her of when they'd first met. He'd had no problem talking to her in Red Rocks. She'd always wondered how he could have been so open there, but not when they returned to Seattle.

"Anything else you want to tell me?" Sarah tried to sound lighthearted. She wasn't sure she succeeded.

"There's nothing left to tell." His gaze raked over her. "Besides, you're tired."

Her chest tightened. She was losing him. He was retreating behind the doctor persona. But she wanted dearly to hang on to the moment. "I'm okay."

He pulled his hand away.

A deep ache welled within her soul. She missed his warmth. She missed…him.

"Your eyelids look heavy," he said in that professional tone of his she was beginning to hate. "It's past time for your medicine."

Despite herself, she stifled a yawn. Now that he mentioned it, her long day *was* catching up to her. But she hated to let things end this way. "I can stay up a little while longer. I'm feeling okay."

His eyes softened, not quite the look a physician gave a patient, but not one a loving husband gave to his wife. Soon to be ex-wife. "The goal is to have you feeling better than okay."

Once she was better, she could return to Bellingham—except right now going back didn't appeal to her as much as it once had. Not when she wanted to recapture the closeness they'd just shared.

Every nerve ending screeched.

What was she thinking? Bellingham was where she belonged. She couldn't allow this moment—this *one* conversation—to change anything. That would be stupid.

Risking her heart again because he'd opened up for a glimmer of what could have been would only hurt her in the end. Sarah had to stay focused on what was best for her. That was getting back to work—the one thing that wouldn't let her down.

She stood. "You're right. I'm more tired than I realized. I'm going to bed."

In the kitchen, Cullen washed his hands, then filled a glass with water. He stretched his neck to each side, but couldn't quite unknot all his tight muscles.

His talk with Sarah hadn't gone as he'd expected. He'd wanted to know what she thought of his friends and the brewpub. He'd never planned on talking about Blaine. No one outside his family and close friends back home knew the truth, but Cullen had been compelled to tell her. He needed to rectify the mistake he'd made by not saying anything about Blaine before. She'd needed to understand that what had happened at Easter wasn't her fault.

He tore a paper towel off the roll, then dispensed her medications.

I've never felt so inadequate in my life.

The pain in those eight words, the tears gleaming in her eyes, had been like daggers to his heart. Cullen hadn't wanted her to cry. She'd been hurt enough.

Because of him.

He'd wanted only to appease his family, particularly his mother, after missing the Easter before. Thanksgiving and Christmas, too. He hadn't considered Sarah's feelings during that trip home. He hadn't considered her much at all when they were together.

Expressing too much emotion equaled loss of self-control, especially around Sarah, who had a way of tearing down his walls. But his silence—not talking and warning her how hard Easter was for his family—had set her up for failure.

He couldn't undo the past, but he wanted to make it up to her somehow. Sarah had difficulty using her laptop and working for more than a few minutes. An idea formed…a way to help her do her job from the cabin. He could take care of that tomorrow.

Cullen walked to her bedroom. He knocked on the closed door, careful not to spill any water. He didn't want Sarah to slip the next time she exited her room.

No answer.

He tried again.

Nothing.

A frisson of worry shot to the surface. He opened the door. "Sarah?"

She was lying on her back in the center of the queen-size bed, sound asleep. Her dark hair was spread across the pillowcase. She'd taken off her jacket and removed her boots, but she was still wearing her jeans and red henley shirt.

I'm a little tired.

A little? Try a lot. Their discussion in the living room hadn't helped matters.

"Sarah." Cullen placed the water glass and medicine on the nightstand. He gently touched her left arm. "Wake up. You need to take your medicine."

Her heavy eyelids cracked. "Must I?"

"You must."

With some effort, she sat. "I thought you were a good doctor."

"I'm a very good doctor, which is why you have to do this."

"I was sleeping fine without them."

"We want you to wake up feeling fine in the morning."

She blinked. "*We?* There hasn't been a *we* for a while."

"That's true." Cullen regretted contributing so much to that happening. "But we're here together now, and we both want you to recover."

Sarah nodded once. She took the pills from him and put them into her mouth.

He handed her the water.

She sipped and swallowed. "Thanks. Now I'm going back to sleep."

"After you undress."

Sarah rested her head against the pillow and closed her eyes. "I'm too tired."

Sleeping in her clothes would be uncomfortable, but she was an adult. Controlling Sarah never was something he'd wanted to do. Or could do for that matter. He wanted only to control her influence on him. "At least get out of your jeans."

Her eyelids fluttered. "I'm not sure I can. I still have trouble with the button when I'm wide-awake."

"Want help?" he offered.

"Please. If you wouldn't mind."

Mind? He wasn't sure what he felt at the moment, but this seemed a light penance for his wrongdoings with her.

His fingers trembled with anticipation and need. He touched the button on her waistband.

Get a grip, Gray.

This had nothing to do with sex. He was supposed to help her. He wanted to help her, if only to make amends for what he'd put her through. But the crazy push-pull of regret versus the physical attraction was giving him whiplash.

Cullen unbuttoned the waistband of her jeans. He tugged down on the zipper. The teeth of the zipper released. This wasn't so hard. He glimpsed a patch of pink lace.

His groin tightened. He jerked his hand away.

They might be soon-to-be divorced and she might be the last woman in the world he should want to be with, but that did nothing to lessen his attraction. His reaction had nothing to do with being celibate for nearly a year. It was Sarah. No one else had ever made him feel like this.

He liked that. Liked how she'd held his hand tonight as he talked about Blaine. Liked how she trusted him to help her in spite of all his failures.

"It's okay. I've got it," she mumbled.

Suck it up, Gray. Any fool could see she was exhausted. He needed to think about her, not himself. "Go back to sleep. I'll take care of it."

That was the least he could do.

Cullen pulled her jeans over the curve of her hips and down her thighs. His hand touched her skin. He ignored the sparks arcing through his fingertips with each brush and slid the jeans all the way off.

Sarah lay on the bed. Her eyes closed. Her lips parted.

Cullen wondered what she dreamed about. Him? If only…

He wanted to crawl into bed next to her and hold her, not only until the sun came up, but…forever. He yearned for the future he'd dreamed of having with her. But that wasn't what she wanted. Even if she did, it might not be the best thing for her. He didn't know how to act or how to be more open. But maybe with Sarah's help, he could learn….

CHAPTER TEN

SUNLIGHT WARMED SARAH's face. She opened her eyes. Light flooded the room through the open blinds. Usually she closed them before she went to bed.

But last night hadn't been usual. Cullen had opened up to her in a way she'd never expected. He'd given her medicine and removed her jeans. But no good-night kiss or even a peck on the forehead.

Sarah had been…disappointed. She chalked up the reaction to exhaustion. The last things she needed were any more kisses.

She shrugged on her robe, tied the strap as best as she could and walked out of her room. She had no idea whether Hannah, Leanne or Zoe would be here this morning. Sarah had a feeling Bill wouldn't be back.

She entered the living room.

"Good morning," Bill said, holding on to a ream of paper.

She did a double take. "You're babysitting me today?"

"Nope, I am." Cullen sat on the floor next to a leather recliner working on a printer.

Sarah looked around the living room filled with cords and boxes, the chair and a table she'd never seen before. "What's going on?"

Bill grinned as if he'd eaten three canaries and two parrots. "You know how your head hurts and arm aches when you work on your laptop?"

She knew the feelings all too well. "Yes."

"Well, we had a great idea—"

"We?" Cullen asked.

The firefighter winked. "Doc had the idea to set up a more comfortable workstation for you."

"You can print pages if the screen gives you a headache," Cullen said.

She covered her mouth with her hands. "This is…"

His gaze met hers. "Not exactly the definition of *fun*."

"It's mine." She studied the oversize leather recliner. "Where did the chair come from?"

He motioned his head toward Bill. "Paulson is good for a few things."

"A lot of things, if you happen to be a lovely lady." Bill ran his fingertips along the buttery leather. "This is my favorite chair. It's yours for as long as you need it."

"Thank you," Sarah said. "Thanks to both of you. But you shouldn't have gone to so much trouble."

Cullen stood. "You need more to do than sleep and walk. Some data analysis won't hurt you if you don't overdo it."

Sarah couldn't believe he'd listened to what she'd said yesterday when they'd spoken about going to Taco Night and done something about it. Something so wonderful.

Her heart swelled with joy. Maybe Cullen had changed. Heaven knew he kept surprising her with each passing day. "I can't wait to get to work."

He brushed his hands together. "Breakfast first."

"What are we having?" Bill asked.

"Omelets and bacon, but I need to run to the store for more eggs."

"I'll go," Bill said, then took off.

She wanted to kiss Cullen and not only with kisses of gratitude. Her heart lodged itself in her throat. "Thank you."

"Your work's important. This will make things easier on you."

And be the perfect distraction. She needed something to keep her from throwing herself into his arms and smothering his gorgeous face with kisses. "Are you working tonight?"

"Nope. I'm caught up on the shifts I missed," he said. "I got lucky. I only missed four shifts while I was away."

She looked at Bill's chair and the table with the printer. Cullen had set up everything on the left-hand side. A rush of affection infused her. "I feel lucky myself."

Last night everything in her world had seemed wrong. Today it felt oh-so-right. Sarah couldn't believe he'd gone to so much trouble. Her heart stumbled.

"It can't be easy having me here, but I appreciate everything you're doing and have done." She couldn't change what had happened in the past, but she was speaking from the heart now. Cullen was her Prince Charming, and she felt like a princess. Albeit a bruised and battered one, but a princess nonetheless. And this might be the closest she ever got to a happy ending. "I hope you know that."

His satisfied smile settled on his lips and spread to his twinkling blue eyes. "I do now."

Over the next week, Sarah slept less and worked more. Interpreting data gave her a sense of purpose and kept her from thinking about Cullen. Okay, thinking about him *too much*. She still dreamed about him and occasionally thought about him kissing her. Thankfully he didn't again.

No matter how compelling the fairy tale was, Sarah knew better than to buy into it again. Others shared true love's kiss and found a happily-ever-after. Not her. She needed to stay focused.

But being with Cullen made it easy to forget her goal wasn't to settle into a comfortable routine here. There might be room for her at the cabin, but there wasn't room in his life. A few conversations didn't make up for all the times he hadn't wanted to talk to her. His kind gestures touched her, but they didn't change anything. She needed to get back to Mount Baker, back to the institute, back to *her* life.

And that was what she intended to do.

Today was her first day alone, a big step on her road to a full recovery. She was enjoying her first taste of independence since the accident. Oh, she'd missed the smell of coffee when she woke and conversations with her friends. But this was what she needed in order to return to Bellingham.

After eating lunch, Sarah downloaded files from MBVI's server. She studied a data stream her boss wanted her to check. The seismometer appeared to be working properly. She'd looked at enough of these squiggly lines to know the difference between ice movement and data glitches, but something didn't make sense. Magma shouldn't move without generating more specific seismic signals. At least, she'd never seen that before.

Sarah opened a new tab on her browser and checked a website listing the many earthquakes that occurred daily in the Pacific Northwest. She scratched her head. "What am I missing here?"

"Me?"

A bevy of butterflies took flight, turning her stomach into a crowded butterfly house. She had missed him, even if she shouldn't.

As he walked toward her, his aquamarine polo shirt seemed to change the shade of his blue eyes, reminding her of Los Tenideros in Costa Rica's Tenorio Volcano National Park, where two different-colored rivers merge. She'd traveled there after receiving her PhD and before starting at MBVI. She'd hoped the trip would heal the wound from her aborted marriage. Hadn't worked. She now wondered if anything could do that.

Sarah couldn't believe how good it was to see Cullen. A part of her wanted to fling herself into his arms, which would be a really stupid thing to do. She remained seated.

He smiled, a wide smile showing off straight white teeth and crinkling the corners of his eyes. He looked gorgeous. Even more so than usual.

She gripped her laptop. "I didn't hear you come in."

"That's what happens when you're concentrating."

His tone teased, but he was right. She'd lost herself in her work and forgotten about everything else. She could lose herself in Cullen if she wasn't careful. "I may be trying too hard."

He stood next to her, looking over her shoulder. "Head hurt?"

His concern warmed her like a fleece blanket. All she'd wanted was to be special to him. But he cared about everyone's well-being, not just hers. That was one reason he'd become a doctor. He'd mentioned Blaine as the other. She hadn't understood why until last week. Cullen might not have been able to save his twin brother, but he was doing his best to save others. "My head is fine. The data is causing me problems."

"Wrong?"

"Data is data. It can't be wrong. But my interpretation might be off," she admitted. "Things are inconclusive right now. I have a suspicion I may have started with too many preconceived notions."

He leaned forward, putting his hand on her shoulder. His male scent wrapped around her. His heat enveloped her. "Why do you think that?"

Cullen sounded interested, as if he really wanted to know what she was thinking. Tenderness and affection and attraction exploded in her chest. She glanced at the graph, trying to ignore her racing pulse, the pooling of desire, the longing for connection squeezing her tight. "Well…"

The numbers and lines blurred. She blinked. Everything was still fuzzy. Her head didn't hurt. It wasn't her concussion. All she could think about, all she wanted to see was…

Cullen.

Her heart pounded as hard as the surf ramming against the coast of Hawaii's Big Island.

Oh, no. She was falling for him.

Realization nearly bowled her over. Not quite the same explosive force of five hundred atomic bombs detonating as had marked the Mount Saint Helens eruption, but enough to send a chunk of molten lava crashing to the bottom of her stomach and taking up permanent residence there.

Sarah struggled to breathe. Whatever happened, she couldn't fall all the way. That would be catastrophic.

"Sarah?"

"I—I thought my gut instinct was correct." She forced words past the constriction in her throat. "I've been looking at data to support a hypothesis. Not looking at the data with an open mind."

Similar to what she'd done falling for him.

He sat on the couch. "It's not too late to go back over it."

"I'm sure I can remedy this."

Because she knew exactly where she'd gone wrong. Tucker wanted her back at the institute ASAP. He'd mentioned it again during their phone call this morning. She should have left by now. But she had stayed trying to work the data so she wouldn't have to go back.

Talk about stupid. She could be the poster child for the movement.

"Sarah?"

"Sorry." If she weren't careful he'd think she'd suffered another head injury. "I'm…frustrated."

She had a job to do. A responsibility to the institute. She'd messed up her analysis. Not to mention allowing her feelings for Cullen to…deepen.

"Hey, don't look so sad. It'll be okay." He touched her hand. "Cut yourself some slack. You're still recovering." He rubbed her hand. His calloused thumb made circles on her skin, leaving a trail of heat and tingles. "You've been working too hard."

Not hard enough. Sarah had become too distracted. She'd disregarded known facts and allowed herself to be caught up in a fantasy. Time to stop with the daydreams and focus on reality.

Cullen might not act the same as he had a year ago, but she hadn't changed. Even if he was willing to give marriage another shot, the outcome would be the same. He would abandon her like everyone else in her life.

Sarah had to be strong. She squared her shoulders. "What are you doing home? I thought you would be at Timberline Lodge all day."

Amusement twinkled in his eyes. "Look out the window."

Big, fluffy snowflakes fell from the sky. "When did it start snowing?"

"A couple of hours ago," he said. "Hughes, Paulson and Moreno are out there now."

"Go join them." And let her try to save face, do her job correctly and get him out of her head and heart again.

Cullen continued to rub her hand. "I can do that another day. I wanted to see how you were doing."

A warm and fuzzy feeling trickled through her.

Pathetic.

Sarah should be immune to him, not reacting like a lovesick teen to every word he said. She tilted her chin. "I'm doing well."

"Well, but frustrated."

He was part of her frustration. That gave her an idea. "You've been working hard. You need a break."

"You're the one who needs a break. Time away from the data so you can relax."

Time away from Cullen to clear her head. That might do the trick. She closed her laptop. "Sounds good. I'll take a nap. Grab your board and join your friends."

"I have a better idea. Let's take a break together."

Her heart rate resembled the data she'd been looking at. Inconsistent and all over the place. "Don't waste your free time on me."

"I'd rather enjoy it with you."

Sarah melted. She couldn't help it. She should decline politely. But the words wouldn't come. Not when her heart was clamoring so loudly it drowned out all sense of self-preservation.

Mischief, as worrisome as a ticking bomb, glinted in his eyes. "I know what we can do. Are you up to checking out Main Street with me?"

Temptation exploded with enough force to do significant damage. Sarah wanted to spend time with him. Be with him. She might regret this. Who was she kidding? She *would* regret this. But she didn't care. "I'm up for it."

As long as Cullen would be with her, she was up for anything.

Half an hour later, Cullen strolled down Main Street with Sarah at his side. She spun to see all the shops and sights. Her excitement added a bounce to his step.

A layer of snow clung to her black parka and colorful wool beanie. The cold air turned her cheeks a cute pink. She looked pretty and, most important, healthy. "This was just what I needed."

"Doctor knows best." That was why he'd suggested this. Her health.

Yeah, right.

He'd been counting the hours—minutes—until he could be with her. She was on his mind constantly when he was away from her. When he was with her, too. "I have a surprise for you."

She rose on her tiptoes. "I love surprises."

Her excitement pleased Cullen. Seeing her upset earlier with a life-as-she-knew-it-was-over expression on her face had made him feel as if he'd failed her somehow. He was relieved she was more like her old self, up for fun and adventure with him. "You'll like this one."

Friends greeted him from across the street. Cullen waved.

"Are you planning to stay in Hood Hamlet permanently?" Sarah asked.

"Yes," he said. "My lease on the cabin is up next month. I might sign another year lease or go month-to-month awhile. I'm considering buying a place."

"That's a big step."

True, but owning a house had always been part of his plan. So had a wife and kids…. He glanced at Sarah and pushed the thought from his mind. "I like living here. It's a buyer's market."

"Strike while the iron is hot."

"Not quite." Cullen had learned his lesson by rushing into marriage. He jammed his hands into his jacket pockets. "I need to do more research first."

"What if you miss out on the perfect house?"

He'd thought Sarah was the perfect woman.

But that hadn't worked out the way he hoped. He didn't want to think about that today. "Then I'll wait for the next perfect place to come on the market."

Her gaze met his. "We're so different."

Understatement of the year. "We had some good times together in spite of our differences."

She nodded. "More good than bad."

Then why had she asked for a divorce? The question echoed through his head. But he knew the answer.

Sarah didn't love him. Oh, she'd never said those exact words when she'd brought up a divorce. She'd told him he deserved better. She'd told him to find another wife who could give him all he wanted.

All what? He'd had no idea what she'd been talking about. He'd wanted only her.

She glanced into the coffee shop. A customer exited. The scents of freshly baked cookies and coffee beans drifted out the open door. "No wonder everyone around here is so active. You need to burn off calories from all this delicious-smelling food."

"You figured out our motivation." Cullen played along. "The more time we spend on the mountain, the more we can eat without guilt."

"When have you ever felt guilty about eating?"

"At the hospital. When you couldn't," he admitted.

Sarah's gaze softened. "You're so sweet."

Brothers and friends were *sweet*. He would have preferred *hot* or *sexy*. But maybe that was where ex-husbands fitted in. He didn't much like the moniker. "Do you know where you want to settle?"

She shrugged. "I'm not sure I'm the settling type."

Not surprising. Sarah had always seemed to have a case of wanderlust. When she'd moved into his apartment in Seattle, everything she owned fitted in her car. "How much longer does your postdoc last?"

"It's hard to say after the accident. I estimate my funding will last a few more months, then I'll have to find a new position. I'm thinking about applying to the Global Volcano Monitoring Project."

The word *global* raised the hairs on the back of his neck. "What's that?"

"A nonprofit group that sends scientists all over the world, particularly to third-world nations, to set up volcano-monitoring systems and teach locals how to use them."

A sense of dread took root in his stomach. "Sounds interesting. Important."

She nodded. "It would be great experience and an adventure. I'd be able to do a lot of good."

"You would." So why did this sound like a bad idea to him? Maybe because he would never see her again. But they were getting a divorce. He wouldn't see her again no matter where she lived.

Cars passed by on the road. Neighbors greeted one another. A woman pushed a baby stroller. A tourist stood in the middle of the street snapping photographs.

"I see why you want to settle here," she said.

"Yeah." This was where Cullen wanted to be. So why couldn't he stop thinking about Sarah living in some remote village in Central America? He realized they'd reached their destination. He stopped and pointed to the wood plaque hanging from the building. "This is your surprise."

Sarah read the words written in gold script. "'Welton Wines and Chocolates.' Two of my favorite things."

"That's why I wanted to bring you here." Chocolate was the second-best way to get rid of Sarah's frustration. The first way was more fun, but not possible with her. He pulled his hand out of his pocket and opened the door. A bell tinkled, announcing their arrival. "After you."

Her eyes gleamed like emeralds. "Thank you."

He followed her inside. "You're welcome."

Warm air greeted Cullen, chasing away the cold. The aromas of chocolate and wine made his mouth water. The atmosphere was comfortable yet not too casual. Zoe Hughes had helped with the interior design. Chocolate was displayed to their left. A wine bar was on the right. In the back were black tables and chairs.

"This could be a dangerous place," Sarah whispered.

Not half as dangerous as her. "Let me have your coat."

Her eyes widened. "We're staying?"

"This wouldn't be much of a surprise if we walked in, turned around and left, now, would it?"

She grinned wryly. "I like your style, Dr. Gray."

Too bad Sarah hadn't liked him enough to stick with their

marriage. No, that wasn't fair. Cullen bore responsibility for the breakup, too. He hung up their jackets on the hat tree by the door.

Christian Welton, a firefighter and Leanne's fiancé, shook his hand. "Good to see you, Doc."

"This is Sarah Purcell," Cullen said. "I wanted her to experience one of Owen's chocolate tastings."

"Great." The firefighter looked at Sarah. His easy smile widened. "I'm Christian Welton. Nice to meet you. Leanne's told me all about you."

Sarah's smile lit up her face. "Your ears should be burning. She said you were smokin' hot, and you are."

Leave it to Leanne and Sarah not to mince words.

Christian's cheeks reddened. "Leanne mentioned the two of you had a lot in common."

"You have no idea," Cullen said.

Sarah's lips pursed. "What's that supposed to mean?"

Christian's gaze met Cullen's in understanding. "It means you and Leanne keep us on our toes."

The bell on the door jingled. More customers entered.

"Take a seat." Christian motioned them to the tables in back. "We're getting set up. The tasting will begin soon."

Cullen and Sarah sat at a small round table sporting a single red rosebud in a glass vase and a lit votive candle. The flame flickered. Romantic. He hoped she liked this.

She looked around. "This is great."

The frown on her face didn't match her words. "You sure about that?"

"I'm a little confused. I thought Christian was a firefighter."

"He is, but his family owns a winery in the Willamette Valley," Cullen explained. "Christian and his cousin Owen opened this shop a few months ago and run it together. Owen is also a chocolatier."

She brightened. "That makes sense."

The bell on the door rang again. More people entered the shop, including Jake and Carly Porter and Hannah and Garrett Willingham, who sat at a table together.

Sarah waved. "Do you want to join your friends?"

Cullen wanted her all to himself. "This is fine."

Christian placed carafes of water, glasses and small plates of crackers on each of the tables. Next came paper place mats with squares numbered one through six and pencils for each taster. "Welcome to Welton Wines and Chocolate. Today we'll be doing a tasting with our chocolatier, Owen Welton Slayter."

Owen limped out from a back room, dressed in a white chef's jacket and gray pants. He also wore a leg brace, thanks to his climbing accident back in November. "Today we'll be tasting six samples, starting with milk chocolate that has the lowest percentage of cacao and ending with our darkest, most complex one. We've provided water at room temperature so it doesn't affect the chocolate or dull your taste buds and unsalted crackers to cleanse your palate between each sample."

"Is it a law all males must be attractive to live in Hood Hamlet?" Sarah whispered.

At least she still found him attractive. That pleased Cullen. "You'll have to ask the sheriff."

As Christian placed chocolate samples on the place mats, Owen lectured about the history of chocolate, beginning with the Mayans and Aztecs and the journey to Europe.

"This is in-depth." Sarah sounded impressed.

"Only the best for you, Lavagirl."

Her startled gaze met his.

Cullen understood her reaction. The words surprised him, too. But he meant them.

She opened her mouth to speak. "Cull—"

He touched his finger to her lips. So soft and smooth. Nothing like they'd been at the hospital. "Not now."

"Allow me to give you a few pointers about tasting chocolate," Owen said to the group. "Examine each sample. Look at the color and the texture. Smell it. Snap the sample in half. Does it sound sharp and crisp, soft and quiet or something in between? After you place the sample in your mouth, don't chew. Let the chocolate melt on your tongue so you can experience the flavors as they unfold. If you have any questions, just ask."

As Sarah looked at the place mat, her brows lowered.

Cullen scooted his chair closer to her. He wanted her to enjoy this, not be all tense and wary. "Let's have fun."

With a nod, she tasted sample number one, following Owen's instructions as if she were doing an experiment in the laboratory.

"What do you think?" Cullen whispered.

"This one is smooth, but I prefer a stronger chocolate."

He placed his arm around the back of her chair. "Mark what samples you like so we'll know what to buy later."

She tapped her pencil against the table. "Aren't you going to keep track of your favorites?"

Cullen didn't have to. He was looking at her now. "I'll keep track, too."

Amusement shone in her eyes. "Then you'd better taste your first selection or you'll be playing catch-up for the rest of the session."

He tasted the sample. "You're right. Not rich enough for me."

The next two had deeper flavors. Sarah decided number three was the tastiest. She drew a heart around the number on her placement.

He toyed with the ends of her hair, letting the silky strands slip through his fingers. She glanced up at him, but didn't say a word. He took her silence as permission to continue.

"For centuries, many have touted the aphrodisiac qualities of chocolate," Owen lectured. "Some scientists have tried to debunk this, while others have claimed it's a psychological effect. Feel free to test this by feeding someone at your table sample number four."

Sarah held a chocolate in front of him with a hesitant look in her eyes. "Do you want me...?"

CHAPTER ELEVEN

CULLEN WANTED SARAH more than he could say. But he knew she wasn't asking *that* question. The chocolate would have to do. With a slight nod, he parted his lips.

She sucked in a breath. Her hand trembling, she brought the sample to his mouth.

He didn't know if she was nervous over him or because she was using her left hand. He hoped it wasn't the latter. He liked the idea she might be as affected by him as he was by her.

She carefully placed the chocolate onto his tongue. "What do you think?"

The intense flavor burst in his mouth with a nuttier and buttery taste. The third sample had been more velvety with a hint of orange.

"I like it." He picked up the fourth selection off his place mat. "Your turn."

Something resembling panic flashed in her eyes, but she opened her mouth anyway. He brought the chocolate closer. The tip of her tongue came out. Cullen fed her the sample.

Sarah's lips closed simultaneously with her eyes.

The aphrodisiac effects of chocolate might not be quantifiable, but he was feeling something. When she opened her eyes, the desire flaring in her gaze suggested she was feeling it, too.

He wanted to kiss her. Instead, he scribbled a star next to the number four on his place mat. "We're buying this one, too."

When he glanced back at Sarah, the tip of her tongue darted out once again and licked her lower lip.

Cullen wanted a taste. He leaned closer and kissed her. Gently.

She tensed for a moment, then relaxed and kissed him back. He pressed his lips harder against hers, enjoying the warmth, the sweetness and the touch of spice that was uniquely Sarah. As with the chocolate samples, the flavors unfolded one after another.

Her kiss filled the loneliness in his heart. He'd missed her so much. He didn't want her to go back to Bellingham or anywhere else.

"Let's move on to sample five," Owen said.

Cullen drew back, even if would rather have skipped the rest of the tasting and continued kissing her. The confusion in her eyes matched how he felt.

He'd kissed her. He'd been with her a large chunk of the day. And he hadn't felt himself losing control. If anything, he was finding himself. He wanted to be a better husband, even if he wouldn't be one for much longer.

He marked his place mat with the pencil. "I'm going to want another taste of number seven."

Her eyebrows bunched. "There are only six samples."

"Seven, if I count you."

She smiled shyly at him through her eyelashes.

He leaned closer. "I have a strong feeling number seven is going to be my favorite."

Gratitude glistened in her eyes and something else. Something resembling…hope. "Mine, too."

The tasting continued. Cullen forced himself to concentrate. All he wanted to do was stare at Sarah and kiss her again. Not in that particular order. But she was paying attention to Owen, so Cullen did, too, while wondering how he could keep things going so well between them.

Number five was delicious with a coconut, sugary taste and went on the to-buy list. Number six was too bitter.

As the tasting came to an end, people discussed their observations. Everyone liked something different about the samples.

Cullen rubbed her back. "Enjoying yourself?"

"What are we doing?" she said in a low voice.

"Tasting chocolate."

"I mean…" She glanced around as if to see if anyone was listening. "You're acting like we're…"

"What?"

"Married."

"We are."

"For now." She glanced over at the table where his friends sat. "But you're doing all this lovey-dovey, couple stuff. I'll be honest. I'm enjoying it. But I'm sure your friends have noticed. What are they going to think?"

She enjoyed it. Good. Him, too. So much so he didn't want the lovey-dovey stuff, as she called it to end. "I don't care what they think."

"You said you told them about us."

He nodded. "They know I filed for divorce."

Sarah's face paled. "You filed?"

She sounded shocked. He moved his hand off her back, but kept his arm on her chair. "I mentioned I'd gotten things started when you were at the hospital."

She nibbled on her lip. "I'm sorry. You did, but I hadn't realized that meant you'd filed."

Okay, he was confused. What else would starting a divorce proceeding mean?

"No big deal who filed, right?" Except at the moment, when all he wanted was to kiss her again, he was wondering if he'd been premature in setting the divorce into motion. "I hope you're not upset."

"Not upset." Her smile would have looked more natural on a mannequin. "I wasn't clear on what you meant. Probably the concussion."

"Probably." But doubts clamored to surface. Hope spread. In a flash, dreams and plans he'd long since suppressed surged to the forefront of his mind. His heart battered against his rib cage. "You still want a divorce, right?"

As soon as he'd spoken the words aloud, he regretted them, afraid to hear her answer. What if she said yes? What if she said no? Even if he wanted to try again, how could he ever trust she would want to stick around long-term? Especially with her life in Bellingham and his in Hood Hamlet. Logically divorce was the best—the only—option. And one of these days his heart would catch up to his head and agree.

It was taking her a long time to answer. Too long.

Cullen stood, disgusted with himself for thinking they might stand a chance. "I'm going to buy some chocolate while you think about it."

You still want a divorce, right?

If today was the benchmark for the future, then no, Sarah didn't. She tapped the pencil so fast against the table she might as well have picked up Cullen's and done a drum roll. But one day didn't make a marriage. Nor did two, the amount of time they'd spent together before eloping.

Even if things went well, how long would it be before Cullen realized he could do better or got tired of her and took off?

She dropped her pencil. Probably not long.

The sooner she could get out of here the better.

And she didn't mean this shop.

Carly walked up to the table with a big smile on her face. "It's so good to see you and Cullen here."

Hannah joined them. "I can't believe how much better you look. You're glowing."

"Thanks." Sarah didn't want to have to smile and make conversation with *Cullen's* friends who knew more about her marriage—make that the end of her marriage—than she did. But these women had become her friends, too. She could smile at them. And did. "The doctor's pleased with my progress."

Carly winked. "The good doctor seems very happy."

"The two of you look great together," Hannah said. "Seems like more is healing than your injuries."

Sarah pressed her toes into the ground so hard she was sure she'd split one of the floorboards. She understood these two women believed in a forever kind of love. They meant well, but she didn't know how to answer them. "Anything can happen."

She hoped that satisfied them.

"Especially here in Hood Hamlet," Hannah said.

Carly beamed. "Christmas magic in June."

Sarah had no idea what Carly was talking about. "Magic doesn't exist. It's nothing more than an illusion."

The two women shared a look.

"Of course you feel that way now. You're a scientist," Hannah said. "But after you've been in Hood Hamlet awhile, you'll change your mind."

Carly nodded. "It happens to everyone. Including Cullen."

Sarah remembered he'd mentioned Christmas magic when they'd arrived in town, but this was too woo-woo for her analytical brain. Magic no more existed than did everlasting love.

A good thing. She couldn't allow herself to be lured in by any yearning, whether it was to believe in magic or in love or a happily-ever-after. "I won't be in town long enough for that to happen."

"It doesn't look like Cullen's ready to send you back yet," Carly said.

Hannah nodded. "You have more healing to do."

"I do." But that wouldn't change her beliefs. She was a scientist grounded in fact. She had to stand firm. If she weren't careful, if she allowed herself to believe, her heart could be obliterated.

She glanced over at Cullen, wishing he would hurry so she could escape the scrutiny of his friends. But he was engrossed in a conversation with Jake, Garrett and Christian.

Cullen's gaze caught hers. The happiness in his eyes did painful things to her stomach that had nothing to do with her surgical incision or broken ribs. She struggled to breathe.

What was going on? The man had filed for divorce, and he still had this effect on her? A divorce she'd brought up, a little voice taunted.

Regret assailed her.

She looked back at the two women, who hadn't missed the exchange. Their enthusiastic smiles suggested they might think the divorce had been put on the back burner.

Sarah opened her mouth to clarify things, but no words came out.

This surprise was turning into a nightmare. She wanted to go home—strike that, back to the cabin—and hide away in her—the guest—bedroom until he had to go to work or on a mission.

Cullen walked over. He held up a white bag with gold lettering. "I've got the chocolate."

Good. Sarah could scarf down the entire bag once she was in her room. She stood, eager to escape this place.

"I don't know if you have dinner plans for tonight, but we'd love for you to join us," Hannah said, much to Sarah's regret. "Jake and Carly are coming over with Nicole, so this will be a kid-friendly menu. Nothing fancy, just lasagna."

"Sarah loves lasagna," Cullen said.

She was touched he remembered and annoyed he'd bring it up now. She forced a feeble smile.

"I'm bringing dessert," Carly added.

Cullen looked at Sarah. "What do you say?"

Darn him. He'd left the decision up to her. Sure, she had an easy out if she said she was tired. People would understand. Too bad she was confused and wary and apprehensive, but not tired. How could she lie to a woman who had done so much to care for her? "Sure, sounds fun."

As much fun as more surgery.

Hannah grinned. "Great."

Yes, great. At least Hannah was happy. Sarah's face muscles trying to keep her panic from showing, but her smile never wavered. She had a feeling this would be a long evening. At least she had one of Carly's desserts to look forward to at the end. And Sarah realized there was one bright spot ahead—she wouldn't be spending the evening alone with Cullen.

She tugged on her ear. Maybe dinner out wasn't such a bad idea after all.

"The lasagna was great, Hannah." Cullen enjoyed being at the Willinghams' house. Nothing like sitting at a crowded dinner table with good friends, tasty food and his beautiful wife. His arm rested on her chair. The ends of her hair tickled his skin with each turn of her head. He could get used to this. "Thanks for inviting us over."

"Everything was so delicious," Sarah agreed, as did Jake and Carly.

Cullen's thigh touched Sarah's. He thought about shifting positions to break the contact, but she wasn't scooting away. Might as well stay put, even if his blood was simmering.

He wished it could always be like this with Sarah. Hanging out with other couples. Kids running around.

Going out with others was something they'd never done in Seattle. With such busy schedules, they'd kept to themselves, spending any free time with each other. Maybe that had been a mistake.

Hannah wiped the mouth of her two-year-old son, Tyler. The boy squirmed and scrunched up his face. She didn't miss a beat. "Would you like dessert now or later?"

"Later," all the adults said at the same time.

"Then let's go into the living room," Hannah said. "Cleanup can wait."

Garrett leaned over and kissed his wife. "I'll take care of it for you."

Her older children—Kendall and Austin—bolted from the table. Tyler and fifteen-month-old Nicole, Jake and Carly's daughter, toddled after them, nearly crashing into each other twice.

Carly laughed. "At least diapers provide padding when they fall."

The adults followed the kids into the living room and took seats on the worn but comfortable furniture. Pieces from a jigsaw puzzle covered the coffee table. Crayons and Lego lay scattered on the floor.

This was the kind of house Cullen wanted to buy. Warm and cozy, well-built and designed for a family. But his dreams about having a family had always included Sarah. Never any other woman, only her.

She sat on the couch with Carly.

He wished Sarah had sat by him on the loveseat instead.

The two women joked about something wedding-related.

He understood why Sarah had wanted to elope after being jilted on her wedding day, but he'd never asked if she wanted a reception or a party to celebrate their marriage. They'd never taken a honeymoon, only short climbing trips. They'd never shared a bank account, either.

Framed photographs covered the fireplace mantel. The wedding pictures drew his gaze. He and Sarah had two wedding photographs, one with the Elvis impersonator and one of the two of them. It had seemed enough at the time. And too much when he'd been moving out.

Jake and Garrett fiddled with the stereo until music played.

A picture of a climber standing atop Mount Hood with a big grin on his face caught Cullen's attention. The gear, over ten years old, dated the photo. That must be Nick Bishop, Carly's brother, Hannah's first husband and Kendall and Austin's dad, who'd died in a climbing accident on Mount Hood.

The women laughed over something borrowed. Or was it blue?

Kendall, who was around twelve, carried in a cardboard box and set it at Sarah's feet. "My mom says you're a volcano scientist."

"I am," Sarah said enthusiastically. "At Mount Baker Volcano Institute. My specialty is seismology."

The girl's face fell. "Bummer. I need someone to help me who knows something about lava flow."

The corners of Sarah's mouth twitched, but she kept a serious expression on her face. "I know something about lava. What do you need help with?"

"My science-fair project."

Hannah touched her daughter's thin shoulder. "Sarah is a guest. Let's not bother her with your homework."

Kendall shrugged away from her mother's hand. "But you and dad know nothing about volcanoes."

"I'm happy to help," Sarah said, much to Cullen's surprise, given her pensive mood and how inexperienced she seemed to be around kids. "I've given some talks at schools and led geology field trips around Mount Baker."

As Kendall dug through the box, Hannah mouthed the words *thank you* to Sarah. Austin showed Jake his newest hand-held video game. Carly played peek-a-boo with Nicole and Tyler. Garrett adjusted the stereo volume.

Sarah gave Hannah a quick nod, then focused on Kendall. "Let me see what you have."

The girl showed her the box jam-packed with maps, a plastic bucket and other things Cullen couldn't quite recognize.

"Looks like you've got plenty to make a project," Sarah said. "Is there a quieter place where we can work?"

"Yes. I know just the place." Kendall, all limbs and hair, scrambled to her feet. "Follow me."

As Kendall jogged out of the living room carrying her box with her little brother Tyler chasing after her, Sarah stood. "How much help is Kendall allowed to have with the project?"

"She's supposed to do the majority of the physical work herself," Garrett said. "But she can have as much assistance as needed with the concepts and science behind the project."

"Got it," Sarah said.

"Tyler went back with Kendall. If he's in the way, let me know," Garrett added.

Sarah waved her hand. "No worries. We'll find something for him to do."

Her willingness to help surprised Cullen, given her awkwardness with his nephews and nieces during that Easter. Maybe spending more time with kids on field trips had made a difference. He remembered what she'd said to him during their conversation in his living room.

I wanted to help with dinner. I tried to help. But I only got in their way. They kicked me out of the kitchen and told me to go find you.

Had his family treated Sarah the same way when it came to the kids? Granted, they hadn't been happy when he'd eloped because they worried his behavior had been too reckless. But surely his family wouldn't have taken their concerns out on Sarah.

Except that was what he'd done, he realized with regret. He'd blamed Sarah for his impulsive behavior in Las Vegas. Even though it had made him feel better, happy, complete.

Hannah stared down the hallway. "Sarah doesn't have to do this."

"She knows that," Cullen explained. "But given the choice between volcanoes and doing something else, she'll pick volcanoes every time."

But the words didn't quite ring true to him. She'd had research to do with her dissertation and other obligations at the university. But she'd worked around his schedule as much as possible. He hadn't felt like a priority because he hadn't wanted to be one. He'd wanted her to be busy so he had reason to be busy, too. Busy…distracted. He rubbed the back of his neck.

Carly picked up Nicole. "You know, the USGS Cascade Volcano Observatory isn't that far away."

Jake held a bottle of beer. "Vancouver, Washington, isn't exactly close."

"It's closer than Bellingham, where Sarah works now," Hannah countered.

Garrett shot his wife a pointed look. Something Cullen hadn't expected from the button-downed CPA who was also OMSAR's treasurer. "Drop it."

Jake nodded. "You, too, Carly. Doc doesn't need you interfering in his life."

"Especially his marriage," Garrett added.

"What? We haven't done anything." Hannah raised her palms. "Carly and I thought we'd mention it in case Cullen and Sarah want to be closer."

Closer, huh? The muscle cords in Cullen's neck tightened. Sarah had been right. His friends had noticed what was going on at the chocolate tasting and had made their own assumptions. Wrong ones. Though a part of him wished they were correct. Sarah had never answered his question about still wanting the divorce. "Sarah and I aren't back together."

"Not yet anyway." Carly spoke as if she knew a big secret. "Anyone can see the two of you are perfect together."

He'd thought that once himself. Now…

Jake blew out an exasperated breath. "Be careful, Doc, or you'll find these two playing matchmaker."

Hannah placed her hands on her hips. "We aren't that bad."

"That's because you haven't been given the chance," Garrett said. "They mean well, Doc, but don't let them get away with anything or you'll have an avalanche on your hands."

Cullen gave both men a nod. He stood. "Appreciate the warning, gentlemen. I'm going to see how the science project is coming along."

And get out from under the would-be-matchmaking reach of the ladies.

"Just follow the sounds of wailing and gnashing of teeth and you'll find Kendall," Hannah said.

Carly made a sour face. "Hey, that's my niece you're talking about."

"Wait until Nicole turns twelve," Hannah said. "You'll understand. I can't imagine what it'll be like when she turns thirteen."

Cullen left them to discuss teenagers. Walking down the hallway, he didn't hear any wailing, but a few giggles and squeals pierced the quiet. He followed the sounds until he came to a garage.

He stood in the doorway.

The three sat on the concrete floor with the contents of the box spread out in front of them. Tyler played with an empty toilet paper roll. He couldn't seem to make up his mind whether it was a sword or a bugle.

"This is going to be so cool." Kendall knelt, leaning forward with an excited gleam in her eyes. "If it works."

"It'll work." Sarah pointed to a piece of paper on the floor. "You need to attach this onto the topographic map."

"Like this," the girl said shyly.

Sarah gave Kendall the thumbs-up sign. "That's perfect."

Tyler mimicked the action.

Grinning at the little boy, Sarah pulled him onto her lap. "You are too cute."

The boy gazed up at her with pure adoration.

Cullen's heart stuttered.

As Tyler examined her cast, Sarah touched Kendall's shoulder. "You're doing an excellent job."

Kendall beamed. "That's because I have you."

"You're doing all the work." Sarah sounded like a mom.

Cullen couldn't breathe.

"I'm simply your scientific adviser," she added.

"Is it fun being a scientist?" Kendall asked.

Sarah's beaming smile hit Cullen like a blast from a laser gun. He leaned against the doorjamb to keep from falling on his ass. Because that was the next place he'd be. No doubt about it.

"Being a scientist is the most fun job in the world," she said, and explained what she did at MBVI.

Kendall held on to Sarah's every word. He didn't blame the girl. He was the same way.

"Is it better than being a wife and mom?" Kendall asked.

Sarah's tender gaze washed over the two children. "I don't have kids, so I don't know about that, but being a wife can be fun, too."

Cullen listened in disbelief, held spellbound by the woman he'd married. His life plan swirled inside his brain, reconfiguring and amending itself by the second.

Kendall fiddled with a piece of plastic. "I can use water for the lava."

"You could, but molasses would work better due to its viscosity."

"My mom has molasses in the pantry." Kendall looked up at Sarah. "But I'm not sure what *visc*...whatever word you said means."

"Viscosity."

Kendall repeated the word. "Viscosity."

Sarah nodded. "Viscosity is the measure of a fluid's resistance to flow."

"Huh?"

"Imagine you have a cup of water and a cup of honey. Which drains faster?"

"The water. Honey moves slower."

"That's right," Sarah said. "Honey has a higher viscosity than water, so it resists flow more. Same with molasses."

"Makes sense."

As the two worked on the volcano, Cullen was captivated by how much Sarah had changed from being awkward and uncomfortable around his family at Easter to at ease with Tyler and Kendall.

This different side, this new side of Sarah appealed to him at a gut level. He pictured her with children of her own, nurturing them, mothering them. All the heady dreams he'd had when they'd first married rushed to the forefront of his mind. Sarah pregnant with his child. A girl with her laugh. A boy with her sharp wit. They would be a family.

His family.

Cullen's heart ached with yearning so strong he started walking toward Sarah. Until he realized she would be the mom of some other guy's kids.

He balled his hands.

You still want a divorce, right?

She hadn't answered him, but that didn't matter.

Forget pride. Forget everything.

He didn't want to lose her, but how could he convince her to give their marriage another shot? What if she didn't want to try again?

His heart thudded. But what if she did?

CHAPTER TWELVE

CULLEN UNLOCKED THE front door of the cabin. "You were amazing tonight."

Sarah walked inside. She wanted to be unaffected by him, yet all she wanted to do was kiss him. She couldn't give in to her impulsive side. Not with her heart at stake. "I didn't do that much."

"You only made a kid's night by helping her put together what will be the winning science project."

Sarah had never felt like such a part of a community, of a family, until tonight. She'd loved every single second of being at the Willinghams' house, from eating dinner to helping Kendall with her volcano model to holding Tyler with his ever-sticky hands. For the first time in Sarah's life she'd wondered if she could be a good wife and mother in spite of her past.

Sadness trembled down her spine. Too bad Hood Hamlet wasn't her community. She would never have a family with Cullen here. She swallowed a sigh. "Anyone would have helped."

"But you did."

She shrugged off her jacket. "I don't know why you're making such a big deal about this."

"The last time you were around kids, you looked like you wanted to run and hide."

Easter. The right sleeve got caught on her cast.

Cullen removed it for her. He hung the jacket on the hat tree by the door. "Tonight was the antithesis of that."

Sarah crossed her left arm over her chest and rubbed her cast. "Tonight was more real than Easter with your family."

With his hand at the small of her back, he led her into the living room. "Easter was real."

She sat on the couch, and he sat next to her. "Okay, it was real, but everything was scheduled with military precision. We moved from one thing to the next without having a chance to enjoy the moment. No chance to catch our breaths. No time to think about anything. I understand now that's the whole purpose of the holiday being so over-the-top. The day is so jam-packed with things Blaine doesn't have a chance to enter your minds."

He rubbed his palms on his thighs as if drying them off. "I told you it's a coping mechanism."

"Yes. But remember, I hadn't a clue then." She needed to get this out, if only for her peace of mind. "All I saw were little kids who wanted to play with their Easter baskets and eat candy, not do crafts, be forced into organized games and march in a parade. I mentioned it to your mom, who snapped at me. Your sisters jumped all over me, too."

His nostrils flared. "Why didn't you tell me?"

"You never wanted to talk about anything." Sarah kept her voice low and steady, even though her emotions and stomach churned. "Why would this be any different?"

"I…" He hung his head. "It's probably too late to apologize."

Sarah touched his hand; his skin was rough and calloused and warm. "It's okay. Addiction does crazy things to people, and this is how your family deals with what happened to Blaine. But it would have been easier knowing going in, and it would have saved a lot of heartache."

He nodded. "I'm not one for doing a lot of talking."

"You had no problem talking to me in Las Vegas."

"Vegas was different."

"Yes, it was." Those two days had been a fairy tale. But once back in the real world, they couldn't sustain the fantasy. "It was easy there. We could be what each other needed. Back in Seattle, not so much."

His eyes darkened to a midnight-blue. "That's—"

"The truth."

Cullen didn't say anything, but his chin dropped.

A nod of agreement? She couldn't be sure.

"We're been doing better now," he said. "Talking. Trying."

"Yes, but this isn't real. I mean, I'm still recovering. It's almost like I'm on vacation."

"Like in Red Rocks."

Disappointment squeezed her heart. She nodded. "But you're not on vacation. You're home. I realized Hood Hamlet's real appeal to you tonight."

Cullen's gaze met hers.

Sarah's pulse skittered.

"What's that?" he asked.

"The community, the people. They're one big extended family. You take care of one another and have each other's backs, like your sisters had your mom's with me. Or Leanne wanting to know about our marriage."

"Or Hannah and Carly mentioning the volcano observatory in Vancouver wasn't that far away."

Sarah's mouth gaped. "They didn't."

"They sure did." Cullen sounded amused. "Much to Garrett and Jake's dismay."

"No wonder you found your way back to the kids and me."

"I was afraid to stay in the living room any longer."

She laughed.

"Maybe I should have listened to what they had to say. Because they're right about one thing." He raised her hand to his mouth and kissed it. "You belong here."

Her heart stumbled.

"In Hood Hamlet," he continued.

Sarah thought he was going to say with him. Hoped he would. But he didn't. She ignored the disappointment. "I live in Bellingham. MBVI is there."

"I live here." He faced her, his gaze trapping hers. "We should be together."

The poles shifted. Her world spun off its axis. Air rushed from her lungs. "Together?"

He nodded with a determined set to his jaw. "A couple."

Surprise clogged her throat. It took a second to find her voice. "We already tried that."

"We're good together."

"Sometimes."

"That's a start."

If only... No. Too much separated them. Too high a wall to climb, too wide a river to cross. "We're too different."

A seductive fire blazed in his eyes. "Opposites attract."

He leaned closer. His heat enveloped her.

She felt light-headed. "They can also repel."

One side of his mouth lifted in a sexy grin. "We definitely attract."

She struggled to breathe.

"I'll prove it to you." His lips swooped down on her. He kissed her hard until her toes curled, sparks ignited under her skin and she was gasping for air. "Enough of a data point, or do you need more?"

Oh, she had all the information she needed to make a conclusion. That brief but oh-so-hot kiss reminded her of the time they'd first met. His kisses had stripped her bare, leaving her naked and emotionally vulnerable and wanting another kiss. All her dormant fairy-tale fantasies had clamored to be heard.

But Sarah didn't need to be rescued. She couldn't fall under Cullen's spell the way she had in Las Vegas. The way he'd—they'd—been acting tonight made it so easy to believe they could be a couple again, not the same as before, but like Hannah and Garrett or Carly and Jake. The way Sarah had always dreamed.

But how long would that last?

Her parents had abandoned her. Dylan, her ex-fiancé, too. She found it hard—okay, impossible—to believe Cullen would stay the distance. And when he left her...

She couldn't let him make her believe in magic or happy endings. "I can't."

He stroked her cheek with his knuckle. "You're going to have to give me more than that."

That was what she was afraid he would say. "I'm tired."

He wrapped a finger around a loose curl. "We can have this conversation lying down."

Warning bells clanged in her head. "Cullen."

"Nothing wrong with the horizontal position," he said. "You used to like it."

Loved it. Heat pooled low in her belly and spread outward, making her limbs feel like liquid silver. She swallowed.

"Come on." He pulled her up from the couch and tugged her gently forward by a wayward curl. "Get ready for bed. Then you can tell me why you 'can't.'"

Can't. Can't. Can't. The word echoed through Sarah's head.

She was tired, but took her time in the bathroom. A mix of procrastination and nerves, each vying for victory. But she didn't imagine there would be any winners tonight.

Apprehension coursed through her veins. She put her robe on over her pajamas. An extra layer of protection. Not from Cullen. From herself.

In her room she crawled into bed, then pulled the covers to her neck. She willed herself to sleep. Hard to talk if she was asleep.

Cullen entered the room wearing only pajama bottoms. His muscular arms and smooth chest and his defined abs made her mouth water. He looked as though he'd been sculpted to her specifications.

She itched to run her fingers over his skin, to feel his strength and his warmth. To have his hands touch her all over.

Sarah shivered with need.

He took a step toward her.

"I'm not having sex with you." The words fell from her mouth like a glacier calving.

His lopsided, sexy grin appeared again. "Who said anything about having sex?"

The man was sex with a stethoscope. Well, if he had one with him. "Just setting some ground rules."

"That's rule number one. Any more?"

She narrowed her gaze. "Maybe."

Laughter sparkled in his eyes. He turned off the light.

Darkness filled the room. She couldn't see or hear him. As he stretched out beside her, the mattress dipped.

She tightened her grip on the blanket. "Stay on top of the covers."

"Your wish is my command."

Sarah gulped. That was what she was afraid of. Because she wanted him. Now. Here in his house. In this bed.

He cuddled against her.

Every muscle tensed. "What are you doing?"

"Getting comfortable for our conversation."

That would be impossible for her to do. Even with the covers, a robe and pajamas separating them, she felt the warmth emanating from his body. And it felt good.

"So why can't we be together?" he asked.

"You're serious about having this discussion in bed?"

"You sound surprised," he said. "Did you think I was going to put the moves on you?"

"Yes." She'd hoped. And dreaded. And, well, she was about as confused as she could be right now.

He guffawed. "O, ye of little faith."

"I have only past experience to go by." She inhaled, then exhaled slowly. "That's why I can't be with you. I'm no good at relationships."

Sarah expected him to offer up a counterpoint. He didn't. The crushing weight of disappointment settled on her chest.

The house creaked. The heater came on, shooting warm air through the vents. Outside the wind blew.

He brushed his fingers through her hair. "Why do you think that?"

She doubted he wanted to stay up all night to hear the long list of reasons. Might as well cut to the chase. "I haven't told you much about my parents."

"You said they've each been divorced multiple times and they're no longer part of your life."

Sarah remembered the last time she saw her mother. It still hurt to think about. "I was an only child, and my parents should have never had me. I think they regretted it. But one thing was clear. They didn't care about me."

"What do you mean?"

"They never wanted me around. After the divorce, they shuttled me back and forth."

He pulled her closer. "That's no way to treat a child."

"No, but that's what they did." The numb tone of her voice matched the way she felt. Resigned. Indifferent. That was how she wanted to feel about what had happened. "I've never seen a successful relationship or experienced one. Only broken ones."

"You saw two tonight at dinner."

"A glimpse." She shivered, and his arms tightened around her. "Being jilted and having my parents walk away has skewed my view."

"You don't have to tell me."

"I want to." She should have told him long ago. "I wanted you to talk to me, but I wasn't so eager to do the same myself."

"We both share the blame. I didn't ask you a lot of questions," he admitted. "So your folks…"

"My mom's fourth husband made a pass at me. It's something that had happened before with men she was dating, so I always kept myself scarce so I wouldn't get hurt, but it had never happened with one of my stepfathers."

Cullen brushed his lips over her hair. "I'm sorry it had to happen at all."

"I told my mom because I was scared, but my stepfather lied. Claimed I was trying to seduce him. My mom believed him and kicked me out of the house. It was heartbreaking, humiliating, you name it."

The memory burned through her.

"Shame on your mom. That's horrible for choosing a man over her own daughter." He squeezed her. "Did you go live with your dad?"

"Yes, but I bounced around a lot. I was still in high school. I ended up spending a lot of time with Dylan."

"You were with him a long time."

She nodded. "He was all I had. When I turned eighteen, my

dad remarried again. His new wife, Caylee, was uncomfortable having a stepdaughter who was just four years younger than her. After I graduated high school, I never saw my dad again."

"Sarah—"

"It's okay. I ended up with a pair of not-so-great parents, but at least they didn't beat me."

"They did in other ways." His warm breath caressed her neck. "I can't believe I'm saying this, but it's good they're out of your life. Neither deserves a daughter like you."

And she didn't deserve Cullen. Because he needed someone who knew how to make relationships work. She didn't.

Tears stung her eyes. Sarah blinked them away.

"But you're not destined to repeat what your rotten parents did," he said. "You can have what they've never had—good, solid relationships. Ones that last."

"Maybe I can do better than my parents." But no way would any relationship last. The result would be the same. She would end up alone and brokenhearted. The way she always had. "But I've learned my lesson. I can't jump back into something…"

"That something is our marriage."

"You know what I mean."

"I do," he said. "But here's the deal. We don't have to jump back into anything. We did that the first time around. It didn't work. There's nothing to stop us from going slower this time."

A vise tightened around her heart. "I'm not going to be here much longer. We don't live in the same state."

"Long distance can't be any worse than being apart for the past year."

A flutter of hope emerged. "I suppose that's true."

"It is true. But don't decide right now," he said to her relief. "Think about it. Think about what it'll take to turn your 'I can't' into an 'I want to.' Will you do that for me? For us?"

Affection for Cullen deepened. He might have been a stranger when they got married, but she'd picked a great guy to marry even if he had a few faults. "Yes, I will."

He squeezed her shoulder. "Now get some sleep."

She wanted him next to her all night. "Will you stay, please?"

"You're going to have to kick me out. Though I can't promise you I won't sneak under the covers if it gets colder."

"You can get under them now."

"Let's not test my self-control too much." He kissed her forehead. "Sweet dreams, Lavagirl."

Sheltered in his arms, Sarah had a feeling she would have very sweet dreams. Maybe a couple of hot ones, too, starring the handsome and incredibly fit Dr. Gray. She hoped she woke up knowing the answer to his question.

What would it take to turn her "I can't" to "I want to"?

The next day, Cullen put away the dishes while Sarah looked at the newest data from Mount Baker. Everything she'd told him last night tumbled around in his head. He couldn't believe they'd been married and knew so little about each other.

I've never seen a successful relationship or experienced one. Only broken ones.

He ached for her. But he needed to know stuff like that if they wanted their marriage to work. Sarah needed help. Therapy, perhaps, maybe together the way his family had done. That could help her move forward so they could work things out. If she wanted to work things out…

All he could do now was wait and hope.

The next two days passed quickly. Too quickly for Sarah. She had no idea what to say to Cullen. Fortunately, he'd been working at the hospital and on a ready team, so she could avoid the confrontation. But she couldn't put it off much longer.

Rays of morning sunlight streamed in the kitchen window. Sarah made herself a cup of chamomile tea. Cullen sat at the kitchen table reading the paper. Today was the beginning of three days off for him. He was looking forward to it. She had mixed feelings. "Want something to drink?"

He lofted a smile her way. "No, thanks. But I'll take another blueberry muffin. Then maybe we could talk."

She picked up a muffin for him, but nerves made her almost

drop it. If Christmas magic did exist, in June or December or whenever, she wished it could come to the rescue now.

He glanced over the paper at her. "Sean invited us to a BBQ tomorrow night. Everyone will be there. I went ahead and told him we'd attend."

She hoped people wouldn't want to talk about her and Cullen. But given the phone calls after the dinner at the Willinghams' house, she knew the chances of that were slim to none.

Her cell phone beeped with a text message.

"Must be Tucker," she said. "He's early this morning."

"Tell him you're still recovering, if he wants you back."

"I'm nearly self-sufficient now."

His gaze locked on hers. "You ready to go back?"

"No."

With a little smirk, he returned to reading the paper.

Sarah's cell phone rang. Tucker's ring tone. That was odd. Considering the text was most likely from him.

She walked to the recliner, picked up her phone and saw the words *Steam Blast* on the screen. Her heart slammed against her chest. Forcing herself to breathe, she hit the answer button. "What's happening up there?"

CHAPTER THIRTEEN

SARAH'S WHITE-KNUCKLE grip on the phone, her stiff posture and the rise in her voice told Cullen all he needed to know. It was time for her to go. A weight pressed down on his chest, right over his heart.

She disconnected the call.

He took a deep breath. "Tucker wants you back."

"Another steam burst occurred this morning." She gathered her papers and shoved them into her laptop bag. "Tucker needs me there. Now."

No. The word positioned itself on the tip of Cullen's tongue ready to spring out into the world. Sarah couldn't go to Bellingham. She wasn't healed enough. Not exactly true, but he would do or say whatever he had to in order to make her stay. He wasn't ready to let her go. If she went away, she might not come back. Especially with things so up in the air between them. "Now?"

"Tucker would have preferred having me there yesterday, but since we don't have a time machine handy…"

Cullen's cell phone vibrated. He pulled it from his pocket to turn it off. He glanced at the screen.

Damn. A rescue-mission call out. "I don't believe this."

She stopped her flurry of activity. "What?"

"Missing climbers."

Someone needed help on the mountain, but Sarah needed help here. Priorities waged battle against loyalty. He had a duty—two actually. The physician and mountain rescuer wanted to be part of the mission, to help whoever was in need. The husband wanted to be with his wife because he might not have much time left with her.

Cullen stood. "The unit's gathering at Timberline Lodge, but I can skip this one and drive you to Bellingham."

"You're needed on the rescue."

He could be. "I don't know the mission specifics. It might not be anything. I've missed missions when I was in the middle of a shift and couldn't get someone to cover for me. They'll have plenty of rescuers."

"You're the only doctor."

His throat thickened. "I'm driving you."

Their gazes locked. Neither moved or said a word. Stalemate.

"How long will your mission take?" she asked finally.

"I don't know."

She wrapped her fingers around her laptop. "What if I wait until you get back? I need to pack all my things. I can look at data here until you return."

His heart swelled with relief, gratitude and affection. "That would be wonderful. I'll be back as soon as I can."

"Don't rush on my account." Concern clouded her gaze. "Please be careful."

He wanted to wipe the worry away, wanted to take her in his arms and hold her close, wanted to tell her how much her waiting meant to him. Instead, he kissed her lightly on the lips, forcing himself not to take the kiss deeper. But he'd make up for it…later. "Always. We don't take needless risks up there."

The pink tip of her tongue darted out and moistened her lips. "I'm holding you to that."

He wanted to run his tongue along her lips. Hell, he wanted to taste her all over. *No time now.* "Please do."

His gear was packed due to an upcoming ready team, but he double-checked the equipment. He filled his thermos. "I'll have someone check on you."

"Thanks, but there's no need. I've been through this when you were with the rescue group in Seattle. I'll be fine. As long as I know…"

"Know what?"

Sarah's tender gaze washed over him. "That you're safe."

Her words tugged at his heart. Cullen didn't want to leave her. He didn't want her to leave him. "Rescuer safety is priority number one. Our mission plans are built around that."

"I know." Sarah didn't sound convinced.

He didn't want her to worry about him. "If you don't want me to go—"

"Go." She cut him off. "I'm being…silly."

He ran his index finger along her jawline. "You're pretty cute when you're silly."

She stuck her tongue out at him.

Cullen laughed. If only it could always be like this. But she was needed in Bellingham. For now. Maybe not for long. Her postdoc position wouldn't last forever. He kissed her forehead. "Pack your things. I'll be back before you know it."

When he arrived home, he would tell her that she always had a place here with him. That he hoped she would return soon. That he hoped she would want to stay. Because he wanted her with him. He hoped she felt the same way.

At two o'clock, snow fell from the darkening sky. Sarah couldn't believe another storm was hitting in June. Especially with three climbers missing and rescue teams searching for them.

More data downloaded from MBVI's server. Tucker wasn't happy she wasn't on her way, but she was doing all she could from here.

She pressed her cheek against the window. The cold stung her skin, but she kept her face there. Cullen had to be freezing wherever he was. Wet, too. She prayed he was okay.

The doorbell rang.

Sarah jumped. Maybe Cullen had finished with the mission. She hurried to open the door.

A woman in her forties with short curly hair stood on the front porch. "I'm looking for Sarah Purcell."

Brrr. It was colder than Sarah had realized. Goose bumps covered her skin. "I'm she."

"I have a delivery from this company." The woman pointed

to the name Haskell, Thayer & Henry printed on a large white envelope, then handed it to Sarah. "Please sign this acceptance of service acknowledging you received the papers."

Sarah tucked the envelope under her arm. She scribbled her signature.

The woman thanked her and walked toward her car.

Sarah backed into the cabin, as if moving in slow motion. Her fingers gripped the envelope. She didn't need to open it to know what was inside. Well, she was 99.99 percent certain.

I knew you were busy, so once I established residency in Oregon I got things started there.

They know I filed for divorce.

Divorce papers. Her stomach roiled. Sarah thought she might be sick. Okay, he'd filed before her accident, but it still hurt.

Sarah plodded into the kitchen and placed the envelope on the breakfast bar. She'd wait until Cullen returned to open it. She had too much to worry about, with him on the mountain in a storm and the second steam blast on Mount Baker.

Hours passed. Sarah looked at data and spoke with Tucker over Skype. But what she wanted was to hear from Cullen. A phone call. A text.

The doorbell rang.

She was almost afraid to answer the door again, but she did. The wind whipped. Snow fell in a solid sheet of white. Carly, Zoe and Christian Welton stood on the porch, bundled up in parkas and hats.

Sarah invited them in. She assumed Cullen had asked his friends to check on her. She was glad he'd done that even though she'd told him not to. She needed the company. "I can't believe you three ventured out in this kind of weather."

"We wanted to see how you were doing." Zoe removed her hat, scarf, coat and mittens, then hung them on the hat tree. "We also have some news."

Sarah forced herself not to hold her breath. "Good news, I hope."

Carly hung her coat. "Rescue Team 4 found the missing climbers and brought them down."

Relief flowed through Sarah, loosening her tense muscles. "That's wonderful. Everyone will be home soon."

Forget about the divorce papers. Sarah wiggled her toes with anticipation. She wanted to see Cullen.

"Almost everyone," Christian said. "Teams 2 and 3 are stuck on the mountain. They'll be down once there's a break in the weather."

"Is Cullen on one of those teams?" she asked.

Carly nodded. "Sean, Jake, Bill, Tim and Cullen are hunkering down in a snow cave. They're fine, but the conditions are pretty bad up there."

The hair on Sarah's arms stood on end. That didn't sound good at all.

"The guys made the smart decision, given the conditions," Christian said. "Leanne and the rest of Team 3 made it to the Palmer lift station before the whiteout made it too dangerous for them to continue. They'll stay there tonight."

Worried, Sarah chewed on her lower lip.

"Everyone is fine," Carly reiterated. "But staying put will keep them safe tonight."

Sarah had slept in a snow cave, part of an alpine mountaineering course she'd taken. A snow cave would protect the team from the elements. That was crucial in this kind of weather. But she would rather have Cullen home.

Zoe raised a paper sack. "We brought dinner."

"No reason to sit alone when we're all in the same boat," Christian explained.

Carly nodded. "We stopped by Tim's place, but Rita and Wyatt are at her parents' house in Portland. The other guys on Rescue 3 live down the mountain."

Sarah appreciated their thoughtfulness. Food was the last thing on her mind, but she needed to eat. To keep up her strength. She wanted to be strong for Cullen. "Thanks. This is so nice of you."

Carly touched Sarah's arm. "It's good for all of us."

"Where's Nicole?" Sarah asked.

"With Hannah and Graham," Carly said. "Jake and I were supposed to have a date night."

"Skip the barbecue tomorrow night and go on your date instead," Zoe suggested.

Carly hugged Zoe. "Thanks, but we'll find another night to go out."

As the four of them prepared dinner, Sarah realized in the short time she'd been in Hood Hamlet, she'd made good friends. Some of that was due to her job, but part—a big part—was the change in her. She didn't let people get close. In Hood Hamlet, that didn't stop people from butting their noses into her life anyway. Maybe that wasn't such a bad thing.

Zoe set the table. "I'm happy we're doing this tonight. When I'm at the base helping out, I'm not so impatient. But I hate waiting."

"Me, too." Sarah would give anything to touch Cullen right now. "I really wish it would stop snowing."

"Rescuer safety is the priority when they're on a mission," Zoe explained. "Sean tells me that over and over again."

Carly nodded. "Jake, too."

Christian prepared chicken marsala. "Add Leanne to the list."

Sarah sighed. "Cullen said the same thing to me."

Zoe placed napkins at each of the four place settings. "What they don't seem to understand is no matter what the conditions are, it's hard not to worry when the love of your life is up on the mountain."

Sarah nodded in agreement.

Wait a minute.

The love of her life? Cullen?

Truth scorched like the hot lava from Kilauea in Hawaii.

Oh, no. She wasn't falling for Cullen. She'd fallen.

She loved him. Truly loved him. With all her heart, body and soul.

What had she done? She folded her left arm over her stomach.

Zoe rushed to Sarah's side. "You're so pale. Sit."

She sat.

Christian knelt, taking her pulse. "Does anything hurt?"

"No." Her voice cracked.

Carly touched Sarah's forehead with the back of her hand. "You don't feel warm."

"I'm not sick." Not unless you wanted to count being lovesick. "Give me a minute. I'm a little light-headed."

A worried look passed between Carly and Christian. His forehead wrinkled. "Put your head between your legs."

Sarah did. She hated making her friends worry when the problem wasn't her injuries. But what could she say to them? That she'd just realized she loved her husband? Loved him to the point nothing else mattered?

"Feel better?" Carly asked.

"Yes."

Physically Sarah did. But emotionally…

This was the worst thing ever. Loving Cullen gave him complete power over her, to hurt her when he no longer wanted her. And he wouldn't want her to be with him forever. How could he? No one else had.

Building a volcano and playing with a toddler didn't mean she would be a good mother. She didn't know anything about being a mom let alone a decent one. Not to mention being Cullen's wife. She could try, but she would end up failing as before. And that would hurt both of them.

Zoe handed her a glass of water. "Take a sip."

Sarah raised her head and drank.

Christian's gaze never left her face. "Your color's returning."

"I'm feeling better," she said.

But her heart was breaking. Thank goodness her things were packed. If Cullen asked her to stay, she wouldn't be able to leave him. That would turn into a disaster. The longer she stayed, the more it would hurt when it ended. She couldn't do that to Cullen. She wouldn't do that to him.

Or herself.

She had to end things now. No going back again. No matter how tempted she might be.

Sarah glanced at the envelope containing the divorce papers. She didn't know whether they needed to be signed or what. But once she figured it out, she could leave. Cullen hadn't tried to win her back before. He wouldn't this time.

Her heart cried out at the thought.

No, she wouldn't let emotion overwhelm her.

This was for the best. Sarah wasn't strong enough to survive being left again. She wasn't sure she was strong enough to leave him on her own. She would have to leave before he got home.

Sarah drank the rest of her water. "I'm okay now. Really."

The relief on her three friends' face coated her mouth with guilt. But this was for the...best. She would be out of here before Cullen returned.

Coward, a voice inside her mocked.

Not a coward. Smart. Proactive. This was the best way—the only way—to break the hold Cullen had over her and keep her heart safe.

Cullen supposed there were worse places he could be than a snow cave in the middle of a blizzard on Mount Hood with four of his closest friends. Someday he might laugh about this, but not tonight.

At least they were safe. And so were the missing climbers. Three lives had been saved today. No sense risking theirs. As soon as the weather cleared, they would head down. Until then, they would make the best of it.

He sipped from his water bottle. The liquid—melted snow—warmed his insides on this chilly night. He'd rather be cuddling in bed with Sarah.

He missed her. He would miss her more when she left Hood Hamlet.

But Cullen understood. Mount Baker was blowing off steam. He didn't blame her for wanting to be back at the institute.

"Whose bright idea was it to sleep out here?" Hughes asked.

"Paulson's," Porter, Moreno and Cullen said at the same time.

"Just a suggestion." Paulson hunkered down inside his sleeping bag. "I didn't think anyone would take me seriously."

"You know Doc," Porter teased. "He's always serious."

Cullen stuck his water bottle inside his sleeping bag to keep it from freezing. "Someone needs to be serious around you clowns."

Hughes grinned. "I'm sure Doc's all fun and games when he's with Sarah."

"She does keep me smiling." Cullen would give anything to be with her now, to feel her warm body and soft curves snuggled up against him. The thought raised his temperature a degree, maybe two. That might work to his advantage here.

"Being opposites is good," Moreno said. "Rita can't stand anything I like to do except hike. And only when it's sunny and warm. But we're about to celebrate our eighth anniversary."

"Rough life having one gourmet meal after another cooked for you," Hughes said. "Unlike me with a gorgeous wife who can't boil water without the fire department showing up."

"It's amazing Moreno isn't pushing three hundred pounds," Paulson teased.

Moreno smirked. "I burn off the calories other ways."

"Yeah, chasing little Wyatt," Hughes joked.

"That's right," Porter said. "Kids make those long, lazy mornings spent in bed a thing of the past."

Moreno unwrapped a granola bar. "Unless the kids are with you."

Porter nodded. "I can't wait to see my girls. I'd love one of Carly's cookies right now."

"She'll have a plateful at the base when we get down," Hughes said.

Moreno nodded. "And Zoe will be there with piping-hot cups of coffee."

A faraway look filled Hughes's eyes. He tightened the cord on his jacket's hood. "Too bad she can't deliver up here."

Paulson made a sour-looking face. "Marriage has turned you all into a bunch of saps. Well, except Doc. He's the same as always."

Cullen wasn't sure that was a compliment. He wiggled his fingers to keep them warm.

"Nah," Hughes said. "He smiles more now."

"I actually heard him laugh," Porter teased.

"Very funny, guys," Cullen said.

Things might be up in the air between him and Sarah, but for all their troubles, he couldn't deny he was a better man for having her in his life. She brought spontaneity to his life and tried to make him see what was important, that there was more to living than making plans. Just because he lost control, whether a little or a lot, didn't mean he was going to fall over the edge like Blaine. He wouldn't with Sarah as his anchor.

Even though he was stuck up here, Sarah was the one who kept his thoughts focused. She was good for him. Not dangerous.

Sarah was the one who had soothed his fears about Paulson. She'd been the reason Cullen had opened up when that was the last thing he wanted to do.

Being open was his biggest fear, not being reckless. The people he was closest with, people like Sarah and Blaine, could hurt Cullen the most and send his emotions out of control. But this second time around with Sarah, being more open with her had made him stronger, not weaker. The same with Blaine's memory.

But Cullen hadn't realized that. Not until now. Would his acknowledging it be enough to keep Sarah from leaving? He didn't know, nor did he care. But he knew one thing. Love was worth the risk.

With a trembling hand, Sarah removed the papers from the white envelope. She scanned each page of the dissolution of marriage petition. Neither of them had any assets the other wanted to claim, so it was pretty cut-and-dried. If she agreed with the petition, she didn't have to respond. The paperwork would go before a judge and their marriage would be over.

With a blue pen in her left hand, she set the tip against a piece of paper. Tears stung the corners of her eyes. Her heart didn't want her to write this note. But she'd learned long ago she couldn't trust her heart.

Sarah refocused, ignoring the pain in her chest. Her heart thudded like a bass drum. The steady beat made her think of a post-battle scene when those who had survived the melee gathered the bodies of dead soldiers. She pushed the graphic image from her mind.

This wasn't war. More like a surrender, a quiet one without any fanfare.

With a shaky hand she wrote what needed to be said and scribbled her signature at the end of the note.

There. She dropped the pen. It was done. Over.

She inhaled, thinking she would feel better. Instead she felt worse.

For the best, Sarah reminded herself. She'd better get busy. The shuttle would be here soon to take her to the airport.

She placed the divorce papers back in the white envelope and set them on the breakfast bar. She placed the note on top.

Last night she'd pulled her wedding ring out of the zippered pocket in her toiletry kit and stuck the gold band on her finger. She'd wanted to wear it one last time. For old times' sake…

Sarah slowly removed the wedding band. The ring slipped off her finger as easily as it had gone on. She placed the gold band with the note and the white envelope. And her heart wept.

CHAPTER FOURTEEN

HOME.

Anticipation pulsed through Cullen's veins. He dumped his backpack in the garage. He would unpack his gear later. All he wanted was to see Sarah.

He entered the house. "Sarah."

She didn't answer.

He searched for her, trying to ignore a sense of foreboding. She wasn't there.

Shoulders hunched, Cullen walked back to the living room. He understood Sarah's need to return to Bellingham, to her job at the institute. Reporters had been abuzz with news of more steam blasts and earthquakes from Baker. Granted he'd been stuck in a snow cave overnight, but to take off without so much as a goodbye…

A white envelope on the breakfast bar caught his attention.

A two-ton weight pressed down on him. He trudged to the kitchen, feeling as if he were wading through quicksand. He saw a note and a gold wedding band sitting on top of the envelope. With unsteady hands he unfolded the piece of paper and read.

Dear Cullen,

I appreciate all you've done for me these past weeks. Hood Hamlet has been the perfect place to recover. Thank you for opening your home to me and introducing me to your friends.

I know you wanted to drive me home to Bellingham,

but after being stuck overnight in a snow cave the last thing you need is to be stuck in a car making the long drive there and back.

The dissolution of marriage petition was served yesterday. I do still want a divorce. I agree with everything in the paperwork and will not be filing a response. Very soon there will be nothing stopping you from getting your life back on track.

I wish you the best. Heaven knows you deserve better than someone like me. I'm sure you'll find her and she'll be exactly what you want in a wife!

Sarah

No! Cullen crinkled the page into a tight ball. He wanted to scream, shout, hit something. He threw the note. It bounced off the wall and fell to the floor.

Familiar anger and resentment exploded. Hands shaking, Cullen picked up her wedding ring. He ran his fingers around the smooth gold band. Sarah hadn't seemed like the sentimental type, yet she'd kept hers. As he'd kept his. He set the ring on the bar.

The silence and emptiness of the cabin matched the way he felt inside.

Was this how Sarah had felt when she'd arrived home from doing research on Mount Baker and discovered he'd moved out while she was away? Cullen didn't want to know the answer. She didn't deserve any sympathy.

Damn her. Couldn't Sarah see they had something special? Why would she walk away like this?

He stiffened.

Walk away like he had when she'd brought up a divorce.

Cullen retrieved the wadded-up note, smoothed the wrinkles from the page, then reread it. Again and again. Her words sank in. Something clicked.

Sarah wasn't leaving him for something better. She wanted him to find something—someone—better than her. This wasn't about him or them, but her. For some reason she didn't think she was good enough.

Just like the last time. But he'd been too hurt, too full of pride to realize it.

Snippets of conversations rushed to the surface.

I've never felt so inadequate in my life.

I wasn't anything special. I would have held him back. I don't blame him for not wanting to marry me.

They didn't care about me. They never wanted me around. After the divorce, they shuttled me back and forth.

All the pieces had been there, but Cullen hadn't put them together. Until now.

He needed to go after her and show her how special she was, how much he needed her. Something her mom and dad had never done, or her idiotic fiancé or...

Him.

His chest tightened, squeezing the air out of his lungs. He'd let Sarah down a year ago. No, he'd let her down from the time they'd returned to Seattle from Las Vegas and he'd tried to remain in control after she had rocked his neat and tidy little world. He'd kept parts of his life separate from her. He'd been afraid of losing control, of following in Blaine's footsteps and losing himself to something that would be bad for him, so Cullen had held on tight to what he could and kept her out. What had the family counselor called it? *Compartmentalizing.* He'd taken it a step further. He'd built walls, remained silent and run away.

When Sarah had mentioned divorce, he'd jumped at the chance to make a clean break, then retreated like a turtle into its shell to lick his wounds. What he'd failed to see was how good Sarah was for him. Damn good.

He wasn't going to make the same mistake again. He would go to Bellingham and convince her they belonged together. Do whatever it took. Fight for her if he had to.

At this point he had nothing to lose except...everything.

Sitting at her desk at MBVI, Sarah studied the seismographic signals. Around her, the atmosphere crackled with energy, phones rang at an almost frenetic rate and people carried equipment out of the building in order to set up additional monitoring stations a safe distance away from the volcano.

Seismic activity from inside Mount Baker's crater had quadrupled in frequency since yesterday's steam blast. Whatever was going on could fizzle out, but until that happened she had work to do. Anticipation over the possibilities ahead buzzed through her, but something kept her feet firmly planted on the ground.

Not something. Someone. Cullen.

She leaned back in her chair, not wanting thoughts of him to swamp her.

The new and exciting seismic signals should be her only concern, but Sarah kept thinking about Hood Hamlet. She missed the town, the people, Cullen. She'd left with so many unknowns.

Had he and the rest of the rescue team made it off the mountain safely? Had he arrived home, read her note? Did he hate her?

Sarah rubbed her tired eyes, then refocused on the data.

Tucker placed a steaming cup of coffee and a chocolate bar on the left side of her desk. "You've been working hard."

The candy reminded her of the chocolate-tasting with Cullen, of his hot kiss. He would never be kissing her again. A knife twisted inside her.

Maybe caffeine would help her concentrate. She took a sip of coffee. "That's why you hired me."

"I hired you because you're qualified and smart." Tucker sat on the right edge of her desk. Her boss was in his late thirties, wore jeans and a T-shirt. He looked more like a rugged cowboy than a nerdy, calculator-toting scientist. "You're also still recovering. Don't overdo it."

"There's lots of data to review."

"And more coming," he admitted. "But you don't have to get through it all right now. Think of it as job security."

She looked up at him. "My funding runs out soon."

"I always have an ace or two up my sleeve. And I have a feeling I'm going to need you around." Tucker had built MBVI from the ground up with lots of sweat and begging and a generous donation from a mysterious anonymous benefactor. He glanced in the direction of Mount Baker. "I'm just relieved you're back. I half expected to receive a call from the Cascades Volcano Observatory asking for a reference so they could hire you."

She flinched. "Why would you think that?"

"Cullen. He was very worried about you at the hospital."

Memories stirred beneath her breastbone. Of him, of her, of them. No, she couldn't go there. "He's a doctor. *Concerned* is his middle name."

"He was more than concerned."

How would Tucker know anything about that? "It doesn't matter. The divorce petition has been filed. I'm not challenging anything. It's over."

"I'm sorry for both of you, but that's one less thing to take you away from here." Tucker stood. "You have one more hour to work. Then go home and sleep."

Her muscles tightened. Steam was still rising from the crater. "I'll sleep when Baker sleeps."

"Now that you're back, I can't afford to lose you."

Her boss's words made Sarah straighten, but they didn't fill the emptiness inside her. Once she'd found total fulfillment in her work. Now she realized she'd been masking the loneliness, the hurt, the ache left by the failure of her marriage. The loss of Cullen.

"We have to figure out when something else might happen up there," Tucker continued. "You need to be in top form. Rested. Ready for anything. Got it?"

Sarah knew that tone. No worries. She could work remotely from home. "Got it."

"And no working from home, either."

Darn. "Yes, sir."

She returned to the data. Thirty minutes later her forehead throbbed. Eyestrain, tiredness or…a broken heart? Most likely a combination of all three. She massaged her temples.

Maybe Tucker was right about going home. She closed her laptop and slid it into her bag. She said goodbye to her coworkers, then exited the institute.

Outside, she glanced up at Mount Baker. The plume of steam contrasted against the blue sky. A gray, overcast day would have matched her mood and the volcano's much better.

"Sarah."

The sound of Cullen's voice sent chills through her. She turned. He leaned against the building. The sight of him in a pair of faded jeans and short-sleeved T-shirt made her mouth go dry. She had to be way more tired than she realized if she was imagining him here.

Sarah blinked. Still there. She wasn't hallucinating. She pinched herself. Not dreaming, either.

She pursed her lips. "Why are you here?"

He straightened. "You forgot something."

No way. Sarah had been extra careful when she packed, to make sure she had everything that belonged to her. "What did I forget?"

Cullen raised his chin slightly, his jaw tight and his eyes dark. "Me."

Her mouth gaped. The air whooshed from her lungs. She couldn't breathe.

He walked toward her, slowly, as if each step were planned, calculated, with intent and purpose. "You're busy with important work, so I brought me to you."

She tried to speak, but couldn't.

He reached forward and ran his hand along her cheek.

Sarah fought the urge to sink into his touch. She had to be strong. For both their sakes.

His gaze ran the length of her. "You've been working too hard. You have a headache."

How did he know that? Her brain whirled with questions and fatigue and a heavy dose of confusion. "I don't understand why you're here."

Cullen pulled something from behind his back. It must have been tucked in the waistband of his jeans. A white envelope. The divorce papers. "You left these for me."

Her heart thudded with dread. "We'll be divorced soon."

He held the envelope out in front of him and tore the top portion.

She reached forward to stop him. "What are you doing?"

"What I should have done a year ago and put an end to any talk of a divorce." He ripped the envelope in half. "Worst money I ever spent."

She stared, stunned. "It doesn't matter. The petition has been filed."

"I told my attorney to halt the proceeding."

Her mouth gaped. She closed it. "We'll have to start over."

"That's all I want. For us to start over."

Her heart pounded against her chest. Disbelief and hope warred inside her.

"I don't want a divorce, Sarah. I've never wanted one, but I was too hurt to realize it. I love you. Only you."

"Love is…"

"The only thing that matters." He took her left hand. "I haven't been the best husband. After what happened to Blaine I was afraid to lose control and wind up like him. You overwhelmed me from the moment we met. It was great at first. I felt whole again, but I got scared. Clung to control where I could. Ran away when I couldn't. Didn't open myself up. Compartmentalized everything. My work. My emotions. Our marriage. You. That wasn't right. Or fair. No wonder you wanted to leave. You deserved better from me. I'm finally ready to give it to you. If you want it. Want me."

Cullen's words sent a gush of warmth flowing through Sarah's veins. She fought the urge to soak up the love he was offering. "Oh, I appreciate this. You'll never know how much. But I've seen what's happened with my parents and stepparents. Even if we wanted to make it work, marriage doesn't last."

He squeezed her hand. "I know you've seen marriages fail. You've lived through it way too many times. But the divorce rate isn't one hundred percent. Some marriages do last. Ours can if we're willing to work on it. Fight for it. I know you're a fighter. So am I."

She wanted to believe, but something—fear, maybe—held

her back. "Even if we fought for it, I don't know how to be a good wife like Hannah, Carly and Zoe. You need someone who's worthy of you. Perfect for you. That isn't me."

"You might not think you're the perfect wife, but you're the perfect wife for me." Cullen pressed her hand against his mouth and kissed it. "I was afraid of losing myself in you. The way Blaine lost himself in drugs. What I failed to see is how good you are for me. You're the best thing that's ever happened to me. You fill me up and set me free. You make me stronger. Nothing wrong with that at all."

Her heart sighed. Still more protests rose to her lips. "But—"

"I don't care that you'd rather be covered in mud or ash than wear something frilly. Or that you prefer cooking on a glacier than in a gourmet kitchen. I love that you're willing to run toward an erupting volcano if it means getting the data you need while everyone else is running away. That's the woman I love, the woman I married, the woman I want to grow old with."

Tears stung the corners of her eyes. Feelings of inadequacy shot arrows through her. She sniffled. "But you deserve better."

"You do, too. I'm far from the perfect man or husband. I tend to see things my way. Sometimes I'm too serious."

That made her smile. "Sometimes?"

He grinned. "A lot of times. I don't have a clue how to show how I'm feeling."

Love for this man bubbled in her soul. "You're doing a pretty good job right now."

"It isn't easy," he admitted. "But you're worth it. We both have a lot to learn and work to do. A lot of things can go wrong, but we can make this work. I have no doubt. But we'll never know unless we're willing to take a chance. I am. If you are, I trust you'll stick it out even if things get a little rough. Up for it?"

Hope was starting to win. "I would love to believe our life, our future, could be spent together, not apart."

He kissed her on the lips. "Believe it. Stay my wife."

If ever she had a chance at a forever kind of love, it would be with Cullen. His coming for her proved he knew her, understood her, sometimes better than she knew herself. But fear kept whispering all the things that could go wrong. She was afraid of being disappointed, of being left. But fear wasn't a good enough reason for walking away from something that had the potential to be so wonderful.

"Yes." Sarah was afraid, but willing, oh-so-willing. She kissed him, a kiss full of her hopes and dreams for the two of them. "I love you. I want to make this work more than anything."

His warm breath caressed her skin. He hugged her. "We are going to make this work."

Hope overflowed from her heart. "So what happens now?"

He removed two gold bands from his pocket. He slid hers on her ring finger. "Your turn."

She placed the other on his finger.

"You'll need to show me where we live," he said. "Then I need to get my résumé together and drop a copy off at the hospital."

She stared at him in disbelief. "What?"

"I love living in Hood Hamlet, but I love you more. I want to be where you are, whether it's here by Mount Baker or wherever you end up. Most places need doctors. And we can always go back to Hood Hamlet someday. Or not. Let's play it by ear and see what happens. Plans can be so overrated."

Her heart swelled with love and respect for her husband. "You are amazing, Dr. Gray."

"You're not so bad yourself, Lavagirl."

As Cullen kissed her, the ground trembled. Another earthquake from Mount Baker.

Contentment and joy flowed through Sarah. She didn't need the sparkling castles with gleaming turrets she'd read about as a child. A steam-blasting volcano in the northern Cascades was the perfect backdrop for the beginning of her and Cullen's fairy tale and true love's kiss.

* * * * *

IN HER
RIVAL'S ARMS

ALISON ROBERTS

For the Maytoners, with love, in recognition of the
magic you have all brought into my life. xxx

CHAPTER ONE

No WAY WAS he a genuine customer.

Suzanna Zelensky had no need to call on any intuitive powers she might have inherited from her bloodline. Even the dark silhouette of this stranger, caused by the slant of late afternoon sunshine through the window behind him as he stepped further into her domain, radiated a palpable scepticism. He wanted nothing to do with anything this business represented. The impression wasn't all that uncommon in the gypsy shop Spellbound and it was almost always emanated by males, but they were invariably dragged in a by a female partner.

This man was alone and yet he moved with a determination that suggested he had a good reason for entering her world. Alarm bells rang with enough force to make the back of Zanna's neck prickle. Who was he and what did he want?

She had seen him well before he'd had the chance to see her. Had caught a clear glimpse of his face in that heartbeat of time from when he'd come through the door until he'd stepped forward into that shaft of light. Strong features with a shadowing to his jaw that accentuated uncompromising lines. A harsh but compelling face. This man wouldn't just stand out from a crowd.

He would render those around him virtually invisible. He was different. Beautiful…

Having other customers to attend to was fortunate. Zanna had time to think. A chance to consider the implications of this unusual visit and an opportunity to gather her emotional resources. She turned back to the teenage girls.

'You'll need a burner to use the essential oils as aromatherapy. We have a good range over here.' The heavy silver bangles Zanna was wearing gave the movement of her arm a distinctive, musical accompaniment.

She could feel him looking at her now. A predatory kind of appraisal that should have raised any hackles she possessed but instead, disturbingly, she could feel a very different kind of response. Her skin prickled as though every cell was being stirred. Coming alive.

'How do they work?' One of the girls was reaching for a burner.

'A small candle goes in the base.' Zanna risked a quick glance behind her, maybe because she had sensed she was no longer under scrutiny. Sure enough, the man was moving, staring at the objects on display. For a moment, Zanna stared blankly at the object in front of *her*. What had she been talking about?

'You put water in the bowl above it,' she managed, 'and sprinkle a few drops of your chosen oil on the water. As it heats, the scent is carried in the vapour.'

'What do these ones do?' A dark-haired girl picked up a tiny bottle.

'Those ones are designed to complement zodiac signs. They increase your personal powers.'

He was watching her again. Listening? Quite likely, given the increase in the strength of scepticism she could sense. Scathing enough to bring a rising flush of heat to her neck. Zanna had always loathed the fact that she blushed so easily and she particularly didn't appreciate it right now.

'I'm Sagittarius,' the blonde girl announced. 'Can I open the bottle and see what it smells like?'

'Sure.' Zanna moved away as the girls tested the oils. Despite being acutely aware of the movements of the stranger within the shop since he'd entered, she had made no direct acknowledgment of his presence. As far as he was concerned, he had been totally ignored, which was not a practice she would normally have employed with any potential customer. They couldn't afford to turn away business.

But this man wasn't a customer. The dismissive rake of his glance across shelves of ornate candle holders and chalices, stands of incense and display cases of Celtic jewellery, even before the flick of a finger against a hanging crystal prism that sent rainbow shards of light spinning across the ceiling, had confirmed that his mission did not include any desire to make a purchase.

He didn't look like someone who might have been drawn in for the refreshments available either. She could imagine him ordering a double-shot espresso to go, not lingering over herbal teas and organic cakes and cookies. Had he even noticed the blackboard menu as he'd raised his gaze? Had he been caught by the play of light on the ceiling from the prism or was he inspecting the intricate pattern of stained glass in the fanlights above the main windows?

He was moving away from her now, towards the selection of crystal stones in a basket near the window. He was tall. She knew he was over six feet in height because the circular feather and twine dreamcatchers suspended from the ceiling brushed the top of his head as he walked beneath them. His hair was black and sleek, the waves neatly groomed, with just enough length to curl over the collar of a well-worn black leather jacket. His jeans fitted like a glove and the footwear was interesting. Not shoes—boots of some kind. Casual clothing but worn in a way that gave it the aura of a uniform. Of being in command. A motorbike helmet was tucked under one arm.

Zanna could almost taste the testosterone in the air and it made her draw in a quick breath and take a mental step sideways.

Maybe those alarm bells had been ringing for a more intimate purpose. Perhaps her intuition had been overwhelmed by the raw sexual energy this man possessed. A subtle but determined shake of her head sent a lock of waist-length copper-coloured hair over one shoulder. She brushed the errant tress back calmly as she moved towards the stranger.

'Can I be of any assistance?'

Dominic Brabant almost dropped the stone he was weighing in a careless hand. He'd only seen the profile and then the back view of this woman when he'd entered the shop because she'd been busy with her customers. He'd had a good look at that back, mind you, while wrestling with the annoyance that two silly schoolgirls presented such an effective barrier to having a private conversation.

He could wait. He'd learned long ago that patience could be well rewarded.

Maybe he would go to one of the small wooden tables, screened by bookshelves, and order one of the teas described on the blackboard menu.

A ginger tea for its energising properties, perhaps?

No. He had more than enough energy. The motivation for being here in the first place had been validated in those few minutes he'd had to take, standing out there in the street, untangling the overload of memories and emotions. He could feel it fizzing in his veins and gaining strength with every passing minute. It had to happen. Fate had provided the opportunity and it felt like the inspiration had always been there, just waiting to be unleashed. The desire to succeed was more powerful than any that had preceded his achievements so far in life.

This was personal. Deeply personal.

He blew out a breath. Maybe a soothing chamomile tea might be the way to go. He couldn't afford to make this any more difficult than it had to be. And he wasn't even sure that this was the woman he needed to speak to. She might simply be a shop assistant who was paid to wear that ridiculous dark purple robe and improbable hair that had to be a wig. Nobody had real hair that could ripple down their back like newborn flames.

It was just part of the image. Like the flowing clothes and heavy silver bangles. The assumption that she was probably large and shapeless under that flowing fabric and that the hair under the wig was steely grey was blown away somewhat disconcertingly by the sound of her voice at close quarters.

The witch—if that was who she was, according to the information he'd been provided with—was young and the lilt in those few words created a ripple that was reminiscent of the silky fall of that wig.

He cleared his throat as he turned to meet her gaze. 'I'm just looking at the moment, thanks.'

A flash in her eyes let him know that she recognised

the ambiguity as he continued to look at her rather than what was for sale in the shop.

The sustained eye contact was unintentional. This wasn't the time to intimidate anyone—especially someone whose co-operation might be essential—but the proximity of the window gave this corner of the shop much more light than the rest of the candlelit interior. Enough light to see the copper-coloured rims around those dark, hazel eyes and the dusting of freckles on pale skin. And the hair was *real*. Or was it? Nic had to suppress an outrageous desire to reach out and touch the tendril caught on the wide sleeve of the robe. Just to check.

'Are you looking for something in particular?' Zanna held the eye contact with difficulty. The hint of a foreign accent in the stranger's deep voice was only faint but it was as intriguing, not to mention as sexy, as her earlier observations. The feeling of connection was more than a little disturbing. How could such an intensity be present so instantaneously?

And, yes…he was looking for something in particular.

Something he had promised when he'd been only six years old.

'When I'm big, Mama, I'll be rich. I'll buy that big house next door for you.'

Disturbingly, he could almost hear an echo of his mother's quiet laugh. Feel her arms holding him. The sadness that would always give her voice that extra note.

'Merci beaucoup, mon chéri. Ce sera merveilleux!'

'No.' The word came out more forcefully than he'd intended. He summoned at least the beginning of a smile. 'Nothing in particular.'

His eyes were dark. Almost black in this light. Inscrutable and unnerving. Resisting the instinct to look away was almost unbearable. The strength of will this man possessed was a solid force but she couldn't afford to lower her guard until she knew what his motives were in coming here.

He was bouncing the crystal in his palm. Zanna had the uncomfortable notion that it wasn't just the rock he was playing with. He had a purpose in coming in here. He wanted something from her. He wanted...*her*?

The ridiculous notion came from nowhere. Or was she picking up a well-hidden signal?

Whatever. It was strong enough to make her toes curl. To send a jolt right through her body, sparking and fizzing until it melted into a glow she could feel deep in her belly.

Desire? Surely not. That was a sensation she thought she might have lost for ever in the wake of the London fiasco with Simon. But what if it was? What if something she'd feared had died had just sprung to life again? She couldn't deny that the possibility was exhilarating.

It was also inappropriate. She knew nothing about this man and he could well represent a threat, both to herself and the only other person on the planet she had reason to cherish. Knowing she had to stay in control in the face of the power this stranger had the potential to wield over her physically was going to be a challenge.

And that was just as exhilarating as knowing she was still capable of experiencing desire. These last weeks, alone in both the shop and the house, had been lonely. Stifling, even.

The challenge was irresistible.

'You're holding a carnelian crystal.' She was pleased to find she could keep her tone pleasantly professional.

If she gave him something concrete to dismiss maybe he would reveal his true motive for being there. 'It's considered to be a highly evolved mineral healer that can aid tissue regeneration. It enhances attunement with the inner self and facilitates concentration.' She smiled politely. 'It opens the heart.'

'Really?' He couldn't help his sceptical tone. His own concentration had just been shot to pieces and he was still holding the stone.

Did some people really believe in magic?

Like they believed in love?

He released it to let it tumble back with its companions in the small wicker basket. He wasn't one of them.

'Excuse me.' The teenage girls had given up on the essential oils. 'What's in all those big jars?'

'They're herbs.'

It was hard to turn away from the man and that was a warning Zanna needed to listen to. A few moments to collect herself was a blessing but the task was made more difficult because the girls were staring at the man behind her now, their eyes wide enough to confirm her own impression of how different he was.

'Common ones like rosemary and basil,' she added, to distract them. 'And lots of unusual ones, like patchouli and mistletoe and quassia.'

Zanna never tired of looking at her aunt's collection of antique glass containers. They took pride of place on wide, dark shelves behind the counter, the eccentric shapes and ornate stoppers adding to the mysterious promise of the jars' contents. They had always been there. Part of her life ever since she'd arrived as a frightened young girl who had just lost both her parents. As grounding as being here, in the home she loved.

'They can be burned for aromatherapy or drunk as teas. They can also be used for spells.'

'*Spells.*' The girls nudged each other and giggled. 'That's what you need, Jen. A love spell.' They both sneaked another peek behind Zanna and Jen tossed her hair.

'Have a look at the book display,' Zanna suggested, unhappily aware that her tone was cool. 'There's some good spells in that small, blue book.'

'You have got to be kidding.'

The deep voice, unexpectedly close to her shoulder, startled Zanna and made her aware of another jolt of that delicious sensation. Cells that had already come alive caught alight. She could actually imagine tiny flames flickering over every inch of her skin.

'Got some eye of newt in one of those jars?'

Here it was. The first open evidence that this man was not a genuine customer. Zanna turned, her smile tight. 'No. We find that currants are a perfectly acceptable substitution these days.'

The giggles suggested the girls were oblivious to the tension that Zanna could feel steadily increasing. She cast a quick glance at the grandfather clock near the inner door of the shop. Only another ten minutes or so and she could close up and stop wasting her time with customers who either had no intention of buying anything or schoolgirls who couldn't afford to. At least the girls were enjoying themselves. The stranger wasn't. She could sense his irritation with the girls. Why? Was he waiting for them to leave? So he could be alone with her?

The flames flickered again but it was beyond the realms of possibility that the strength of the physical connection she could feel was being reciprocated. He wanted her for something, though… Of *course*…why hadn't she thought of that the moment she'd seen him come in, looking as though he had ownership of whatever—and *whoever*—was around him? As if he had the power to snap his fingers and change her world? To give her exactly what she wanted most.

Or to take it away.

Zanna stilled for a moment. Could he have come from the offices of the city council? They were as keen as the owner of the dilapidated apartment block next door that this property be sold and both the buildings destroyed in order to make a fresh development possible. There'd been veiled threats of the council having the power to force such a sale.

There was no sound of movement behind her either. Just a deep silence that somehow confirmed her suspicion and made her apprehensive.

Maybe the girls picked up on that. Or perhaps they'd seen Zanna look at the clock.

'Have you seen the time?' one of them gasped. 'We're going to be in *so* much trouble!'

They raced from the shop so fast the door banged and swung open again. Zanna moved to close it automatically and, without really thinking of why she might be doing it, she turned the sign on the door around to read 'Closed'.

She turned then. Slowly. Feeling like she was turning to face her fate.

And there he was. Relaxed enough to have one hip propped against the counter but watching her with a stillness about him that suggested intense concentration. Zanna felt a prickle of that energy reach her skin and she paused, mirroring his focus.

Something was about to happen.

And it was important.

His smile seemed relaxed, however. Wry, in fact, in combination with that raised eyebrow.

'You don't really believe in any of this stuff, do you?'

'What stuff in particular?' Zanna's heart picked up speed. If he was admitting his own lack of interest, maybe he was going to tell her why he was really here. 'There's rather a lot to choose from. Like aromatherapy, numerology, crystals, runes and palmistry. And the Tarot, of course.' Mischief made her lips curl. 'I would be happy to read your cards for you.'

He ignored the invitation. 'All of it.' His hand made a sweeping gesture. 'Magic.'

'Of course I believe in magic. I'm sure you do as well.'

The huff of sound was dismissive. *'Pas dans un million d'années.'*

The words were spoken softly enough that Zanna knew she had not been intended to hear them but the language was instantly recognisable. He was French, then. That explained the attractive accent and possibly that aura of control, too. She might not have understood the words but the tone was equally recognisable. Insulting, even. *Why* was he here—when he felt like this?

She'd had enough of this tension. Of not knowing.

'Are you from the council?'

As soon as the words left her mouth Zanna realised how absurd they were. It wasn't just because he was French that he had that quality of being in charge. A confidence so bone deep it could be cloaked in lazy charm. This man didn't work for anyone but himself. To suggest he might be a cog in a large, bureaucratic organisation was as much of an insult as dismissing everything that science was unable to prove. No wonder she could sense him gathering himself defensively.

'I beg your pardon?'

'You've come about the house?'

His hesitation spoke volumes. So did his eyes. Even if she had been close enough, those eyes were so dark already she might not have picked up the movement of his pupils but he couldn't disguise the involuntary flicker.

She'd hit the nail on the head and, for some reason, he was reluctant to admit it. Another possibility occurred to Zanna. He could be a specialist consultant of some kind and perhaps this was supposed to be an undercover inspection, in which case she might have been well advised to simply play along with the advantage of her suspicions. But this was too important to risk playing games. Honesty couldn't hurt, surely?

Disarming…*charming* this man, even, might get him on side. *Her* side.

'The historical protection order,' she said. 'I've been expecting someone to come and want to see the house.'

'Ah…' He was holding her gaze and, for a heartbeat, Zanna had the impression he was about to tell her something of great significance. But then his gaze shifted and she could sense him changing his mind. He nodded, as though confirming his decision. 'Yes,' he said, slowly. 'I *would* like to see the house.'

Should she show him? How dangerous would it be to be alone with this man? But what if he did hold the key to saving this place? How good would it be to have its safety assured by the time Maggie got home? She owed her beloved aunt so much and a protection order would be a gift beyond price.

For both of them.

Zanna took a deep, steadying breath. And then she mirrored his nod. 'I'll have to lock up,' she told him. Moving to collect the key from behind the counter took her even closer to him and she felt that odd curl of sensation deep within again. Stronger this time. That heady mix of desire laced with…danger.

She was playing with fire.

But, oh…the heat was delicious.

'I'm Zanna,' she heard herself saying. 'Zanna Zelenksy.'

'Dominic Brabant.' It was only good manners to extend his hand and his smile disguised the satisfaction of confirming that she was the person he'd been hoping to meet. 'Nic.'

'Pleased to meet you, Nic.'

The touch of her hand was as surprising as hearing her voice had been. That familiar *frisson* he noted would have been a warning in years gone by but Nic had learned to control it. To take the pleasure it could offer and escape before it became a prison.

Not that he'd expected to find it here. Any more than he'd expected this opportunity to appear. Fate was throwing more than one curveball in his direction at the moment. But how was he supposed to handle this one?

He watched as Zanna dipped her head, holding her hair out of the way, to blow out the numerous candles burning on the counter. With swift movements she divided and then braided the hair she held into a loose, thick rope that hung over her shoulder. Pulling a tasselled cord around her neck released the fastening of the purple robe. Skin-tight denim jeans appeared and then a bright orange cropped top that left a section of her belly exposed. There was a jewel dead centre. Copper coloured. It made him remember her extraordinary eyes. And as for her skin…

His gut tightened in a very pleasurable clench. The notion of her being a witch was too absurd. He was quite certain he would be unable to discover a single wart on that creamy skin.

Anywhere.

Mon Dieu… His body was telling him exactly how he would prefer to handle this and it didn't dent his confidence. It was a given that he would win in the end because he had never entertained the acceptance of failure since he'd been old enough to direct his own life, and this new project was too significant to modify.

Could what was happening here work in his favour?

Be patient, he reminded himself. He needed to go with the flow and see what other surprises fate might have in store for him.

The ripple of anticipation suggested that the reward would be well worth waiting for.

CHAPTER TWO

Stone gargoyles sat on pedestals, guarding the steps that led to the shop's entrance. While Zanna fitted an old iron key into the lock and turned it, Nic took another stride or two onto the mossy pathway beneath massive trees.

Having already admitted his interest, he didn't have to stifle the urge to look up through the branches to get another look at the house. Zanna's distraction was fortunate because it gave him a few moments to deal with a fresh wave of the turbulent emotions that memories evoked.

It had to be his earliest-ever memory, running down a brick pathway just like this, summoned by the creak of the iron gate that announced his father's return home. Being caught in those big, work-roughened hands and flung skywards before being caught again. Terrifying but thrilling because it was a given that nothing bad could happen when Papa was there.

He could hear the faint echo of a small child's shriek of laughter that blended with the deep, joyous rumble of the adult.

Piercing happiness.

Nothing bad *had* happened while Papa had been there. Life had been so full of laughter. Of music. The sounds of happiness that had died when Papa had been snatched away from them.

The memory slipped away, screened by filters the years had provided. And he could help them on their way by focusing on the house and using his professional filter—an extensive knowledge of architecture and considerable experience in demolishing old buildings.

It really *was* astonishing, with the unusual angles to its bays and verandas that gave it the impression of a blunted pentagon. It was iced with ornate ironwork, intricately moulded bargeboards and modillions and, to top it all off, there was a turret, set like a church spire to one side of the main entrance, adding a third storey to the two large rooms with rounded bay windows.

A secret, circular room that begged to be explored.

Especially to a small boy who had gazed at it from over the fence.

The shaft of remembered longing was as shiny as that moment of happiness had been. The filters were like clouds, shifting just enough to allow a bright beam to shine through. Bright enough to burn.

The emotion behind this current project would be overwhelming if he let it surface. Not that his mother was here to see it happen but that only made it more important. This was going to be a memorial to the one woman he'd ever truly loved. To the man she'd loved with all her heart. To the family he'd had for such a heartbreakingly short breath of time.

He swallowed hard.

'It's amazing, isn't it?' Zanna had joined him on the path. 'The most amazing house in the world.'

A leaf drifted down from one of the trees and landed

on Nic's shoulder. Zanna resisted the urge to reach up brush it off.

'It's certainly unusual. Over a hundred years old. Queen Anne style.'

Had she been right in guessing that he was a specialist in old houses? 'How do you know that?' she asked. 'Are you an architect?'

'Used to be. Plus, I've done a lot of study. The style was taken up in the 1880s and stayed popular for a long time. The Marseilles tiles on the roof make it a bit later because they weren't introduced until about 1901.'

The brief eye contact as he glanced at her was enough to steal Zanna's breath for a moment. The connection felt weird but gave her hope. He knew about old houses. Would he fall in love with *her* house and help her fight to save it?

'I didn't know about the Queen Anne style until recently,' she confessed. 'I had to do some research to apply for the historical protection order. It's all about the fancy stuff, isn't it? The turret and shingles and things.'

It didn't matter if he didn't admit that consideration for protection was the reason he was here. Zanna was asking the question partly because she wanted him to keep talking. She loved his voice. It reflected the dark, chocolate quality of his eyes. And that faint accent was undeniably sexy.

'It was also known as free classical,' he told her. 'The turret *is* a bit of a signature. Like those dragon spikes on the roof ridges. It looks like it was designed by an architect with a strong love of fairy-tales.'

'Or magic?' Zanna suggested quietly.

He shook his head, dismissing the suggestion, but the huff of his breath was a softer sound than she might have expected. 'Typical of New Zealand to adopt a style and make it popular only after it was considered passé by the rest of the world.'

'So you're not a kiwi, then?'

'By birth I am. My mother was French. A musician. She came across a kiwi backpacker who'd gone to Paris to trace his own French ancestry. She found him sitting in a park, playing a guitar, and she said she fell in love with him the moment she heard his music.'

Why was he telling her this? Were memories coming at him so hard and fast they had to escape? No. Maybe it was because he'd had more time to process these ones. They'd been spinning and growing in his head and his heart for days. They'd inspired this whole project.

'She came back here to marry him and I was born the same year. He…died when I was five and I got taken back to France a year or so later.'

Turning points. When life had gone so wrong. He couldn't fix that, of course. But he could honour the time when it had been perfect. Not that he could share any of that with Zanna. Maybe he'd already said too much.

'I still have a home there,' he finished. 'But I also live in London.'

Zanna's eyes were wide. 'I've lived here since *I* was six. My parents got killed in a car accident and my aunt Magda adopted me. I've only recently come back, though. *I've* been in London for the last few years.'

The point of connection brought them instantly that little bit closer and Nic was aware of a curl of warmth but then, oddly, it became an emotional seesaw and he felt disappointed. So they'd been living in the same city, oblivious to the existence of each other? What a waste…

Another leaf drifted down. And then another. Zanna looked up, frowning.

'I'd better get some water onto these trees. It's odd. I didn't think the summer's been dry enough to distress them.'

'Maybe autumn's arriving early.'

'They're not deciduous. They're southern ratas. They don't flower very well more than once every few years but when they do, they're one of our most spectacular native trees. They have bright red, hairy sort of flowers—like the pohutukawa. The street was named after them. And the house. But they were here first and they're protected now, which is a good thing.'

'Why?'

'The trees are big enough to make it harder to develop the land—if it's ever sold.'

'You're thinking of selling?' Maybe this mission would end up being easier than expected. Done and dusted within a few days, even. Strange that the prospect gave him another pang of...what *was* that? Like knowing that he'd lived in the same city as Zanna without knowing about it. Not quite disappointment...more like regret?

Yet he knew perfectly well that the world was full of beautiful women and he'd never had trouble attracting his fair share of them. What was it about Zanna Zelenksy? Her striking colouring? Those eyes? The strong character?

She certainly wasn't feeling it. Her face stilled and he could see a flash of strong emotion darken her eyes.

'Not in my lifetime. This is my home. My refuge.'

Refuge? What did she need to run and hide from? Was there a streak of vulnerability in that strength? Yes...

maybe that was why his interest had been captured. But Zanna ignored his curious glance and began walking down the path.

'It's part of the city's heritage, too,' she flung over her shoulder. 'Only the council's too stupid to recognise it. They'd rather see it pulled down and have some horrible, modern skyscraper take its place.'

It wouldn't be a skyscraper.

It would be a beautiful, low building that echoed the curve of the river.

The Brabant Academy. A music school and performance centre, funded by the trust that would bring brilliant musicians together to nurture young talent. A serene setting but a place where dreams could be realised. A place of beautiful music. And hope for the future.

Nic followed her along the path. Heritage was often overrated, in his opinion. A smokescreen that could hide the truth that sometimes it was preferable to wipe out the past and put something new and beautiful in its place.

And this was one of those times. A final sweeping glance as he reached the steps leading to the main entrance of the house revealed the cracked weatherboards and faded shingles. Peeling paint and rust on the ironwork. Poverty and neglect were stamped into the fabric of this once grand residence and it struck deeply engrained notes in Nic's soul.

A new memory of his father surfaced.

'Why on earth would we want a grand old house that would take far too much money and time? We have everything we need right here, don't we?'

The tiny cottage *had* contained everything they'd needed. It had been home.

The shock of moving to the slums of Paris had been all the more distressing. The smell of dirt and disease and...death.

Yes. The hatred of poverty and neglect was well honed. Memories of the misery were powerful enough to smother memories of happier things so it was no surprise that they were peeking out from the clouds for the first time ever. Maybe he would welcome them in time but they were too disturbing for now. They touched things Nic had been sure were long dead and buried. They had the potential to rekindle a dream that had been effectively crushed with his mother's death—that one day he would again experience that feeling like no other.

The safety of home. Of family.

Zanna found she was holding her breath as she turned the brass knob and pushed open the solid kauri front door of her home.

First impressions mattered. Would he be blown away by the graceful curve of the wide staircase with its beautifully turned balustrade and the carved newel posts? Would he notice that the flower motif on the posts was repeated in the light switches and the brass plates around the doorknobs—even in the stained glass of the windows?

Maybe he'd be distracted by the clutter of Aunt Maggie's eccentric collections, like the antique stringed instruments on the walls above the timber panelling and the arrays of unusual hats, umbrellas and walking sticks crowding more than one stand on the polished wooden floorboards.

He certainly seemed a little taken aback as he stepped into the entranceway but perhaps that was due to the black shape moving towards them at some speed from out of the darkness of the hallway beneath the stairs.

Three pitch-black cats with glowing yellow eyes. Siblings that stayed so close they could appear like one mythical creature sometimes. She could feel the way Nic relaxed as the shape came close enough to reveal its components.

'Meet the M&Ms.'

'Sorry?'

Zanna scooped up one of the small, silky cats. 'This is Marmite. The others are Merlin and Mystic. We call them the M&Ms.'

'Oh…' He was looking down at his feet. Merlin, who was usually wary of strangers, was standing on his back feet, trying to reach his hand. He stretched out his fingers and the cat seemed to grow taller as he pushed his head against them.

Artistic fingers, Zanna noted, with their long shape that narrowed gradually to rounded tips. If Aunt Maggie were here, she'd say that this man was likely to be imaginative, impulsive and unconventional. That he'd prefer an occupation that gave him a sense of satisfaction even if it was poorly paid.

He'd said he used to be an architect. What did he do now? Consulting work with organisations like the historical protection society? It certainly seemed to fit.

Those artistic fingers were cupped now, shaping the cat's body as they moved from its head to the tip of the long tail. Merlin emitted a sound of pleasure and Zanna had to bury her face in Marmite's fur to stifle what could have been a tiny whimper of her own. She could almost *feel* what that caress would be like.

It was Mystic that started the yowling.

'They're hungry,' Zanna said. 'If I don't feed them, they'll be a nuisance, so would you mind if we start the tour in the kitchen?'

'Not at all.'

She led him into the hallway—shadowy thanks to the obstructed light and the dark timber panelling on the walls. What saved it from being dingy was the large painting. A row of sunflowers that were vivid enough to cast an impression of muted sunshine that bathed the darkest point.

She knew that Nic had stopped in his tracks the moment he saw it. Zanna stopped, too, but not physically. Something inside her went very, very still. Holding its breath.

It doesn't matter what he thinks. What anybody else thinks...

The involuntary grunt of sound expressed surprise. Appreciation. Admiration, even?

Okay. So it *did* matter. Zanna could feel a sweet shaft of light piercing what had become a dark place in her soul. Not that she could thank him for the gift. It was far too private. Too precious.

Opening the door to the sun-filled, farmhouse-style kitchen—her favourite part of the house—accentuated the new pleasure. The knowledge that Nic was right behind her added a dimension that somehow made it feel more real. Genuine. Even if nothing else came of this encounter, it had been worth inviting this stranger into her world.

The surprise of the stunning painting had only been a taste of what was to come. Nic had to stop again as he entered the huge kitchen space, blinking as he turned his head slowly to take it all in. It should be a nightmare scene to someone who preferred sleek, modern lines and an absence of clutter. It was only a matter of time before he experienced that inner shudder of distaste but at least he knew it was coming. He would be able to hide it.

Cast-iron kettles covered the top of an old coal range and the collection of ancient kitchen utensils hanging from an original drying rack would not have been out of place in a pioneer museum. The kauri dining table and chairs, hutch dresser and sideboard were also museum pieces but the atmosphere was unlike any such place Nic had ever been in. Splashes of vivid colour from bowls of fruit and vegetables, unusual ornaments and jugs stuffed with flowers made the kitchen come alive.

The shudder simply wasn't happening. Instead, to his puzzlement, Nic found himself relaxing. Somehow, the overall effect was of an amazingly warm and welcome place to be. It felt like a place for…a family?

Abandoning his helmet on the floor, he sank onto a chair at one end of the long table as Zanna busied herself opening a can and spooning cat food into three bowls. When she crouched down, her jeans clung to the delicious curve of her bottom and the gap between the waistband and the hem of her orange top widened, giving him a view of a smooth back, interrupted only by the muted corrugations of her spine. He could imagine trailing his fingers gently over those bumps and then spreading them to encompass the curve of her hip.

Oh…*Mon Dieu*… The powerful surge of attraction coming in the wake of those other bursts of conflicting and disturbing emotions was doing his head in. He needed distraction. Fast.

Maybe that curious object wrapped in black velvet on

the table, lying beside a wrought-iron candelabra, would do the trick. Lifting the careful folds of the fabric, Nic found himself looking at an oversized pack of cards.

Witchy sort of cards.

The shaft of desire he was grappling with morphed into a vague disquiet. It was very rare to feel even slightly out of his depth but it was happening now. There was an atmosphere of mystery here. Of eccentricity that had an undercurrent of serenity that had to come from someone who knew exactly who they were. Or some-*thing*, perhaps, because he couldn't be sure whether the vibe was coming from Zanna or the house.

Weird…

'We keep them wrapped in black.' Zanna's voice was soft. And close. Nic looked up to see she had a pair of wine glasses dangling by their stems in one hand and a bottle in the other. She held it up in invitation and he nodded.

'Sure. Why not?'

The wine was red. Blood red. His disquiet kicked up a notch.

'Why?' he asked.

'It just seemed like a good idea.' Zanna wasn't meeting his eyes. 'A glass of wine is a nice way to wind down. We could go into the garden, if you like.'

He followed the direction of her gaze. French doors provided a glimpse of a bricked courtyard between the kitchen and a tangle of garden. An intimate kind of space.

'I'm fine here.' Nic cleared his throat. 'I meant why do you wrap those cards in black?'

'It's a neutral colour that keeps outside energy away.' Zanna had filled her own glass and she sat down at right angles to Nic.

'It's black magic, right? Witchcraft?'

The flash in those extraordinary eyes was enough to make Nic feel unaccountably apologetic.

'I don't believe in witchcraft,' Zanna said, her voice tight. 'And calling any of this black magic is an insult to my aunt. Her family can trace its roots back to the sixteenth century. They travelled around and made their living by things like fortune-telling. Aunt Maggie has a very strong affinity with her heritage. I've grown up with it and I love Maggie enough to respect it. I see it as another dimension—one that adds some colour and imagination to life and can help people cope with the hard stuff.' She closed her eyes and sighed. 'Sorry…I get a bit defensive. We've had people try and twist things into something they're not and then use it against her. Against us.'

Nic said nothing. He had a feeling he knew who those people might be. But they were out of the picture now. He was the one who got to decide how things would be handled from now on. Except that he had no idea. Yet. He stared at the cards.

'I've always thought of it as a load of rubbish,' he admitted. 'The fortune-telling, that is.'

'Depends on how you look at it.' Zanna reached out and touched the pack of cards with her fingertips. 'It's about symbols. They demand an active response. You have to think about how you really feel and trying to relate to an unexpected symbol like the picture on a card can make you consider a totally new dimension to a problem. I like to think of them as a tool for self-knowledge. A way of centring oneself, perhaps.'

'Seeing the future?' He couldn't help the note of derision but she didn't seem to take offence.

'I don't believe the future can be seen…but I don't believe things are necessarily fated to happen either. There
are choices to be made that can radically alter the direction you take in life. Big choices. Little choices. So many
that you don't even notice a lot of them but it pays to be
aware. Some people think they have no control and they
blame others when things go wrong. If you've made an
active choice and things go wrong, you can learn from
that experience and it's less likely to happen again.'

Like falling in love with the wrong person…

Inviting a complete stranger into your home…

'If you don't believe the future can be seen, how can
you tell a fortune and say something's going to happen?
Like a new job or overseas travel or…' he snorted softly
'…meeting a tall, dark, handsome stranger?'

Was that a reference to himself? Was he *flirting* with
her? Zanna knew the rush of heat would be showing in
her cheeks. Did he know how good looking he was?
Probably. Nobody could be out there looking like that
in a world full of women and not find it incredibly easy
to get whatever he wanted. Maybe toying was a better
word, then. It made her remember the way he'd been
looking at her when he'd been playing with that crystal
in the shop. It made her remember the way he'd made
her feel. That reawakening of desire.

How far could that go?

How far did she want it to go?

'Okay…' She avoided meeting his eyes. 'First off, I'd
probably say that there was an opportunity of a new job
or travel or something. You might not have been thinking about it but the idea would be planted and you'd be
more open to new ideas because of that suggestion. You
might recognise an opportunity and then you'd have a

choice. Something would change. You'd either take that opportunity or be more content to stay where you were.'

'Do you tell your own fortune?'

She smiled. 'Occasionally. If I have a problem I want to think through. I prefer to have Aunt Maggie read my cards, though. It's great fun and the best way I know to have a really meaningful conversation. That's how this whole business started. Way back, before my time here, but I've had plenty of people tell me about it. They came to have their cards read and Maggie became a magnet for anyone with a problem. And she's such a warm and loving person she would offer them tea and cakes at the same time and it all just grew into a way she could make her living.'

She took a sip of her wine and Nic couldn't look away. He watched her bottom lip touch the glass and the way her throat rippled as she swallowed. He picked up his own glass to find it contained a surprisingly good red wine.

'Back then,' Zanna continued, 'before the city centre spread and the houses gave way to office blocks and hotels, there were streets and streets of cottages. Houses that had big gardens with lots of fruit trees. People kept chickens. Mr Briggs down the road even kept a goat. So many people. This was the big house but everyone was welcome. They all adored Maggie and this place was like a community centre. I remember it being like that when I was young.'

'But the houses have gone. There's no community now.' Okay, it was sad but things changed. Progress happened.

'Some of the people still come back and talk about the old days. They can't believe that the house and Maggie are just the same as ever and they love sharing the memories. She always promises she'll still be here the next time they come.'

She wasn't here now. If she was, Nic might have been tempted to ask to have his cards read so that he could see if she was as amazing as Zanna made her sound. Had she really helped solve problems for so many people?

'Can you read the cards?'

Her eyes widened. Surprise or shock? 'I've grown up with them…yes… I'm not as good as Maggie but I can certainly read them.'

'Would you read them for me?'

The hesitation was obvious. 'Are you sure you want me to?'

So that they could have a really meaningful conversation? So that he could sit here a while longer and put off thinking about why he was really here? Maybe even find a solution to his own problem?

Nic held her gaze. Long enough for a silent message that had nothing to do with fortune-telling. He wanted more than his cards read and that want was getting stronger by the minute.

'Yeah…' His voice was husky. 'I'm sure.'

CHAPTER THREE

HE HAD NO IDEA, did he, how much could be revealed in a reading? He was drinking his wine, leaning back in his chair and watching curiously as Zanna went through the ritual of lighting the five fat candles on the arms of the candelabra and opening a drawer to extract a tiny bottle of lavender oil that she sprinkled on the black velvet square.

'To cleanse the space,' she explained.

'Right…' The corner of his mouth quirked but his gaze had enough heat that she could only handle the briefest contact.

Was it what she was doing that had captured his attention so intently or was he watching *her*? Adding the impression to wondering what she was about to find out about *him* made her feel oddly nervous. She needed another mouthful of her wine.

'The first thing I need to do is pick a card to represent you as the significator.'

'The what?'

'Significator. The querent. The seeker of knowledge.' This was good. She could hide her nerves by doing something she knew she was good at. She spread the cards, face up, in front of her. The sound Nic made was incredulous.

'But they're beautiful… They look like artwork reproductions.'

'This set is based on one of the oldest known packs. Tarot cards have been around for five hundred years. The first known cards were painted in Italy during the Renaissance. Back around the second half of the fifteenth century.'

Was he impressed with her knowledge? Why did she *want* him to be? Zanna glanced up but Nic was staring at the cards. Many pictures depicted people and each card had a title.

'I don't like that one,' he muttered. 'I hope Death isn't going to appear in my line up.'

'The meaning isn't necessarily literal. The death card means that something must come to an end. Whether or not it's painful depends on the person's capacity to accept and recognise the necessity for that ending.' The words came easily because they'd been learned many years ago. 'Sometimes you have to let go of an old life in order to take the opportunity of a new and more fulfilling one.'

'That's very true.' Yes, he was impressed. 'Something I've always lived by, in fact.' There was a question in his eyes now. Or was it an accusation? 'Do *you*?'

Zanna blinked. This wasn't supposed to be about her. She retreated into card lore as she looked away. 'The cards are designed to portray a story. Kind of the rites of passage of an archetypal journey through life. Everybody faces the same sorts of challenges and problems— the same as they did five hundred years ago. People don't change and it's often a surprise to find how similar we are to those around us. Every situation is different but the challenges can be the same.'

'You don't really believe you can predict the future, do you?'

This time, Zanna was able to hold his gaze. 'I believe that particular choices and situations have led to where one is in life and the response to that position presents future choices and situations. Understanding why and how some things have happened is the best way to cast a more conscious influence on the future.' She gave herself a mental shake. 'Are you over forty years of age?'

That made *him* blink. 'Do I *look* like I'm over forty?'

A bubble of laughter escaped. 'You could be a well-preserved specimen. How old *are* you?'

'Thirty six. How old are *you*?'

'That's not the least bit relevant. You're the one I need to find a card for.'

'Hey…I answered *your* question.' There was an unguarded tone in his voice. A peep at a small boy having a playground conversation perhaps. It gave her a soft buzz of something warm.

'I'm twenty-eight,' she relented. 'Oh, yes…This is definitely you.' She picked up the card. 'The King of Pentacles.'

'Why?'

'He represents a strong, successful individual with a gift of manifesting creative ideas in the world. He also represents status and worldly achievement and has the Midas touch.'

He looked taken aback. Did he think that wearing well-worn leather and jeans would disguise his obvious lack of any serious financial hardship? That jacket had been expertly tailored to fit so well and the nails on the ends of those artistic fingers were beautifully manicured. His casual appreciation of the special wine she had chosen had been another giveaway. She placed the chosen card on the centre of the black cloth. Then she scooped up the rest of the pack and began shuffling the cards.

'That's a lot of cards.'

'Seventy-eight.' Zanna nodded. 'The major Arcana that is the depiction of the journey and then the minor Arcana. Four suits of Cups, Wands, Swords and Pentacles. They represent elements and experiences.' She spread the cards in a fan shape in front of Nic, facing down this time. 'Formulate your question or think about a problem you want clarified,' she invited. 'You don't have to tell me what it is. Then choose ten cards and hand them to me in the order selected.'

She placed the cards in set positions in the form of a Celtic cross. 'This card over yours is the first one we look at. It's the covering card. Where you are at the moment and the influences affecting you.' She turned it over. 'Hmm…interesting.'

He was sitting very still. He might think this was a load of rubbish but he was unable to stop himself buying into it.

'Why?'

'Page of Wands. It suggests that it's time to discover a new potential. Also suggests restlessness at work. Something's not going the way you want it to.' She touched the card at right angles to the one she'd just read. 'This is the crossing card. It describes what is generating conflict and obstruction at the moment.' She turned the card face up.

The oath Nic muttered was in French but needed no translation.

'You're taking the pictures too literally,' she told him.

'The Hanged Man is a symbol. It suggests that a sacrifice of some sort might be needed. Maybe there's something that would be difficult to give up but it needs to go because it's blocking progress.'

He was giving her that odd look again. As though he was including *her* in whatever thought processes were going on.

'This is the crowning card,' she continued. 'It represents an aim or ideal that is not yet actual.'

'The future?'

'Potentially.'

'What's the Queen of Wands?'

Should she tell Nic that the Queen of Wands was the card that had always been picked as the significator for her own readings?

'She's industrious, versatile, strong-willed and talented.' Zanna kept her eyes firmly on the card. 'She's also self-contained and stable. She holds her great strength and energy within, devoting them to the few things to which she chooses to give her heart.'

The moment's silence was enough to make her realise that she didn't need to tell Nic about her own relationship to this particular card. He was joining the dots all by himself.

'It may not mean a person, as such,' she added. 'It could mean that it's time to start developing her qualities yourself. Things like warmth and loyalty and being able to sustain a creative vision.'

He wasn't buying that. He'd made his mind up, hadn't he, and she could sense his immovability when that happened.

The card depicting the immediate future suggested a dilemma to be faced with either choice leading to trouble and the card representing the kind of response that Nic could expect from others was one of her favourites—the Lovers.

Nic clearly approved of it, too. 'Now, why didn't that one show up for my immediate future?' he murmured. 'That would have been something to look forward to.'

The tone of his voice held a seductive note that rippled through every cell in Zanna's body like a powerful drug. She hadn't felt this alive for so long.

Maybe she never had.

Had this man come into her life to teach her to feel things she didn't know she was capable of feeling?

What would she do if he touched her with the kind of intent that tone promised?

Could she resist? Would she even try?

Maybe not. Zanna did her best to quell the curl of sensation deep in her belly. The anticipation. 'You're being too literal again. This card is the view of others. It could be that you're doing something to make them think as they do.'

She could sense his discomfort and it was disturbing. *He may not be who he seems to be. Take care...*

She knew he might be dangerous. It was reckless to be taking pleasure from his company. From this anticipation of what might be going to happen, but maybe that was what was making this such a thrill. Adding something wild and even more exciting to this chemical attraction.

It was an effort to keep her voice even. 'This particular card might mean that you have to make a choice and it probably concerns love. It might be choosing between love and a career or creative activity. Or it could be that you're involved in a triangle of some sort. Or that someone's trying to get you to marry in a hurry.'

He was shaking his head now. 'I never have to choose between love and my career. I've never even thought about marriage and I avoid triangles at all costs.'

He walked alone, then? He was unattached?

The thought should have made him seem more attractive but something didn't feel right.

Zanna read a few more of the cards before she realised what was nagging at the back of her mind. It was too much of a coincidence that she felt so involved with every interpretation he was making. For whatever reason, Nic had included *her* in the question or problem he had brought to this reading.

Why?

'This card represents your hopes and fears.'

'The Fool? Who isn't afraid of making a fool of themselves?'

'The fear might apply to the fact that a risk of some kind is required. It suggests that a new chapter of your life might be about to begin but it needs a willingness to take a leap into the unknown. It fits with a lot of other cards here.'

'What's the last one?'

'That position is the final outcome. It should give you some clues to answer the question you brought into the reading.' Her own heart picked up speed as she turned it over. 'Oh…'

The tension was palpable. Nic didn't have to say anything to demand an explanation.

'The Ace of Swords means a new beginning,' she told him quietly. 'But one that comes out of a struggle or conflict.'

He drained his glass of wine. It was all rubbish. So why did it feel so personal? It was obvious that Zanna was part of his immediate future. That it was going to be a struggle to get what he wanted. But did she really need to be sacrificed?

The thought was disturbing. She was part of this place and it felt like a home. A kind of portal to those memories buried so far back in his own story. Nic looked away from the table, his gaze downcast. It was the first time he'd noticed the floor of this space. A background of grey tiling that resembled flagstones had been inset with mosaic details. Starburst designs made up of tiny fragments of colour that dotted the floor at pleasingly irregular intervals.

'It's not original, is it?' he queried. 'The floor?'

'Depends what you mean by original.' Zanna was refilling his glass. 'The old floorboards became unsafe because they were rotten. Maggie and I have always considered our creative efforts pretty original, though.'

'You made this floor?'

'Yes.' She topped up her own glass. 'Took ages but we loved doing it. In fact, we loved it so much we did flagstones for the garden, too. And a birdbath.'

Nic shook his head. Extraordinary.

'Maybe it's something to do with gypsy blood. Making do with what you find lying around. We dug up so much old broken china around here that it seemed a shame not to do something with it so we broke it up a bit more and used it for mosaic work.'

'Taking an opportunity, huh? Dealing with a problem.'

'Yes.' She was smiling at him as if he'd understood something she'd been trying to teach. The sense of approval made him feel absurdly pleased with himself.

'So you really do come from a gypsy bloodline?'

'Absolutely. It's only a few generations ago that my

family on my father's side was travelling. Maggie was my dad's older sister. My great-grandfather was born in a caravan.'

'Where does the name Zelensky come from?'

'Eastern Europe. Probably Romania. That's where my aunt Maggie's gone now. She was desperate to find out more about her family before she's too old to travel.'

The smile curled far enough to create a dimple. 'What's funny?' Nic asked.

'Just that Maggie's got more energy and enthusiasm than most people half her age have. She's the most amazing woman I've ever known and I never fail to feel enormously grateful that she was there to rescue me when I got orphaned.'

Suddenly Nic wanted to change the subject but he wasn't sure why. Maybe he didn't want to be reminded that she was vulnerable. That she'd been a frightened child. That this place was her home. Her *refuge*. Because it would give her an advantage in the conflict he knew was coming?

That was weird in itself. Nic didn't let emotions sway business decisions.

This was hardly a business decision, though, was it? It couldn't be more different from the luxury resorts he'd become known for designing and developing in recent years. And the impulsive decision to buy into Rata Avenue had unleashed so many personal memories. This had nothing to do with business, in fact. This was deeply personal. A step back in time to where he'd spent the most vulnerable years of his own life.

Was that why this house felt so much like home?

He cast another glance around the kitchen. No, this was nothing like the fragments of memory he still had.

The kitchen in the cottage had been tiny and dark and it had taken a huge effort from Maman to keep it sparkling clean. There was something about this space that tugged hard at those memories, however. Some of those old utensils, perhaps—like the metal sieve that had holes in the shape of flowers? He dropped his gaze to the floor. To the fragments of the old china embedded in the tiles.

Blue and white were prominent but many had small flowers on them. Like that one, with a dusty pink rose. He almost didn't recognise his own voice when he spoke.

'Where did you say you got all the china?'

'We dug it up. Some of it was in our own garden but most came from next door where the park is now. There was a cottage there that was even older than this place. The council acquired the land and demolished the cottage before I came here but it was a long time before the site was cleaned up so it was like a playground for me. I knew I wasn't allowed to go too close to the river but once I started finding the pretty pieces of broken china, I didn't want to. It was like a treasure hunt I could keep going back to. I think that was where my love of flowers came from.'

But Nic wasn't listening to her words. He wasn't even thinking of how musical that lilt in her voice was. He was thinking of a china cup that had pink rosebuds on it and a gold handle. He could see his mother's hands cradling it—the way she had when she'd become lost in her sadness. He could see the look in her eyes above the gold rim of the cup that matched the handle. He could feel the sensation of being so lost. Not knowing what to do to make her smile again. To bring back the laughter and the music.

'When I'm big, Mama, I'll be rich. I'll buy that big house next door for you.'

How could grief be so sharp when it had been totally buried for so many years?

Maybe it wasn't Zanna's vulnerability he needed to worry about at all. It was his own.

The pain was timely. He was here for a reason—to honour his parents—and he couldn't let anyone else dilute that resolution. No matter how beautiful they were.

'I should go.' He glanced at his watch. How on earth had so much time passed? 'It's getting late.'

'But didn't you want to see the house?' There was a faint note of alarm in Zanna's voice. 'There's still time before it gets dark.'

'Another time perhaps.' Except the words didn't quite leave his mouth because Nic made the mistake of looking up again.

The sun was much lower now and the light in the room had changed, becoming softer and warmer. Shards of colour caught in his peripheral vision as the light came through stained-glass panels and bounced off cut crystals that were hanging on silver wires.

It made that amazing colour of Zanna's hair even more like flames. Glowing and so alive—like her eyes and skin, and that intriguing personality.

There was no point in seeing the rest of the house but he didn't want to leave just yet. He might not get another time with her like this. Before she knew who he was or what he wanted. And being with her—here—might be the only way to get more of those poignant glimpses into his own past. As painful as they were, they were also treasure. Forgotten jewels.

Was it wrong to want more?

Quite possibly, but—heaven help him—he couldn't resist.

'Sure,' he heard himself saying instead. 'Why not?'

Maybe it hadn't been such a good idea to give Nic a tour of the house.

It might have been better to let him wander around by himself. But how could she have known that he would pick out the features she loved most herself? That the feeling of connection would gain power with every passing room?

He commented on the graceful proportions of the huge downstairs rooms, the ornately carved fireplaces and the beautiful lead-light work of the stained-glass fanlights. He knew more than she did about old houses, too.

'Those ceiling roses were more than a decorative feature.' With his head tilted back to inspect the central light surround, the skin on his neck looked soft and vulnerable. Zanna could imagine all too easily how soft it would feel to her fingers. Or her lips...

'They're actually ventilators. Those gaps in the plasterwork were designed to let out hot air.'

'Useful.' Her murmur earned her a glance accentuated by a quirked eyebrow. Could he feel the heat coming from her body?

No. It definitely hadn't been such a good idea to do this. Zanna froze for a moment at the bottom of the staircase. The rooms on the next level were far more personal. What would he say when he saw more of her handiwork? Could it take away that sweet pleasure that his reaction to the sunflower painting had given her?

He hadn't stopped moving when she did so his body

came within a hair's breadth of bumping into hers. Her forward movement was an instinctive defence against such a powerful force and there was only one way to go.

Up the stairs.

Maggie's room was safe enough. So were the spare bedrooms but the bathroom was next and she stood back to let Nic enter the room alone. Folding her arms around her body was an unconscious movement that was both a comfort and a defence.

So far, the features of this house had been expected. Period features that were valuable in their own right. Things that could be salvaged and recycled so they wouldn't be lost and he wouldn't need to feel guilty about their destruction.

But this…

Nic was speechless.

The fittings were in keeping with the house. The claw-foot bath, the pedestal hand basin and the ceramic toilet bowl and cistern with its chain flush, but everything had been painted with trails of ivy. The tiny leaves on the painted vines crept over the white tiled walls from the arched window, making it appear as though the growth had come naturally from outside the house. The floor was also tiled in white but there were small diamond-shaped insets in the same shade of green as the ivy. The interior of the antique bathtub was also painted the same dark green.

'*C'est si spécial…*'

Reverting to the language of his heart only happened when something touched him deeply but he didn't translate the phrase as he walked back past Zanna. She didn't move so he kept going towards the last door that opened off this hallway.

Directly over the shop, this room shared the feature of a large bay window but here it had been inset with a window seat that followed the semi-circular line. A brass bed, probably as old as the house, had a central position and the colours in the patchwork quilt echoed those of the tiles in the nearby fireplace.

The walls were lined with tongue-and-groove timber that had been painted the palest shade of green. Dotted at random intervals, but no more than a few centimetres apart, were reproductions of flowerheads. Every imaginable flower could be found somewhere on these wooden walls. From large roses and lilies to pansies and daisies—right down to the tiniest forget-me-nots.

'The hours this must have taken…' Nic murmured aloud. 'It must have cost a fortune.'

'It was good practice.'

Startled, Nic turned to find he wasn't alone in the room any longer. That feeling he'd had earlier of being potentially out of his depth had nothing on the way the ground had just shifted beneath him.

'*You* painted these?'

The shrug was almost imperceptible but the modesty was appealing. 'Maggie gave me an encyclopaedia of flowers for my twelfth birthday. I added one almost every day for years.'

'And the ivy in the bathroom?'

'That was a wet May school holiday.' Another tiny shrug came with the hint of a smile. 'Maggie said it would keep me out of mischief.'

He stared at her. 'Do you know how extraordinary you are, Zanna Zelensky? How *talented*?'

She simply stared back at him. As though he'd said something wrong and she was trying to decide what to do about it. The moment stretched but Nic couldn't break the silence. The air hummed with a curious tension but he had no clue as to what might have caused it.

Finally, she spoke.

'There's one room you haven't seen yet.'

His nod was solemn. His mouth felt dry and he had to lick his lips.

The turret. The one room he'd wanted to see inside for as long as he could remember. The child buried deep inside was about to have his dearest wish granted. But… what if it was a disappointment? If it was nothing more than, say, a storage area?

He forced his feet to start moving. To follow Zanna up the narrow, spiral staircase that led to the secret room beneath the witch's hat of the turret. If it was less than he hoped for, he'd cope. He had with every other childish hope and dream that had been crushed, hadn't he?

Opening the small door at the top of the stairs, Zanna walked ahead of him. She said nothing. She didn't even turn around as she walked over to one of the arched windows and stared out as if she was giving Nic some privacy.

And maybe he needed it.

Despite the now rapidly fading day, the light was still good in here thanks to the skylights in the sharply sloping, iron roof.

He was in an artist's studio.

Zanna's studio.

Works stood propped against the walls. A half-finished canvas perched on an easel and there was a strong smell of oil paints and solvents. The overwhelming first impression that struck Nic was the sheer vitality of the colours around him. Muted, sun-baked hues in what looked like a series of work based on old European town streets that made him think of Italy and France. More vivid colours were in the flowers, like the deep blue of hydrangeas and the scarlet shades of poppies. Black cats could be seen concealed amongst the blooms. A series of sketches that the M&Ms must have inspired lay scattered on a table. Black cats—sleeping, washing themselves, jumping and playing. Even her pencil lines caught a sense of movement and vitality.

For a long, long time Nic didn't speak.

He didn't need to ask if she'd been the one who had painted that stunning row of sunflowers that made a dark hallway downstairs glow but it would have been an easy way to break the silence.

He actually opened his mouth to ask the rhetorical question but, as he did so, he shifted his gaze to where Zanna was standing and there was something about her stance that made the words evaporate.

Was she even aware of him being here?

CHAPTER FOUR

GOD...THIS WAS so much harder than she'd expected it to be.

She'd wanted him to fall in love with her beloved home. To understand why it was so important to save it. And this room was an integral piece of the architecture of the old house...

But it was so much more than that. The house was the home of her heart—where she felt loved, *safe*—but this room...

This was the room of her soul.

Her absolute refuge. It wasn't just paint smeared over those canvas sheets. They all contained fragments of *who* she was.

Not that he could know how much of a risk she was taking right now.

Zanna stared through the window as the shadows deepened but she couldn't see the huge rata trees below as they became dark and vaguely menacing shapes. There were other pictures in her mind.

Her best friend, Brianna, who'd travelled to London with her three years ago, when she'd graduated from art school. The bottle of champagne they'd splurged on when Brie had scored that job in a big gallery.

The show opening where she'd met Simon and fallen in love for the first time in her life. It had been a given that they would be living together within weeks. Planning their wedding and the rest of their lives.

More champagne as Brie and Simon had conspired to get Zanna to have her own show and they'd toasted her sparkling future as an artist. Not that she could show the *craft* that she'd previously engaged in, of course. Anyone could paint cute cats and flowers but they would coach her into producing *real* art. The kind that the critics would take notice of.

Had they known what kind of notice that would be taken? The humiliation of having her work ridiculed so publicly?

Of course they had. They'd been laughing about it that day, hadn't they? When she'd come home to find them in bed together.

Such a long, lonely trip back to New Zealand but it had been the only thing to do. She'd needed to heal and there had only been one place for that—in the comfort zone of her past. Maggie and the house. The shop with its magic and *this* room—the studio Maggie had created for her because she'd believed in her.

Even with all that faith and love and the solid grounding of the link to her past, it had taken a long time for her to climb those stairs again. To pick up a brush and start the work she had to do because it was who she was.

And now she'd allowed a stranger in here.

A potential critic.

Maybe she'd read too much into his impressions when he'd seen the sunflowers in the hallway and her immature efforts in the bathroom and on her bedroom walls. He might be too polite to reveal his opinion now that he was faced with her real work but she'd know the instant she looked at his face.

And she couldn't put it off any longer. Good grief… it felt like she'd been standing here for ever and there hadn't been a sound behind her.

She could hear something now, though. A quiet footfall on the bare, wooden floorboards. A long, slow inward breath. The faint squeak of leather in motion. By the time she turned, he was so close that she would see exactly what he was thinking. Especially with the way a last ray of the setting sun was angling directly through the window.

The unexpected explosion of colour as that sunbeam caught Zanna's hair took Nic's breath away and something else ignited deep in his belly, making arousal an overwhelming force.

Those astonishing eyes were wide. Vulnerable. She was waiting for his reaction to her art, wasn't she, but how could he begin to put the emotions they evoked into words?

To do so would mean opening a part of himself that he never looked at, let alone shared with anyone. The place where abandoned dreams were locked away. Where there was unconditional love and the warm comfort of a place called home.

Where a sunset meant far more than the passing of another day because you could shut off the rest of the world and simply be with the people who mattered most.

Nic felt like he was being dragged into that place— that's how much of an effect this room and what it contained had had on him.

Had he really intended to persuade Zanna to sell this property to him so that he could tear the house down to make way for something new?

Yes. It had to go, didn't it? It was a part of a dark past for him. A symbol of a time when the world had spun on its axis for a small boy and started the downward spiral to unbearable misery.

But it was part of Zanna's past, too. Part of who she was and she was…amazing.

There was too much to think about and it was too much of an emotional roller-coaster.

Confusing.

Right now, all Nic could think was that he wanted to make it all go away so that he could simply be with Zanna. If he could spend more time with her, maybe it would all fall into place.

He had to try and find some words. He couldn't just stand here and stare into her eyes.

'I…I don't know what to say,' he admitted. 'It's… You're…'

Something in her eyes seemed to melt. Were tears gathering? No…her lips softened as well, though you couldn't call it a smile. She lifted her hand. Placed a fingertip softly against his lips.

'You don't need to say anything,' she said softly. She drew in a breath, her next words no more than a sigh as she released it. 'Thank you…'

His hand captured hers and held it as she took it away. He lifted his other hand, without thinking, to mirror her action and touch *her* lips. Of their own accord, his fingers drifted sideways until they reached the angle of her jaw, with her chin cradled by his thumb.

Repercussions simply didn't exist in this moment. He

had to kiss her. That would undoubtedly make the rest of the world disappear, at least temporarily.

His touch was light. He would have felt the slightest flinch or withdrawal and there could be no mistaking his intentions as he slowly lowered his head so maybe she was feeling the same overwhelming pull?

The conviction that—unbeknownst to him, anyway—choices had already been made?

He was going to kiss her.

Or maybe he was merely responding to *her* desire to kiss him?

Why did she want it so badly?

Because it was a fitting way to thank him for the unspoken gift of validating her work? Words couldn't have encompassed what she'd seen in his eyes—the way her paintings had made him feel.

Because she needed so badly to have him on her side? To present a case that would not only mean that the house would be safe from the council's determination to get rid of it but that financial help would be available to restore Rata House to its former glory.

Maybe it was simply because she wanted to feel desirable again. That somebody wanted what she had to offer. That that somebody was the most gorgeous man she'd ever seen would only make it more special. Was that wrong enough to be ringing alarm bells?

Good grief, she could actually *hear* those bells as Nic's mouth hovered over hers, so close that she could feel their heat.

But then they got louder and Zanna gasped. She felt her mouth graze Nic's lips as she jerked her head sideways.

'It's the phone… I have to get that…' She was already

moving. She could see the stairs. 'It could be Maggie and the phone lines in Romania are awful.' She raised her voice as she flew down the narrow staircase. 'I've been worried about her for weeks.'

The spell had been broken and maybe that was for the best.

The memory of how he'd felt when he'd been a heart-beat away from kissing Zanna could be shoved into that space where the other broken things were stored. It would help if he got out of this room.

Nic shut the door of the studio behind him. When he reached the bottom of the spiral staircase he could hear her voice drifting up from somewhere downstairs.

'Maggie? Is that you? Oh, thank *goodness*… How are you? *Where* are you?'

Yes. The phone call had been timely. He could use a few minutes here to try and clear his head. Her voice got fainter, making it easy to tune it out as he paced the length of the hallway and back again and then paused beside a wide window at the end to peer out.

Maybe he needed to find a reconnection to the real world?

He could see his new acquisition from here—the ugly apartment block. It would be no great loss to the world to put a wrecking ball through that architectural disaster.

On the other side of Zanna's house was the small park where his first home and other cottages had long since been removed. If he *could* get this land, there couldn't be a more ideal place for the music school—bordered by the river and blending seamlessly into the pretty park. Perfect.

The motivation for the project was as strong as ever.

Unshakeable, in fact. This was something he *had* to do but there was no denying that niggle of guilt. That doubts were brewing.

This house might be a symbol of crushed dreams for him but for a lot of other people it was a symbol of something far more positive.

A place that inspired creativity.

A place to have their problems solved.

A place that oozed warmth.

Love…

Maybe that was where the doubts were originating. For the first time, Nic was tapping into memories that were worth cherishing. Feeling things he had denied himself for longer than he could remember. Would that portal be damaged if he obliterated the past to make a clean slate?

Compromise. Maybe that was the key.

What if he made a gallery of beautiful photographs in the entrance foyer to the school to honour the house that had been on this site? With a plaque to record its history and importance to a community that had long gone?

People could still visit.

Zanna could make a new studio somewhere else. He could help her find one.

He was still standing there, lost in thought, when Zanna came back up the stairs. 'We got cut off,' she said. 'But it doesn't matter. At least I know she's all right. More than all right, it seems.'

'Oh?' The sound was polite. His mind might be clearer now but his body was drifting back into a haze of desire. He had to consciously keep his hands on the windowsill behind him so that they didn't move in the hope of touching Zanna.

This was more than the kind of physical attraction he was used to. Maybe she really *was* a witch and he was the victim of some kind of bizarre manipulation.

Even her voice seemed to cast a spell.

'I didn't realise how worried I'd been, not hearing from her for so long. It's no wonder the phone lines are a bit of an issue, though. She's been in Bucharest and as far as the border to Ukraine near the Black Sea.'

Her hands seemed to be trying to follow an invisible map of Romania. She was speaking quickly and tiny flickers of her facial muscles added to the impression of vitality. *Passion…*

Did she look like this when she was immersed in her painting?

'Anyway, one of her second cousins runs some kind of a B&B. There was another guest there. A man called Dimitry. He owns a castle, it has no plumbing but I think she's in love…'

How had they managed to exchange so much information in such a short time? Was her aunt just as passionate in the way she talked or did they have the kind of connection that allowed communication on a level that needed very few words?

'With the castle or Dimitry?'

'She says it's the castle but I suspect it's both.'

Not that it mattered. Or maybe it did. In either case, surely a new dream would need funding. It could be an ace up his sleeve if the offer to buy this property was generous enough to allow for a new studio for Zanna and some money for her aunt to put into a castle restoration project as well.

'So she might not want to come back?'

The glow faded with disconcerting speed from Zanna's face. He could almost see her withdrawing—as if she'd revealed too much or said the wrong thing. She was putting up some kind of defensive barrier. Dammit. He wanted to see her smile again. To hear the voice that made him think of a rippling stream. To watch those compelling movements of her hands and face. But he couldn't even see her face now. She had taken a step forward to stare at the shadows of the world outside beyond his shoulder.

'It's probably just a holiday romance. There hasn't been anyone in her life for as long as I've known her. She's just…lonely…for something *I* can't give her.'

Nic's breath caught as he heard the echo of her tone. He had to turn towards her.

Was Zanna lonely, too?

There was a harsher note in her voice as she spoke again.

'Ugly, isn't it?'

He blinked. 'What is?'

'That apartment block next door. It's had nothing done to it for decades. The only people that live in it are the occasional squatters.'

'Needs pulling down.'

'That would cost money.' There was still passion in her voice but this was the flip side of the joy he'd heard when she'd been talking about her aunt. There was an undercurrent of something dark now. Something he could recognise all too easily.

Hatred. Contained but deeply rooted in the fear that something precious was going to be taken away from her.

'The owner doesn't want to spend that money until he gets what he *really* wants.'

'Which is?' The question was no more than a quiet prompt.

'*This* place. Enough land to make it worthwhile.'

Nic chose his words with care. 'You know the owner?'

'It's a company. Prime Property Limited. They specialise in development, though why they picked this place is a mystery. They usually make millions by ruining some gorgeous beach by building posh resorts. It's run by a man called Donald Scallion and his son, Blake. The scorpions, Maggie and I call them.' She flicked him a glance that might have been apologising for her tone. 'There's been…trouble…going back a fair few years now.'

'I'm sorry to hear that.'

It wasn't hard to make that sincere. This would all be so much easier if so much damage had not been done. It had been a mystery to Nic as well why Prime Property had bought the apartment block in the first place but if they hadn't, he wouldn't have seen that file sitting on Donald's desk when he'd come over to discuss another one of those lucrative resort developments they had worked together on more than once. He wouldn't have seen the image of a house he'd only seen in dreams for decades.

No. They'd been nightmares. Glimpses of the absolute security and happiness of his earliest years. People he couldn't touch and the sounds of music and laughter that he couldn't hear because of the invisible barrier that was closing in and suffocating him.

Now that mystery had taken a twist. It was only days ago that Donald had had his own turn to be mystified.

Why on earth would you want it, Nic? It's a millstone.

The land's not big enough for a decent hotel and next door won't sell. We've tried everything, believe me...'

Nobody had to know why. Not yet.

Even Zanna?

Maybe especially Zanna.

The sincerity of his words was still hanging in the air between them. They had diffused the strength of Zanna's anger. That hatred. Flipped it, even?

Yes...the way she was looking at him now suggested that she believed he could help her.

And maybe he could. The image of one of the cards that had shocked him flashed into his head. That hanged man. She'd explained that a sacrifice could be needed sometimes. Something that would be difficult to give up but needed to go because it was blocking progress.

Maybe she just needed to understand...

But how could he persuade her? It was getting difficult to think again as her gaze held his so unwaveringly.

The spell...or force of attraction or whatever it was was gaining power again.

He wanted to persuade her...

He wanted her to understand...

He wanted...*her.*

It was as simple—and as complicated—as that. Maybe everything else could just wait a while longer.

He spoke quietly. 'Try not to worry, Zanna. Things will work themselves out.'

He could see hope in her eyes now. More than that. Faith? In *him*?

That gave him an odd squeeze of something he couldn't identify. Made him want to stand taller. Be a better person?

He could make this right in the end somehow. He could give Zanna what she needed.

Somewhere else.

Somewhere better.

It felt like he was floating, rather than consciously moving closer to Zanna. Close enough to touch. To pick up where they'd left off before the interruption of that phone call but, this time, he moved with a deliberate, delicious intent.

The curl in her hair had been enough to hold the braid together without any kind of fastening, the long end twisted into a perfect ringlet. He slipped his fingers into the braid just above the ringlet and, surprisingly, he could drag them down without meeting any resistance. Her hair was so soft it was easy to tease the coils apart as he worked his way up the long braid. His head was bent close to hers so he could whisper in her ear.

'Maybe you're not the only one who can see into the future.'

He'd reached the base of the silky rope that was virtually separating itself now, so that when he pushed his fingers through the thick waves, they touched the soft skin behind her ears. Impossible not to caress it. Zanna's inward breath was a tiny gasp.

'And perhaps it's a good thing that your aunt is having a break,' he continued. 'That she's found happiness.'

'With a man she's only just met?' Zanna's eyes had drifted shut. There was a tiny frown on her forehead as if she was trying to concentrate and he could see the effort she made to swallow. 'She's old enough to know better.'

Nic's hand was cradling that slim neck, locked in place by a soft tangle of copper waves. He lifted his other hand to trace the outlines of her face—drawing a fingertip with exquisite tenderness over each eyebrow, across her cheekbones, down the line of her jaw and, finally, over her lips.

'And you, Zanna?' he murmured. 'Are *you* old enough to know better?'

The touch of that fingertip was like the path of a slow-burning fuse.

Oh, yes…she was more than old and wise enough to know better. But there was a trail of fire that was sending heat throughout her entire body. She'd kept her eyes closed. Stifled a sigh that could have been one of pure pleasure escaping but the touch on her lips was too much. Her eyelids flickered open and it was a shock to find Nic's face so close to her own. To meet the gaze that was locked onto hers.

This man was a stranger. One who she might never see again after tonight. Only hours ago the idea of a one-night stand would have shocked her but that had been before the reawakening of physical desire that was so strong it was painful.

Deliciously painful.

She'd never felt it this strongly.

Maybe that was because she'd been so closed off since she'd left London. But maybe it was because this man had connected with her on a level that no one else ever had.

He understood her work.

He *got* her.

It felt like they'd already connected on an intimate level. What would it be like to make that connection physical as well as emotional?

His eyes were darkened to black by a desire she recognised instantly because she was sharing it. Her lips
parted to utter the word that should have been the only
sane response to his soft query but no word emerged.
Instead, her tongue touched that fingertip and her lips
closed again, taking it prisoner.

Had he groaned, or had that sound of unbearable need
come from somewhere inside herself? The tension was
morphing into movement and Zanna braced herself for
an explosive release of whatever was containing that
shared desire. This kiss had the potential to be uncon-
trollable and bruising.

But when his lips touched hers, that first time, they
did so with a softness that was heartbreakingly tender.
A totally unexpected gentleness. A tiny gap of time and
the pressure increased to soar into something as uncon-
trollable as she'd anticipated. A taste of something new
and powerful enough to be frightening in its intensity
but that tiny gap of time couldn't be erased.

It had only been a heartbeat of such gentleness but it
had been long enough to win her trust.

She was lost.

Her bedroom.

It was the obvious choice, given that its door was open
just down the hallway and it offered a surface where they
could resume this amazing kiss without the distraction
of having to stay standing.

Taking her hand by threading his fingers through hers,
Nic led Zanna into the room with the painted garden of
a thousand flowers. *Her* room. He felt the sudden tension in her hand that could have become hesitation and
he lifted it smoothly to her neck, keeping their fingers

locked as he kissed her again, his tongue dancing with hers. Then he released her hand, using his own to hook the hem of her top to lift it and peel it off over her head.

The scrap of orange fabric fell to the floor and Zanna felt his hands tracing the knobs at the top of her spine. Shaping the dip of her shoulder blades and ribs and then sliding around and coming up so that his thumbs slid over the curve of her breasts and grazed nipples already so hard they ached. The brief stroke sent an exquisitely painful jolt of sensation that went straight to another ache building much lower, in her core.

Did he sense that? She could feel the strength and purpose in those large hands as they went to the fastening of her jeans. He popped the stud but didn't touch the zipper, merely holding the waistband and pulling to separate the fabric. Zanna heard the groan of the metal teeth parting and then his hands were on her back again, sliding beneath the denim. Beneath the flimsy fabric of her knickers so that he was cupping bare skin.

Dear Lord…she had never done anything like this in her entire life. Sex with a total stranger.

Except he didn't feel like a stranger. Some sort of connection had been there from that first moment, hadn't it? The way he'd looked at her after he'd spent all that time looking at her paintings. A haunted—and haunt-*ing*—look. He'd been touched in a deep place.

A tender place. As tender as that first kiss that had won her trust had been.

Even after months together, Simon had never been able to touch her like this. To touch her body or her soul like this. But Nic *was* still a stranger. A gorgeous stranger who was, clearly, a very accomplished lover. This was new—and dangerous—but instead of making her want to run and hide, it was simply adding another dimension that made it irresistible.

Until now, she'd merely clung to him, the passage of time irrelevant. There was no going back. Zanna wanted it all.

And she wanted it *now*.

'*Nic…*'

The hoarse whisper was a plea that he couldn't refuse. Going as slowly as he might have liked was no longer an option as he felt her hands slide from his neck to fumble with the buckle of his belt.

He could give her exactly what she wanted. What they both wanted.

He caught her hands and held them. Tipped her back towards the bed and let her fall gently, catching her jeans as she slid through his hands to tug them free.

He stripped off his leather jacket, reaching into the pocket in the lining to extract the small, foil packet he knew was there. He saw the way her eyes widened. Did she think he carried a condom because he made a habit of spur-of-the-moment sex with a complete stranger?

The assumption would be wrong. He might have had the opportunity—more than once—but he'd never indulged in meaningless encounters.

Including now. How this had become so meaningful in such a short blink of time was beyond his comprehension but he wasn't going to waste a moment more than it took to shed his clothes by trying to think about it.

He didn't want to think about anything other than this amazing woman. How she would feel and taste as he made love to her. What he would see in those incredible eyes as he took them both into paradise.

CHAPTER FIVE

SPELLBOUND...

Maybe there *was* some kind of magic in the air around here.

That could explain the vivid dream Nic had just woken from and the way his hand reached out to see if the woman he'd just been kissing so intensely in his sleep was actually real. To try and keep feelings he hadn't known existed pumping through his body for a bit longer?

But the other side of the bed was empty. Still warm but empty. As though someone had waved a wand and made Zanna simply vanish into thin air. The fragments of that dream became elusive and evaporated into the air as well. An overall impression of the last hours remained, however, and it had been—easily—the most memorable night of his life so far.

That pleasure also seemed destined to evaporate as Nic opened his eyes and blinked in the morning light. He was alone in a strange bed and he had potentially made a complicated mess of what should have been a straightforward business proposition.

He needed to buy this house and then put a bulldozer through it.

Admittedly, that would come after salvaging some

of the architectural antiques but there was no getting around the fact that he would be destroying this house.

Zanna's house.

Guilt took a hefty swipe at him out of left field. Something about this house had been absorbed enough to get under his skin. Or maybe it was something about Zanna that he'd absorbed.

Tasted and revelled in, more likely.

Mon Dieu...

Nic threw the bed covers back and pushed himself to his feet. He'd find that ivy-covered bathroom and take a quick shower. It would be helpful if he was fully clothed and couldn't smell Zanna Zelenksy on his skin before he initiated the conversation he needed to have with her.

The one where he persuaded her to sell him her house.

There was still no sign of Zanna as Nic went downstairs a short time later and he could feel the emptiness of the big old house. Not that it felt oppressive. However unhelpful it was to think about it, houses like this had real character and this one gave him a picture of an elderly and much-loved grandmother in a rocking chair, quite content with what life had to offer and waiting patiently, knowing that there were more good things to come.

Oblivious to the fact that there was a time for everything to die?

It didn't have to die, though, did it? Nic had the power to save a life here. The ridiculous notion was dismissed with a grunt. This was a *house*. If he wanted to wallow in the analogy of life and death, all he needed to do was focus on the birth of the new and beautiful creation that would take the place of this outdated dwelling.

Yes, Zanna would hate him for it but that wasn't his

problem, was it? It wasn't as if he'd ever see her again after his business was concluded here. His life was in Europe and New Zealand was a whole world away. There were countless other beautiful women in that world. He didn't have to forget about her—she could just join the ranks of others who had briefly touched his life in a memorable fashion.

Except she was nothing like any of the others, was she?

Her beauty was unique with that flame-coloured hair and those extraordinary eyes and milky skin. Her passion was unique, too. Her talent mind-blowing.

She's flaky, he reminded himself. Her unusual bloodline and upbringing put her on the outskirts of what rational people would find acceptable. An outcast, almost.

That wasn't helping to clear his head.

Nic knew what it felt like to be an outcast.

The kitchen was deserted but the French doors to the garden were open so Nic went outside. Into the bricked courtyard garden beyond the French doors. There was a wrought-iron table and chairs here and a clay chiminea that looked as though it was well used as an outside fire. A clear blue sky held the promise of a beautiful day but it was early enough for it to still be a little crisp. Following a brick pathway through an arch that was almost invisible beneath a riot of dark red roses, he turned a corner to find Zanna crouched in a large vegetable garden.

She was wearing those jeans again that clung to her long legs like a second skin but the orange top had gone today. Today's choice was a close-fitting, white singlet and, from this angle, Nic was getting a view of cleavage that took his mind straight back to the pleasures of last night. He wouldn't have thought it was possible but it had been even better the second time…

Layered over the singlet was an unbuttoned, canary-yellow shirt. Another flame colour to tone with her hair and that sharpened the memories of the heat that had been generated between them. The sleeves of the shirt were rolled up to her elbows and her hair was loose—the way he liked it best.

Whoa…the thought had an edge of possessiveness. Permanence, even. How disturbing was that?

And suddenly this had all the awkwardness of the morning after, with the need to escape without causing offence, compounded by the guilt of knowing he had infiltrated a rival's camp under false pretences.

He cleared his throat. 'Hey, there…'

'Hi, Nic.' Zanna stood up with graceful ease, a fistful of greenery in her hand. 'I was finding some parsley. I thought you might like some scrambled eggs for breakfast?'

One of the black cats appeared from beneath the giant leaf of a rambling pumpkin vine to rub against his ankle. Then it flopped onto its back, inviting a tummy scratch.

'I've never seen him do that before.' Zanna stepped carefully between the splashes of colour a row of marigolds made. The other two cats were close on her heels. 'Merlin really likes you.'

'You sound surprised.'

'He's very picky when it comes to people.' Smiling, she kept moving until she stood close enough for her body to touch his. Then she stood on tiptoe and lifted her face. Nic felt the bunch of parsley tickle his ear as she kissed him lightly. 'Just like me.'

The touch of her lips was a spell all on its own. For

a few seconds it was enough to wipe out the awkwardness. Enough to shove that guilt into a mental cupboard
and slam the door. Nic slid his hands beneath the yellow shirt and held Zanna's waist as he kissed her back.
Disturbing echoes of warnings that he was only making
things worse faded to nothing as he was sucked back
into the present moment. The softness of those lips and
the feel of her breasts against his chest...

Zanna felt the parsley slip from her fingers as the kiss
took her straight back to last night.

The most amazing night of her life.

The strength of this attraction and her response to
it was unnerving. Unreal. She could feel herself being
dragged back into a place where nothing else mattered
and no one else existed. Fighting the distraction was difficult but it had to be done. She knew she was risking
too much, too soon, to trust how he made her feel. Not
only that, she'd made a resolution out here in the garden—to talk to Nic about why he was really here. To be
honest about how much they needed the financial help
a historical protection order could provide.

To ask for his help...

'Eggs,' she murmured against Nic's lips. 'Scrambled,'
she added a few seconds later.

'Mmm. With parsley.'

'It's here somewhere.' Zanna slipped free of his arms,
crouching to collect the fallen sprigs.

They walked past the old apple and pear trees on the
small lawn that divided the vegetable garden from the
courtyard beyond the archway. The cats stayed as close
as they could to her feet without getting stepped on.

'Look at that. The grass is almost dead. Which reminds me, I need to give the rata trees a good drink.

This is the best time of day to put some water on. Do you mind waiting a bit longer for breakfast?'

'You don't have to cook for me.'

'I'd like to.' Zanna looked up. 'There's something I'd like to talk to you about.'

He held her gaze. 'I've got something I'd like to talk to you about, too.'

Her heart skipped a beat. Could it be that they were on the same page? That she wouldn't even have to ask for his help because he already intended to offer it?

Leaving the parsley on the arm of a wooden bench seat, Zanna headed for the front of the house and Nic followed her. He needed a few minutes to think about what he was going to say and it was helpful to catalogue more of the degeneration of the building as they walked. The paint wasn't just peeling, it was clearly falling off rotten weatherboard. Guttering was hanging loose and he could see the remnants of broken roof tiles pushing more of it out of place. It wouldn't be that long before the house was uninhabitable.

The hose lay coiled like a solid snake near the outside tap. The sprinkler was inside a galvanised bucket with hose attachments and an old iron key. He held it up.

'Lost something?'

'No. It's the spare for the front door. Maggie's a great one for losing keys and she's convinced nobody would think of looking in the bucket. Leave it there. The sprinkler's all we need at the moment.'

She showed him where to place it. They stood under the rata trees amidst a steady drift of leaves and one of the cats took a swipe as a leaf fell nearby.

'Good grief…it's *raining* leaves.' Nic was staring up at the canopy of the tree. He shaded his eyes with his hand, already well into a damage-locating frame of mind but this was an unexpected bonus. 'What's *that*?'

'What?'

Nic moved to touch the trunk. Nearly hidden by the twisted bark was a large hole.

'If that hole was made by a beetle, I hope I don't come across it. It's *huge*.'

'There's another one.' Nic pointed further up the trunk. He stepped out of sight behind the tree. 'And there's more.'

'No wonder the trees are looking sick. They're infested.'

Nic's face appeared again. 'I don't think it's beetles.' Going back to the first hole at head level, he ran his fingers around its edge.

'These holes have been deliberately drilled,' he said quietly. 'And I'm guessing they've been filled with some kind of poison.'

Zanna could feel the blood drain from her face. 'Who would do something that awful?' she whispered. 'These trees are so special. A lot of people supported the bid to have them protected. There was quite a fuss about it and it was an election year so the city council had to take some notice.'

'How long ago did that happen?'

'Ages. Before I went to London. Maybe five or six years ago? Just after the apartment block was sold and we started having trouble, I guess.'

'If someone had been upset about the decision to have the trees protected and did something, it's more than long enough for poison to have an effect, even on such big trees. Let's have a look at the other one and see what we're up against.'

We?

Was this a declaration of whose side Nic was on?

The shock was wearing off by the time they returned to the kitchen but Zanna didn't bother collecting the parsley on the way past. She felt sick. Grief and anger twisted themselves into a painful knot in her belly.

'There's no hope for them, is there? Either of them.'

'I wouldn't think so.' Nic was watching her intently. 'Someone's done a thorough job.'

'What's it going to be next? Will they poison the cats to try and drive us away?'

He gave her an odd look. 'Nobody's going to poison your cats, Zanna.'

'You don't know that. They warned me that they'd win in the end.'

'Who?'

'The scorpions. Prime Property. The owners of the horrible apartment block next door. They want this land and, clearly, they're going to use any means they can to get it.'

He turned away from her and paced a couple of steps as though he didn't want to have any more to do with this situation.

Well…why would he? He'd been sent here to do a simple job and it was suddenly getting complicated and unpleasant.

What if last night had only been a one-night stand as far as Nic was concerned? If the prospect of emotional involvement sent him running for the hills? Maybe he was appalled at the thought of dealing with a weeping woman.

Zanna might be more than a little upset but she wasn't about to burst into tears.

She was angry. And it was too easy to turn at least a

part of that anger onto someone who wanted to simply walk away. What had happened to that *we* he'd mentioned?

When Nic turned back to face her, he knew his face was grim. This was the time to tell her a few home truths. That the trees would have to be felled. That the house was disintegrating around her. That the only sensible thing to do was to take an offer that would be generous enough to make it easy to move on to something that wouldn't generate increasingly stressful problems.

'No, they're not.' Tension made the words come out as almost a snap. 'They're not even in the picture any more. But—'

'How would *you* know?' Zanna's voice rose as she interrupted him. The flash in her eyes made him remember just how passionate this woman could be. And she was being threatened now, albeit in an underhanded way that had probably happened a long time ago. It might have had nothing to do with the Scallions' determination to acquire the property. Maybe there was someone out there who simply didn't like trees.

'Because…' Nic ran his fingers through his hair, blowing out a breath as he looked away from her again. 'Zanna…I…' He was struggling to think of what to say. *Because I own that apartment block now?* He could see exactly where that would go. She would see him as no more than the replacement of a Prime Property representative. Somebody determined to force her to give up her property. And she'd be right.

It would hurt her and…dammit, maybe it had to happen but he didn't have to like hurting her, did he?

And…maybe—just maybe—there was a way around this. A solution…

He could feel the way she was staring at him but the idea was embryonic and there was no point even suggesting it if it wasn't possible. He wasn't even thinking about her now. His mind was racing. He had a lot of work to do before he would know if this idea had merit.

Zanna could feel her eyes narrowing. He was looking for an excuse to get away, wasn't he? Fine. She had other people to worry about.

'How am I going to break this news to Maggie?' She didn't expect an answer. 'She'll be heartbroken. She'll feel like she has to come home and that'll spoil a trip of a lifetime for her.'

'Zanna… Listen to me. I—'

But she didn't want to hear any more of his well-intentioned reassurances. Not when he didn't actually care. Or have a clue how serious this was. She held up a hand as a signal to stop him speaking. She needed time to think. To get past this visceral reaction and plan what to do about it. A glance at the wall clock made the means of finding that time easy.

'It's nearly nine o'clock. You'll have to excuse me. I have to open the shop.'

She wasn't going to let him say anything, was she? His best intentions of letting her know that he wasn't the person she thought he was and that he had his own interests in this property were fading with every interruption.

'I've got things I need to do as well.' Nic followed her gaze at the clock, then he looked at the door.

Zanna shook her head. He really couldn't wait to get away, could he?

'Did you need anything else from me?'

A split second of searing eye contact reminded her of what he'd needed from her last night. What she'd needed from *him*. But it was gone so quickly she could have been mistaken.

'What?'

'The house. Did you need anything else?' He would need to file a report on the historical value of the house, wouldn't he? 'Like any documents or photos?'

Oddly, he blinked as if he had no idea what she was talking about. Then he closed his eyes slowly and nodded.

Of course. He was well down a new track mentally but Zanna still thought he was here on behalf of a historical protection society to document the merits of preserving this old house. And, thanks to the shock of finding the trees had been poisoned, she was so focused on the immediate issue that she would automatically block any suggestion of stepping back to look at the bigger picture.

Nic could see it very clearly and it gave him a completely different angle on which he might be able to base his pitch. He already had a dozen things buzzing in his own head that needed attention. They could talk later. When she'd had some time to calm down and he was armed with more information.

'Yeah… A few photos might be useful. I'll use the camera on my phone.'

Disappointment was just as strong as her anger. Painful, even. He would walk out the door any minute now and that might be the last time she ever saw him. She couldn't help the chilliness of her next words.

'That's not very professional, is it?'

'Sorry?'

'I would have thought that an official report would need more than that.' She gave an incredulous huff. 'How many jobs like this have you actually done, Nic?'

Good grief…how frustrating was this? He couldn't afford to tell her the truth now. She'd throw him out on his ear and he'd never get a second chance. 'I do know what I'm doing, Zanna.'

She'd annoyed him now. Oh, help… How had things changed so dramatically in such a short time? It seemed like only minutes ago that the world had stopped turning while they'd been kissing in the vegetable garden and now here they were, practically glaring at each other. This clearly wouldn't be a good time to ask for his help, then.

A flash of pure desperation made her open her mouth to do just that or at least to ask if she was going to see him again but Nic wasn't even looking at her. Was he trying to work out how to access the camera on his phone?

Words failed her.

What would she say? *It was nice to meet you* or *Thanks for last night and how 'bout you write a report that will help me save my house?*

Would he think that she'd offered him her body as some kind of bribe?

She could feel her colour rising. It was her turn to look away now. To eye the door as a means of escape.

'Well…you'll know where to find me if you need anything else, I guess. Just pull the front door closed when you're done. It'll lock itself.'

CHAPTER SIX

ZANNA HEARD THE ROAR of a powerful motorbike being revved a short time later as she finished lighting the candles on the counter.

So he was gone.

He'd made her feel so special.

Desirable.

Talented.

Loved…

A few hours. No more than a blip in a lifetime but she knew she would never forget those hours for as long as she lived.

They had been precious and they should be enough.

He'd given her two amazing gifts. He'd reawakened desire. So effectively that Zanna knew it was going to be possible to fall in love again. He'd shown her that there was an oasis in the desert it felt like her heart had become.

And he'd given her faith in her art again. Her real art.

Either one of those gifts were priceless. She should be feeling enormously grateful instead of this crushing sense of loss that she would never see Nic again. An almost desperate longing for more…

People came and went in the shop. Being so close to

the central city, there were a lot of hotels nearby and tourists were drawn to the anachronism of the old, dilapidated house that didn't belong where it was any more. They didn't buy much but at least the distraction was enough to stop her thinking so much about Nic.

The day still dragged, however, and Zanna had to try hard to keep focused. She smiled at the tourists and wondered if stocking a few souvenir items like kiwi toys and paua shells might help the profit margin. No. Maggie would hate that. She still mourned the time when Spellbound had been more about the tearoom and the people who'd come together here.

But they both had to make a living. More than make a living. Somehow, they'd have to find enough money to deal with the trees. To do something more than temporarily patch up the worst of the damage time was doing to the house. Manuka honey that was known for its medicinal properties wouldn't be so out of place amongst their stock. Zanna needed to ring her essential oil supplier among others today. Maybe one of them would know a reliable source for the honey.

By late afternoon, she'd had enough. The arrival of the teenage girls who'd been here yesterday made her spirits sink even further. They weren't genuine customers, any more than Nic had been. And they'd been in the shop when he'd arrived so it was impossible not to think of him. To cast a glance at the door with the forlorn hope that history might repeat itself and he would be the next person to appear.

'Jen wanted another look at that book of spells,' the dark-haired girl explained. 'The little blue one.'

'Knock yourselves out.'

It was quiet for a few minutes. Zanna breathed in

the lavender of the oil she had chosen today in the hope of calming her mind. It didn't seem to be working. She still felt churned up about the discovery of the poisoned trees. Maybe she should burn a bit of sage to eliminate any lingering negative energy. Except that it was more likely that a good part of that uncomfortable sensation was stemming from knowing she wouldn't be seeing Nic again and sage wasn't going to help.

'Hey, this is cool.' The girl sounded excited. 'You can make Stevie call you, Jen. Look—it's easy. First you just have to choose a colour that represents him.'

'How do I do that?' The blonde girl called Jen directed her question at Zanna rather than her friend.

'There's a colour chart in the book.' Zanna automatically went to help them, taking the book and flicking through the pages. 'Here. You choose a colour that represents his characteristics.'

'Stevie's orange for sure,' Jen declared, moments later. 'Able to make friends readily. Generally good-natured, likeable and social.'

Orange was her favourite colour. Would she pick it to represent Nic's characteristics? Likeable was too insipid a word to apply to him. With his beauty combined with that confidence and ability to display tenderness, the attraction went way beyond *liking* him. It would be all too easy to fall head over heels in love with him.

Maybe she already had…

'I reckon he's red,' her friend countered. 'They form opinions rapidly, express them boldly and choose sides quickly but may be swayed easily from one viewpoint to another.'

Nic could be red. He was certainly bold. It had felt like he'd chosen her side, too. Had he changed his mind when it had become apparent that the road might get a bit too rocky?

'Stevie's not loud enough to be red.'

'He's your boyfriend, I guess. Or he will be—if this spell works.' The girl grinned at Zanna. '*Does* it really work?'

'I haven't tried it.'

Maybe she should…

'So what do I do now that I've picked the colour?' Jen sounded breathless.

'You've got a photo of Stevie, haven't you?'

'Yeah…I cut it out of the school magazine.'

'Okay, then. You need some orange thread and an orange jellybean and the photo. You tie the thread around the photo and leave it for at least one hour to absorb his energy. Then you use the same thread to tie the jellybean to your phone.'

'And then what?'

'And then he rings you up and asks for a date, of course.'

'Oh…' She looked at Zanna with a hopeful expression. 'Do you sell jellybeans?'

'No. There's a petrol station down the end of Rata Avenue. They'll have some.'

'Hey, thanks so much.' Jen's smile was shy. 'I'll let you know if it works.'

'Good luck.'

With the excited energy of the young girls gone, the shop became almost oppressive and time slid by even more slowly.

What did you do with massive, dying trees? Would they turn into skeletons that would make the house look like a Halloween prop or would some official person come and say that they were required to have them taken down because they could present a danger to the public?

How much would that cost?

She wouldn't tell Maggie about it, Zanna decided. She couldn't bring herself to dampen the joy her aunt was experiencing. She'd been left in charge. More than that, because Maggie had signed a power of attorney, giving her absolute control over everything to do with the house and shop while she was overseas. And the trees had probably been on death row for years. A few more months wouldn't make any difference.

It was simply another obstacle to overcome. It wasn't the final straw—not by a long shot.

Zanna picked up the book of spells the girls had left on the counter and went to put it back on the display shelf. She could close up soon and go back into the house. She needed to do some baking. The organic chocolate-chip cookies were always popular. So was the banana bread. Would it be better than being in the shop with the ghost of Nic's energy lurking?

No. It would probably be worse. There could be far more of that energy lingering in the hallway where he'd given her that first gift of knowing that her art was meaningful…

In the kitchen where she'd read his cards…

In her bedroom…

Zanna closed her eyes, trying to gather some inner strength.

And then she heard it. The roar of a powerful engine in the street.

The silence that followed was enough for her to be able to hear her own heartbeat as it picked up speed and thumped against her ribs.

He'd come back.

The joy of that knowledge took her breath away.

The bell on the door jangled.

'Hey…' Nic's tone was light but there was an underlying tension that was still making it impossible to breathe. 'You're due to close, aren't you?'

Zanna could only nod. She stared as he stepped closer. He had his helmet tucked under his arm but he had something else in his other hand. Another helmet.

'Put this on,' Nic directed. 'And come with me. There's something I want to show you.'

Zanna had never been on a motorbike. She had no idea where Nic might be planning to take her or what it was he wanted to show her.

This was crazy but she felt her hand reaching out to take the helmet.

It didn't feel like she had a choice. Or maybe that choice had already been made, in that instant when she'd invited Dominic Brabant to step into her life.

This time, Zanna could feel as well as hear the engine as Nic kick-started it into life with her sitting on the back of the bike. She'd been so sure that she'd never see him again when she'd heard it only that morning but the shocked delight of hearing him return had blown that misery out of the water.

Now she had the rich rumble of the huge machine between her legs and her arms tightly wound around Nic's waist with her chest pressed against his back. It felt dangerous and wildly exciting and incredibly sexy. She could see the road flashing past the wheels and feel the ends of her hair whipping in the wind. The first time he leaned into a corner and she felt the bike tipping was terrifying but then they were upright again and she was safe.

Because she was with Nic.

He'd come back and she felt safe again.

It took very little time to weave through the rush-hour traffic of the central city and then cut across one of the outer suburbs. This was the green belt where the wealthy could have lifestyle blocks and indulge hobbies like breeding alpacas or making boutique wines. A gorgeous, lush valley with hills and a river and pockets of native bush like small forests.

Halfway along the winding road the bike slowed and turned through some old, ornate wooden gates. They rolled past a small lake bordered by weeping willows that had a faded, wooden rowboat moored by a miniature jetty. An ancient, stone building that might have been stables long ago had a backdrop of tall, native trees but at the end of the pebbled driveway, there was nothing but a smooth stretch of grass like an inner-city park.

What on earth did he want to show her?

A perfect spot for a romantic picnic? It seemed unlikely that the small storage compartment on the bike could be hiding a hamper.

Climbing off the bike, Zanna was already missing the contact of Nic's body but his hands brushed her neck and jawline as he helped ease the helmet off her head. Even better, he then dipped his head and kissed her.

Long and slow. With that mind-blowing tenderness that had captured her heart so completely.

It was hard to suck in a breath. Even harder to think of something to say. She could feel her lips curving into a smile.

'Nice. But you could have shown me that anywhere.'

He took her hand. 'Come with me.'

They didn't stop until they'd walked up the gentle slope to reach the middle of the grassed area. Nic was still holding her hand but he wasn't looking at her. His gaze travelled slowly to take in the whole scene from top of the hill to the lake and the patch of forest and the old stables. His nod was satisfied.

'It's as good as they told me it was,' he said. 'Perfect.'

'It's certainly gorgeous,' she agreed. 'Idyllic. But what's it perfect for?'

'A house. This land is for sale. Not on the open market yet but when it is, it'll be marketed internationally. It's special, isn't it?'

Zanna blinked. Was Nic thinking of buying this property? 'You're going to build a house? You want to *live* here?'

His expression was unreadable. 'The idea of having a New Zealand summer instead of a European winter every year is certainly attractive but, no, I'm not thinking of building a house.' It looked like he was taking a deep breath. 'I was thinking of helping someone to *shift* a house.'

Zanna's jaw dropped. An image of Rata House on this land appeared in her head with astonishing clarity. With space all around instead of being dwarfed by high-rise buildings. Air to breathe that wasn't full of the fumes of inner-city traffic. A garden that could include a whole orchard instead of a couple of tired fruit trees. The serenity of a view that encompassed a tranquil lake and cool, shady forest. Stables that could be a gallery or beautiful tea rooms.

A dream scenario but…it simply wasn't possible.

The shake of her head felt violent enough to send a

painful twinge down her spine. She let go of Nic's hand as if it was burning her and stepped backwards to create more distance.

'No...'

'I know it's a big idea.' Nic was watching her carefully. 'You need a bit of time to get used to it.'

Zanna shook her head again. 'You're wrong. It's not a new idea. Someone suggested it years ago and Maggie was really upset about it. She said the damage would be too great and the spirit of joy from all the lives that had touched the house would be broken. It's what it is because it's *where* it is.'

'No.' His gaze was steady. Compelling. 'It's what it is because of the lives that have touched it and that's happened because of the people who live in it.' Nic's voice was quiet. As calm as his face. 'But it's dying slowly because of where it is. Getting more and more hemmed in and out of place and you must know how much it's crying out for some restoration. Wouldn't it be better to save it? Shifting it would be the ideal opportunity to repair and strengthen it. You and Maggie could still live in it. Still have the shop and the tea rooms. The people who know the house could still visit. It's not that far.'

'It's too big. It couldn't be done.'

'Anything's possible. I have a mate—Pete Wellesley —who's a specialist in shifting houses. He owes me a favour. I have tickets on hold and he could fly over from Sydney first thing tomorrow to have a look. He's already seen the photographs I took and he reckons it's doable. They'd take off the roof and turret and cut the house into pieces, separating the floors. Then they'd put new foundations down on the new site and put it all back together. With enough people on the job it would only take a few weeks.'

'It would cost a fortune.'

'The land it's on is worth a fortune. I could make sure you get enough to cover any costs.'

'Why?' Zanna's head was spinning. There was too much to think about. 'Why are you doing all this?'

He hesitated for a long moment. 'I want to help. And I know what's going to happen.'

It was what she'd wanted, wasn't it? To persuade him to help? This wasn't what she'd had in mind, though. And there was something ominous in his tone.

'What do you mean—what's going to happen?'

'I've been talking to people on the city council today.'

Of course he had. It was what he'd been employed for.

'And?'

'There's been an unofficial vote that could become official very shortly. The council feels that the house is in the way of what could be an important development for the inner city. Their words were that it was inter-fering with their approved developmental mission for the inner city. They could enforce a sale to them and the value they would assign is likely to be a lot less than what it would be worth if you sold it privately. Also, any legal costs of trying to object would be taken out of a compensation package.' He was holding her horrified gaze. 'The clock's ticking, Zanna. Time's running out.'

She was so scared.

Oh, she was holding herself admirably straight and the tilt of her chin suggested she would fight to the death for something—or someone—she loved but Nic could see the fear in her eyes.

The need to protect her was overwhelming. The beautiful thing was that he could do that without hurting his own interests. This was a win-win situation for everybody involved. He'd spent the day networking harder than he ever had on a project. Finding the right people to talk to and calling in favours from all over the show but he'd pulled it together. The germ of the idea he'd had that morning was coming together so smoothly that it felt like it was meant to happen.

Just as surely as Zanna Zelensky had been meant to come into his life?

Right on the heels of the need to protect came the urge to comfort and reassure. It took only a step or two to fold Zanna into his arms and hold her close. She needed time, that was all. The solution was here—for all of them. It was a stroke of extremely good fortune—and his inside contacts in the real estate industry—that had made this piece of the countryside available and Zanna had seen it without being prejudiced by knowing the agenda. She would see the location of her beloved house through a very different lens when he took her back there now because she wouldn't be able to help imagining it here.

He knew better than to push too hard. This was the time to back off. As counter-intuitive as it seemed on the surface, he needed to actually distract Zanna and let the concept take root subconsciously. He could take her out to dinner somewhere. Take her home and make love to her again. And again.

His arms tightened around her.

It might be part of an automatic game plan but it was also a bonus he wasn't about to resist, despite the niggle of the guilt that hadn't been entirely vanquished by working on this superb solution.

He hadn't said a word that wasn't the truth. He just hadn't told her the whole story—that the development the council members were so excited about was the concept of his music school. That planning permission would be a given and that enforcing a sale of Rata House would only be set into action if he had problems acquiring the necessary extra land.

He could wait and purchase the land from the council, probably for less than he intended to offer now. He was doing *this* part purely for Zanna. He'd also told the truth when he'd said the house was slowly dying. They couldn't afford the repairs it needed and they were unlikely to get council permission for any major structural work even if they could have afforded it. He did want to help. To look after her. He knew better than to put her back up by voicing the desire, however. This was a woman who could look after herself and instinct told him it was going to be tricky to win her complete trust.

While he couldn't allow it to jeopardise his project, the desire to win her trust was surprisingly strong.

And bubbling somewhere beneath the fire he'd thrown all those irons into today was the idea that it might be simple to merely fudge a timeframe. If he'd acquired the apartment block *after* buying the Zelenksy property then nobody—well, a particular somebody that he was holding close right now—could accuse him of having a conflict of interest.

Could it even be considered a conflict when it was such a perfect solution?

Yes, he was treading a fine line but it wasn't the first time. The biggest risks often generated the biggest rewards.

Time *was* running out. He'd allowed himself a week

to sort this project. It was only day two and if he could pull it off, he was on track so that everybody could win. Even better, he would have a whole week with Zanna that he could remember for the rest of his life.

'Let's go home,' he whispered into her ear. 'And sleep on it.'

Nic wouldn't let her talk about it that evening.

'Wait until you have all the information you need,' he said. 'Until the idea stops spinning in your head for long enough to see it properly. I've given Pete the nod to jump on a plane in the morning. He'll be able to answer questions better than me. Then it'll be time to talk.'

He distracted her, instead. With food and wine, at a gorgeous restaurant that had beautiful music and a dance floor.

It was no surprise that this astonishing man could dance so well. What was a surprise was the sheer bliss of drifting in his arms to the music. Of being with him.

Of wanting to be with him…for ever?

That made her head spin as much as the crazy idea of shifting her home to the most idyllic location possible.

They were dreams. Too good to be believable.

Either of them.

But, oh…it was heaven to play with them for a while.

He wasn't going to let her sleep on the concept in a hurry either, when they finally returned to Zanna's bed.

They were comfortable with each other's bodies now. Enough to touch and explore and discover new things. Nic's leisurely tracing of her body came to a halt as his fingers brushed the stone in her navel.

'I meant to ask last night,' he murmured. 'What is it?'

'A topaz,' she told him. 'My birth stone.'

'It's perfect for you. It's got the colours of flames in it. Just like your hair.' He stroked a soft curl back from her face. 'And your eyes...' He moved in to kiss her softly and she felt her lips curl beneath his.

'Why are you smiling?'

'This stone is supposed to enhance emotional balance.'

His lips were so close she could feel the word more than hear it. 'And?'

'And I'm not feeling particularly balanced right now.'

There was a moment of absolute stillness then. As if the world was holding its breath—waiting for her to tell him that she was in love with him?

She couldn't. Not yet. It was all too new to trust and too big to mess with. But it was hanging there, unspoken.

'Same,' Nic whispered.

Another moment of stillness could have made the atmosphere way too intense but then she felt his lips curl into a smile.

'I think I like it.'

Zanna was more than ready to sink into the kiss. 'Same.'

CHAPTER SEVEN

Sleep had finally come but the first fingers of light from a new dawn found Zanna awake again.

Her head was still spinning.

Or maybe it wasn't. Maybe her head was just fine and it was the world spinning around her. Changing its axis. Presenting her with possibilities that should be elusive and only dreams but were actually close enough to touch.

Nic was close enough to touch. Sprawled on his back with one arm flung above his head. For a long minute Zanna simply gazed at him. She loved the rumpled disorder of his wavy hair and the tangle of dark lashes kissing the top of those chiselled cheekbones. His lips were slightly parted and so deliciously soft looking amidst the dark shadowing of his jaw she had to consciously stop herself reaching out to touch them.

Instead, she slipped quietly from the bed. She needed a bit of time to herself to walk around the house and think. To compose a careful text message that wouldn't panic Maggie and make her think she had to come home but would still let her know that there was some urgency to make some big decisions.

It was Saturday, which meant she could close the shop

at midday and that would be about the time Nic returned from collecting Pete from the airport. They had the rest of the day before Pete's return flight to Sydney but the pressure was going to be on for her to make some kind of decision by the time he left, at least on whether or not she might be interested.

Of course she was interested. The idea didn't even seem so farfetched any more by the time she was introduced to Pete Wellesley. Nic's friend made Zanna think of a pirate, with his dreadlocked hair and a ring through one ear. With his easy smile and dancing eyes, it was impossible not to like him.

He had nothing like the controlled, bad-boy biker vibe that Nic had exuded at first sight but the combination of the two personalities was a force to be reckoned with. Pete's hint of mischief balanced Nic's intensity. Nic's attention to detail focused Pete's enthusiasm. She felt safe with Nic and inspired by Pete. They were both so confident and focused on the job at hand and they both seemed experts in their fields.

'We went through architectural school in London together,' Nic told her. 'And we both did a course on building heritage conservation. Pete took it further and did the thesis for his master's on relocation.'

'Did you do a thesis, too?' Zanna added a jar of olives and some cheese to the array of food she'd put together for a picnic-style lunch in the courtyard garden.

'His was on how to make money,' Pete told her.

'It was about blending modern architecture to the immediate physical environment,' Nic corrected.

'AKA how to make money.' Pete raised the bottle of beer he was holding in a toast. 'And good on you, mate. You do what you do very well.'

Zanna frowned. 'I thought you were an expert in *old* houses.'

The two men exchanged a glance. Then Nic caught Zanna's questioning gaze.

'My career has been all about developing luxury international coastal resorts and boutique hotels in the last few years but this is a special project,' he said.

His eyes added another message. That it was more than special. That he was completely invested in it because it was about someone he loved.

Her breath caught—held by the wave of emotion that swept through her. How long did it normally take two people to fall in love? If it happened this fast, did that make it an illusion?

A dream that she would have to wake up from?

The dream of saving her house might have taken an unexpected twist but, as the day wore on, it began to seem more and more possible.

'Turn of the century, you said?' With lunch and the introductory process complete, Pete had thrown himself into a thorough examination of the house, which had involved taking a lot of photographs and measurements. Having spent most of the afternoon exploring every inch, inside and out, they were finally back in the kitchen, sitting around the table as Pete entered data into his computer program. 'Do you know the exact year?'

Zanna shook her head. 'Nic seemed to think it was later than 1900 because of the Marseilles tiles. Does it matter?'

'Building styles varied a bit. If platform framing was used, which I expect it was, it means that the walls for each floor were framed separately above and below the first-floor joists. That makes it much easier to separate the floors for removal.'

Nerves kicked in again at that point. Alarm bells, even. 'I still can't believe you can chop a house up without doing enormous damage somewhere along the line.' There would be no going back if she agreed to this. No way to repair the damage if it turned out to be a mistake.

'But you saw the pictures of Pete's recent projects over lunch,' Nic reminded her, gesturing towards the tablet computer that was the only equipment Pete had brought with him other than a laser device for taking measurements. 'Even blowing up the images you couldn't tell where they'd been put back together.'

'This is a big house,' Pete said. 'It would need to go into six or maybe eight pieces. The only thing I can say for certain will get damaged are the roof tiles but you would have been looking at a replacement roof within a few years anyway.'

'That's true. There's been a leak in one of the spare bedrooms recently.' And they would never be able to afford a new roof so the damage would only accelerate.

'Slate would look good,' Nic suggested. 'Even better than the tiles.'

'It's wider than eighteen metres,' Pete continued, 'so it would need cutting twice. Where we cut depends on where the load-bearing walls are inside and any particular features that need protecting. Like the staircase.'

'And the turret,' Nic put in. 'That's got to be protected.'

'We'd remove that separately.' Pete was still tapping notes into his computer. 'Take it off with a crane. We'd separate the top storey. The ceiling of the ground floor stays with the floor of the upper storey so we'd have to put in bracing beams to hold the shape of the lower rooms together.' He stared at the screen for a long moment and then looked up to flash a grin at Zanna. 'It's doable,' he pronounced. 'And I have to say I'd relish the challenge. But you're lucky that those trees have been killed.'

Lucky? Was he serious?

'Those trees are hundreds of years old. Protected. There's nothing lucky about losing them.'

Pete raised an eyebrow in Nic's direction before turning towards Zanna. 'If they were still healthy there'd be no way you'd be allowed to take them down, and without taking them down there'd be no way of moving the house because of the high-rises around it and the big trees in the park.' He turned back to Nic. 'Are you going to give me another ride on that shiny toy you've hired and take me out to see the potential site for relocation? They're the last boxes I need to fill to get an estimate of costs.'

And then it would be a done deal.

'Sure.' Nic looked as though he was on the point of high-fiving Pete. 'And then I can drop you back at the airport. You okay with that, Zanna? I'll be a couple of hours.' He got to his feet, heading towards where he'd left the bike helmets on the floor near the French doors.

'No.' Zanna was surprised to hear the word coming out of her mouth but not nearly as startled as the two men looked.

'No,' she repeated, more firmly. 'I don't think I am okay with any of this.'

An awkward silence fell as Nic met her gaze. And then another significant glance passed between the men.

'How 'bout I meet you outside?' Pete suggested quietly.

A single nod and then they were alone.

'What's going on, Zanna?' Nic was careful not to sound impatient. 'I thought you were on board. That you liked the idea.'

It had felt like a done deal, in fact. The estimate of costs was not important. Nic was more than prepared to cover whatever it was going to cost. The goalposts were in sight and he could smell success.

'It's all happening too fast. I haven't had a chance to think about it properly, let alone talk to Maggie. I feel like I'm being railroaded. Bullied, even… And I made a promise to myself that I would never let that happen again.'

What on earth was she talking about?

'What do you mean…*again*? I'm not trying to railroad you. Quite the opposite. I didn't even talk about it last night because I wanted to give you time to think about it without feeling pressured, but…' He ran his fingers through his hair. It was a risk but if he didn't push things here, there was a real danger of all the work he'd done so far being for nothing. 'There *is* a time limit. You need my help and I can't be here much longer. We've only a few days to get it all sorted.'

'I wasn't talking about you.'

Something in Zanna's eyes gave Nic that feeling of wanting to protect her again. Of wanting to make everything all right. For a heartbeat it was actually stronger than what he wanted for himself.

Long enough for him to hold her gaze and close the gap between them. To take her hands and hold them.

'So tell me who you are talking about. Trust me, Zanna.' She wouldn't be disappointed if she did. He'd make sure of that. 'Please.'

'That's the problem,' she whispered. 'Trust…'

Nic knew that Pete was waiting for him outside beside the motorbike. Probably impatient to get going and get this project kicked into some real action. As impatient as he was himself.

But this was important.

Vital, in fact.

He led Zanna towards the table and invited her to sit. He was ready to listen and solve any problem that was about to make an appearance. He was good at that. Not that Zanna seemed in a hurry to get to the point.

'I never thought I could make a living out of my art,' she told him. 'It was a dream that seemed too good to believe in. I didn't even go to art school for years. I did a degree in art conservation first. I imagined myself working in a museum and getting up close and personal with the work of famous artists.'

Nic made an encouraging noise.

'But the more time I spent around art, the more I loved doing my own work. It was my best friend, Brie, who persuaded me to do a postgraduate art degree in London, and Maggie took out another mortgage on the house to pay for it. She'd always believed in me, she said, and when I was rich and famous I could pay her back.'

Nick waited, slotting away the information that there was more than one mortgage on the house. No problem. He could make the offer even more attractive.

'Brie came to London with me. She scored a job in a big gallery and that was how I met Simon. Brie started a campaign to get him interested in me. He was a big wheel in the European art scene and the careers of artists he picked as up and coming really took off.'

Nic didn't like the way she closed her eyes and took a deep breath. He had the feeling that this Simon was important to Zanna and he didn't like that. Good grief, was that unpleasant prickle of sensation jealousy?

'Brie's campaign worked a treat,' Zanna said. 'He chose me for more than just my art. We were living together in a matter of weeks. Talking about getting married.'

Yep. It was jealousy.

'He really wanted to help my career but he said that the kind of work I did—the flowers and cats and everything—was craft more than art. I needed to try something more contemporary. Edgier.'

Nic snorted. The man was an idiot. Had he not really looked at Zanna's paintings? Could he not appreciate how they could make people feel? Not that he knew anything much about art but surely the emotional impact was what mattered?

'It didn't feel right,' Zanna continued quietly. 'But this was my best friend and my fiancé who were trying to persuade me and I was in love so, of course, I trusted them. I let them push me in a direction I would never have chosen for myself and they pushed hard. I spent months working on a collection for an exhibition. Huge paintings. I must have gone to every old cemetery in London to choose the gravestones I based the work around.'

'Gravestones?' Nic's jaw dropped. 'You had a theme of death in your work?'

'Pretty much.' Zanna shrugged. 'It was edgy. Dark. Art, not craft.'

Nic thought of the rich colours in Zanna's paintings. The warmth. The feeling of movement and life captured in those sketches of the cats.

'They didn't know you very well, did they?'

Zanna's breath came out in a huff. 'Maybe they knew me very well. Maybe the campaign had never been about getting my career as an artist off the ground.' She shook her head. 'I'm not sure I really believe they set out to destroy me. Maybe it was a game that took on a life of its own. Or maybe it came from a subconscious need to get me out of the way. Anyway—' her voice became harsh '—it worked. They got what they wanted out of it.'

'Which was?'

'Each other, of course. The humiliation of the awful reviews my exhibition got was only part of it. I went home after a particularly horrible day to find Simon and Brie in bed together.'

'*Merde*...' Nic wanted to find this Simon idiot and ruin him. The way he'd tried to ruin Zanna. 'So that was why you left London?'

She nodded. 'I came home to the one person I knew I could trust absolutely. To the place I felt safe.'

Her refuge. He'd known there was something huge behind her use of that particular word. It had been that glimpse of her vulnerability that had touched something unexpected deep within him. Had been the catalyst for everything that had filled the time they'd had together since.

And he was expecting her to pick that refuge up and shake it in the hope of keeping something so precious safe. He was asking her to trust him when he wasn't even being entirely honest with her.

He could see something in himself in that moment that he wasn't proud of and the sensation was even more unpleasant than any twinge of jealousy. He'd had moments in his life when he'd hated himself and this took him back to feeling inadequate. Totally powerless. Angry instead of sad that he was losing something—no, some*one*—precious to him.

He tightened his grip on Zanna's hands. Held her gaze. If he could put this right, he might know that it was possible to do more than let her know it was okay to trust someone. He might discover that it was possible to be a better person himself and escape from a legacy that he'd thought would always haunt him. But he'd gotten in so deep—how could he even start to fix things without doing more damage? If Zanna thought she had misplaced her trust again, would she hide behind a protective barrier for the rest of her life?

She deserved better than that. How could you truly love someone if complete trust was missing? She deserved the chance to give her love without reservation and the man who was lucky enough to win that love deserved to know all of Zanna because she was so special. Unique.

'I need to take Pete out to see the land,' he said slowly. 'But that doesn't mean I'm trying to push you in a direction you don't want to go. If you decide you don't want to do this, that's fine.'

He meant every word. He might have the power to make sure he got what he wanted here but if it was at the expense of abusing the trust he was asking Zanna to put in him then he would back off. He would find another way to create a memorial to his parents.

Zanna nodded. 'I'll try and get hold of Maggie and talk to her about this. See how she feels.'

The timing of Maggie's phone call couldn't have been better.

Nic had been gone for more than two hours and Zanna had been pacing, her mind darting back and forth over a confusing spectrum.

Nic was nothing like Simon. He wasn't trying to change her into someone she wasn't. He was offering to help secure the place where she was herself most of all. He *got* her work. Unconditionally. It didn't matter a damn to him if the people who knew about art dismissed it as craft.

If she went ahead with this new plan, she would have a studio in an idyllic location that would be safe to live in for ever. With a business that could support her even if she never had the courage to try selling her work.

And he'd been right. He wasn't pushing her into agreeing with his idea. He'd backed off completely to give her space to think about it. Filled that space with the reassurance that it was safe to trust him, in fact.

To love him?

He wasn't Simon and he'd made her feel amazing things again. She would only hurt herself if she let Simon's legacy destroy something this beautiful and, if she let that happen this time, she could be setting a precedent that meant she would never truly trust anyone again.

She wanted it to happen. Both the house relocation and possibly finding a relationship that was strong enough to overcome the obvious logistical problems like living on different sides of the world, but it was terrifying to be getting this close when so much could go wrong.

What if Nic didn't feel the same way about what they'd found with each other?

What if Pete had found something about the potential site that was going to make it not doable or too expensive?

What if Maggie flatly refused to entertain the idea of such a radical sideways move to save the house?

Maybe it wasn't surprising that she burst into tears the moment she heard her aunt's voice on the phone.

Of course Maggie knew exactly the right things to say until Zanna calmed down enough to start talking. And then she listened without interrupting, other than to encourage her, as Zanna poured out everything she needed to say. Her voice was choked with tears when she told her aunt about the trees and it wobbled when she relayed the information that the council's decision to enforce the sale could be imminent.

'But Pete says it's lucky the trees have been killed,' she finished, 'because otherwise we couldn't even think about shifting it. And Nic says that the spirit of the house is about the people, not the place it's sitting, but…this is so huge, Maggie. How do I know that I can trust him?'

'You need to listen to your heart, darling. It will tell you all you need to know. You had your doubts about Simon right from the start, didn't you? You couldn't understand why he'd chosen you. You felt you had to change to deserve him. He's the one who needed to change. He didn't deserve *you*.'

A smile tugged at Zanna's lips for the first time in this conversation. Nic didn't want her to change. He wanted her to be safe to be herself. This whole plan was about protecting the things that were most important to her.

Her smile grew. 'Oh, Maggie—you should see the land that he's found for sale. It's just out of town and there's a lake and a forest and—and it's all *so* gorgeous. There's an old stable block that could become the shop and tea rooms. You'd love it.'

'*You* love it, darling, and that's all that matters.'

'It's not just up to me. This was your house long before I came to share it. It's your business. This has to be your decision and whatever you decide, I'll support you, you know that.'

'I know. So don't be upset when I tell you what I've decided, will you?'

A prickle of fear sent a shock wave down Zanna's spine. She was going to veto the project?

'I've decided to stay here,' Maggie said softly. 'Dimitry's asked me to marry him.'

'*What?* Oh, my God…' Zanna had to back up against the wall to find some support and she still found herself sinking to a crouch. '*Maggie*… You've only just met him. You can't possibly be sure about something that huge.'

'Oh, darling…' There was laughter in her aunt's voice. 'I've waited my whole life to find this. Do you think I didn't recognise it instantly? The only thing I wasn't sure of was whether Dimitry felt the same way. When it's right, you just know… Well, I did anyway. I have had a lot of practice in reading people.'

'Oh…' Zanna was closer to tears now than she had been in talking about the trees. A roller-coaster of emotions was going at full speed in her head and her heart. Happiness that Maggie had found the love of her life. Sadness that they were going to be living so far apart and that the closeness of their relationship would inevitably change. Jealousy, even, that there was someone else who would be Maggie's first priority. And running beneath all those dips and swoops were the rails of something that felt like…hope?

That Maggie was right? That there were no rules about how long it should take to know if you'd met the love of your life?

That what she'd found with Nic could be *real*…

'I gave you power of attorney, my love, and now I'm giving you more than that. The house is yours to do whatever you want to do with it. All I ask is that you take care of those cats of ours and keep the things you'll know I want to come back for safe. Now...' Even on the end of a phone line, half a world away and without the benefit of the card ritual, Maggie seemed to be able to read her mind. 'Tell me all about this Nic.'

Zanna was smiling again. 'He's French, Maggie. His full name is Dominic Brabant...'

'Brabant?' Maggie sounded startled. 'Where have I heard that name before? Oh, no...it couldn't be... Or maybe it could...'

'Here it is.' Nic pulled the folded sheet of paper from an inside pocket of his leather jacket. 'A formal estimate of the cost of shifting the house and repositioning it and a pretty generous estimate of what we think the costs of complete renovation would be.'

Was it his imagination or was Zanna sitting curiously still at the kitchen table, her fingers resting gently around the stem of a crystal glass? An open bottle of wine was beside the flickering candelabra, an empty glass beside it. Nic raised an eyebrow as he shed his jacket and her half-smile was an invitation so he poured himself a glass and sat down. He unfolded the sheet of paper and pushed it closer to Zanna.

'We got it printed out at the business centre in the airport lounge. And I've added the asking price of the land as well. See?'

'Good grief.' Zanna touched the paper as if she couldn't believe what she was seeing. 'That's nearly two million dollars.'

Nic covered her hand with his own. 'That's why I'm going to offer you three million for this property.'

This was the first step in putting things right. To make sure that Zanna understood that the dream solution he had presented was possible. That life would be secure in the future for both herself and the aunt she clearly adored.

The next step would be some honesty.

The silence that followed was unnerving. So was the way Zanna was looking at him. The way she slid her hand out from beneath his so very carefully. As if he'd done something unforgiveable.

'Why, Nic?'

'What do you mean?'

'Why would you offer me so much? The last registered valuation for this place was way less than half of that. The last offer Prime Property came up with was only six hundred thousand. Why do *you* want it so much?'

There was something in her tone that told him the game was up. That the opportunity to be voluntarily honest had been lost. His mouth suddenly dry, Nic took a long swallow of his wine.

'I've been talking to Maggie,' Zanna told him.

'Oh… She's not happy about the idea, then?'

The shake of Zanna's head dismissed his response as irrelevant. 'Was your mother's name Elise?'

CHAPTER EIGHT

IF HE WAS SHOCKED, he was hiding it well.

There was, in fact, a softening in his eyes that looked curiously like joy.

'Maggie remembers her?'

It made it worse that Nic seemed happy to have been found out. It was rubbing salt into what felt like a very raw wound.

How could he? Just a breath after she'd bared her soul and told him about how devastating Simon and Brie's betrayal had been. How hard it was for her to trust anyone's motives.

He wasn't even considering how she might be feeling right now but maybe he'd realise if she kept talking. Surely the strain in her voice was obvious?

'She said she was very beautiful, with long dark hair, but she was very shy because she thought she didn't speak English very well. And she didn't need anyone else in her life, anyway, because she totally adored her husband.'

The way she could have adored Nic. Not that he had any idea that she'd been ready to give him her whole heart. Her trust.

She couldn't go there now. No way.

Stupidly, though, her heart hadn't caught up with what her head was telling her in no uncertain terms.

And Nic was oblivious. He was hanging onto every word she spoke. This was important to him. Far more important than picking up on the sense of betrayal Zanna was fighting with because he hadn't told her about any of it.

It was a real effort to keep her voice steady. 'She remembers that she was a brilliant musician and she gave piano lessons to local children. She could sing beautifully too and your father played the guitar and she would hear them at night, singing French love songs in the garden.'

And how easy would it have been to hear that when it was coming from the garden right next door? From the people who'd lived in one of the small cottages that had been removed to make the public park.

His eyes were so dark. They caught the candlelight just then. Because of the moisture of unshed tears? The accusation that had unmistakeably laced her last words seemed to have gone as undetected as how upset she was.

'They had a baby they called Dommi. Maggie said she'd never seen such a happy little family.'

He looked away from her and his mouth tightened. Was it painful to hear this?

Good. Why should she be the only one suffering here?

'You said you were taken back to France when you were six years old.'

A single nod but Nic didn't say anything.

'You didn't tell me it was because your mother got evicted from her cottage because she couldn't manage her rent. That your father had been killed in a tragic accident at his work a year or more before that.'

'No.' The words were raw. 'I didn't tell you that.'

Her heart made her want to reach out and touch him because she knew he needed comfort. Her head made her throw an even bigger verbal spear.

'It's a bit of a coincidence that the historical protection society sent you to evaluate this house, isn't it?'

There was an accusation in her tone that grated. Zanna had no idea what fragile ground she was treading on here. How intrusive it felt to let someone else into this part of his life. To trust someone enough to share any of this story. And it was being forced on him before he was ready.

There was anger to be found there. Nobody had managed to force him to do anything once he'd been old enough to gain control of his own life.

But she knew already. The protective walls around that hidden place had been breached.

And she had trusted him, hadn't she? She'd opened her heart and shared the pain of the life she'd thought she'd had in London imploding.

Dommi. He hadn't heard that name since he was twelve years old and his mother had died. He'd become Dominic with the formalities of going into care and he'd chosen Nic when he was sixteen and found work that enabled him to become independent. To take control and steer his life towards a place where he'd never have to feel that kind of pain any more.

Nobody knew. Not even Pete—his closest friend—knew more than sketchy details of his background. And Pete had no idea why he'd decided to take on this project, although he'd guessed straight off that he'd been hiding something.

'I wasn't sent here to evaluate the house. I never told you that.'

'You knew that was what I thought. You didn't tell me the truth.'

Nic closed his eyes. 'No.'

This was it. The destruction of trust. He wasn't going to come out of this feeling like a better person. He was going to think less of himself. How on earth had this happened? He'd spent so many years building up defences against precisely this and somehow this woman had slipped under his skin and had the power to leave him unprotected and vulnerable.

'Why not, Nic?' The faint wobble in her words cut straight through his heart. 'Did you think I wouldn't understand?'

His eyes snapped open. Was it possible that she *did* understand? That she could forgive him for the deception?

She'd been through her own childhood trauma, hadn't she? She'd been lucky to have found a loving home so she couldn't know how soul destroying it was to be handed around like an unwanted parcel, but she did know what it was like to lose your parents.

'Do you remember what it was like when your parents were killed, Zanna? How you felt?'

She nodded slowly. 'It was like the world had ended. I was lost and very, very frightened.'

'It was like that for my mother and me when Papa was killed. And my world *had* ended as I'd known it. Maman couldn't get over it. She got sick. The children who came for lessons went away. She took me back to her home country but there was no way she could find work. She got really sick, with cancer that went undiagnosed until far too late. I think she wanted to die, so that she could be with Papa again.'

'Oh…*Nic*…' Zanna could hear the bewildered child behind those words. Feel the pain of thinking you couldn't make things better. That you weren't good enough or something. Her heart was definitely winning the battle over her head now and the urge to comfort was getting overwhelming. Being fuelled by an urge to forgive? 'How old were you when she died?'

'Twelve.'

'So you got taken into care?'

His nod was terse. He wasn't going to talk about those years. Ever.

'I'd already learned to stop remembering when life had been good because it only made things worse. I got very, very good at it. I hadn't even thought about any of it for years and years. Until I saw this house again. The next-door house that had the scary lady living in it.'

That brought a wry smile to Zanna's lips. 'Yeah… I thought she was pretty scary at first, too. Larger than life, that's for sure. Nothing like anybody I'd ever known.'

Zanna was nothing like anybody Nic had ever known. After watching the play of emotions on her face he had to focus again on what he needed to say.

'I did come to New Zealand for an entirely different reason,' he admitted, 'and the memories were hard to handle because I hadn't expected them. I'm ready now. To remember.' He swallowed hard. 'To honour those memories.' He met Zanna's gaze. 'I couldn't share them. They were too raw. Too personal. And…I didn't know you.'

'But you do now.'

'I do.' Her eyes were so soft. He hadn't seen an expression like that since…since his mother had told him how much she loved him. The squeeze in his chest was so painful he had to look away.

'Would you have told me—if I hadn't found out?'

'I was going to tell you tonight. I couldn't *not* tell you. Not after you told me about what happened in London. I…don't want to hurt you, Zanna.'

He was starting to gain the skill of reading her. He could see the flicker in her eyes that told him she could hear the truth in his words. The softening of something in her face that let him know that trust might have been bruised but it was still intact. Just.

He could certainly feel the tension ebbing rapidly.

'What do you want to do to honour those memories? Is that why you want to buy this property?'

'Yes.' Nic took a deep breath and then he told her about the vision for the music school. How it would sit beside the river and the park and look like it was meant to be there. How the sound of music would drift across the tiny patch of the earth where his parents had been so happy. Where he'd been so happy. He wanted to put a beautiful bench seat in the park with their names on it so that people could sit and listen to the music. He told her about the gallery he wanted to put in the foyer of the school to honour Rata House.

He wasn't sure at what point he'd taken hold of Zanna's hands. Or maybe she'd taken hold of his. It didn't matter. She listened to every word and there were tears on her cheeks when he finally stopped talking.

'That's so beautiful, Nic. We were fighting so hard to save this house partly because we knew that if it went in the future when we weren't here, something horrible might take its place—like a huge hotel or another apartment block like next door. But your music school…that's exactly what should be here. Oh, Maggie will love that.' A smile broke through the tears. 'Maybe fate kept us fighting just so that it would be here for you.'

It was hard to swallow past the lump in his throat. Hard to breathe against the constriction in his chest. And Nic had to blink hard to clear the prickle behind his eyes.

She *did* understand.

And he knew he could love her for that.

This was a gift. Did it even matter that he hadn't told her about owning the apartment block?

Yes, his head said. It could change everything.

No, his heart said. It could change everything.

Trust would not survive a second blow. Not before it had had time to get stronger. Maybe he should have told her that was what had brought him here in the first place instead of clouding it with a vague reference to an entirely different reason. If she'd asked what that reason had been, he would have told her.

But it was too late now. Saying anything else might dilute this incredible feeling of being understood. Of having someone beside him. Sharing his dream because she understood exactly why it was so important.

Or was it too late? If she understood as well as she seemed to, she would see how the purchase of the apartment block had been the catalyst for all of this and it could be dismissed along with the deception of having let her assume he'd come onto her property on behalf of the city council.

But there was a new light in Zanna's eyes now. Excitement.

'How soon can we start the ball rolling?'

'We can get the papers drawn up on Monday.' How much easier was it to buy into that excitement and silence the argument going on between his head and his heart? 'No…I've got legal contacts. Someone will be happy to work on a Sunday if they get paid well enough.'

'I'll call our solicitor,' Zanna said. 'Keith Watson. We've known him for years and years and he's helped us a lot. Given us free advice every time we've faced trouble from the council or needed to know how to handle harassment from the Scallions. He loves this house. He'll be thrilled to know it's going to be reborn.'

'Once the agreement for sale and purchase is finalised, we can give Pete the green light. If we make an immediate possession date, we can get started as soon as you're ready.'

'What am I going to do with all the stuff in the house and shop? It'll all have to come out for the removal process.'

'We'll find a storage facility. Get packers in.'

But Zanna shook her head. 'I'll need to sort everything. Maggie's going to want a lot of her things and they're precious. Like those antique instruments. I'd want to pack and shift those myself to make sure they're safe. I promised her I'd keep them safe.'

'We'll make sure they are.' The excitement was gaining force. Bubbling between them—the future so bright with the potential for amazing things to happen.

The conviction that he could do anything with Zanna by his side took Nic by surprise. He'd walked alone for ever and this feeling of shared anticipation was something new. It felt like he'd put a magnifying glass on the satisfaction he'd always felt when a new challenge was falling into place. How much greater would the joy be when it was complete?

He wanted Zanna by his side, then, too. He wanted to open the door of her restored house to take her for a tour. He wanted her holding his hand as they cut the ribbon for the opening of the Brabant Music Academy.

He couldn't imagine *not* wanting Zanna.

It was as simple as that.

And he felt like he was looking into a reflection of how he was feeling as he gazed into Zanna's eyes.

Conversation had died. Tomorrow would be soon enough to start talking through the thousands of details. Tonight was for celebrating what was going to be achieved.

Together.

Words wouldn't be enough, anyway. There was only one way that Nic could show Zanna how much it meant to him to have someone sharing this part of his soul.

Zanna couldn't tell where her body left off and Nic's started as he rose from the table to lead her upstairs. Maybe that was because she had started to move at exactly the same moment, with exactly the same destination in mind.

Any sense of betrayal had long since been extinguished. Of course he'd been unable to let a stranger into a place that he'd kept hidden for so long, even to himself. How could she blame him for taking an opportunity to protect that privacy when she'd made it so easy?

But he'd invited her in now.

He trusted her.

Maybe, this time, she could really trust her own instincts. Trust *him*. Trust the inherited wisdom that generations of seers had given Maggie.

When it was right, you just *knew*.

CHAPTER NINE

THE NEXT FEW DAYS passed in a blur.

Looking back, Zanna knew she would remember only bits of it but they were memories that she would always treasure.

The night together after he'd told her so much about what had made him into the person he was. How being invited into such a personal space had made her love him so much more.

The way Nic had looked when the contract had been signed and that first, major step had been taken. Not that she'd agreed to be paid so much more than the property was worth. Two million was enough. He could put the rest into the music school.

The surprise of discovering how well Nic could play a guitar when they were packing up Maggie's old instruments. Listening to him singing her a French love song late at night, out in the courtyard, with the chiminea and candelabra providing all the warmth and light they could need.

Knowing that this was where she always needed to be. By Nic's side.

She'd started some packing in the shop now, too. Boxes of stock were being sent to join others in the storage facility they'd hired. There was a notice on the door explaining why Spellbound would have to close in the near future but she was happy to assure customers that the business would start again before too long in an even better place.

The cats were unsettled by all the unusual activity and seemed to be always underfoot, seeking reassurance.

'It's all okay,' Zanna kept telling them. 'I know it's a worry but you guys are going to be so happy in the country. There'll be trees to climb and lots of mice to catch. You probably won't even want your tinned food any more.'

They didn't seem to want it very much at the moment. On Tuesday night, Zanna tapped the spoon against the bowl but there was no streak of black coming from any direction.

'Where are they?'

Nic glanced up from his laptop. After meetings that morning with the council planning department to apply for various permits and checking out storage facilities, he'd started preliminary plans for the music school and had been absorbed for the rest of the afternoon while Zanna had been busy in the shop. 'I haven't seen them for hours. Not even Merlin.'

'That's weird. I'd better check that I didn't lock them in the shop by mistake. They were hanging around when I was packing in there earlier.'

The cats had, indeed, been accidentally locked in the shop. Maybe they'd been asleep on the pile of clothing behind the stack of boxes Zanna had filled that day. It was Merlin who jumped into her arms as she opened the door but Marmite and Mystic glued themselves to her ankles, competing for attention with plaintive cries of having been imprisoned.

Zanna was laughing as she tried to get down the steps without the cats tripping her up but the laughter died the moment she felt the hairs on the back of her neck prickle.

She wasn't alone.

The shop was dark and empty behind her. The front door of the house was open not far away but Nic was in the kitchen at the back and probably too far away and too focused on what he was doing to hear her even if she screamed.

Maybe she was imagining things. The light of the day was almost gone and the wind had picked up so the shadows cast by the massive, dying trees and the sound of creaking branches was spooky.

Then she looked beyond the trees. The streetlights would come on at any moment now and, when they did, the figure standing beside the lamppost just outside the gate would be instantly obvious.

A male figure. Just standing there. Even without being able to see him clearly, she knew he was staring at the house.

At her.

A tourist out for a walk, she told herself. Someone had stopped to look at the curiosity the house had become.

Except that a tourist wouldn't feel like such a threat. They wouldn't be standing with such...nonchalance? And they certainly wouldn't emit a sound like low laughter. Merlin stiffened in her arms and responded with a hiss.

'Evening, Miss Zelensky.' He made her name sound like an insult. 'How's it going?'

The cats at her feet were gone in a streak, heading

for the safety of the house. Merlin's claws dug painfully into Zanna's arms as he launched himself in the wake of his siblings. Following them herself might have been a sensible option but it wasn't the way she responded to a threat. Instead, she became very still. Centring herself and gathering her strength.

'Blake. What are you doing here?'

'Happened to be in town. Just wanted a look.'

'You've looked. You can go now.'

The man Maggie had always referred to as the junior scorpion took a step closer. The rusty, wrought-iron gate was permanently ajar. Another step and he would be on the brick pathway.

'There's nothing here for you. The property's sold.' She couldn't help the note of satisfaction that coated her words. 'To someone else.'

'I know.'

Zanna felt that prickle in her spine again. A premonition of danger. She tried to shake it off. Prime Property couldn't threaten them any longer. Or was that why Blake was here? Was he angry that they'd lost their long battle?

He didn't seem angry. There was a smugness in those words.

'It's none of your business.'

He laughed again. 'You sure about that?' He turned, as if intending to walk away. 'Tell Nic I'll give him a call tomorrow. We need to talk.'

The prickle turned into a chill that sent ice into Zanna's veins. This time it was her moving to narrow the gap between them.

'Why would I do that? What makes you think he would want to have anything to do with the likes of you?'

Blake turned back. She could see the gleam of his teeth as he smiled.

'We've been partners for years, sweetheart. Dad and I were only too delighted to get rid of having to deal with you and your aunt and obviously he managed to do what we couldn't. In record time, too. What was so attractive about what he had to offer, Suzanna?' The tone was a sneer. 'As if I couldn't guess.'

'I don't believe you. Get out, Blake. I don't ever want to see you or your father again. Set foot on this property and I'll call the police. You could still be charged with malicious damage after what you did to our trees.'

'We could sue you for malicious damage right back. You've got no idea of the grief you've caused us, sweetheart. It's lucky that the heart attack didn't kill Dad. At least he'll get the pleasure of seeing you gone. Of seeing this house knocked flat.' He took another long glance upwards. 'Good riddance, I say. Good on you, Nic.'

This time when he turned he kept moving. The streetlights came on in time for Zanna to see his silhouette fade as he walked past the apartment block.

No. She couldn't believe that Nic would be in partnership with the Scallions. He would tell her how ridiculous the very idea was as soon as he heard about it. She started walking towards the front door of the house but then stopped.

It made sense.

Nic had said that his career was usually about luxury international coastal resorts—exactly the kind of developments that Prime Property was famous for.

He had hidden his connection to the property from the moment he'd walked in. Sure, she knew the story about his background was true, thanks to Maggie, but didn't that make it worse? He had come here with a single purpose in mind and perhaps the motive of knowing even a hint of association with Prime Property would have made him unwelcome to set foot in the house had been stronger than a desire to keep his background private.

And he'd gone so much further than merely setting foot in her house…

Oh…*God*…

Had she been played? Sucked into going in a direction she'd never intended? The way Simon and Brie had persuaded her to change her art? What if she was heading for an even bigger fall that she'd never be able to come back from? That she'd trusted someone enough to reveal her humiliation only to find that history was repeating itself?

Her mind raced on to imagine the worst. What if it turned out that the house fell apart when they tried to shift it? It would only be her loss, wouldn't it? They'd still have their patch of land. *Two* patches of land. Enough for the biggest hotel in town, and maybe that was the real agenda. Maybe Nic's connection to this property had just been a fortunate coincidence. That the music school would be deemed uneconomic or something before it got past the planning stage.

No. The things Nic had told her were true. They'd come straight from his heart. She *believed* him.

She'd believed Simon, too.

Maybe her instincts couldn't be trusted.

Or maybe she'd been ignoring the warnings those instincts had issued. She could hear an echo of his voice. Of hers as well, during that card reading.

'Sometimes you have to let go of an old life in order to take the opportunity of a new and fulfilling one.'

'Something I've always lived by... Do you?'

There had been a moment of warning she hadn't ignored, even then.

He may not be who he seems to be. Take care...

It was Nic who'd spotted the holes in the trees.

And who just happened to have a mate who specialised in relocating old houses. She'd noticed those odd glances between the two men that day, hadn't she?

But it had all worked, hadn't it? She'd signed legal contracts. No wonder Blake had sounded so smug.

If only Maggie was here, Zanna thought desperately. She felt so alone. She could be on the point of losing everything. Losing the house would be bad enough but she had the horrible feeling she was about to lose Nic as well.

Merlin jumped onto Nic's lap but he pushed him off as the tail cut his view of the computer screen in half. Offended, the cat started washing himself but Nic didn't notice. He'd finally got the line just right. The curve of the building as it echoed the line of the river. The software program he was using allowed him to layer the plan on top of the aerial photographs of the area that he'd already removed both Rata House and the apartment block from. He could circle it now and get an idea of how it sat from both the street side and the river side.

He heard Zanna finally come back but still didn't turn his head.

'Come and look at this. I think I've nailed it.'

It was the silence that finally broke his concentration. Nothing like the quiet serenity that Zanna was capable of generating sometimes. This was a heavy silence. Ominous. When he looked up and saw her face, he uttered a low oath.

'What's wrong? What's happened?'

Had one of the cats been run over or something? Merlin was sitting nearby, licking a paw and then scraping it over his face. And, yes…there were two cats still engrossed in eating.

Had she had some bad news about her aunt? Surely someone must have died to make her look like that. So shocked. Drained of any vestige of colour.

'Are you part of Prime Property, Nic?' Her voice was flat. 'A partner?'

'No.' His chair scraped on the wooden floor as he pushed it back to get to his feet. 'Hell, no…' He started to walk towards Zanna but she held her hand up and it felt like he'd hit a force field. He stopped in his tracks.

'I just found Blake Scallion standing outside the gate. He said he'd call you tomorrow because you *needed to talk.*' He could see Zanna's throat move as he swallowed. '*He* said you'd been partners for years. I didn't believe him but then I thought…it could be true. Maybe you had been sent to *deal* with the little problem that Maggie and I represented.'

'I'm not a partner of Prime Property. Yes, I've worked with them. They've used my designs to develop coastal resorts. The way other property development companies use my expertise all over the world for all sorts of projects. That was why I was in New Zealand in the first place. They've bought a huge block of land on the Hibiscus Coast and they want me on board to get another resort off the ground.'

This was the explanation he should have given her long ago but it was too late now. Way too late.

'But you've bought this property.' Zanna's expression was frozen. She wasn't prepared to believe anything he was going to say to try and explain. 'The one that Prime Property's been trying to get hold of for the last ten years. They still own the one next door. Another *coincidence*?'

'They don't own next door any more. I couldn't have started the project for the music school unless I had both properties.'

'So *you* own the apartment block now?' A wash of colour stained Zanna's cheeks. Anger...? Or maybe it was relief. He could defuse this whole situation if he took the opportunity she was offering and let her believe that he'd approached the Scallions to sell the apartment block only after he'd purchased Rata House. 'When did you buy that—or is that why Blake wants to talk to you tomorrow?'

Nic closed his eyes. Deception by omission was one thing. An outright lie was unacceptable. Yes, telling the truth could change everything but he had no choice. And maybe he needed a leap of faith. It would only be a glimmer of hope but she might understand—the way she seemed to have understood everything else about him. He opened his eyes.

'I bought the apartment block ten days ago. Before I came here.'

He had to let the silence extend as Zanna processed what he'd said. He could feel his heart thumping and it skipped a beat completely when she finally spoke again because her voice sounded so tightly controlled. Cold.

'So you came here knowing that you couldn't go ahead with your plans unless you persuaded me to sell?'

He didn't need to say anything. She could see the truth in his eyes.

And it hurt so much more than she'd tried to prepare herself for.

'Is there really going to be a music school, Nic, or was that part of the grand plan? Get me on side with the sob story of your unhappy childhood? Pete said you're good at making money. Wouldn't a really *big* apartment block or a hotel or something be more in your line of work?'

She could see that her accusation had hit home but the flash of shock in his face was quickly masked. A barrier was going up between them. A huge, impenetrable barrier.

That hurt, too.

A *sob story*? Had he really thought she understood? He'd let her into the most private part of his soul and she was dismissing it as being some sort of manipulative device.

Nic could feel his head taking over completely from his heart. Putting him in a professional mode. This was what he'd come here for, wasn't it? A business deal. And he'd succeeded. It should be enough.

Clearly, it would have to be enough.

'You're getting what you wanted out of it, aren't you? Yes, I wanted the land but when I met you and saw how you felt about the house I knew it shouldn't be simply demolished. You were right in wanting to save it but you wouldn't have won in the long run when you can't afford to even maintain it where it is. I came up with a solution that gave us both what we wanted. I made that solution possible. Do you think you could have done this without my contacts? Like Pete? Like the estate agent who told me about land that wasn't even on the market yet?'

'You were holding all the cards. You were hiding the truth. Did you just happen to spot those holes in the trees or did you already know they were there? Had you been in on those plans, too? *Years* ago?'

'No. I had no idea Prime Property had any interest in this place until I saw a file on Donald's desk two weeks ago. The picture of a house I could never forget. They have no idea why I wanted to take over the project. I haven't even told Pete what I've got in mind here. You're the only person who knows that. Knows why it matters.'

The only person who understood that he was chasing a memory. Trying to catch and preserve a fragment of how it had felt to be loved and safe. Surely she could remember how it had felt to be in each other's arms that night? That they were the only two people in the world who could share the pain of that particular loss and the joy of turning it into something meaningful?

Zanna couldn't miss the intensity of his words. She knew what Nic was trying to tap into—that shared vision of honouring both their pasts with the music school and its gallery. The trust he'd won from her by sharing his secrets.

But it wasn't going to work this time. Trust wasn't something you could keep breaking and then gluing back together. This time she was going to protect herself more effectively. And it wasn't a total disaster, was it? Maybe she wasn't going to lose the house. She might end up with that dream property in the green belt, with her house and the business intact and a place that could inspire her real work with her art.

Was that enough to make up for what she was definitely losing here?

That trust? The ability to love somebody with her entire heart and soul?

He'd come here with the same agenda that the Scallions had always had. To get her out so that they could have what they wanted. He'd lied to her. More than that…

Shame and anger curdled the grief of loss.

'Do you often have to sleep with potential sellers, Nic?' It was hard to force the words out because every one of them hurt. 'Get them to fall in love with you so that they'll be only too happy to fall into line?'

That shattered the barrier for a heartbeat. Good grief…had he really not had *any* idea how she felt about him?

Did he think she'd been playing some kind of game, too? *Acting?*

'Bit silly of me to persuade you to offer less, wasn't it?' Zanna finally broke the distance she'd held between them. She walked to the table and picked up the sheaf of papers that was her copy of the sale and agreement purchase. She ripped it in half.

She only had to lean a little to snap shut the lid of Nic's laptop.

'Game over,' she said calmly. 'Get out, Nic.'

And then she turned and walked out of the room.

Into the hallway beneath the sunflower painting, but she didn't let herself remember the way Nic's reaction to seeing it had made her feel. Had mattered so much.

She couldn't trust anything she felt any more and, as if demanding recognition, there were overwhelming emotions boiling up inside. The pain of betrayal. The grief of loss. The shame of being deceived. Broken love. All competing with a desperate desire not to believe any of them but to trust how she felt about Nic. Any one of them was powerful enough to make her shake like this.

She had to keep moving so she didn't sink into a quivering heap that Nic would have to step around on his way out of the house. She ran up the wide stairs and still she kept going. There was only one place she could go to find some sort of release from the storm. A refuge that would allow her to clear her head and start to think instead of being battered by this crashing emotional surf.

She slammed the door at the top of the spiral staircase behind her.

And then she locked it.

CHAPTER TEN

GUNNING THE ENGINE of the bike was a satisfying echo to the anger heating Nic's blood. Opening the throttle as soon as he escaped the city's speed limits and leaning into the blast of cold air finally cooled that heat enough for the shock waves to stop blasting him from all directions.

He was miles out of the city now. In a small town whose main street boasted a motel, a Chinese takeaway restaurant and a liquor store.

Perfect. A bed for the night, something to eat and a bottle of even halfway decent Scotch and he could sort this whole mess out. He could start defining exactly what was making him so damn angry and that was a very necessary first step before he decided what he was going to do next. Anger had no place in making rational decisions.

An hour or two later and being dismissed by Zanna Zelensky in the wake of her ripping up their contract was top of the list of what was making his blood boil.

The knee-jerk reaction was that *il n'avait pas d'importance*—it made no difference. It was only a copy of a legally binding contract and his solicitor held the original. He still owned the property in Rata Avenue.

Yes, it would be time consuming and expensive to have to take it to court but he would win. He would still get exactly what he'd come to Christchurch for.

But it did make a difference, didn't it? Pouring another shot of whisky into the cheap tumbler, Nic paced the soulless motel room.

The satisfaction of achieving exactly what he'd set out to achieve would always be tainted by the dispute. The planned gallery to pay homage to Rata House would be nothing more than a victory crow—an insult to Zanna.

The knock-on effects on his career were enough to anger him all on their own. He was going to have to delay meetings on projects that were starting to line up. A boutique lakeside hotel in Geneva. A warehouse redevelopment on the banks of the Thames in London. The ambitious resort planned for the stretch of beach on the Hibiscus Coast north of Auckland in New Zealand that had been the reason he'd come here for the talks with Prime Property two weeks ago.

Well…that wasn't going to happen now. He had no intention of working with the Scallions again. A short phone call to Donald was all it took to let him know that he couldn't continue to work with a company that resorted to underhanded and illegal tactics like poisoning protected trees. He left Donald in no doubt about how stupid his son had been to come here and try and put the boot in and gloat over the fact that Zanna's property had finally changed hands.

He didn't add that he would never forgive the fact that Blake had unwittingly managed to destroy the connection he'd found with Zanna because it was none of their business. But by the time he ended the call Nic knew he had identified the real core of his anger.

He couldn't win in the end on this one because he'd lost something that had nothing to do with business. Something huge. Yes, the land was the only real connection he still had with his parents and that almost forgotten life but, if that was all he had, there would only ever be memories of how special it had been. Fragments of emotion that would be fleeting echoes of how it had felt to have a home. To belong.

Pour aimer et être aimé.

To love and be loved.

When he was with Zanna, the feeling wasn't a memory. It was real. More than real because it held the magic of a promise that it could always be there. That place was irrelevant because that feeling of home and safety was to do with who Zanna was, not where she lived.

He didn't need a handful of cards spread out beneath a flickering candelabra to read his future if he lost what he'd found so recently. It might be full to the brim with professional satisfaction, public accolades and more money than he could ever spend, but on one level it would be meaningless.

That level had been safely locked away for as long as he could remember but it had been released now and it was too big and too shapeless to ever catch and restrain again.

He loved Zanna. It was as simple as that.

And hadn't she all but said that she'd fallen in love with him?

Do you often have to sleep with potential sellers, Nic? Get them to fall in love with you so that they'll be only too happy to fall into line?

With a groan, Nic reached for the bottle again and unscrewed the metal cap. Poised to pour another shot, he paused. His gaze shifted to the Formica bench of the kitchenette with its electric jug and sachets of probably dreadful coffee.

He let go of the bottle.

Strong coffee was what he needed now. And a bit more time before it was safe to hit the road again.

To go back to where he belonged.

With Zanna.

The house was no emptier than it had been ever since Maggie had set off for her journey of discovery weeks ago.

But it felt different.

Zanna could feel the cavern of that emptiness below her from the eyrie of her studio in the turret.

The spirit of joy the house had always contained was gone, destroyed by a tidal wave of anger and grief.

It was just a house in the end, wasn't it? Without the people, it was haunted by ghosts. Maggie's. Nic's. The ghost of the frightened child she had been when she'd come here and the broken person she'd been when she'd returned from London last year. Maybe the most unbearable ghost right now was the person she was when she was with Nic. The person she had wanted to be for the rest of her life.

She still needed to keep moving because, if she didn't, these emotions would suffocate her. Her hands moved of their own accord to select brushes and paints. The only available canvas was large but that was fine. She had something huge inside that needed to come out. She couldn't have consciously chosen a subject if she'd tried so she didn't spare a thought for a preliminary sketch or even a mental image of where she was headed. This was just an exercise to release some of her anguish. To channel it into a symbol of some kind, perhaps, so that she could then choose to either remove it from her life entirely or keep it as a reminder to make her future choices with more care.

The subject chose itself and it wasn't really a surprise to discover that it was going to be a portrait of Dominic Brabant. What was surprising was how well imprinted he was on her soul for the perfect shape of his face and hands and body to be emerging with such ease and precision. Cruel of her subconscious to pick the scene it had but she knew better than to mess with what was happening inside her head and her heart by trying to change what needed to be expressed.

And besides…this could quite possibly be the best painting she had ever done. As the minutes ticked into hours Zanna was aware of an excitement stealing into the turbulent mix of her emotions. It was a rare thing to find that her mind and hands and spirit were in synch enough to be producing something that felt so right from a creative point of view.

She had caught the moment perfectly and she had to blink away tears as she added the final touches to the work. The twilight of a late summer's evening. The flickering light of small logs burning in the chiminea and echoed by the candelabra on the small table. The posture and intensity of the man holding the guitar. She could almost feel the softness of the tousled waves of his hair. Hear the notes of those words of love in the most beautiful language of the world.

Feel the way those hands had touched and held her soul.

It hadn't all been an act, had it? An expert lover could have learned how to inflame a woman's desire by unbraiding her hair and touching her face as though his fingers wanted to know her features as intimately as his eyes did, but could passion be combined with such... tenderness if it was simply playing a role?

No. She didn't believe she had imagined that he felt as strongly as she did. She had felt the truth in that moment of silence when he'd admitted that he felt as emotionally unbalanced as she did.

But could she trust what she believed?

Given her track record, probably not.

Given how exhausted she was, having channelled an excess of energy into her painting, this wasn't the time to even try and decide what she could trust.

She had to sleep but the thought of going down to her own bed and sleeping alone only brought another wave of misery. Better to stay here and curl up on the antique chaise longue that had been donated to her studio when it had become too ratty to grace the formal living room downstairs. It would be softer than the floor and she was tired enough to consider that a viable option.

Zanna didn't need to leave the lights on to have the image she'd just painted as her last thought before she slipped into an exhausted slumber.

Without needing the adrenaline rush of speed to burn off anger, it took a lot longer to get back to the city.

Propping the bike on its stand, Nic pulled off his helmet and hung it over the handlebars, before turning to look at the silent silhouette of Rata House. It was completely dark from where he was standing. Hardly surprising when he checked his watch to find it was after three a.m.

Zanna would be sound asleep.

Would she be frightened by a knock on the door? He didn't want to frighten her.

Would she guess that he had come back because he couldn't stay away?

But she didn't know he loved her, did she? Would she even believe him when he told her?

Of course she'd been upset. He'd known how fragile that trust was—how it wouldn't survive an additional blow.

He'd hurt her and it was unbearable.

His feet took him, unbidden, through the wrought-iron gate and up the mossy, brick pathway. The stalk of a rough leaf, propelled by a stiff breeze, hit his cheek hard enough to sting and he could almost smell the decay of the dying trees as he veered towards the veranda of the main part of the house.

He peered through the stained-glass panels on either side of the front door, hoping to see a glimmer of light from the end of the hallway that led to the kitchen, but he could see nothing. He could still smell something, though. The musty, decayed smell of the trees seemed to be getting stronger and it was oddly pungent, as though some of those mysterious herbs in Zanna's shop were being burnt.

Sure enough, a glance towards the door of the shop entrance showed a flicker of light. The kind of light that candles would produce and Zanna was very fond of candles, wasn't she? He could remember how many of them had been burning on the counter that day he'd gone in to see her. And the way she'd held her hair back, out of danger, as she'd leaned in to blow them out.

Was she in the shop? Unpacking some of the stock, perhaps, because she believed the deal was off and she needed to reopen her business? He retraced his steps and went to knock on the shop door.

'It's only me,' he called, as he knocked. 'Nic. I need to talk to you, Zanna.'

The only response was the tapping of the 'Closed' sign on the glass of the door as it reverberated to his knock. There were stained-glass panels here, too and the candlelight was much stronger.

So was the smell.

The tendrils of smoke coming from the gap beneath the door were unmistakeable evidence that something was terribly wrong.

Spellbound was on fire.

'*Zanna…*' Nic pounded on the door with a clenched fist. He wrenched at the handle but the door was firmly locked.

Was she even inside the shop?

Down the steps again and Nic stared up at the house. Her bedroom was directly above the shop and below the turret room that contained her studio. Smoke rose and he'd heard somewhere that more people died of smoke inhalation than got burned to death in a fire.

Where was she?

The sound of a sharp crack and then a fizzing noise as though some flammable material had exploded came from within the shop and suddenly he could see the shape of flames through the coloured panels. The smoke gushed out and curled away into the night air.

Running, Nic made his way back to the house door.

He pulled out his phone and punched in the three digit emergency number.

'*Fire*,' he yelled. 'Number thirty-two, Rata Avenue. *Hurry*—there's someone inside the house.'

For a few seconds Nic made a panicked search for some kind of weapon he could use to break a window and get access to the house. A branch from one of the rata trees? The trees were virtually dead so it would be easy to break off a thick piece of wood.

Dying trees…water…the galvanised bucket. The connection took only a microsecond and it felt like Nic had the spare house key in his hand almost by the time he'd completed the thought process. Muscles in his jaw were bunched so tightly he could feel his teeth aching as he finally turned the key and shoved the door open.

The hallway was black. Even if he'd been able to locate a light switch it wouldn't have helped much but enough light was coming from behind to illuminate the thick smoke that was already obscuring half the sweep of the staircase. So much light Nic's head swivelled. Had the emergency services arrived without the use of any sirens?

No. To his horror, he saw that one of the glass panes in the bay window of the shop had blown out. It looked as though flames were hurling themselves into the night air, seeking fuel like some kind of famished, wild animal. The dry leaves and branches of one of the rata trees were close enough to provide exactly what was being sought. Spurts of flame were shooting upwards into the tree and expanding like a mushroom cloud. Illuminating the witch's hat of the turret and the dark windows beneath it.

Any thought of how dangerous it would be to go inside the house simply didn't occur to Nic. In that moment it wouldn't have mattered how quickly he might be overcome by smoke or whatever horrible fumes it might contain.

Zanna was in the house and nothing else mattered.

Nic bunched up the soft fabric of his T-shirt to try and make some protection to cover his mouth and nose. He ran into the smoke and took the stairs two at a time. The heat around him increased but there were no visible flames in here. Holding onto the carved newel post at the top of the stairs, he took a moment to orient himself.

Maggie's room. The bathroom. A spare bedroom. Zanna's room was two doors down on the right just before the spiral stairs that led to the turret. Directly over the shop and where the inferno was gathering pace. He pushed himself on. He had to take a breath and even through the bunched fabric he could taste the smoke and feel the heat and the inadequate level of oxygen the air contained.

But he was in her bedroom.

'Zanna? *Zanna*…' The effort to shout required another breath, which made him cough and draw more smoke into his lungs.

The bedroom was empty.

Smoke had now reached as far as the narrow spiral staircase and it felt thicker here than it had anywhere else. Of course it did. Smoke rose and this was the very top of the old house, in a direct vertical line from where the fire had started.

The door at the top of the stairs was closed. He had to feel for the handle. He turned it and pushed.

No…

The door was locked?

Why?

Nic banged on the wood. 'Zanna. *Zanna*… Are you in there?' She had to be in there because the door was bolted from the inside. 'There's a *fire*…'

He could hear the approaching wail of sirens now. He could hear the sound of glass breaking and then people shouting. What he couldn't hear was any sound from within the round room in the turret.

Zanna's room. Her refuge. This was where she would have gone when she couldn't bear to be in the same room as him, he just knew it.

Was she already unconscious from breathing in too much smoke?

Bracing himself, Nic gathered all the strength he could muster and slammed his shoulder against the door.

And then he did it again.

Zanna had never been so deeply asleep. So deeply drawn into the dream that had begun with the last image she'd seen before slipping into unconsciousness. She was in her courtyard garden, surrounded by the sound of the song Nic was singing as he plucked the strings of that old guitar. She was dancing by the light of the candelabra, wearing something soft and floaty—the soft velvet robe she'd been wearing the day Nic had first walked into Spellbound?

She could smell the aroma of the wood burning in the chiminea. Could feel its heat. She could even hear the words of the song Nic was singing. She knew they were in French but she could understand them so easily.

Ne me quitte pas…don't leave me…

She could hear her own name in the chorus. That was new…

Zanna…*Zanna*…

The dancing in her dream had to stop. The ground was shaking. As Zanna's mind was reluctantly dragged back into consciousness she pushed her eyelids open. Where was she?

She could make out the bare wooden floorboards that looked familiar enough but everything else was so hazy. She was surrounded by her paintings but they seemed obscured by a thick fog. The smell of the fog was weird and Zanna realised how short of breath she was. It was an effort to fill her lungs and when she tried, it was uncomfortable enough to make her cough. And that sucked more of the fog in and made her cough again even more harshly.

Nic heard the cough. The mix of relief that Zanna was in the room and fear that she might already be too overcome by the smoke somehow gave him the strength to summon a last burst of reserves. With this final punishing blow, the wood splintered around the doorhandle and Nic fell into the room, along with an enveloping cloud of thick, hot smoke.

He was on his knees but he could see the shape of Zanna, hunched on the floor beside the old couch. Pushing up with his arm sent a vicious shaft of pain through the shoulder he'd used to batter down the door. It hadn't been possible to keep his face covered while he'd been trying to break through the door and he'd inhaled enough smoke to make his lungs burn painfully as well. The coughing was constant now and a wave of dizziness assaulted him as he crawled towards Zanna to pull her into his arms.

'Fire…' He choked the word out. '*Have to…get… you out.*'

Zanna was stumbling, racking coughs making her double over. Nic kept a grip on her arms that went beyond firmness. A part of his brain registered the fact that he could be causing her pain but it couldn't be helped. Somehow, he had to get them downstairs and there was no way he could carry her down that narrow spiral staircase. Not with only one arm that was obeying commands.

There was a fire escape outside her bedroom window. A wrought-iron ladder that was attached to the weatherboards and ran down to the roof of the veranda. Or would that be unusable now? Had the flames from the burning tree crossed the gap and joined with whatever horror was rising from the shop below?

The passage down the spiral stairs was a barely controlled fall but he caught Zanna with his uninjured arm at the bottom and cushioned her impact. With one arm around her waist he crawled forward, dragging her with him. It was too difficult to breathe and Zanna seemed barely conscious. He couldn't remember what direction they needed to go in. He just knew they had to keep moving.

To stay still would mean certain death for both of them.

Zanna was only dimly aware of what was happening. She knew she was in Nic's arms. She could feel the soft smoothness of that leather jacket and the strength of his muscles as he tried to carry her. But she could feel that strength ebbing as well. The dizziness was overwhelming and her eyes were stinging so much it was impossible to open them. Fear was there, too. She knew something terrible was happening.

But she was in Nic's arms so how bad could it be? She just had to try and help him. Had to stay close.

Then she felt the grip of those arms loosen and the smoothness of that soft leather slip away. There was new pressure now. Stronger. Heavily gloved hands that were pulling her upwards. Roughly clad arms that were holding her. Alien faces obscured by masks, making sounds that resembled speech but were totally incomprehensible.

There was movement, too. Rapid and purposeful. The temperature changed and became cold. More hands were pulling at Zanna, tangling themselves in her hair painfully. Something was on her face, covering her mouth and nose. She tried to push it away because she needed to breathe. *Had* to breathe. She was suffocating.

'Leave it on.' The voice was suddenly clear. 'It's oxygen, love. You need it. You've inhaled a lot of smoke.'

Zanna tried to open her eyes. She tried to say something but the effort only provoked a new fit of coughing. She could hear someone else coughing nearby. There were sounds of people shouting and heavy activity. Generators or engines humming. Water gushing and hitting solid objects under pressure. Someone talking more quietly, right beside her.

'Just concentrate on your breathing, Zanna. I'm putting a clip on your finger so we can see what the oxygen level in your blood is doing. Then I'm going to listen to your chest. Are you hurting anywhere?'

She shook her head. How did they know her name? Who were these people? She made a new effort to open her eyes and caught a glimpse of uniformed people surrounding her. One was holding a stethoscope. Another was wrapping a cuff around her arm. She was on a stretcher and there was another one within touching distance if she reached out.

Nic was sitting on that stretcher.

Oh…thank God…Nic was here. Those patchy memories of being held so tightly in his arms hadn't been a dream. She had sent him away but he was here again.

He'd come back. The way he had that first time when she'd been so sure she wouldn't see him again.

Why had he come back this time?

To apologise, perhaps? To say goodbye?

How hard would that be?

She didn't want him to stay. She couldn't trust him. But it would have been better to have never had to see him again.

But hadn't he just saved her from something terrible? How could you not trust someone who had saved your life?

Confusion exacerbated the dizziness that was already clouding her brain.

Nic's face was blackened. He was holding a mask to his mouth and nose and coughing wretchedly. Someone was touching his arm and he gave an anguished yell of pain that Zanna was sure she could feel herself.

'Looks like it's dislocated, mate. Hang on and we'll get you some pain relief before we do anything else.'

The paramedic was blocking her view of Nic now but knowing he'd been hurt made her chest tighten and it was even harder to try and breathe.

Through the narrow windows above his head Zanna could see flashing lights. In the split second before the dizziness took hold again and forced her eyes shut, she looked out of the back doors of what she realised was an ambulance.

She could see the fire engines parked close by. A crowd of heavily uniformed figures were bustling about, dealing with equipment and hoses. And she could see the charred branches of the trees, devoid of any leaves now, and she could even see the black holes that had been the windows of Spellbound—missing teeth in a broken face.

Her house had been burned. Her home was gone.

The tears felt like overheated oil as they seared Zanna's eyes. She held them tightly shut. This was way too much to cope with.

'The cats.' Her words came out as a harsh croak and she didn't even recognise them herself. She caught the arm of the paramedic who was taking her blood pressure. The movement was agitated enough to make him abandon the task and lift the mask from her face.

'You'll have to say that again, love. I couldn't hear you properly.'

'*Cats...*'

'Sorry?'

'Cats.' Nic's voice came from behind the paramedic. 'There are three cats. Black.' He coughed and Zanna could hear the rasp as he sucked in a new breath. 'They would have been inside the house. You have to find them.'

'I'll pass it on. Nobody's allowed in the house yet. They're still trying to make sure the fire's contained.' The mask was fitted back to Zanna's face. 'Try not to worry. Someone will find your cats.'

She let her eyes drift shut again.

Nic was here but she didn't know why.

Her beloved house was destroyed.

Maggie was on the other side of the world.

And the M&Ms were missing. Dead?

Her brain hurt from trying to take it all in. Her lungs hurt from trying to breathe. But most of all her heart was hurting.

And it was unbearable.

CHAPTER ELEVEN

HE HADN'T FELT like this since his mother had died and they'd come to take him away.

So alone, with an unknown future that was huge and empty and forbidding.

Except this time *was* different.

He really had been alone then and he'd learned to rely only on himself. Not to let anyone close enough to make it a problem if they disappeared.

But then he'd met Zanna. How had she got so close, so fast? As if there'd been a Zanna-shaped hole in his soul that she had just slipped into?

He could have lost her last night and the enormity of facing that made everything else meaningless in comparison.

Was this love? This feeling that he could never be the best person he was capable of being without her? That an unknown future could be bright and enticing instead of something that had to be faced with grim fortitude?

Nic had the curious feeling of coming full circle. Of finding what he'd resisted searching for all his life, only to discover it had been back where he'd started. Physically and emotionally. In the only place he'd known a family. With the only person he'd ever fallen in love with.

He had to tell Zanna.

They'd been separated as soon as they'd arrived at the hospital. The first attempt to relocate his shoulder had been unsuccessful and then there'd been X-rays and drugs that had taken a long time to sleep off.

With his arm in a sling he'd finally been able to trace where Zanna was in the hospital, only to be told that she was currently asleep and not to be disturbed. When he went back again, she was awake but talking to a police detective who was investigating the fire.

'Come back in a couple of hours,' the nursing staff advised. 'Miss Zelensky's not going anywhere just yet. She needs a good rest.'

She was still asleep when Nic returned yet again but this time he wasn't going anywhere. He sat on a chair near her bed and listened to the faint rasp of her breathing.

And waited.

Sleep was the best escape.

There had been visits from doctors. A portable X-ray machine had been brought in to take images of her lungs and a respiratory technician had taken a long time to test their function. The interview with the police detective had been tiring and upsetting because nobody could tell her whether the cats were okay. It had been such a relief to drift back into unconsciousness.

Being awake meant too many things clamouring for attention. Practical things like whether she still had any clothes available and if there was enough money in the bank to cover temporary accommodation. Physical things like how long it would be before it felt easy to breathe again and how soon she would have enough of a voice to call Maggie so that she could tell her about what had happened now. The emotional things were the worst, though. That horrible feeling of knowing that something disastrous had happened and the future had changed for ever. A bit like that emotional tornado she'd found herself in after finding Simon in bed with Brie. A lot like the terrifying abyss of knowing she would never see her parents again.

She'd had Maggie then but now she had nobody. Not here, anyway. Not close enough to hold her and make her believe that it would all be all right in the end. She had a blurry memory of Nic being in the ambulance with her but she hadn't seen him since.

He'd risked his life to save her. The police detective had told her that and the nursing staff obviously thought he was a hero.

'He did come,' someone told her. 'But you were asleep. He'll be back.'

To say goodbye?

Maybe she didn't want him to come back.

She saw him the moment she opened her eyes. Sitting in the chair, slumped forward a little with his elbows on his knees and his hands shading his eyes, as if he was trying to find a solution to the problems of the world.

For a moment she just gazed at him, remembering the first time she'd seen him. When he'd walked into her shop and she'd felt the blast of testosterone and the thrill of thinking he wanted *her*.

Amazing that someone could still exude that kind of masculine power from such a relaxed position. Could still seem commanding when his clothes were streaked with grime and there was a big tear in his jeans. Could still be so incredibly sexy with a couple of days of stubble and lines of weariness etched deeply into his face.

Nobody would ever guess the vulnerable part of him that was so well hidden but, for Zanna, that knowledge would always be there. He needed her love but already she could feel it being locked away. A part of the past. Was that for the best? He might not have wanted it anyway.

Her inward breath caught and made her cough and Nic's hands dropped as he lifted his head.

For a long, long moment they simply held each other's gaze.

'Hey...' Nic's voice was quiet. A bit croaky. 'You're awake. How are you feeling?'

'Oh—okay, I think.' Her voice was still hoarse. She pushed herself more upright in the bed. 'Are you?' He had his arm in a sling.

The single nod was familiar now. 'I dislocated my shoulder. It's been put back. I just need to be careful with it for a bit.'

'No bike-riding, then.' Zanna tried to smile but it wasn't going to happen.

'No.'

A silence fell that she didn't want to continue because that could be the moment that Nic told her he was leaving. That he was giving up on his music-school project or whatever it was he'd come for because it had become all too messy and that he was going back to London. Or France. Somewhere as far away from her as he could get.

Some things had to be said, however.

'I hear you saved my life,' she managed. 'Thank you.'

'I just happened to be in the right place at the right time. It wasn't a matter of choice.'

'There's always a choice. You didn't have to put your own life at risk.'

But Nic shook his head. His look suggested she was missing the point.

'Have the police talked to you yet?'

'No. I saw an officer at the house. He was making sure nothing got looted but he let me in when I told him why I was there. I've got your bag and wallet and things. And some clothes for you. They might smell a bit smoky but they're okay.'

'You've been to the house?'

'Yes. I needed to do something while you were asleep.'

'Did you find the cats?'

'No. Sorry. I've left some food out in the courtyard for when they come back.'

'How...how bad is it?'

'I couldn't get into the shop. That's where the worst of the damage is and there was a fire investigation crew in there. As far as I can see, it's only smoke and water damage in the rest of the house but...it's not pretty, Zanna. I've called Pete. He's going to come over and see whether it makes a difference to whether it can still be moved but he can't come for a few days.'

But Zanna didn't seem to be interested in whether the project would have to be abandoned. Like she hadn't realised how stupid it had been to suggest he'd had a choice about whether or not he'd go into a burning house.

She'd been inside. Of course he'd had no choice.

'They're saying the fire was deliberately lit.'

'*What?*'

'There's apparently clear evidence that an accelerant was used. In the shop.' Zanna coughed again and reached for the glass of water on the bedside locker.

'I've told the police all about Blake being there. About all the trouble there's been.'

Had she told them about him as well? About the apparent deception that had led to her agreeing to sell the house?

It didn't matter. Nic's opinion of himself probably wasn't any worse than what the police would think.

'This is my fault.' He pressed his fingers to his forehead before pushing them through his hair. 'I called Don. I told him that I wouldn't be working with him again. I knew they'd be angry. I suspect the company will be in big financial strife if the new resort project gets canned. And he knew I'd bought your place. They would have made a lot of money out of that if they'd ever got hold of it.' He had to get to his feet. 'But to do *that* as some kind of revenge… You could have died, Zanna.'

'It's not all your fault, Nic.'

'What's not all his fault?'

Two police officers were standing in the door of the room. Zanna recognised one of them as the detective she'd spoken to earlier.

'Did you find him?' she demanded. 'Have you arrested Blake Scallion?'

'We've talked to him, yes.'

'And?' Nic was scowling.

'He denies any involvement. He's telling a rather different story, in fact.' The detective turned to Nic. 'You're Dominic Brabant, I assume?'

The single nod answered the query.

'And you've recently purchased thirty-two Rata Avenue from Miss Zelensky?'

'Yes.'

'And you own the adjoining property?'

'That's correct.'

'I understand you're into property development. That you've worked with the Scallions over the last few years off and on.'

'Not any more. Not after what I've learned about how they've treated Zanna and her aunt. They—'

'What did you intend to do with the house? It would be in the way of any development, wouldn't it?'

'Are you suggesting *I* set the fire?' Nic's tone was dangerous. 'When Zanna was inside?'

'And you were conveniently there to rescue her?' The detective's expression said it seemed plausible.

'That's ridiculous.' The fierceness of her words made Zanna cough again. 'We're...we're...'

What were they, exactly? Or what had they been? Friends? Lovers? Soul-mates? She didn't know what they had been and it made her feel helpless. Knowing that whatever it was wasn't there any more made it all seem irrelevant anyway. She shifted her gaze to Nic as if that could help her make some kind of sense of what had happened between them but he was glaring at the detective who was speaking again.

'The suggestion came from Mr Scallion but it's not an unreasonable scenario. I imagine the house is insured. It would be more profitable to make a claim than pay demolition costs. And hasn't a fair percentage of the contents already been put into storage?'

'Blake's lying,' Zanna said fiercely. 'He's been threatening us for years. He poisoned our trees.' She made a frustrated sound. 'You don't know what you're talking about. The house is going to be shifted, not demolished. We've bought land...'

Except that contract hadn't been signed yet, had it?

The papers had all been drawn up but the owners were overseas until next week so couldn't add their signatures.

'And of course Nic was around,' Zanna added. 'He's been staying with me since...'

Was it only last week? Would they ask how long she'd known him before she'd let him stay?

This was all crazy and she seemed to be making it worse. Zanna pressed her lips together and shut her eyes. She needed to think.

'We'd like you to come down to the station, Mr Brabant. We need to ask you some more questions and take a statement.'

'Fine. The sooner we get this sorted the better. I'd like a solicitor present as well.'

Zanna's eyes snapped open. Were they *arresting* Nic? What evidence did they have, other than circumstantial? Not for one moment had she thought he'd had anything to do with the fire but—just for a heartbeat—she could feel the roller-coaster of the doubts and perceived betrayal she had been riding for the last few days.

Was there something in what the police were suggesting?

Something she just didn't want to see because part of her still wanted to believe in Nic?

She'd ripped up the contract and potentially made it impossible for him to achieve his dream. He would have been angry about that, wouldn't he?

He'd worked with Blake before. Was it so impossible to imagine he would do it again?

But why would he have risked his own life to save her from a fire he'd started himself?

Or had he misjudged the timing of events?

Nic chose that moment to turn and look at her. He

seemed about to say something but then he met her eyes and his mouth closed.

He turned again, without saying a word, and accompanied the police officers out of the room.

Zanna was pushing her bed covers back as a nurse came into the room moments later.

'What do you need, love?'

'I need to go home,' Zanna said, her voice breaking. 'Now. Could you help me find my clothes, please?'

CHAPTER TWELVE

THE TREES WERE BARE.

Whatever leaves had still clung to their branches had either been burned away or just given up the battle and fallen to the ground. The trunk of the tree closest to the shop was blackened and the smaller branches were gone, their stumps poking into a grey sky that threatened rain at any moment. The house looked naked without the leafy screen. Exposed to the eyes of curious onlookers who stood behind the bright orange 'Police Emergency' tape that circled the front of the house and peered at the evidence of trauma with morbid fascination.

One of those figures was familiar. It was only days ago that she'd seen her solicitor, Keith Watson, and that meeting had been a celebration of a secured future for Rata House. A future that looked as if it had been snatched away.

'Suzanna.' Keith came towards her as the taxi pulled away. 'I couldn't believe it when I heard about the fire. Are you all right?'

No. Zanna was a very long way from being all right. Force of habit made her stand a little straighter, though.

'I was lucky,' she told Keith. 'I got rescued. It could have been a lot worse.'

'Indeed it could. How on earth did the fire start?'

'Apparently it was arson.'

Keith looked shocked. And then he looked around them as though worried that someone might have overheard. 'Are you allowed inside?' He gestured towards the police officer who stood on the path on the other side of the tape.

'It's my house. Why wouldn't I be allowed inside? I need to see how bad it is.'

Keith lowered his voice. 'If they know it was arson, then it's a crime scene. Let me have a word with the officer.'

Zanna waited on the edge of the crowd, thankful for the hood of her sweatshirt giving her a perceived privacy. This was hard, not being alone when she had to cope with the shock of seeing her home like this. She wasn't even sure she wanted to go inside yet.

Steeling herself, she looked past the ruined trees. The glass panes of the bay window of Spellbound were broken and had been roughly boarded over. The weatherboards of the house were blackened and larger pieces of debris from the shop had been piled in a charred heap at the bottom of the steps.

Despite herself, she was drawn closer. She needed to see the worst of it.

She was closer to the rest of the onlookers now. Beside a trio of high-school students.

'Oh, my God,' a blonde girl said. 'I can't believe this.'

'It's awful,' her companion agreed. 'Where are we going to go after school now, Jen?'

Zanna's head turned. Holding Jen's hand was a lanky youth with a flop of hair that covered one eye.

'I told you about this shop, Stevie, didn't I? It was so cool.'

'Bit of a mess now. Let's go and get a burger or something.'

'It must have been one of those candles.' Jen still sounded fascinated by the drama. 'On the counter, remember? Maybe one of them didn't get put out. It's really sad, isn't it?' She leaned closer to the boy, who obligingly put his arm around her shoulders as they turned to leave.

Zanna had to blink back tears. Maybe the jellybean spell had worked but there wouldn't be a stream of teenage girls coming into Spellbound as word of mouth spread.

There wouldn't be anyone coming in for herbal tea and organic cake either. Spellbound, as it had been, didn't exist any more.

Keith was waving at her. Holding the plastic tape up with his other hand. 'We can go in and get any necessities you might need but we can't stay long. And you can have a look but we're not to go beyond the tape or touch anything in the shop. They haven't finished the investigation yet.'

Zanna nodded. She was thankful that Keith was here. A kindly, middle-aged man who had known both her and Maggie for years. He would look after her if she couldn't cope and right now she wasn't at all sure how well she was going to cope.

They started with the shop, skirting the pile of debris and climbing the steps to look over the tape past the half-open door.

Water still dripped from intact but charred beams in the ceiling of the room. The smell of the fire was still overpowering. The dead, unpleasant odour of charred wood, wet ashes and a peculiar mixture of pungent oils and herbs. A blackened, stinking layer of rubbish covered the floor and what was left of the counter.

Zanna shut her eyes. Had she shut the door properly last night or had she been distracted by that horrible sensation of being watched and then forgotten completely when she'd gone in to confront Nic with what she'd been told? What if the cats had gone back to their favourite new sleeping place on that pile of clothing?

She choked back a sob and Keith put his arm around her shoulders.

'Let's go into the main part of the house. It can't be as bad as where the fire started.'

It wasn't as bad. Or maybe Zanna was being protected by the numbness she could feel enveloping her brain and her heart. Fatigue washed into every cell in her body and it was an effort to make her legs move to follow Keith. She just needed to get this over with and then she could find somewhere to curl up and go to sleep again for a while.

Everything looked black and dirty and smelt horrible. How could smoke do so much damage in such a short space of time? It was like someone had taken a colour image of everything and then made a very bad job of trying to turn it into an arty sepia print. The colours were all wrong on the flowers on her bedroom wall and when she touched one, all she did was make a blackened smear that obliterated the lines of the petals.

It was heartbreaking.

'Do you want to look upstairs? In the turret?'

Zanna shook her head. The last thing she remembered clearly from last night was finishing that painting—an image torn from her soul. She couldn't bear to see that ruined.

'I don't need to see any more,' she said quietly. 'I just want to check to see whether the cats have been back for any food and then I'll have to find somewhere to stay.'

'We'll organise a motel. Or you could come home with me. Janice would love to be able to look after you.'

It was a kind offer. She should feel grateful but the numbness was blunting any kind of response and Zanna was actually grateful for that. If she couldn't feel small things, maybe she'd stop feeling the huge, overwhelming things as well.

'Have you contacted your insurance company?'

'No.'

'It might be best if I do that for you. It's going to complicate things a bit that the property's been sold so recently. And that the fire was deliberate. It could get messy.'

Zanna simply nodded. She couldn't face any of the bureaucracy that this situation would create. She didn't have the energy and what was the point? Everything was ruined.

The food that Nic had left in the courtyard for the cats hadn't been touched. As if that was the last straw, Zanna sank into one of the wrought-iron chairs and closed her eyes, gathering that comforting numbness around her like a cloak.

'Have you been in touch with Maggie? Does she know about this?'

Zanna shook her head again.

'Would you like me to do that for you?'

'No. But I haven't got my phone. I don't imagine the landline will be working?'

'I wouldn't think so. They will have turned off the

services to the house after the fire. I'll have Maggie's number in my phone. Would you like to use that?'

Zanna wanted to shake her head again. She didn't want to have to tell Maggie about this. Didn't want to have anything pierce the anaesthetic cloak that was working so well to numb her emotional pain. It would be the middle of the night over there and Maggie would answer her phone already knowing that something was very wrong.

'She'll need to know,' Keith said gently. 'And I'm sure she'd want to know as soon as possible. This has been her home for a very long time and we both know how much she loves it.'

So Zanna nodded instead of shaking her head and let Keith find the number and call it. Then he handed her the phone and walked back into the kitchen to give her some privacy.

It rang and rang and went to voicemail. Hearing Maggie's voice was enough to stab a huge hole in the numbness and suddenly all Zanna wanted was to hear the voice for real and not on a recorded message so she ended the call and immediately pushed redial.

This time it was answered but then there was only silence.

'Hello? Maggie—are you there?'

She could hear something. Someone speaking faintly in a language she didn't recognise. Russian? No…it must be Romanian. Had Maggie lost her phone?

'Hello?' The query was more tentative now. 'Can someone hear me?'

'Ah…' A rich male voice was clear. 'At last. It's hard to work a different phone. Is that Suzanna?'

'Yes…' The English was perfect but heavily accented. 'Is that…Dimitry?'

'Yes. I am so pleased you called. I have been trying to find your number but couldn't access the contacts menu.'

The numbness was evaporating painfully fast, as if it was being peeled away from Zanna's skin.

'Where's Maggie, Dimitry? What's happened?'

'Maggie is in a hospital in Bucharest. I brought her here earlier in the night because I was so afraid for her and it seems that she may have had a heart attack. She is having a procedure at the moment but she gave me her phone before they took her away. She asked me to call you.'

'Oh, my God… *No…*'

Keith must have heard her agonised cry because he came out of the house swiftly. With one look at Zanna's face he took the phone from her shaking hand.

'Hello? My name's Keith Watson. I'm with Suzanna. Please tell me what's going on.'

'I do apologise for the length of time this has taken, Mr Brabant. But you understand we had several lines of enquiry to follow up.'

'So I can go now?'

'You won't be needed again until Mr Scallion's trial begins. That probably won't be for a month or so.'

'Did you get hold of Zanna? Does she know about the CCTV footage from the petrol station on Rata Avenue that shows Blake buying the can of petrol?'

'We've been unable to contact her. She left the hospital some hours ago, shortly after we brought you in for the interview. She visited the house but left in a hurry about an hour later, according to the officer we have on the scene. Her mobile phone isn't being answered. It's either switched off or dead or out of range.'

Nic could only nod. His shoulder ached abominably and it felt like days since he had slept. They'd offered him food while he'd been here at the central police station but he hadn't been hungry. The physical discomfort he was in was pale in comparison to the utter weariness of spirit weighing him down.

He would never be able to forget the way Zanna had looked at him from her hospital bed.

As if she thought he could have been responsible for the fire that had almost killed her.

He was too exhausted to feel hurt any more. Or angry, which had been the best way to deal with the hurt. Now he just felt empty.

And a bit lost.

There was only one place in this city that he felt remotely connected with and it wasn't a long walk from the city's biggest police station so it was no real surprise that he automatically headed in the direction of Rata Avenue. He would have to do something about sorting the bike still parked on the street, anyway, given that he wouldn't be riding it back to the hire firm himself.

It was late afternoon now, and beginning to rain, which made the scene of the fire all the more bleak when he arrived there. The broken and boarded windows of the shop made the house look derelict. Haunted, even.

A police officer was sheltering from the rain on the veranda.

'The owner's not here but there's a bloke in there who says he's her solicitor if you want to talk to him.'

Nic didn't bother telling him that he, in fact, was the owner. Or was he? The possession date had been yesterday, hadn't it? Did something like this put an immediate injunction on legal proceedings? Keith would know.

He found Keith in the kitchen, finishing a phone call.

'You can start tomorrow. Nine o'clock. I've arranged a cleaning firm to be here at the same time, so the items for storage can be cleaned before you transport them. I'll be here as well. I want to make sure that everything salvageable is removed.'

He turned to Nic as he ended the call. 'You look terrible.'

'Cheers.'

His tone was grim but Keith's face softened. He stepped forward to grip Nic's uninjured shoulder. 'I've known Suzanna Zelensky since she was six years old,' he said quietly. 'A frightened little girl that Maggie was determined to keep safe. You saved her life last night and—on behalf of Maggie—I want to tell you how much that means.' His voice cracked. 'Just in case Maggie never gets the chance to tell you herself.'

He let go of Nic and cleared his throat. 'I'm sorting out getting the house cleared for you.'

'So the property is legally mine?'

'The possession date was four p.m. yesterday so it was well past by the time the fire started. There's a grey area concerning insurance on the house because nothing had been arranged to cover that separately. I'll talk to the insurance company and we'll start working through that tomorrow. I'll have to look into the purchase of the new land as well, but it looks as if that might have to fall through. Suzanna's not going to be here to sign anything.'

'Why not?' A chill ran down Nic's spine. 'Where is she?'

'Right now she's on a flight to Auckland. She's heading for LA and then London, where she can connect to a flight to Romania. It's going to take too long but it was the best we could do and the airlines have done their best to accommodate a family emergency.'

'What emergency?' Was it the mix of pain and exhaustion that was making his brain feel so sluggish?

'Maggie's had a heart attack. We have no idea how bad it was. Or even if she'll still be alive by the time Suzanna gets there.' Keith shook his head. 'As if the poor girl didn't have enough on her plate as it is. She looked a lot worse than you, Nic, but there was no stopping her.'

A smile tugged at the corner of Nic's mouth. 'She has an amazing spirit. Nobody would stop Zanna being with a person she loved who needed her.'

Keith gave him a curious glance that lingered long enough for Nic to wonder what the older man was thinking.

'I've got a few more calls and notes to make. You might want to have a wander around. I imagine you need a bit of time to decide what you need to do next.'

That was true enough. So many things would have to be put on hold. He might own the land but nothing could be started for the music school until the house was gone and that belonged to Zanna. It would be a couple of days before Pete could get here and give his opinion on whether it could still be moved but Nic didn't want to think about what would happen if it was decided that the damage was too great.

And it wasn't, surely?

With more purpose in his movements, Nic followed Keith's suggestion of wandering around. He took in the revolting mess of the room that had housed the shop but damped down the feeling of defeat the smell and sight of the damage evoked and looked more closely. The windows could be replaced and the stock certainly could. The gap in the internal wall that had let so much smoke into the main part of the house could also be repaired but how complicated that would be depended on how much damage there had been to the supporting beams.

He looked up. The solid beams would always be scarred from the charring but they looked strong enough to be structurally sound. If he went to the room above and tested the floor, he might get an even better idea of whether additional strengthening would solve any issues.

His path took him up the main stairway. He could feel his heart thumping against his ribs as he remembered the last time he'd come up here. The overwhelming fear for Zanna's safety that had driven him through the heat and smoke.

The feeling like it was his own life he was trying to save.

Being in her bedroom added a tightness to his throat that reminded him of how hard it had been to breathe. And no wonder. How much smoke had made it in here to blacken the walls like this? How sad would Zanna have felt to have been standing where he was? All that work. The painstaking hours that encapsulated the birth of a passion. The emerging talent that was such a huge part of who she was. The flowers were ruined.

Or were they?

Rubbing one gently with his finger only made the black smudge thicker but when he licked his finger and concentrated on one tiny patch, the delicate blue of a forget-me-not appeared amongst the grime as if a miniature spotlight had been focused on it. He looked around.

This could be fixed. How would Zanna feel if she could walk in here again and see them as they had been? He could imagine how still she would become. The wonder in her face that would morph into joy.

He could add a lump to the tightness in his throat as he turned away. The odds of him seeing that were virtually nil.

There was no real reason to climb the spiral staircase but maybe he needed some closure. To view the door that was responsible for the pain he was in. To see where Zanna might have died if he hadn't been able to break in.

The smoke had been thick enough to be dangerous but not as bad as it had been a floor below. The sketches and paintings weren't obscured by grimy residue. The images of the cats reminded Nic that he needed to have another look for the M&Ms before he left. The image on the easel was a different one from what had been there the last time he'd been in here.

He stepped closer. And then he stepped back again.

Something huge was squeezing the breath right out of him as he stared at the painting. At his own image that could have been a photograph except that it was too rich for that. He could hear the notes of the guitar strings being plucked. The words of the classic song he'd been singing for Zanna.

Ne me quitte pas.

Don't leave me.

How could she have captured him so perfectly without knowing him well enough to see into his soul?

And if she could really do that, there was no chance she could have believed he would ever do anything to put her in danger.

All that was needed was a chance to be together

again—without something traumatic obscuring what
needed to be seen.

Of course Zanna needed time with Maggie right now
but soon…

Maybe soon, what she would need would be a reason to come back.

How long would she be away?

Too long?

Or not long enough?

CHAPTER THIRTEEN

'LADIES AND GENTLEMEN, please return to your seats. We will shortly be starting our preparations for landing.'

The announcement came while Zanna was trying to freshen up in the cramped confines of the plane's toilet. She had dragged a brush through her hair, washed her face and managed to apply enough make-up to hide the physical evidence of a long and tiring journey. The train trip through Romania had been enough of a trip in itself but the ensuing roundabout connection of flights from Bucharest to Germany to Singapore and finally back to New Zealand had taken over thirty hours.

As she returned to her seat and complied with the preparation for landing instructions by putting her safety belt on and shoving her bag under the seat in front, the pilot's voice came over the engine noise again.

'Going to be a gorgeous day, folks. Light north-westerly breeze, clear skies and an expected maximum temperature of twenty-eight degrees Celsius. A real Indian summer's day.'

Just as well she'd chosen to wear her favourite orange crop top, Zanna decided—one of the few items she had grabbed during that frantic scramble to pack a bag a month ago, when she'd been so afraid she wouldn't arrive in time to see Maggie alive.

So many panicked hours with no way to communicate with anyone until she'd reached Dimitry, who had been there to meet her flight. Not only was Maggie still alive, she was back at home in Dimitry's castle. The heart attack had been minor and the treatment meant that, with a few lifestyle changes, she would probably be healthier than ever. The moment Zanna had walked into her aunt's embrace she had known that that place was exactly where she needed to be. Where she needed to stay until some healing—both physical and emotional—had taken place.

She might not have come home this soon if Keith hadn't made contact to let her know she was required to give evidence at Blake Scallion's trial for arson. The cards had told Maggie that the conclusion to the trouble was coming and she was already satisfied that karma was intact. Keith had told them that Prime Property had gone into liquidation in the last few days. The Scallions were ruined.

It wasn't the only forecast that had come from the treasured set of cards Zanna had brought over for Maggie.

'The Empress? But she's about marriage and birth…'

'Perhaps it's the birth of a creative child, darling. You might be about to start a period of artwork that will provide fulfilment. I miss your paintings so much. Especially the sunflowers under the stairs. And the ivy in the bathroom.'

That had brought tears to Zanna's eyes but she still wasn't ready to talk about it. Those paintings were gone and she missed them too. Especially that last one. She hadn't wanted to talk about Nic either. It was over. Gone, along with her dreams for the house and her studio.

The plane's wheels jarred on the tarmac and the engines howled as it slowed.

The cards had played a cruel trick, putting up the King of Pentacles as a forthcoming influence for Zanna, but she wouldn't allow herself to see it as representing a person.

Because that would always be Nic's card?

He hadn't even called.

And why would he, when he'd been left thinking that she didn't believe in him?

On top of her drama-queen performance of ripping up that contract and telling him to get out?

She'd been so hurt by the idea of him being associated with Prime Property. She'd felt so betrayed. With the benefit of hindsight she could see that it had been a necessary twist of fate that the unexpected availability of the apartment block had been the catalyst for the inspiration of the music school. If he hadn't purchased the neighbouring property first, he would never have had reason to come to a city that would never boast a coastal resort.

Where was he now? Probably on site at the location of a new project or back in London or France, waiting for decisions to be made so that they could all move forward. Of course the sale of the property hadn't been affected by her ripping up what had only been a copy of a legally binding contract.

The plane had stopped now. The snap of seat-belts being released accompanied movement as everyone began to gather their belongings.

The King of Pentacles was probably to do with all

the money that was waiting in an account after the sale had been finalised. A Midas touch, thanks to Keith, who had been taking care of everything that had needed sorting. At first unbearably weary and then feeling too sad, Zanna had let Maggie take over the intermittent conversations about what was happening and simply accepted her reassurance that things would be as they needed to be in the future. Her beloved aunt needed time to recover herself and she deserved to enjoy the happiness she'd found with Dimitry without having it tainted by worry about her niece's disastrous love life.

And it seemed that there was no hurry. Zanna could take a look while she was here for the trial and the really big decisions could wait until after that. Until she was ready.

Finally, she was. It was time to move forward, in more ways than one.

Hearing herself being paged as she emerged from customs led Zanna to an information desk.

'There's a message for you, Miss Zelensky. A Mr Keith Watson has arranged an elite taxi for you. It's the first one on the corporate taxi rank.'

Zanna smiled her thanks. It was a pleasant surprise not to have to arrange her own transport into the city. Had Maggie made the suggestion during one of those quiet conversations with their solicitor?

The walk to the taxi rank was short but there was enough time to look up and marvel at the clarity of the air here compared to the permanent haze of Europe. This was home and quality of light was something she wanted to infuse into her paintings for the rest of her life. Regular visits to the fairy-tale castle in the Transylvanian

Alps would be a must but this was where she wanted to be based.

She would just have to find somewhere to live.

The first car on the rank was a sleek, dark BMW with a discreet elite logo. Zanna opened the back door.

'Is this the taxi ordered by Watkins and Associates? Going to the Park View Hotel?'

The driver nodded into his mirror and muttered something about luggage that she had difficulty hearing. He was wearing a uniform that included a peaked cap and his mirrored sunglasses were all that she could see in the rear-view mirror.

'Don't worry about luggage. This is the only bag I have.' Sliding onto the comfortable leather upholstery, she dropped the overnight bag beside her. She fastened her safety belt as the car pulled smoothly away from the stand and then tilted her head back and closed her eyes. It was only a short ride into the central city but Zanna didn't feel inclined to engage in meaningless small talk. She needed some time to centre herself and prepare for the emotional impact that would come at some stage today when she had to go to Rata Avenue and make a decision about the final fate of her house.

The ten minutes seemed to stretch longer than even bad traffic could account for. And when she opened her eyes it took several seconds for Zanna to register what part of the city she was in. Or rather what part of the city she was *not* in. They were nowhere near the CBD. She was being driven out of town, in fact, with the last pocket of suburbia now behind them.

What was going on? Zanna's tiredness evaporated, the alarm raised by a potentially dangerous situation providing more than enough fuel to burn it off. She sat up straight as the car slowed to turn off the main road.

Maybe she wasn't being abducted. The last time she'd been on this road had been on the back of Nic's bike when he'd brought her out to see the land that would have been the perfect location for Rata House.

Had Keith arranged this, too? She'd assumed that the sale and purchase agreement for the land out here had been shelved, along with all the other plans in the wake of the fire, but maybe there was something that needed discussion. Was Keith meeting her there?

Her guess about the destination was correct, at any rate. The car slowed again at the ornate wooden gates she remembered and then rolled up a driveway newly shingled with small white pebbles. Past the lake with the willow trees and jetty and the little rowboat and there was the old stone stable building, but Zanna barely registered it. She remembered the stretch of grass like a small park and she could remember imagining Rata House in the middle of it.

Her fatigue must be a lot worse than she'd realised for her imagination to be playing a trick like this. For her to be seeing exactly what she had imagined. Her house—only it couldn't be her house because this was a younger version. Freshly painted, with a new slate roof, copper guttering and downpipes and new, wide veranda steps flanked by tubs of brilliant orange, red and yellow nasturtiums.

Even more fantastically, there were tendrils of wisteria already climbing up the wrought-iron of the veranda decoration and borders around the house were filled with the kind of old-fashioned flowers Zanna loved best. Roses and lavender and pansies. A profusion of colour that wrapped the house with a ribbon of joy. Most amazing of all were two large rata trees planted in front.

Completely lost for words, Zanna climbed out of the car very, very slowly after the driver opened the door for her. For a full minute she just stood there, completely stunned.

And then she looked around for someone to tell her what on earth was going on. How this magic had happened. But she was alone with her chauffeur.

'Do you know?' she asked. 'Who did this?'

In response, he shrugged off the uniform jacket to reveal a black T-shirt. Took off the peaked cap he was wearing. Removed the mirrored sunglasses.

And Zanna gasped.

'*Nic.*'

Oh, dear Lord, he looked exactly as he had in every dream she'd had of him in the last month. The rumpled hair and those gorgeous dark eyes. The shadowing on his jaw and that sexy hint of a slow smile that hadn't surfaced yet.

'What do you think?'

'I…' Zanna's head swerved to check that she hadn't imagined the house and then it swerved back because it was more important that she wasn't imagining that Nic was here. 'But I don't understand… How did you do this? *Why*?'

'I wanted to give you something to come back for.' The words were quiet. 'I wanted to see you again.'

'Oh…*Nic*…' Laughter was warring with tears. 'You could have just asked. If I'd known you wanted to see me I would have gone anywhere.'

She saw understanding dawn in his eyes and the lines of tension dissolve in his face. She saw the beginnings of that smile but then he was too close to see any more and she didn't need to see because she could feel. The strength of his arms around her as he held her so tightly. The softness of his lips as he kissed her and then kissed her again.

And then he took her hand. 'Come and see,' he invited. 'I want to show you everything.'

But Zanna stopped before they'd even reached the veranda steps. 'How?' She demanded. 'How on earth was this even possible?'

'It was a logistical nightmare,' Nic admitted. 'Pete and I have been working pretty much twenty-four seven since we started, which was probably about when you arrived in Romania. We've had up to a hundred contractors on site since the house was positioned, to get the renovations done. They only finished planting up the borders under floodlights last night.'

'But I hadn't even paid for the land.'

'Keith sorted it. Along with Maggie and me. She's quite some woman, your aunt, isn't she?'

'You've been *talking* to Maggie?'

'I wanted to talk to you but Maggie didn't think you were ready to listen at first. And then she came up with the idea of surprising you. Showing you that you hadn't lost as much as you thought you had.'

'Including you?'

'Especially me.' Nic kissed her again and his breath came out in a sigh that sounded like relief. 'That was why I agreed to the plan to keep it a secret. I had to know I could pull this together because I didn't want to promise something I couldn't deliver. I don't want you to ever again doubt that you can trust me.'

'I don't. I didn't… I was confused, that was all. There

were too many things happening all at once and they were too big… I couldn't take it in fast enough.'

She looked around her again. 'I still can't take *this* in. Whose idea were the nasturtiums?'

'Mine.' Nic was smiling again. 'They're the colour of flames and they make me think of you.'

'Oh, Nic… You have no idea how much I love you.'

'I don't know about that.' Nic bent to kiss her yet again. 'But I hope it's at least half as much as I love you.' When he lifted his mouth he touched his forehead to hers for a long, solemn moment.

'Je t'adore, ma chérie.'

She needed no translation. 'I love you, too,' she whispered back.

With her hand held within the circle of his fingers, Nic led Zanna inside. He had poured his heart and soul into this project for weeks and he'd never been so tired. Or so nervous about the result. Had he done justice to the home she had lived in for most of her life and loved so much? Changes had had to be made but that was life, wasn't it? You let go of some things and that meant you could choose the best and treasure them.

The interior walls of the house had been relined and painted in soft, pastel shades of lemon and cream. New carpets had been laid but the design and colours fitted the period of the house perfectly. New curtains graced windows with wooden framing that glowed richly after the timber had been stripped and restored.

'It feels so different,' Zanna murmured. 'So *light*…'

'It's not hemmed in by high-rise buildings any more. We've positioned it so it will get maximum sunlight, even in the winter.'

'You got everything out of storage. You've even put

the antique instruments back in the same places. And Maggie's hats… Oh, I'm glad we put them into storage before the fire. They wouldn't have survived the smoke.'

The beams in the room that had been Spellbound were the only reminder of the fire. They had been cleaned and polished but would always be misshapen and stained.

'Because you can't wipe out the past,' Nic said softly. 'And sometimes you have to honour it because it's what has made you what you are today.'

Every new surprise was a delight. Her bedroom with the painting she had done of Nic playing the guitar hanging over the head of the bed they had shared. The flowered walls intact and the blooms as bright as when they'd first been painted.

'We got lucky and found an electrician with a bit of imagination. He found places for the new plugs without having to ruin a single flower. And a plumber who looked after the ivy in the bathroom.'

Even the tiled floor in the kitchen had been saved and relaid. A new courtyard of recycled bricks lay beyond the French doors with the chiminea set amongst a collection of terracotta pots. The old rustic table and chairs were waiting. A bottle of champagne stood in an ice bucket with two stemmed glasses in invitation.

But Zanna didn't see them. Her hand gripped Nic's hard enough to cut off the circulation in his fingers as she stared at the terracotta pots filled with flame-coloured geraniums. To where there were three black shapes emerging from between the pots and coming towards her.

Letting go of Nic's hand, Zanna dropped to a crouch and gathered the wash of black fur into her arms. Tears of joy were on her cheeks as she looked up at him.

'They're alive…' she whispered.

'I found them the day we were lifting the house. Or Merlin found me.'

'He's a clever cat. He knew you were special right from the moment he met you.' Zanna was on her feet again. 'Like I did.'

He took her into his arms again. He never wanted to let her go.

'Is it all right? Is it how you imagined it could be?'

'Better. Unbelievable. I still have no idea how you could possibly have pulled this off.' Zanna's smile was misty. 'I know I really do believe in magic now.' She pulled away far enough to catch Nic's gaze. 'But I don't want to live here.'

His jaw dropped. Time stopped.

'Alone,' Zanna added. 'I couldn't live here without you, Nic. This place is perfect but…it's a house and—'

'And home is where the heart is,' Nic finished for her.

Her nod was solemn. 'Mine is with you,' she said. 'For ever.'

It was too hard to find words. Too big. All Nic could do was tilt his head in a single nod to signal his agreement. To kiss this woman he loved so much in a way that would let her know he felt exactly the same way.

For ever was going to start right now.

EPILOGUE

A year later...

THE SPEECHES WERE over and the crowd poised to applaud.

Nic's hand covered Zanna's so that they were both holding the oversized ceremonial scissors they were using to cut the wide scarlet ribbon.

The Brabant Music Academy was officially open.

The beautiful, curved building that echoed the flow of the river was being hailed as one of the most significant new assets of the city. The acoustic masterpiece of a concert hall would cater for the most discerning musicians and their fans. The numerous, soundproofed tutorial rooms would give the students what they needed to be nurtured into the futures they dreamed of. The later addition of the café and courtyard garden would encourage others to step into a world they might not otherwise have entered and the space tagged for after-school and holiday programmes might inspire members of a new generation.

Members of the symphony orchestra were playing in the concert hall as the invited guests toured the academy. Herbal tea, champagne and organic canapés were available in the café.

Nic was still holding Zanna's hand as they mingled and talked to people. So far, they hadn't made it past the foyer that housed the gallery of beautiful black and white photographs of Rata House—the captions below sharing the history of the land on which the school now stood. One of the images was in colour. And it was a painting rather than a photograph. A scene of the house reborn, with the lake in the foreground and the back-drop of the native bush.

'This is one of your paintings, Zanna?' The mayor looked impressed. 'I must get to your next exhibition. I'm told your first was a sell-out.'

'Of course it was.' The pride in Nic's voice was matched by the loving glance between the couple.

The mayor continued to admire the painting. 'It looks like it was always meant to be there. I'm delighted to see that someone had the vision to preserve such a special part of our city's heritage. And in such spectacular fash-ion. I suspect you're a bit of a magician, Nic.'

'No magic involved. Just a dream and a lot of hard work.'

'I'll bet. You deserve the privilege of having it as your home.'

'One of our homes.' Zanna smiled. 'We intend to spend half our year in France, where we have another house.'

'Ah…' The mayor nodded. 'I heard that was where you went to get married?'

'No,' Zanna laughed. 'We got married in a castle. In Transylvania. Let me introduce you to my aunt Magda and her husband. They've come all the way from Ro-mania for this opening ceremony.'

Maggie was delighted to meet the mayor. 'I can't tell you what a lovely surprise it was to find the council has planted rata trees on the avenue. Such lovely, big specimens, too.'

'Mr Brabant got the biggest one available. Have you seen it out there on the lawn?'

'We're heading that way now.' Zanna linked her arm with Maggie's and smiled at Dimitry. 'Let's go and find you both a glass of something bubbly so we can celebrate properly.'

There was so much to celebrate but Zanna wouldn't be drinking anything more than a cup of herbal tea. She met Maggie's gaze over the rim of her cup a short time later.

'So the cards were right.' Her aunt smiled. 'I had a feeling the Empress was there for more than the birth of a creative child.'

It was too early for it to be any more than a guess but there was no point in trying to keep it a secret.

'We only just found out.'

'Congratulations.' Dimitry's eyes looked suspiciously moist. 'Such happy news.'

'I think it will be a girl,' Maggie pronounced.

Zanna looked up at Nic. 'If it is,' she said softly, 'I'd like to name her Elise.'

He had to take her away then. To a quiet spot away from the crowd. To the bench seat that had been placed on the river side of the rata tree on the lawn. The seat with the small brass plaque that carried his parents' names.

So that he could kiss his wife and tell her again just how much he loved her.

So that he could hear her tell him the same thing.

He'd been wrong in telling the mayor that no magic had been involved. And hadn't he told Zanna within the first few minutes of meeting her that he wouldn't believe in magic in a million years?

Well…he had just changed his mind. It was the only word to describe this—the alchemy of finding the person you wanted to be with for ever that only happened when they felt exactly the same way.

There was more magic to be found as well. Very strong magic that meant this was one spell that would never be broken.

Ever.

* * * * *

ROYALLY
SEDUCED

MARIE DONOVAN

To my own Eleanor of Aquitaine.
A sunny French book for a sunny girl.
With much love always.

1

LILY ADAMS STOOD in front of her New Jersey apartment building shivering in the predawn morning skies. Although it was July, the air was still damp and chilly at four in the morning. Her cousin Sarah and her cousin's husband Curt should be here any minute to take her and Sarah to the airport. She and Sarah were less than a year apart in age. Sarah's dad was the brother of Lily's late father, and he had done his best to act as a stand-in dad. Although Lily and Sarah had grown up in different suburbs of Philadelphia and gone to different schools and colleges, they had gone to summer camp together and shared major milestones.

And now they were sharing a fabulous trip together. Lily shivered again, this time in anticipation. Her first time in Europe! Sarah had studied in France and was a high-school French teacher, but Lily was a total newbie. A European newbie, so to speak.

After graduating from college with a somewhat-less-than-lucrative journalism degree with an even-less-lucra-tive English-literature minor, Lily had decided to remedy a childhood of never going anywhere by starting a modest career as a travel writer. So far, she had done several ar-

ticles on her native city of Philly and had branched out to
New Jersey and New York.

But writing articles for the local parenting magazine on
top ten historic sites for kids in Philly was shooting fish in
a barrel. Adventure lay outside the Tri-State area, so she'd
scraped together enough money for a trip to France. Just
her and Sarah for the next few weeks.

She craned her neck. Yes, that was their car, a dark
sedan that glided smoothly to the curb. Sarah hopped out...
in her pajamas? Comfort was important for flying, but,
well, okay. Lily didn't much care what their fellow passengers thought of her cousin's baggy pink T-shirt and red
flannel pants, complete with monkeys dangling off palm
trees. It was all good, as long as Sarah could pass through
security without being tagged for crazy.

But Sarah also looked like death warmed over, her
short brown bob scraped back by a linty black headband
that looked like an Alice in Wonderland reject. Her face
was pale even in the dim light, and her lips were dry and
cracked.

"Um, are you okay?" Stomach flu on an international
flight would be kind of dicey.

Sarah's mouth spread into a wide grin and then she
burst into tears of all things, clutching Lily as she sobbed.
Curt hopped out of his side of the car and hurried to them.
"What the heck is going on, Curt?"

"No!" Sarah jerked her head up, her expression alarm-
ingly close to a snarl. "Don't you dare say a word!"

Curt and Lily cringed. "Of course not, darling. It's yours
to tell, precious." He wrapped his arm around his wife's
shoulder and kissed the top of her limp hair.

Darling? Precious? Curt was usually about as romantic
as a rock.

"Sarah?" Lily said cautiously. She wasn't sure what was

going on, but she had a nonrefundable ticket to Paris leaving in about four hours.

Her cousin's face smoothed out until it was almost beatific. "Lily, I'm pregnant!"

Lily shrieked loud enough to wake the neighbors, who wouldn't bother calling the cops even if it were some mad strangler coming into her apartment. "Pregnant!" She started to jump up and down but quickly stopped when she saw the queasy look on Sarah's face.

"I know, I know! After all these years, all those times when it didn't work out…"

Lily gave her a quick kiss, remembering Sarah's several miscarriages until the damn doctors had figured out she'd had a blood clotting disorder all along. This trip to Europe was supposed to be a kind of decompression from the pain and stress of her infertility and losses—no pressure to conceive with a husband five thousand miles away. "But how did you find out?"

Sarah giggled. "I'd been feeling kind of off for the past week but I figured it was a touch of flu. Then last night about eight, I started throwing up hard, and Curt was worried. He took me to the E.R. They put in an IV but also ran a pregnancy test." She shrugged, her face splitting into a grin. "And here we are."

"Well, of course you can't go." Lily wouldn't have her cousin risk her baby on a strenuous overseas trip.

Curt's shoulders sagged in relief. He had obviously expected some hassle.

"But, Lily, how will you manage all by yourself? You don't speak a lick of French, and you've never been anywhere."

Great for her self-confidence. "Didn't you tell me that if you ever got pregnant again you would need very close prenatal care along with anticoagulant shots right from the start?"

"Yes," Sarah admitted. "But I feel so terrible about abandoning you."

"Please," she scoffed. "I'm a big girl. I have my itinerary and my French phrasebook."

Sarah winced. Lily had a terrible accent, being unable to master the sheer nasality of the language. "Well, at this time of year there are always English speakers roaming around if you get into a bind. And Curt and I will take you to the airport like we planned. I wish I had given you more notice than this," she fretted.

"I wouldn't change anything," Lily told her, and that was the truth. Later on in the pregnancy, when her cousin felt more secure, Lily would inform her she was going to be the godmother. Maybe she would bring back a little French toy for the baby and keep it hidden until he or she was born.

Curt loaded her things into the trunk and they headed for the Verrazano Bridge to cross into New York. JFK Airport sat on a bay overlooking the Atlantic Ocean in Queens. At that early hour, the miles passed quickly and Lily found herself deposited on the sidewalk with all her luggage.

Sarah reached her hand out the window to grab her cousin's hand. "Lily, Lily, please take care of yourself." Her eyes were filling up. Lily's were, too, only she didn't have early pregnancy hormones to blame, thank God.

She blew Sarah a kiss. "Everything will be fine. I'll text you once I land. You just concentrate on taking care of yourself—and your baby."

Sarah waved as Curt pulled away from the curb. Lily took a deep breath and hefted her backpack onto her shoulders before pulling her medium-size rolling suitcase into the terminal.

Her first major trip anywhere. France, land of wine and roses, perfume and pomp. Wow, that sounded good. She grabbed her phone and quickly entered that phrase. She had her laptop all tuned up and ready for the great stories that would fall in her lap.

Lily was going to take France by storm.

JACQUES MONTFORD HOPPED off the Métro stop a few blocks from the family mansion on Rue de Faubourg St-Honoré. His mother, the Dowager Countess de Brissard, had wanted to send the family car to meet him at the airport, but he needed more time. Time to get out of the closeness of the airplane, the craziness of Charles de Gaulle Airport, time to get some fresh air—as fresh as Paris could provide.

He climbed the stairs to the street. Ah, the *parfum de Paris* in the summer. More than a hint of auto exhaust and pollution, but also a touch of garden from behind the high walls he passed. Jasmine, definitely rose and a touch of lily. But no lavender.

The only lavender in Paris was in the buckets in the flower market and maybe in a clay pot in some less sophisticated neighborhood than the one he walked through.

For real lavender, Jacques would have to leave Paris and go to Provence.

The idea of another trip at that point seemed exhausting. More exhausting than staying with his mother in Paris? That remained to be seen.

He rounded the corner to the house and took the steps before knocking on the wide wooden door. He hadn't bothered to take his key ring on his trip to the Southeast Asian typhoon disaster area. As a relief-work physician, he'd had plenty of important medical supplies to carry with him. It was typical to bring one backpack of personal items and a couple of large suitcases filled with medicine, bandages and emergency surgical instruments. In fact, he was wearing his trusty backpack right now. He couldn't wait to drop it in his suite of rooms, take a shower and grab something to eat in the large kitchen. A quick knock, the door opened and he was officially in hell.

"Surprise!" A crowd full of people he didn't know greeted him, slapping him on the back and shaking his hand.

His mother, her hair an exact color match for his thanks to the hairdresser, fought her way to him, kissing him on both cheeks twice and crying prettily, though not enough to either ruin her mascara or redden her eyes. "Jacques! *Mon petit* Jacques is finally home!" she announced. His mother's guests cheered again.

He was a rich lady's prize poodle being trotted out for admiration. *And for his next trick, he will administer oral rehydration salts and give measles vaccinations!*

He felt like turning around and leaving. But the crowd filled in behind him and Bellamy was taking his beat-up backpack from him.

His mother clutched his shoulders. "Ah, Jacques, your hair. Why so long?" She fingered his long ponytail of chestnut-brown hair. "And *la barbe* that hides your handsome face?" She tapped his beard. "You look like one of those scruffy men who live in the subway." She, of course, was impeccably turned out in a flowing silk peach-colored lounge suit, the perfect outfit for an evening party at home.

"*Maman,* please." He took her hand away from his face but kissed the back of it so she wouldn't fuss.

She dimpled at him. "Someone else is waiting to kiss you," she said coyly.

He had no idea who. "Bellamy?" He was their ancient butler and the idea of being kissed by the old English fossil made him crack the first smile of the evening.

Unfortunately his mother misunderstood. "Oh, you funny boy. But that smile tells me you know who I mean."

"Actually, *Maman,* I don't…" he began, and then his teeth clicked together in shock at the person she intended him to kiss.

He'd rather have dysentery again.

"Nadine." It was difficult to pronounce his ex-fiancée's name from a clenched jaw, but he did just fine.

She took that as an invitation instead of an expression of dismay. "Oh, *mon amour!*" She flung her expensively dressed arms around his neck and tried to kiss him, but he turned his head and was happy to see her spitting out strands of his hair instead.

He took her by the upper arms and tried to set her away from him, but her grip reminded him of a gecko he'd watched while lying in a hospital bed in Thailand. That sticky-footed lizard could walk upside down on the ceiling and even across glass without falling. Of course it could also lick its eyes with its tongue, something that Nadine had not mastered—as far as he knew. What she did with her tongue was none of his business anymore. It was what she had done with it while it *had* been his business that had caused their breakup.

So why was she here, reenacting *The Hero's Welcome* from a black-and-white postwar movie? Jacques looked around at his proud mother and her well-lubricated guests eyeing him and beautiful blonde Nadine fondly. Nadine wisely decided not to kiss him again and instead threaded her arm through his, snuggling into his side. A hired waiter pressed a glass of champagne into his hand that wasn't suctioned to Nadine, and his mother raised her own glass.

"To my son, Jacques Charles Olivier Fortanier Montford, Comte de Brissard." As usual, she forgot the title he valued the most—doctor.

But the guests cheered anyway. Perhaps his beard hid what had to be a sour expression. *Huzzah, huzzah.* All that was needed was a rousing orchestral version of "La Marseillaise" as the weary warrior came limping back to Paris. He started to sing under his breath. *"Allons, enfants de la Patrie..."*

Nadine gave him a strange look and he remembered his precarious situation. She wanted nothing better than to be Madame la Comtesse de Brissard, and Jacques's paltry wishes were the only impediment to her desire to enter the *noblesse*.

He detached himself from Nadine and raised his glass in fake cheer when he caught his mother staring at them. "Come with me, Nadine."

He hurried her into the small hallway leading to the back stairs. Nadine looked at him apprehensively but reached out her arms to him.

Jacques folded his. "Nadine, what the hell are you doing here?" She started to pout, but he ignored it. "Were you hoping I'd developed amnesia along with dysentery?"

"Jacques!"

He was too tired to be kind anymore. "Go away, Nadine. I don't know what you've been telling my mother all these months, but it doesn't seem to have been the truth."

"But, *mon cher,* we just had a little misunderstanding before you left. If you had stayed instead of going to that dreadful typhoon, we would have smoothed things over in no time."

His jaw fell. "Nadine, I caught you having sex with your personal trainer. In our bed."

"I know, I know." She pasted an anguished expression

on her face. "And I feel terrible about that. I made a mistake."

I, I, I. Or as his Portuguese friend Francisco would say, *Ay, ay, ay.* It was all still about her.

"No, Nadine. We were through as soon as you undressed for that hairless, muscle-bound refugee from the tanning salon."

Her lips tightened, and he realized the Neckless Wonder might still be her "workout partner." She scoffed, apparently deciding to take the offensive. "Jacques, you know marriages among our class are not necessarily exclusive. Don't be so bourgeois."

"Genetically impossible, *chérie.* As you well know, I am the Count de Brissard," he taunted her.

The look in her eye made him glad the guillotine had been retired two hundred years ago. "You have the soul of a *peasant.*" And she meant it to sting.

Too bad for her he spoiled it by laughing. "I take that as a grand compliment. As a rule, peasants do not cheat and then have the gall to mock the person they cheat on." Although he had had a few months to come to terms with her infidelity, it still angered him and he started to raise his voice.

"You are the most selfish man I ever met!" she shouted at him.

"Selfish? Because I do not care to share my fiancée sexually?"

"Pah! If you would have stayed in France for more than two weeks, perhaps I wouldn't have needed to find companionship elsewhere."

"*Bien,* so I am selfish for leaving this mansion and going to the absolute hellholes of the world to help people who have nothing? Sick people? Dying people? *Et toi,* how do *you* help anyone but yourself?"

"Eh, *oui,* Saint Jacques of Paris. Any more of your 'good works' and they will be carving a statue of you for the Cathedral de Notre Dame. Make sure they get your sweaty hippie hair and beard correct. *Cochon!*" Her face reddened.

He didn't know if she was calling him a pig because of his hair or his personality, and he didn't care. "You are unbelievable. I am grateful I saw your true character before marrying you. I'm sure you would have cost me plenty to divorce you once I found out."

Her mouth twisted, about to fire more insults at him, but he couldn't take it—couldn't take *her*—any longer. He rounded the corner leading back to the party and stopped short.

His mother stood stricken in the hall, her hand covering her mouth—like he wished he had done to himself. The guests stood behind her, their expressions ranging from shocked to sly to amused.

Even Bellamy was shaking his dignified gray head. If Bellamy heard them yelling, they must have been loud indeed.

"Maman." He lowered his head to hers. "I am so sorry to ruin…" Out of the corner of his eye he caught a young man with disheveled blond hair surreptitiously taking his photo with his phone.

Was nothing private anymore? He couldn't even talk to his mother in their own home without some idiot and his camera phone?

"Eh, you!" he shouted at the man. "No photos. Give me that phone."

The guy clutched his phone to his chest but Jacques easily wrestled it from him and deleted the picture.

But that first man was not the only one. A larger camera took his picture—several times. Had his mother hired a photographer for the party? No, he noticed a polished brunette standing next to the photographer, taking copious notes.

"Reporters, *Maman?*"

Her stricken expression confirmed it. "Just the society page. They asked to come when we got news of your return."

"I don't want to be on the society page." That was a big reason he didn't stay in France for very long.

"I'm so sorry, Jacques." Her big blue eyes started to tear. "I missed you so much and wanted to welcome you back."

The large room started pressing in on him. "No, *Maman,* I'm sorry for embarrassing you. But I can't stay."

"What?" Her forehead creased. "But, Jacques, you just got home."

"I can't," he repeated. The noise, the bright lights, even the smell of the food was making him dizzy and disoriented. Nadine's theatrical sobs in the background didn't help, either. He pushed his way through the party guests and grabbed his beat-up backpack from near the door.

Ever the professional, Bellamy opened the door. "Good to see you again, milord," the butler informed him. Jacques gave him an incredulous glance considering the *mêlée* coming towards them, but the old man was as unruffled as always.

"If you would permit some advice from a longtime family retainer, I would recommend a sojourn in the country. Perhaps some fresh air and hearty cooking would benefit your constitution."

"That's the best idea I've heard in a long time, Bellamy. *Merci beaucoup.*" Jacques spotted the ambitious reporter and her photographer gaining on him.

"Not to fear, sir, mum's the word." After delivering the

quintessential English promise, Bellamy tipped him a wink before practically shoving him out the double doors.

Jacques darted down the steps and heard a thud against the door. Bellamy was holding off the savages at the pass, so to speak, so Jacques took advantage of the delay and made a beeline for the Métro.

He hopped a train to the Latin Quarter, a quirky neighborhood along the Seine that was home to the famous Sorbonne, the seat of the University of Paris. He knew of a student hostel there, and his scruffy appearance would blend right in. A bowl of soup in the café, a good night's sleep and then out of the city.

He'd had enough of Paris, and he'd only been there about two hours. A new record, even for him.

2

LILY STEPPED INTO the elevator of the youth hostel. At twenty-six, she was a bit older than many of the back-packers, but they were an accepting bunch. She'd never had the money to take a year off and backpack through Europe, so she envied the young students.

Two of them called down the bare-bones hallway to hold the elevator, so Lily stuck her arm out to block the doors.

"Thank you, Lily. Where do you go today?" Blonde and German, Silke and her companion, Hans, had been very helpful since Lily's arrival, pointing out tricks to getting around the Métro and giving her tips on cheap eats. To save money, Lily ate like the backpackers—rolls and *café au lait* at the bakery across the street for breakfast, a loaf of bread and ham along with some cheese and fresh fruit for lunch, and maybe a dinner out at a café if she could find one reasonably priced.

"I'm not exactly sure, but probably to *la Madeleine*."

"Who?"

"*La Madeleine* is a giant church in the Opera Quarter. Napoleon helped design part of it." Lily's stomach growled. "Plus there's a huge food mall and flower market next to it."

"Ah, very good." She gestured to her equally blond companion. "Hans and I are going to the cemetery in Montparnasse."

Hans nodded enthusiastically. "*Ja,* many important writers and thinkers are buried there. Jean-Paul Sartre and Simone de Beauvoir, Charles Baudelaire and—"

"And don't forget Samuel Beckett. He wrote *Waiting For Godot,*" Silke added helpfully, in case Lily wasn't familiar with that mind-numbing play. Thanks to her English degree, she unfortunately was.

"And if we have enough time, we will see the Catacombes. When they ran out of room in the city cemetery a couple centuries ago, they moved everyone there."

"Everyone?" Surely they didn't mean…

"They have walls of skulls and bones. That says so much about what life is all about. In the end, we are just piles of organic matter for others to stare at," Silke finished.

Lily fought back a sigh. How very grimly existential of them. No wonder they were going into raptures about Sartre and Simone de Beauvoir, the king and queen of existentialism. Lily preferred to take a more cheerful view of life, but that didn't seem to be the European way. No wonder they thought Americans were cockeyed optimists. And of course most Americans, if they thought of the French at all, imagined either mimes in white-striped shirts or else morose chain-smoking café dwellers dressed all in black.

Maybe that was a good blog article. "So what do you think of Parisians?"

Silke immediately answered, "Oh, it is very nice here."

"Ja," Hans agreed.

The elevator opened and they walked out to the lobby. "But what do you really think?" she insisted.

Silke looked around furtively. "It is not very organized. Sometimes the attractions do not open on time."

"Twenty minutes late, even," Hans threw in. "And they close for lunch at all hours—not what the sign says."

Lily smiled. Ah, punctuality. The more laidback French attitude did not sit right with German precision. "I can see how that would be a problem. But perhaps some spontaneity is a good thing on vacation?"

They gave her identically puzzled looks. Silke shrugged. "If they want to be open different hours, they should change the signs."

And that was that. Lily waved goodbye as they set off for their sunny Parisian day of skulls and cemeteries.

Lily turned toward the door, but she bumped into another backpacker, a tall, lean man with a long brown ponytail and matching beard. "Oh, *pardonnez-moi,*" she tried her French on him.

"No problem," he replied in perfect English with only a hint of an accent, as he adjusted the straps of his small black backpack.

Rats. "Is my accent that awful?" she burst out.

"What?" He looked at her, startled.

"My accent. My cousin Sarah says I have a terrible French accent, even on basic things like *pardonnez-moi* and *merci.*"

He gave a tiny wince as she pronounced those words.

"You hear it, too, don't you?" she cried. "I must sound like the American village idiot trying to speak your language."

"Hey, hey," he soothed her. "How long have you been living in France?"

"I've been visiting for a couple days."

He raised his shoulders in a typically French shrug.

"And so you think your two days in Paris means you speak French perfectly?"

"Well, I guess not. But you speak English perfectly."

"I should hope so. I lived in Manhattan for ten years."

"Really? I'm from Philly, but I live in New Jersey right now."

"Ah, Joisey," he said in a perfect New Jersey accent. Was there no accent this man couldn't do?

"Hey, don't knock Jersey. Not all of us can afford Manhattan." Although he didn't look like he could afford even the student hostel. And if he'd lived in New York for ten years, he was probably older than the other backpackers, too.

He held up his hands in placation. They were big and nicely shaped, with long, strong-looking fingers.

"Do you play piano?"

"What?" He looked startled again. Lily was single-handedly earning a reputation for all Americans as being slightly crazy.

"Piano." She wiggled her fingers at him.

He looked down at his hands and then back at her. "Why? Do you want me to play a tune for you? Would you like 'Alouette' or 'Frère Jacques'?"

"I can see you must be too busy to make conversation." She lifted her nose like she'd seen her mother's employer do a million times before to an impudent guest. Mrs. Wyndham was one of the grand ladies of Philadelphia's upper crust and Lily's mother was still her housekeeper, in charge of managing the myriad employees and tasks necessary for the smooth running of a historic mansion and busy social activities. "Thank you for your assistance, and have a nice day."

She brushed past him out the door onto the busy French sidewalk. Fresh croissant or *pain au chocolat* for breakfast?

Flaky French chocolate rolls sounded good. Before she could decide, she felt a touch on her elbow.

"Hey, hey." Backpack Guy stopped touching her with his long piano fingers as soon as she stood still. "I'm sorry, *mademoiselle*. You caught me by surprise and I forgot my manners."

"No problem." Lily spotted a café down the street that she hadn't visited yet. "I'm always grumpy before breakfast, and that chocolate roll is calling my name." She eyed his spare frame. She didn't think it was from too many cigarettes since he didn't smell of smoke. In fact, for a guy who looked like he'd been sleeping on a park bench for a month, he actually smelled nice. "If you don't mind my saying so, you could use a croissant."

His mouth pulled into a wry grin. "Probably. Why don't we get some croissants together?"

She leaned away from him and gave him a suspicious stare.

"I was a Boy Scout if that makes a difference."

"Really? There are French Boy Scouts?" She perked up. This was the kind of thing she wanted to learn about his country—something that wasn't in the tourist books.

"Come have a *café au lait* with me and I'll tell you all about *le scoutisme français*."

"*Scoutisme?* Is that a real word?"

"On my honor." He raised his hand in what looked like a Boy Scout sign.

"Well, okay. And maybe you can help me with my French pronunciation."

"I would be happy to."

Lily turned to face him. "All right, I can't call you French Backpacking Boy Scout, so you better tell me your name."

He smothered a laugh. "No, that would be quite a mouthful. My name is Jack Montford."

"Jack? Isn't it actually Jacques?"

"Yes, but I started going by Jack when I lived in New York."

"Smart move. I'm Lily Adams." Lily set off for the café. "Come on, Jack-with-the-Backpack, let's get you a couple croissants—with extra butter."

JACK DIDN'T KNOW quite how he'd wound up going out for breakfast with a woman he'd literally bumped into, but Lily Adams was right—he could use some calories. She'd thought he picked her out as an American from her accent, bad as it was, but he had picked her out as an American as soon as he saw her blond ponytail and cheerful expression. Her hazel-green eyes gazed eagerly at everything, as if she were trying to memorize details for later.

And to think she wanted to learn about French scouting, of all things. Not where to get the best-smelling *parfum* or cheapest designer knockoffs, but actual bits of real French life.

They stepped up to the café counter and Lily cleared her throat. *"Je voudrais deux croissants et deux pains au chocolat. Oh, deux cafés au lait. Merci."*

Jack had to admire her tenacity when she knew she had difficulties with the language. He quelled the cashier's incipient smirk with what he thought of his *comte* look.

Lily, happily oblivious, accepted the bag of pastries and handed him a cup of coffee.

"Merci," he thanked her. "And you say *de rien,* which means, 'It was nothing.'"

She practiced that a couple times as they walked to a bench along a pretty little park. Jack chewed a bit of *pain au chocolat,* mindful that his digestion was still a bit sensitive. Lily dipped her croissant into the milky coffee with gusto, not minding the flaky crumbs falling on her khaki cargo pants.

University students from the nearby Sorbonne argued about philosophy and politics while a young long-haired musician played guitar, his girlfriend staring up at him adoringly.

Nadine had stared at him like that while they were dating, but stopped soon after their engagement. It was as if she didn't need to bother once she had his ring. And of course he had been gone many months out of the year with his disaster relief work. His closest friends in the world, Giorgio, Prince of Vinciguerra, and Francisco, Duke of Aguas Santas in Portugal, had warned him to slow down.

Jack found it easy to ignore their advice. They were ones to talk about slowing down. Giorgio ran his own country and Francisco owned not only a huge, busy estate in the Portuguese countryside but also a private island in the Azores.

If only his friends had grabbed him in person a couple months back, since it wasn't hard to delete their phone and text messages.

He'd slowed down, all right, almost to the point of permanently stopping. When they'd heard he was sick, George and Frank first offered to fly to the hospital in Thailand to collect him. When that hadn't been necessary, they threatened to confiscate his passport so he couldn't leave France until George's sister's wedding.

George, Frank and Jack had met going to university in New York and had set up a nice bachelor pad for themselves when George's parents tragically died in a car crash back in their small country Vinciguerra, on the Italian peninsula. George's distraught twelve-year-old sister, Stefania, had come to live with them, along with a no-nonsense housekeeper.

End of their bachelor pad, but the beginning of the best time of his life. Stevie became one of the gang and the sister he'd never had. And now she was getting married.

Jack hoped she and her German fiancé looked at each other like the young guitar player and his girlfriend.

"Earth to Jack." Lily peered into his face and waved a croissant. "You still hungry? You put away that chocolate roll pretty fast."

He looked down into his lap. A small pile of crumbs was all that remained. Maybe the fresh air and quiet greenery was helping his appetite, but he didn't want to push his luck. "You want to know about the real France?"

She rolled her eyes. "Of course. Who doesn't?"

"Many people. For them, we are France-Land, a giant amusement theme park for them to visit. See the Eiffel, look at the Mona Lisa, hear the bells rung by the Hunchback of Notre Dame, and *voilà!* You have experienced the true France."

She gave him a peeved look. "I don't agree with that at all, and you have a pretty low opinion of tourists for a guy who's backpacking his way around the country. Or is it just a low opinion of American tourists?"

"Well…"

"Aha. You, *monsieur,* are a snob. And see, I know that is a French word, too."

"I am not a snob." He was acquainted with many snobs and he wasn't one, was he?

"When you lived in New York, did you go to the Statue of Liberty?"

"Of course. A gift from my country to yours." Stevie had loved the green lady. If she hadn't been Princess of

Vinciguerra, Jack often thought, she would have become an American citizen.

"And the Metropolitan Museum of Art? And the Empire State Building?"

"Yes to all of those."

"So why can't we enjoy the Eiffel Tower, the Mona Lisa and the bells at Notre Dame Cathedral?"

He gave her a nod of apology. "Again, you have caught me without my manners. We are notably proud of those three things in Paris, and many more, of course."

"So since I have already visited all those places, tell me where I should go next to get a sense of the real France."

Jack made a split-second decision. His other belongings were safely stashed in a locker at the hostel for the day and he hadn't made any firm plans to leave for Provence. What was one more day? The trains were always running to the south of France. "Why don't I show you?"

Her pretty brow wrinkled again. "Show me what?"

"One of the most beautiful parks in Paris that only the locals know about. You like to hike?"

"I love it," she promptly replied. "The Appalachian Trail runs through Pennsylvania, and I've hiked several parts of it."

"Good, this will be easy for you. Do you have a Métro card?"

"All set." She stood and dumped her empty cup into a nearby trash can. "*Allons!* Let's go."

Jack smiled. Her dreadful accent was starting to seem rather cute. He immediately put the brakes on that idea. Lily was a tourist, and he was going back to Provence to sit in the sun, eat and regain his strength.

He grimaced. Kind of like the mangy stray cat his Provençal housekeeper Marthe-Louise had taken in and fattened up last winter. Ah, well, she'd be happy to do the same for him.

3

"I CAN'T believe this is in the middle of the city." Lily gazed around the park in rapture. Fashionable young mothers in silk T-shirts and slim Capri cargo pants pushed babies in strollers, their gladiator sandals slapping the pavement. Older men strolled along the paths, conversing with enough upper body movement to qualify for a cardiovascular work-out. She was the only tourist in sight. "How do you say the name again? The sign says Butts, but that can't be right."

"No, we have no 'butts' here."

Lily sneaked a look at his, but those baggy shorts made it impossible to tell. Probably as lean as the rest of him. Rats! He caught her peeking. She fought a blush, and she hadn't even seen anything. He was kind of cute with his warm brown eyes.

"You would pronounce it 'Boot show-mon.'"

Lily never would have guessed that from the sign that read Parc des Buttes-Chaumont. "What does it mean?"

"*Buttes* are hills and *Chaumont* probably means 'bald mountain.' And *parc* means—"

She elbowed him, interrupting his chuckle. "Yes, thank you, I figured that out for myself."

He wrapped his arm around her shoulders for a brief

squeeze and then dropped it. "I am just teasing you, Lily. I admire your courage in coming by yourself to a country where you do not speak the language."

"I wouldn't have been on my own if my cousin hadn't had wonderful news." She found herself telling him about Sarah's past problems having a baby, and he nodded as if he knew what she was talking about.

"Yes, yes, it was wise for her to stay at home. Pregnancy can be difficult in the first trimester, especially with a history of complications." He cleared his throat. "But of course I am not an obstetrician."

She laughed. He looked as little like any ob-gyn she'd ever met. She pulled out her camera and took a few shots of Parisians enjoying the fine summer day. "Come on, let's walk." She followed the path into the park and was surprised to find herself in almost a forest. "Wow, Jack, look at all these trees."

"Yes, the park was commissioned by Napoleon III in the mid-1800s. Many of the trees were planted then." Jack pointed to a curve. "Ah, turn here."

All the noise of Paris had fallen away as they passed a red brick mansion in the park and crossed a terra-cotta-tiled bridge. "Down the steps?" Lily peered down a dark, cool tunnel.

"Exactement." Jack went down a couple steep steps and extended his hand. "Watch your step. The rock can be slippery."

Lily took his strong, warm hand. As they descended, she was grateful for his steady grip and her sturdy hiking boots. "How on earth did they ever make this park?"

"They shaped it from an old quarry and it took several years to finish."

She concentrated on keeping her footing and only looked up when they emerged onto a long, narrow suspension bridge. It was as if they were in a misty watercolor illustration of a fantasy novel heavy with wizards and princesses. She couldn't resist taking more photos, this time one-handed.

The bridge towered over a serene lake that reflected up the greens, yellows and reds of the surrounding trees. She realized they were still holding hands, but didn't let go. She'd enjoyed Paris, but missed Sarah badly. Sightseeing by herself wasn't as much fun as with someone else. A travel buddy gave her the chance to say, *Wow, look at that,* or even spotting something funny and giving a nudge to share in the joke.

Lily looked sideways at Jack and was surprised to see how much he had relaxed. "You're not much of a city boy, are you?" They started to cross the wooden planks of the bridge, the steel railings making decorative geometric patterns of triangles and rectangles.

He smiled, his white teeth showing through his thick beard. She wondered what he looked like under all that hair. Just her luck, he would have no chin or a weird facial tattoo. "No, I would rather be in the country. Once I have finished in Paris, I am going south, to Provence."

"Provence," she tested the name on her tongue. "You're from there."

"My family is. I don't get there as often as I like." He cleared his throat. "But enough about me. What do you do when you are not traveling?"

Hmm. She didn't want to tell him she was writing travel articles because he might worry she was writing down everything he said. "I'm a freelance writer. I write magazine and newspaper articles on anything I can get paid for—history, local sights—I've even covered school-board meetings and supermarket grand openings."

"Ah." He nodded thoughtfully.

"What, *ah?*"

"That is why you want to learn about the real Paris, the real France. People interest you as much as the places."

"Hmm. I've never thought of it that way. I just wanted to keep busy and keep getting jobs." They came to the end of the bridge and Lily pulled her hand free from his, pointing up to the Roman temple-looking thing on the hill in front of them. "Wow, look at that." She supposed she could have used her other hand to point, but she was starting to like holding his hand a little too much.

Her danger signals were flashing: romantic park setting in Paris—*check*. Hand-holding with a well-spoken, seemingly decent guy—*check*. Not remembering the last time she held any male body part—*check*.

Jack pulled a water bottle from his small backpack and drank. "One more thing to see before we climb." He took a deep breath and headed down the trail toward the lake.

Lily fought a pang of irrational disappointment that he didn't take her hand again, but the man obviously could read mixed signals as fast as she sent them. She followed Jack and stopped next to a weeping willow tree, its yellowish branches and silvery green leaves drooping over the path. "Sing willow, willow, willow. Sing all a green willow will be my garland." She couldn't help grabbing a handful of branches and clutching them to her in pure dramatic fashion. She was such an English major geek.

Jack stopped. "*Othello,* right?"

Her jaw fell. He wasn't even a native English speaker and he knew enough Shakespeare to understand her obscure reference? "Very good." She sounded like Sarah at her most teacher-ish.

"Shakespeare in the Park." Central Park, NYC, that is. He started walking again.

"I went to that once! But they did one of the comedies, not a tragedy. Which do you like better?"

"The comedies, of course. Real life has enough sadness already."

"True. And I never liked the character of Othello. He had everything he ever wanted and tossed it away because Iago preyed on his insecurities. Weak." She shook her head. "And strangling his wife, Desdemona—what a creep."

"The man did die by his own hand in the end," Jack pointed out.

"He should have done everyone a favor and done that first. Or *maybe* he could have even believed his wife was telling the truth about being faithful to him and then gone and kicked Iago's ass for making trouble."

"Unfortunately, marital fidelity and ass-kicking make for dull theater."

"Not if they have a good fight choreographer for the ass-kicking scene. Those guys can make thumb-wrestling look fascinating."

"Thumb-wrestling?"

Aha, so there was at least one American tradition he didn't know about. She was about to lift her hand to show him but realized they'd be holding hands again, albeit in a combative manner. "I'll show you later." She dropped the willow branches and turned toward the sound of rushing water.

Jack stood there gazing up at the tree. "Aspirin is derived from willow bark—the scientific name salicylic acid comes from the willow genus *Salix*."

She turned slowly to stare at him. "How do you know that?"

"Science class."

Lily raised her eyebrows. "You must have paid better

attention in science class than I did." She was lucky to recall that the scientific name for humans was *Homo sapiens.*

"I know you have your own strengths." He moved close and for a second, she thought he would kiss her under the umbrella of the bowing branches. But he must have picked up her hesitation again and withdrew, the gleam in his brown eyes shuttered. *"Allons!* Let's go see the waterfall."

"Okay." She followed him, expecting to see a stream burbling over a shallow drop, but instead they stepped into another grotto, with a high waterfall thundering down to a pool at their feet. "Holy cow, look at that. And this is part of that same quarry?"

He nodded and tipped his face up to the water, little droplets condensing on his cheeks. She closed her eyes and did the same, exhaling deeply as some of her tension flowed away.

Traveling without Sarah had been more stressful than she realized. She had to be constantly alert to where she was and who she was near. And the language barrier— well, that wasn't so bad. Sarah had been right that there were plenty of English speakers roaming Paris.

Like Jack. He was a bit of a puzzle—scruffy-looking but clean and obviously well-educated with a variety of knowledge. She opened her eyes to find him watching her with an enigmatic expression.

"You rarely find places like this in any city."

"No." She shook her head in agreement. "There's nothing like it in Philadelphia or New York."

"That is a replica of the Roman temple of Daphne." He pointed up to the round Grecian-looking building. "It's the highest point in the park and you can see all the way across Paris to the Sacre-Coeur Cathedral."

"Great!" Lily checked her camera to make sure she had

plenty of space on her memory card and set off after him. The stairs were cut into the rock as before and twisted around as they ascended. She was so excited that she didn't realize Jack had fallen behind. He waved her on when she stopped. "Just getting a drink—I'll catch up to you in a minute."

She was too excited to drink and quickly got to the top. "Oh," she gasped. It was just as Jack had said, the best view in the city. She looked down on all the cute neighborhoods and across northeast Paris to the white dome of Sacre-Coeur Cathedral. She grabbed her camera and took shots from every angle, zooming in on the cathedral and the houses below. The bridge made a cool composition with the surrounding trees reflecting in the water. "'A favorite of local Parisians, Parc Butts-Something-Or-Other is a hidden treasure of greenery amidst the noisy city.'" Yes, that introductory sentence sounded pretty good, so she typed it into her phone.

But where was Jack? She peered around guiltily at being so caught up in her work. Had he twisted his ankle? "Jack?" she called, descending several steps. He stood below her, huffing and puffing.

"Stopped to take a drink." He limped up the rest of the stairs.

"Hey, you're gasping. Are you okay?"

"Fine," he gritted out, bending over to rest his hands on his knees and sucking air at a pretty good pace.

Lily looked around, wondering what she should do if he keeled over. They were alone at the highest point of the park and she couldn't exactly toss him over her shoulder in a fireman's carry. "Do you need an inhaler?"

He shook his head. At least he wasn't asthmatic. She could see herself calling the Parisian version of 911 and trying to ask for emergency medical help to come to some park with the word *butts* in the name.

He straightened, his face flushed with exertion and probably embarrassment, too. He pulled a bottle of water from his small backpack and sipped slowly.

She pulled out her own water and pretended they had stopped for a water break. Once he wiped his mouth and met her glance, she shook her head. "Too many cigarettes will kill your endurance."

He gave a dry laugh that turned into a cough at the end. "I am not a smoker, Lily. I am probably the only man in France who doesn't smoke."

She had to agree with him there. The tobacco-free movement was about as welcome as a barge of plague rats floating down the Seine. "Well, you've got that going for you."

"But not much else, eh?" His color seemed to be returning to normal. He spread his arms wide. "Ah, the perfect specimen of French manhood. I cannot even climb a hill without gasping like an old man with emphysema."

"Have you been sick?"

Jack sighed. "Unfortunately, but I was hoping I was better."

"Maybe you're pushing it a bit to come to the hilliest point in Paris, don't you think?"

He grimaced. "You are right. I should have known better."

"What are you getting over, if you don't mind my asking?" She hoped it was nothing awful like cancer or something serious like that.

The first glimmer of humor returned to his brown eyes. "Dysentery."

"Dysentery?" she blurted. She found herself unconsciously stepping back from him, trying to remember if they had shared any food or drink. "How in the world do you get dysentery these days? I thought the tap water smelled a bit funny but I thought it was okay to drink." Was that why everyone carried bottles of expensive spring water? Why didn't Sarah mention this to her before she left? *Don't drink the water!* Wasn't that usually the last advice people shouted out the windows of their cars as they dropped you off at the airport for a journey to a foreign country?

"No, I did not get dysentery in France." He rubbed his cheek as if his beard itched. "I caught it in Myanmar."

"Myanmar? Why on earth would you go there?" She'd never heard anything good about that place nowadays, ever since they stopped calling it Burma. It was definitely not on her list of places to visit.

Jack set off at an easy walk and Lily followed him. "They had a typhoon and I was an aid worker—food, shelter, healthcare, all the fundamental necessities. I accidentally drank some untreated water and…" He held out his arms. *"Voilà."*

"Wow, you went there on purpose?" She realized that sounded kind of rude. "I mean, that's noble work."

"Not so noble when you get as sick as the people you are trying to help. I wasted many resources, especially when they had to take me to the hospital in Thailand."

"You must have been severely ill, then."

"Eh, there were many who would have benefited from hospital care but I was the one who was transferred out."

"Guilt." She raised her index finger to make her point. "You have survivor's guilt."

"What?" He gave her a funny look.

"Sure. You're thinking, 'Why me? Why did I get better medical treatment than the others? Why did I live when others didn't?'"

He glanced down and away from her. "You may be right."

"And what are the answers to those questions?" Lily gave an imitation-French shrug. "No one knows. Come on, you're French. Use a little bit of that national tendency toward fatalism. It was meant to happen that way." She peered into his face and gasped in pretend shock. "Surely you're not an *optimist,* are you?"

A small smile crept across his lips. "Well…"

"Uh-oh." She wagged her finger. "Watch out—someone might mistake you for an American if you're not careful. An optimistic Frenchman. Tsk, tsk, who would have thought?"

"A personal failing." He grinned at her. "Please do not tell anyone. I would like to keep my French passport."

"Don't let it happen again. If French people were all cheerful and friendly, what would tourists complain about?"

"Parisians are Parisians." He gave that uniquely French shrug that she had tried to copy and failed. "You will find if you go to different areas of the country, people are more friendly."

"Like Provence?"

His face softened and he wore a faraway glance. "Exactly. The air is warm and light and the sky is pure blue. The hills are always green, and even the north wind, the *mistral,* brings clear, dry weather in its path."

Lily was memorizing his description as best as she could, his words painting a vivid picture.

"Everything is more in Provence. The food is richer, the wine is crisper, the fish are bigger and the ducks are plumper. Have you ever had a day where everything comes together—the weather, the countryside and the food?"

Lily did. "Once, my mother and I packed a picnic and

drove out to Washington Crossing Historic Park, where George Washington crossed the Delaware River to capture Trenton from the English. There is a huge wildflower preserve on the grounds, and Mom and I sat in the middle of the flowers, smelling the perfume, listening to the bees. The sky was bright blue with white puffy clouds and we ate chocolate éclairs and licked the melted smears off our fingers." Funny how she hadn't remembered that outing in so long. Despite her mother's busy schedule, she carved out time to spend with Lily.

"Almost every day is like that in the Provençal countryside." He sighed. "I have been away too long. But soon I will return."

JACK FELT SLIGHTLY better talking about Provence, but the rest of his morning had been a severe humiliation. He'd finally caught his breath descending from the beautiful Grecian folly, but not without several worried looks from the lovely Lily, who fussed over him as if he were an old man.

He was a man who could land a twin-engine plane on a grass airstrip and immediately trek several miles through harsh jungle terrain, but he couldn't manage a set of stairs in the middle of Paris. *Pathétique.*

But look, there was someone in worse shape than him. He stopped next to a young mother trying to carry her baby down the last set of stairs in one arm and her bulky carriage hooked over her other elbow. "May I help?"

The woman nodded gratefully and handed over the carriage. He carried it down for her but realized he was breathing hard and sweating again. How embarrassing, especially when Lily noticed, as well.

"Careful, Jack, you're still getting over that case of dysentery."

Unfortunately, *dysentery* in English translated to

dysenterie in French and the young mother gave him a look of horror, yanking her carriage away.

"No, no, *madame*. I am all better now," he tried to soothe her in French. She still looked panicked. "Trust me, I am a physician myself."

"Then you should know better, *monsieur*. You should not be going about Paris infecting innocent mothers and babies." She glared at him and scurried away, baby still in one arm and pushing the carriage with a couple finger-tips—probably home to disinfect everything he touched.

He sighed. "Lily, you can't go around telling people I have dysentery. It makes them nervous." That was an understatement. Instead of Typhoid Mary, he was Dysentery Jack.

"You mean she understood me?" she asked eagerly.

"The word is almost the same in both languages."

"Oh. Sorry."

"For that word, you have a perfect French accent."

"Figures." She laughed. "What are some other diseases I can learn in French and terrorize the local populace? How about dengue fever?"

He had to laugh in return. Oh, boy, did he know diseases. Most of them had been eradicated in developed countries, fortunately. "That would be *la dengue*."

"Ho-hum. Typhoid?"

"Typhoïde."

"Boring. Diphtheria?"

"Diphtérie."

"Bubonic plague?"

Ah, he'd barely escaped an outbreak in Madagascar that had popped up just after his team had left a flood scene. Thanks to some heavy-duty antibiotics given in case, none of them had gotten sick. "That is *la peste bubonique*."

"Really?" Her smooth forehead wrinkled. "You French

must be pretty cool customers. Plague is a mere pest for you. And I know more French than I thought. Since you don't want me telling people you're getting over dysentery, if anyone asks me what's bothering you, I can tell them you have *la dengue, typhoïde, dipthérie* or even *la peste bubonique.*"

He groaned, imagining the frantic calls to the Ministry of Health and the tabloid articles—*The Count of Brissard, recently returned from a mysterious hospitalization in Thailand, is rumored to be carrying dengue fever, typhoid, diphtheria and bubonic plague.* "Please do not. I have no desire to be thrown in quarantine for undetermined weeks. I spent enough time in the hospital already."

"Okay, okay, I'm only kidding. You're the only person I know in this whole country. I certainly don't want you quarantined."

"Good. Although I will have to keep on your good side, just in case."

Lily laughed, the sound light and carefree. He hadn't heard nearly enough laughter in how long? Months? There hadn't been much to laugh about in typhoon country.

He wanted to hear more of Lily's laughter. Before his rational, scientific mind could censor his previously undiscovered impulsive side, he blurted, "Come to Provence with me. You want to see the real France? I will show it to you."

4

LILY SWIRLED HER pale golden chardonnay as she sat in a café across from the hostel. Its motion was almost hypnotic as it circled the glass. She was being more pensive than usual, but really, what was the point if you couldn't visit Paris and wax philosophic over a glass of wine?

And she had plenty to think about. Coming to Paris alone had strained the boundaries of her capacity for adventure, but to set off for Provence with a near-stranger? Her warning bells were sending off a few clangs, and unfortunately, being the imaginative type, she could imagine the headlines: American Writer Disappears in Provence; in Unrelated news, the Grape Harvest Is Unusually Heavy in One Lonely Vineyard. Or, Notorious French Criminal Claims to be Aid Worker Recovering from Dysentery. Or would that be *dysenterie?*

But Provence…ooh la la. Summer in the South of France. Perfume, lavender, roses. She was really starting to love France and had even bought some new clothes to better fit in. Tonight she was wearing a floaty peach-colored silk top and a khaki miniskirt—even a pair of the gladiator sandals that she'd seen everywhere.

"Is this seat taken?" a familiar male voice asked.

Lily looked up from her wine. Was that…no, it couldn't be, but it was. "Jack, what did you do with your hair?" she blurted.

"It's in the wastebasket of a barber who wore almost the same look of horror when he first saw me."

No, not horror. Shock and amazement that he would cover up such a nice face with a mop of hair. He was way past good-looking and into the handsome realm. She'd thought he was nice-looking in a kind of shaggy, granola-crunchy way before, but minus the surplus hair? He was downright sexy.

Of course he was a bit pale where his beard had covered, and still a bit too thin, but that actually made him look like he should be modeling fashionable skinny jeans and snug dress shirts with an expression of ineffable ennui.

"What is that?" She stared at his chin. "Do you have a dimple in your chin?"

He sat down across from her. "Hush. Men don't have dimpled chins, they have cleft chins." The waiter appeared and Jack ordered a chardonnay as well. "Would you like another? My treat."

"If you're sure you have money after your haircut." Everything in Paris was hideously overpriced, even barbers and basic chardonnay.

He smiled and her jaw dropped. She pointed a finger at him. "You have dimples in your cheeks, too—and don't tell me they're clefts. I majored in English and there's no such thing as a cleft cheek." He broke into laughter and her heart was pounding.

Oh, boy. His warm, golden-brown eyes lit up and his white, even teeth gleamed in the fading light.

"Ah, Lily, Lily." He used the French pronunciation of her name—Lee-lee. "I have laughed more with you today than I have in the past month."

"Laughter is the best medicine. Chardonnay is the second-best," she quipped as the waiter set down two more glasses.

He raised his glass in a toast. "*À votre santé.* To your health."

She touched her rim to his and drank. He did the same, stared at the wine and wagged his hand back and forth. "Eh, pretty good. You like white better than red?"

"Depends on what the meal is."

"But of course." He started to fiddle with his hair and dropped his hand sheepishly when it wasn't there. "Anyway, I realized that I probably startled you earlier when I invited you to Provence."

"A bit," Lily allowed, strangely disappointed that he might be rescinding his offer—an offer she wasn't seriously considering. Was she?

"Me, I am normally not so impulsive, but I thought if you wanted to see Provence, and I am going there, well, we could travel together. As friends, of course," he hastily added.

"Ah." She'd been attracted to his smart personality despite his shaggy looks—not her usual type at all. But clean-shaven and fashionably trimmed, he was a dangerous combo. "Look." She spread her hands. "You seem like a nice guy, but I didn't just fall off the turnip truck."

He leaned forward. "That is a fascinating American colloquialism. I've never heard that before. It means that you are not naive, no?"

"No. I mean, yes, I am not naive." His French-like use of double negatives was confusing her. "So why would I think it is a good idea to travel alone several hundred miles into remote countryside with a man I met this morning?"

"Of course!" He grinned. "You want my references. This is a very French custom."

"Always glad to be culturally accurate," she said dryly. "But really, you're going to call your friends François or Gérard so they can tell me what a good guy you are? Men will say anything to help other men."

"Pah." He made a disparaging gesture with his free hand. "Men like that are *cochons*. That is a very useful word to know. *Pigs*. Or *swine* if you are in a more poetic mood. But I have an impeccable reference who would vouch for my good character and lack of maniacal tendencies."

"I don't know about the maniacal tendencies. You did go to Myanmar during a typhoon."

"*After* a typhoon." He waggled his finger at her. "There is a grand difference."

"Well, you learned your lesson this time. At least in Provence you can drink the water."

"Why would you, with all the good wine?" He laughed. "Does your laptop have a webcam?"

"Sure." She'd "called" Sarah with it yesterday to assure her cousin she was still alive and walking around Paris. Sarah was still queasy, but that was the worst of it. Her OB had seen her the next day and had been horrified at the idea of an overseas trip.

"If I could borrow it, I can call one of my old teachers who would vouch for me. A lady teacher, if that would be better."

It would. Still not believing she was even considering a crazy side trip like this, Lily fired up the webcam and Jack dragged his chair around next to her. The tables were close together as it was, so he was only inches away.

Up close, he was even sexier as he rested his arm along the back of her chair. She inhaled his woodsy cologne that smelled exotic and…erotic. Her nipples tightened under her thin silk T-shirt, and a long-forgotten throbbing started between her thighs. She crossed her legs to try to tamp that down and forgot she was wearing a skirt and that he was sitting so close.

Her bare leg briefly rested on his thigh—he was still wearing shorts. She pulled away but instead wound up running her calf down the length of his.

That certainly did not help her cool off. Or him, either, apparently. His eyes widened and his nostrils flared. Geez, why didn't she just crawl into the guy's lap?

"Sorry," she muttered.

"No, no, it is very close in here." He took a deep breath and shifted away slightly before turning the computer toward him. "I have an account, so you will not be charged." He logged in and tapped in a web address. "Ah, here we are. Perhaps my former teacher is online now."

The wine in Lily's stomach hadn't sedated the butterflies as she waited for the window to open. What would she decide if she found out Jack Montford was the best thing since sliced croissants?

JACK'S FORMER GOVERNESS appeared in the webcam window on the computer screen. Her gray hair was pulled into a bun as usual, a pencil shoved into it. She was probably working on another editing or translating project from her home in London.

"*Bonsoir,* Madame Finch. How are you tonight?" he continued in French.

"Jacques, it is good to see you in one piece," she replied. "Why are we speaking in French?" Madame Finch was as English as Winston Churchill and had been Jack's governess for many years until he had gone to prep school. They almost never spoke French together because he had needed to practice his English.

"I need you to vouch for my good character to this young lady."

"What?" She wrinkled her brow. "You've never needed my help before to meet women. Surely your sterling personal qualities combined with the cachet of being the Count de Brissard are sufficient to impress the female sex?"

"Madame, I haven't told her about my title. She is suspicious of upper-class men as it is."

"Oh, a smart girl." Madame smirked.

Lily was starting to wonder why they were only speaking French. "So, Madame, I need to assure her of my sterling personal characteristics. Oh, and don't tell her I'm a doctor. She thinks I'm a regular disaster-relief worker."

"Anything else?" she asked dryly. "You must really want her to like you for yourself."

He stopped, struck by the truth of that statement. "Yes, yes, I do."

"If you like her so much, you must tell her about your whole life, more than bits and pieces."

"I will." Madame was correct, as always.

"Good." She switched into English. "Please do excuse our rudeness in speaking French in front of you, *mademoiselle*. I work as a French translator and editor and welcome any practice with a native speaker like Jacques."

Lily smiled. "No problem. I'm Lily Adams, from Philadelphia, but I live in New Jersey now."

Madame nodded. "Ah, an American. Jacques did enjoy his years there. I am Fiona Finch, and I was fortunate enough to be Jacques's teacher when he was young."

Good. She hadn't called herself the governess. That would have raised certain issues.

Lily cleared her throat. "Yes, well, Jack and I just met today."

Madame's eyebrows shot up. "Today? Well, a true *coup de foudre,* right, Jacques?"

"Oh, what does that mean?" Lily asked him innocently.

He gave a strained smile. "A flash of lightning, something unexpected." It also meant love at first sight.

"Yes, that's true." Lily smiled at Madame. "I bumped into him in the hostel lobby, tried practicing my French on him, and he responded in English because my French is obviously not very good. Then we started chatting, he took me to that park with *butts* in the name, and then he asked me to go to Provence with him. But I'm not going anywhere with a guy I met today because I don't want to be one of those international stories that wind up on the twenty-four-hour news networks discussing, 'Where could Lily Adams be?'" Lily wound down her worries, Madame nodding in agreement the whole time.

"I commend you for your sensibility. Unfortunately, Europe is full of handsome, unscrupulous young men."

Jack made a noise of protest, but Lily ignored him, leaning in to peer at Madame. "That's it exactly! I wasn't planning to come by myself but my cousin is having a baby, after all, and she wants me to be very careful because I am alone."

"You brave girl." Madame was ignoring him now as well in a moment of female bonding. "Cads and bounders! Europe's crawling with 'em these days. It's a wonder girls don't go missing by the trainloads considering the trash that dares walk the street."

"Exactly!"

Jack didn't see this going well for him. "But Madame—"

Madame was just warming up. "You should have seen the riffraff I encountered on my last trip. Utterly disgusting the way they act—"

"Madame, please!" Jack interrupted in desperation. "Lily is going to think I'm an axe murderer."

Both women looked at him as if they'd forgotten his presence. Lily muffled a giggle and Madame frowned at him for his poor manners.

"Excuse me, Madame," he apologized.

She sniffed but inclined her head in acceptance of his apology. "So, Mademoiselle Lily, despite the preponderance of dubious characters, my former student Jacques is not one of them. He is diligent, hard-working, courteous and of the highest moral fiber."

"He did say he was a Boy Scout."

"Oh, my, yes. Earned the highest award in the organization. If he has promised to show you around Provence, you can be assured that he will conduct himself with the utmost of gentlemanly qualities. No need to fear he would pounce on you like a panther."

"Oh." Was it his wishful thinking, or did Lily sound a tiny bit disappointed? She sat up straighter. "I'm glad you vouch for his character."

"Absolutely." Madame gave him a steely glare. "And I will give you my phone number. Please call me if you have any concerns. I have many friends in the south of France and they would be happy to come to your assistance." Jack winced—he'd better behave himself. Madame's friends in the south of France were all his own friends and employees, as well.

"That would be wonderful." Lily pulled out her cell phone and entered not only Madame's two phone numbers, but her email address and home address.

"There." His former governess sat back in satisfaction. "You're as safe as you would be with your cousin, my dear. Master Jacques will care for you as if you were his own sister."

"Of course." He gritted out a smile. He didn't have any sisters, and he certainly didn't consider Lily as one. But a promise was a promise.

"Wonderful!" Lily threw her arms around him and kissed his cheek. "The south of France! Provence!"

Madame Finch grinned at him as she reached for her keyboard. "*Bon voyage,* you two. Lily, I am only a phone call away." Jacques could have sworn he heard an evil-sounding chuckle as she terminated the web call.

Lily still had her arms around his neck, her smooth bare legs rubbing his, her thighs firm and tanned as her short skirt had crept up. "I can't believe it—this is so exciting."

He had to agree. Exciting, but damned inconvenient that his libido had come roaring back after being comatose for so long. And he'd promised to take the sexiest woman he'd met in years to the most romantic place on earth—and treat her as a sister.

Lovely. Lovely Lily, with sparkling green eyes and glossy peach lips begging for him to kiss them. For him to pull her into his lap and show her what real French kissing was about. But…no.

He patted her wrist and waved to the waiter for their check. She dropped her arms awkwardly and he pushed her wineglass toward her. "A toast to our trip."

"Cheers." She tapped her glass to his again. "When do we leave?"

"If we take the TGV high-speed train, we can leave early tomorrow and be in Avignon in under four hours."

"Only four hours," she breathed. "I won't get a wink of sleep tonight."

Jack gave her a dry smile. Neither would he, but for a different reason.

5

LILY COULDN'T HELP gawking at the TGV train, luxurious with comfortable red-and-gray seats. The seating arrangement in their car consisted of one seat on one side of the aisle and two seats on the other. There was the option of facing each other over a small table, which was what Jack had chosen when he'd booked their last-minute tickets.

They were on the upper level. Jack had called it a duplex, but Lily thought it was more like a double-decker bus, only with a roof, of course.

Lily handed Jack her suitcase and he tucked it into the bins at the end of the car. She took her purse and laptop with her, figuring the rest of her luggage was safe enough.

Jack settled into his seat across from her and was looking drowsy as the train pulled from the station. Lily was too excited to sleep.

He yawned and closed his eyes as the train gathered speed, passing through the Parisian suburbs.

Lily gasped as the train emerged from a tunnel into the countryside. It didn't seem as if they were going about two hundred miles an hour—unless of course you looked directly at the trees and bushes close to the line. They were a green blur. "Look at that!" But he was sound asleep.

He really had overextended himself with that hike yesterday—no walk in the park for him. Typical man, refusing to admit any weakness.

Lily could sympathize. How many times had she put on the infamous stiff upper lip during a difficult situation? Sometimes best to grit your teeth and soldier on. But now wasn't the time for that. She opened her laptop and began making notes for an entry for their train trip.

After an hour or so, she decided to stretch her legs and stepped into the narrow aisle, nodding to a stylish young Frenchwoman who'd had the same idea. She found the restroom, bought a snack from the bar between first and second class and then made her way back. She was walking at almost two hundred miles an hour—and her old gym teacher said she was slow—ha!

Right before she got back to her seat, she passed the Frenchwoman again. "Excuse me," she said in English.

"Of course. American?"

"Of course," Lily parroted back to her, feeling a tinge of jealousy at the dark-haired woman's overall ease. Ease in English, ease in how her hair fell onto her shoulders, how her clothes were fashionable but comfortable. And how in the world did she keep linen pants from wrinkling on a train ride?

But Lily wanted to be a better person than that. "You have a lovely country."

"Thank you. I have been to New York. Parts of it are nice."

Damned by faint praise. "As are parts of Paris."

But her return crack went over the woman's head because she was staring at Jack. "Your lover is very handsome." She was right—not about the lover part, but about him being handsome. Jack did look particularly gorgeous, almost like a Renaissance painting of a sleeping shepherd boy with his pale skin and reddish-brown hair, which curled slightly around his ears and neck.

Lily's hackles rose and she gave her a tight smile. She was about to say he wasn't her lover, but then realized, why give Frenchie an opportunity? "He is, isn't he?" A little devil made her say, "And wonderful in the bedroom, as well. So inventive." She fought back a blush.

"Frenchmen usually are, unlike American men." *Touché.* But Lily wasn't about to defend the lovemaking abilities of her country's male population, especially since she pretty much agreed.

"But he looks familiar." The Frenchwoman wrinkled her perfect brow as she examined the sleeping Jack.

Nice try, sister, she'd heard that before. "I don't think so. Now if you would excuse me…" She slipped into her chair and deliberately opened her laptop, typing words like *skhjaldhfkjhioeurio* and *dkoiasuejndkjfioadioufi* in an attempt to look busy. She peered at her screen. Geez, the mess looked like a cross between Greek and Old Norse. She backspaced until the nonsense syllables were gone.

Jack had fortunately slept through her bragging on his sexual prowess. She didn't know what had made her do that.

Yes, she did. Her face started burning. She'd been wondering about his sexual prowess ever since he'd turned up sexy and clean-shaven and she'd accidentally rubbed her thigh all over his.

She quickly opened a new document and began a blog post on travelling the TGV—*Train à Grande Vitesse,* the Train of Great Speediness. Like most things, it sounded better in French.

Like her name, Lily. Your average flower that showed up every Easter at the grocery store, like it or not. But it sounded better in French—Lee-lee. And even Jack's full name, Jacques. Exotic and adventurous, or was she reminded of old Jacques Cousteau specials on the nature channel?

"Jacques," she whispered his name, just to hear it from her own mouth.

He bolted upright, his eyes wide and staring. *"Quoi? Qu'est-ce qu'il y a?"*

"Oh, my gosh, I'm so sorry." She grabbed his hand. "I didn't mean to wake you."

"What?" He turned to her, his eyes coming back into focus. "Are you all right?"

"Fine." She patted his hand. "Go back to sleep. We still have a couple hours left."

He rubbed the sleep from his eyes. "No, I'm awake now. I thought I heard someone calling me."

Cringe. "I was chatting with this woman. Maybe you overheard us."

"Maybe. Do you have anything to drink? My mouth is very dry." She passed him a water bottle and he drained it.

"I'll get another." He stood and stretched, his shoulders filling out his thin pale green cotton T-shirt. "Do you need anything?"

Yeah, a cold shower for her libido and a bar of soap to wash her mouth out for lying. But since those weren't options… "How about an orangeade?"

JACK STOOD IN a quiet corner of the train's bar, sipping his own orangeade as he checked his voice mail. Four frantic messages from his *maman,* despite the fact he'd called her after leaving to apologize again for the ruins of her well-meaning, if not well-thought-out, party. He'd made it clear he and Nadine were permanently over, but her romantic soul probably thought they'd had a lovers' tiff. Not one voice mail or text from Nadine. Good. She'd gotten his message, then.

A voicemail from Frank in Portugal and a text from George—who knew where George was? He was traveling frequently back and forth to New York to spend time with his fiancée, Renata, a wedding-dress designer who specialized in vintage styles. Apparently Stevie was wearing one of her creations, and that was how she and George had met.

He hadn't talked to his friends for several days and called Frank first. His friend's yelp of delight was a boost to his dysentery-shriveled ego. Good thing it hadn't shriveled anything else—he hoped.

"Jack, you jerk, don't you check your voice mails anymore?" Frank clucked. He always was a mother hen.

"Nice to talk to you too, *mon ami.*"

"Hold on, I'm talking to George on the other line. Let me see if I can conference call on this new phone of mine." A couple clicks later, the three of them were conversing as if they were all in the same café.

After reassuring his friends that he was not on death's doorstep any longer, he mentioned that he was on his way to Provence.

"Wonderful!" Frank enthused. He loved being in the country himself and disliked city life.

"A diet of that hearty peasant food will fatten you up in no time," George added.

"Nadine called me a peasant the other day," he admitted.

Frank made a choking sound and George groaned. "When did you see that *puttana?*" Not a nice Italian word, but unfortunately appropriate.

He quickly explained about the fiasco at his mother's house.

"You did the right thing to get out of town as soon as possible. I know girls like her. They think the entire country is a wasteland between Paris and Nice. She'll never follow you there," Frank reassured him.

"From your lips to God's ears," Jack replied, having learned that most appropriate plea from one of his Jewish friends in New York.

"Amen," George replied piously. "I have church on the mind, my friends. Stevie and her Teutonic knight have come up with a handful of possible dates, and we are all meeting with the Archbishop Wednesday."

"Already," Jack marveled.

George cleared his throat. "Stefania has a request for you and I promised to pass it along."

"Anything," he replied promptly.

"She has realized her wedding will bring much publicity and wants to use that for the benefit of others. Would you be willing to sell her part of your lavender crop to help make a commemorative perfume to sell for her charity?"

"Sell? I'll give her anything she wants." Jack thought out loud. "Much of the crop is already spoken for, but there are several fields available that would be perfect for her project. Madame Simone Laurent is the master perfumer of the House of Laurent. She would be thrilled to work with your sister. I will inform the farm manager about the lavender."

"Ah, is that still Jean-Claude?"

"Of course." Jean-Claude had worked for his father and had even been a young worker when Jack's grandfather had been alive.

"Stevie will be sure to come to Provence herself. She adores Jean-Claude and his wife."

"Yes, Marthe-Louise is still housekeeper there. She

loves having young women around whom she can teach how to cook all the Provençal favorites."

"Well, you'll have to get on the ball and bring her a young woman to teach."

Jack gave a wry smile. Standing in the crowded bar of the Paris-Avignon TGV wasn't the place to explain that he was indeed taking a young woman to Provence. Frank and George wouldn't understand a brief explanation. "When would I have the chance to meet a nice girl? I don't work as fast as you, George," he joked. George had met his fiancée one day and invited her to Italy the next.

Jack realized with a jolt that he had met Lily yesterday morning and invited her to Provence yesterday afternoon. That put him one up on George.

And he realized he wanted to get back to Lily. "Thank you for checking up on me, *mes amis*. I will be in touch over the lavender."

They said their goodbyes and Jack hung up. He dumped his empty orangeade bottle in the trash and carried a full one back to Lily. She was staring at her laptop, her honey-blond hair escaping her ponytail. Although she was typing with both hands, she clenched a pen between her teeth.

When she saw him, she looked up and smiled at him around the pen. She quickly spit it out and gave him a wry grin. "Old habit. I was an inveterate pencil chewer until I gave that up—too many splinters. But I still seem to write better this way. Strange, huh?"

He sat down across from her, charmed at her little quirk. "What are you writing?"

"My impressions of the TGV, a couple video clips I took with my phone. I hope to get some travel articles published from this trip. I've been publishing a few entries and photos on a blog."

"You're blogging?" Still leery of his run-in with the press, Jack was reluctant to be a feature.

She must have read his demeanor. "Oh, don't worry. I'm only publishing photos of the attractions and a couple of myself when I was able to find somebody to take my photo."

Lily would be a huge attraction for any blog, especially one with male readers. "I would like if you don't show me in those photos. The organization I work for does not like its workers to have online photo presences. It makes us more attractive to would-be kidnappers." It was true. As a French nobleman, he would be the jackpot for any ragtag band of outlaws who'd scraped up an automatic weapon.

He'd dodged the bullet so far but would have to see if his foray onto the social pages would make the aid directors nervous.

Her eyes widened. "My gosh, I never thought of how dangerous that would be. Don't worry, I won't show you. And I mentioned you briefly once but called you Pierre as a pseudonym."

"Pierre?" He chuckled. That actually *wasn't* one of his names. "That was my great-uncle's name. He lived down the road from us and was a true Provençal character."

"Really?"

"But of course. He had his own vineyard and made vats of incredibly strong wine. He also had several mangy-looking hound dogs and would go into the hills in the winter to look for truffles—not the chocolate kind, but the real truffle. A special, underground fungus that only dogs and pigs can sniff."

Lily nodded. "They are quite good shaved over pasta. I've always wanted to try the Italian white truffle, but those are terribly expensive, even more than the black."

Now, how did she know so much about truffles? Most

thought truffles were chocolate bonbons. And many did not care for their earthy, fungal scent and taste. "I've never tried the white truffle myself."

She grinned at him. "We'll save our money and chip in. Last I saw, they were about $10,000 per kilo."

He winced. "Ah, so expensive."

"I know." She tapped the back of his hand with the dry part of her pen. "Between me, a writer, and you, an aid worker, we would have to save for years."

Jack nodded. Part of that was true. He'd refused most of his salary and had donated it back to the aid organization, so he wasn't swimming in cash. His family was loaded, as the Americans liked to say, but most of that was tied up in real estate, farmland and the house in Paris. He had enough for his daily needs and never considered tapping into the long-term investments. God willing, he wouldn't be the last Comte de Brissard, and he didn't want to be known as the profligate count that flushed the family holdings down the loo. "You must have worked very hard to be able to come to France."

She laughed. "You don't know the half of it. My magnum opera include 'How to Potty-train Your Toddler in Ten Easy Steps,' 'Top Ten Organic Dog Food Brands' and 'Ten Historic Heroines of Philadelphia.'"

"I sense a theme."

"Magazine editors love articles with numbers in them, and ten is usually about right. It makes good cover copy."

The first article struck him. "Lily, what do you know about potty training? You do not have any children, do you?"

"Of course not. I researched online and talked to moms and a preschool teacher." She frowned at him. "And what would I be doing here all summer on my own? I'm not one of those upper-class mothers who leaves her children with

the nanny and jaunts off to Europe. No, thanks." She made
a sour face.

Jacques nodded. His own mother had often left him with
not only his nanny but with Madame Finch and Bellamy
when she wanted to travel. It was a typical situation for
children of his class, as Lily had so succinctly explained.

He wondered where she had learned so much about the
moneyed class, like black truffles and absentee mothering. Maybe from American movies and television. They
were notable for their celebrity interest.

She tipped her head to the side. "You know, you bribed
me with telling me about French scouting but never did
get around to that. Time to pay up. I may sell a freelance
article on this." She clicked on her laptop. "Okay, here's a
new file for my notes. Now tell me the French version of
the scouting pledge." She looked expectantly at him.

Jack couldn't decide whether to grin or groan. He was
thinking the least noble thoughts possible at how her
breasts curved under her peach-colored T-shirt and how
her enthusiasm was a bright sunburst compared to all the
cool, collected women he'd known. "Well, there are many
scout organizations in France depending on religion and
politics."

"Fascinating," she murmured, her lips parting and eyes
widening. His breath sped up, as well. "Tell me more,
Jack."

"On my honor," he muttered, remembering his prom-
ise to Madame Finch, the governess with the evil streak.
He could practically hear her laughing all the way from
London.

6

LILY RESTED HER head against the seat in the rental car. They had arrived in the amazing steel-and-glass Avignon train station in less than four hours as promised. It left Jack enough time to show her the famous bridge of Avignon that only extended halfway into the Rhône River due to strong currents as well as the beautiful stone Papal Palace that was the home of several popes during the 1300s.

While they were grabbing a couple sandwiches for a late lunch, Jack had noticed a sign on a public bulletin board that a nearby town was hosting a lavender harvest festival. "Do you want to go?"

"Sure."

He had consulted the board again. "There are several hotels and a hostel. It's not a huge festival, so we should be able to find a couple beds at the hostel."

"Sounds good." A quiver ran through her stomach at the word *beds*. She'd been imagining Jack in a bed since last night. He'd given her nothing more than a couple sidelong glances but she could tell he was interested in her, too.

It had been so long since her last relationship, and the mild spark she'd had with her ex-boyfriend was nothing compared to the fiery sizzle she felt with Jack. She hadn't come to France to jump in the sack with a Frenchman, and it probably would even be counterproductive to her writing efforts.

On the other hand, France was full of examples of artsy types who managed to combine sexual passion and their creations. Look at Van Gogh—no, not him. Creepy. Or the sculptor Rodin and his protégée Camille Claudel—but she wound up in a mental institute. There was a huge Rodin gallery in Philly and Lily remembered that poor woman's story well.

Um, there had to be a happy ending there. Unfortunately, all she could think of were the artists who would have benefited from modern pharmaceutical therapy and the writers and poets who drank too much absinthe, the notoriously strong liquor that was banned in France about a hundred years ago.

Was that a blog post? See, she could combine her writing work and thoughts of him. A veritable romantic multitasker. "Jack, have you ever drunk absinthe?"

"Ah, they call that the green fairy for its color and supposed effects on the mind." He went on to discuss the active herbal ingredients in absinthe while Lily scribbled rapidly. He finished, "But there is little evidence that it can cause hallucinations, and it's now for sale in France again."

She shook her head. "Geez, you know a lot about the medical side of it."

He grinned. "And yes, I have tried it, but I don't care for it. Licorice-flavored, you see." He wrinkled his nose.

"Not a fan of that?"

"No, I prefer sweet things." Was it her imagination or did his gaze flick down to her bare legs and then up to her breasts? He was subtle, though. If she hadn't been so tuned in to him, she never would have noticed.

"If only they made lavender liqueur…" she teased him, wondering if he had meant her when he'd talked about sweet things.

"They do."

"Okay, another blog post for me." She started making notes again.

"You'll have time for writing later." He touched her knee to get her attention and quickly drew his hand back. "I want you to look around now so you can truly see what you're writing about."

She wanted his hand back on her knee, but it was firmly gripping the steering wheel. Instead, she looked out the window at the scenery. They'd just climbed a hill and the world was spread out before them.

Provence was beautiful—as if using that word was even a smidgen bit adequate to describe the land and the air, a crisp quality fragrant with floral perfume. Even better than perfume, because the flowers were alive and growing, putting out their scent with every touch of the breeze.

"It looks just like the paintings," she told him. "I thought those flat orange-and-purple landscapes were stylistically flat. But that's the way it actually looks."

He smiled. "The orange fields are *épautre,* or spelt in English. An old, old grain from the wheat family. It's been grown together with lavender for hundreds of years."

"No wonder you wanted to get out of Paris. This is heaven compared to the city."

"I agree. I'm glad you like it. This area is kind of a purple triangle of lavender growing. It's bordered by the towns of Sault, Banon and Sederon. Different varieties are used for different products, but the best and most exclusive varieties have a special designation, like wine. We take our lavender very seriously here—it's even called *l'or bleu*—blue gold."

"I can see why."

There was a small gravel pull-off area and Jack stopped the car there without asking. She hopped out to take pictures of the panoramic valley below.

He stood next to the front tire and stared out at the fields. Mindful of his privacy, she took a picture of him from the back, only the back of his head visible.

But even that was interesting. She lowered the camera. "Do you have a birthmark there, Jack?"

He rubbed the nape of his neck. "I suppose you can see that now that my hair is shorter. Yes, it's what they call a stork bite. Babies often have them, but they often fade quickly—mine never did."

"And what shape is that?" She came closer to see, her breath ruffling the tender skin.

A shiver seemed to run through him, and she fought the crazy urge to kiss the small red spot.

When he spoke, his voice was scratchy and he had to clear his throat. "I've only seen it in a mirror, but it looks like a heart."

"How cute." She rubbed her thumb over it and he turned, grabbing her hand.

"Sensitive spot." He held her hand for a second and then let go.

Sensitive or arousing? Lily was getting aroused herself, imagining her mouth, her hands on his smooth skin, his strong fingers touching her in all sorts of sensitive spots.

"Enough photos?" He stood next to the driver's door, obviously ready to get moving.

"For now, but I have plenty of camera memory and the will to use it." She hopped in and he pulled out onto the road again.

"Provence is a photographer's dream. In the summer, you can't drive down a village street without seeing someone with a camera. Out in the country, not as much, but you still trip over backpackers and campers."

"Did you grow up near here?"

"Not too far. My father unfortunately passed away when I was young and my mother now lives in Paris."

She wrinkled her face in puzzlement. "Why didn't you stay with her when you were in Paris? Is her apartment too small for the both of you?"

"No, she has a large enough place for me to stay, but she had many guests and I wanted to get away from the noise."

"I can see that about you, Jack. You have a touch of the hermit about you."

He gave a startled laugh. "Hermit? But I am hardly ever alone in my line of work."

Lily smiled. "And that wears you down, doesn't it?"

Jack slowly nodded. "*Oui,* I suppose it does. Sometimes I would bribe my tentmates to go to the mess hall for an extra hour so I could be alone."

"And you came down here for some vine-ripened aromatherapy. All you have to do is open your window and you get a snootful of soothing lavender scent."

He laughed. "But Lily, this is not true lavender here. This is lavandin, a hybrid that is more suited to homemade candles and laundry soap. In fact, the word *lavender* comes from the Latin word 'to wash.' I will show you the true lavender, like I am showing you the true France."

"And I appreciate you doing this for me, Jack."

But he was already shaking his head. "No, no appreciation necessary for me. If you see the real country, your articles will be strong and authentic, better for your career."

"How nice." He was thinking of her writing career? That was even more touching. On one hand, she was an open book, but Jack was still a bit of a mystery. "What did your father do before he passed away?"

"Many things, but his favorite was working in the lavender fields. Everyone works all day, every day, until the harvest comes in and the lavender goes to the distillery."

"A lavender farmer?" Lily gasped in delight. "No wonder you know so much about it."

He gave her a rueful look. "I was not spared due to my tender age. As soon as I was useful, I was in the fields with the men. And before the age of cell phones, I was the messenger boy, running from the fields back to the house to get supplies, check the weather report and most importantly, learn when lunch would be ready. Harvesters eat *a lot*. Probably over four or five thousand calories a day because the lavender is picked by hand."

"Your mother must have been busy cooking for them."

He choked back a laugh and gave her an incredulous look. "My mother wasn't much of a cook. One of the other local women was in charge of meals. Even now, *Maman* prefers parties to farming."

"But this is lavender. It's not exactly pig farming. I've been out in the Pennsylvania Amish country and, believe me, there are much smellier farms there."

"And that was her favorite part of the lavender. Being *from* the farm, not on the farm. She could give gifts of lavender perfume or sachets and pretend she pressed the blossoms with her own hands."

Lily laughed. "Your mother sounds like…" She didn't want to mention growing up in the servants' quarters. It sounded so archaic, and she didn't know if Jack was as egalitarian as he seemed. Some of the French were firmly steeped in the class system and regarded upwardly mobile women as peasant upstarts. "She sounds like a woman my mother knew. She would hire the best party planners, caterers, florists, musicians for her party and then act as if she'd done all the cooking and decorating herself."

Lily herself had served at dozens of Mrs. Wyndham's high-powered functions where local celebrities and politicians were frequent guests. Her mother had often roped her into waitressing if the caterers needed an extra pair of hands. Talk about humiliating—serving hors d'oeuvres to your classmates' parents and cleaning up broken glass and spilled booze when they'd had too much to drink. Worst of all was when her classmates were invited and she had to serve them. She wished more than once that she could wear a wig and sunglasses to those parties.

"Parties here in Provence are more casual. As long as you have plenty of good food and wine, everyone is happy." He turned a corner leading down into the town and they quickly came to a standstill in traffic.

Lily looked around. "I thought you said this wasn't a huge festival. When was the last time you were here for it?"

He grimaced. "Ten years ago."

"Looks like the world has discovered your sleepy little village."

"I suppose they welcome the increased tourist money." But he didn't look thrilled about it.

"Of course. Everyone has to make a living."

Jack nodded. "And times can be hard when you depend solely on the land. Many people here live mostly on what they grow in the garden and hunt in the forests."

"That's the trendy thing to do now—eat locally. And you can't get much more local than your backyard."

"We French are well-known trendsetters." He laughed. "And wild rabbits and wild boar are delicious if cooked for several hours in red wine." He deftly negotiated the narrow cobblestone streets, avoiding pedestrians with a death wish and other cars intent on fulfilling their desires.

"That sounds wonderful. Maybe I could try that this week."

He shook his head. "Eating locally means eating in season, and those are traditional fall dishes. You would have to be here in October or November when the weather cools."

"I'll be long gone by then."

"Ah, yes." They both sat in silence as the cars in front of them inched along. "But since you are here now, you get to see the lavender." He spotted a parking slot and shoe-horned the rental car into it. Lily wouldn't have had the nerve to even try.

"That's true, but I bet every season has something wonderful to see."

"I think so, but of course I am a native son." He turned to smile at her. It was such a sweet smile that impulsively, she grabbed his right hand where it sat on his knee.

His smile faded but he immediately tightened his fingers around hers. "Lily, I am supposed to be a gentleman around you." His voice was low and gritty. "I would not break a promise to you or Madame Finch."

"You are a gentleman, but maybe I'm not much of a lady."

His breath hissed out in anger. "Don't say that about yourself. You are more of a lady than those born to the title."

"And how would you know about titled ladies?" she teased, leaning into him.

His amber brown eyes searched her face, his face taut as if he were in the middle of a great conflict. He seemed to come to a decision and sighed.

She was going to ask him if he were all right, but then he closed his eyes and lowered his mouth to hers.

Her breath caught in her throat as their lips touched. Her eyes fluttered shut and she practically swooned at the soft, gentle pressure of his mouth. He lightly pressed a kiss to her and then, realizing her eager response, deepened it so her mouth was open and moist under his.

Jack groaned in satisfaction, murmuring her name. She grew brave enough to flick the tender inner margins of his mouth with her tongue, and his fingers tightened almost painfully on hers.

He caught her tongue and sucked on it, and she cupped the back of his neck to keep him close. Her other hand slid up from where it rested on his knee to massage his thigh, the crisp hair tickling her fingers.

Jack dragged himself backward, his chest heaving. His glance fell to her breasts. Her diamond-hard nipples pressed against her thin bra and T-shirt. He raised his hand to cup her breast and then dropped it to his side as if he'd lost all his strength. "Ah, *mon dieu.* Lily…"

She muffled his mouth with her palm. "If you are about to apologize…well…" His hot breath against her tender skin made her almost forget what she was going to tell him and she panted a couple times before remembering. "Oh, yeah. Don't apologize, okay?"

He nodded and she started to pull her hand back, but not before his tongue flicked out to taste her. She yanked her hand back in surprise, not offense, and he gave her a dry smile. "You see, Lily? I am not much of a gentleman after all. You may want to get out of the car before I start the engine and drive us somewhere without an audience."

She actually wavered. If that was what he could accomplish in the front seat of a miniature car, imagine what he could do with some working room. But was she ready to hop into the backseat with him?

Her hesitation was enough to break the spell. "Get out, Lily. I'll follow you in a minute."

"But why…" She spotted the front of his shorts and understood why he needed some down time, so to speak. She opened the door and staggered out, not in much better shape herself.

She quickly put on her sunglasses to hide her dazed expression. *Now what, Lily?* Jump into bed with a guy she'd met the day before? Not her style, but then the whole getting-to-know-you routine hadn't worked much for her previously. And it wasn't the whole perfumed air, blue sky and beautiful scenery that was making him appear so sexy. He just *was*.

She had the feeling she'd find him as sexy if she'd met him in whatever jungle he usually lived in. Maybe that was what had saved him from being snapped up? And did she even know if he was snapped up or single?

Nope, and she needed to learn that before she made her decision. She leaned down. "Jack, I'll be right back."

"What?" He started to get out of the car but made a face and sat back down. Lily stifled a giggle. She'd never had such an effect on a man before and it made her feel powerful. Sexy.

She whipped around the corner of an old limestone building and pulled out her phone. The number was the newest she'd input. "Madame Finch, this is Lily. I have a question for you."

She asked her question and got the answer she'd wanted. Now all she needed to do was make her decision.

LILY LOOKED AROUND the perfume factory in wonder. The House of Laurent was housed in a historic building painted the color of ripe cantaloupe with white-shuttered windows. Jack had gone to the hostel around the corner to make a reservation for them for the night. Lily was relieved to put off her decision, for tonight at least.

For now, she was on the clock, so to speak. She couldn't very well come to Provence and not write about perfume, could she? She took several photos of the display of ancient perfume pots, delicate perfumed gloves that had been all the rage in a smellier society, and Art Deco French glass perfume vials and cut-crystal bottles that were works of art in themselves.

She'd been lucky enough to catch two spots on the English tour, but where was Jack? Not that he needed a tour in English, but she found herself wanting to share more and more with him.

They had gathered the group when a hand rested on her waist—he was back.

"Just in time." She smiled up at him. "What's with the hat?" He was wearing an olive-drab, military style sun hat pulled down practically to his eyebrows.

"This? The sun is very strong this time of year and I am a bit pale."

"Oh, true. I have my own sun hat, but it's in the car."

"We can get it after the tour if you'd like." He cleared his throat. "The hostel had two beds left—one in the male bunkroom and the other in the female. I reserved them for us."

"Ah. Good." Right? She tried to ignore her feeling of disappointment. The tour started right after that and Lily was swept away in note taking.

Jack leaned down to her, his brim bumping her head. "If you don't get all the details, ask me later. We learn much of this growing up in the area."

"Great." After that, she relaxed a bit and learned about

different methods of extracting the fragrant oils from plants, such as steam distillation, pressing the flowers into fats and more modern methods such as volatile solvents and pumping gases into the flowers to release the scent molecules. "Very high-tech, isn't it?" she murmured to him.

"Pah. If you have premium flowers, you don't need fancy methods."

"A purist, eh?"

"But of course. You should never settle for less than the highest quality in everything."

"That's a nice theory."

"But not practical?"

She shrugged. "My budget doesn't always allow for top of the line in everything."

"Very true. But a woman's perfume should be an indulgence, something that makes her feel wonderful." He gestured to a case with a frosted-glass bottle blown into the shape of a swan.

"I can see that." This would make a great blog post.

"She lifts the stopper and fragrance fills the air. It reminds her of the last time she wore it because scent is a powerful memory trigger. Did she meet her lover then? Is she meeting him tonight?"

There was that word again. *Lover.* Lily listened to him, spellbound. His mellow baritone voice and his sexy French accent were hypnotic.

He continued, "Then she strokes the stopper over her neck, her throat, the hollows behind her ears, as she wonders what new memory she will make tonight."

"Um, wow." She cleared her throat.

"That is the magic of perfume."

She stared up at him, trying not to pant. "What perfume is your favorite?"

He leaned down to whisper in her ear. "Yours."

"But…but I'm not wearing any."

"I know." His breath feathered over her neck, sending a million nerve endings abuzzing. "The most intoxicating perfume of all is the scent of a woman's skin. Even the most skilled *parfumier* cannot duplicate that."

And if a skilled perfume master could bottle Jack's sex appeal, it would be a bestseller. But then she'd have to share it with another million women, instead of guarding it all for herself.

Lily smiled up at him. Maybe not tonight in the hostel, but soon, she'd open the bottle and make some new memories.

LILY COULDN'T BELIEVE how fast the day passed. A visit to the perfume lab, filled with pristine white furnishings and brown glass scent bottles, a leisurely lunch at a sunny sidewalk table and then walking around the town hand in hand so as not to get separated in the crowd—or so Jack claimed.

He could claim whatever he wanted as long as she could keep his strong fingers wrapped around hers. He showed her many of the historic buildings, including an ancient church, a historically accurate restored lavender press and an ancient plane tree that shaded benches in the town square.

Twilight was starting to fall, the pinkish-purple light bathing them in a rosy glow. Lily was tired from the sun and wine, but her nerves felt almost raw and jittery. She took some deep breaths. Tonight they would stay in the hostel and tomorrow was another day, as Scarlett O'Hara was wont to say.

She muffled a yawn with her free hand and rolled her neck.

"Tired?" He moved behind her and started rubbing her shoulders.

She moaned at the exquisite sensation. "Oh, yes, Jack. Harder, harder."

His fingers tightened and she realized how erotic she'd sounded. That wasn't far off the mark. She stepped away and turned around, not wanting to embarrass herself further. "Thanks, that felt great. What would you like to do for dinner? I have some granola bars and dried fruit in my backpack."

His pained expression made her laugh. "We will be able to find something more substantial than that." But after stopping in several restaurants around town where the crowds were standing-room-only and the wait for a table was hours, Jack was forced to admit defeat. "I suppose we could find something at the hostel, although packaged noodles and sandwiches isn't my first choice."

"Food snob." She handed him a granola bar, which he ate grudgingly on the way to the car to pick up their luggage.

The hostel was an old limestone building that looked suspiciously like a school. Jack confirmed her guess when she asked. "Yes, it was the local primary school for many years but the village built a bigger, more modern school at the edge of town. A couple years ago, an investor bought the property and had it remodeled into a hostel."

"Now we can legitimately sleep at school." He laughed as they went up the steps. "I feel like I should check in at the principal's office."

And the main office was now the front desk, the clerk a jolly older woman, unlike any principal that Lily had ever met. Jack greeted her and her face fell. She spread her arms wide and shrugged expressively, replying to his question.

Whatever they were talking about, it wasn't good news for them. His polite insistence didn't get him anywhere, only more expressive shrugs.

Lily touched his elbow. "What is it?"

He pursed his lips and puffed out a sigh. "She says when we didn't arrive in time, she gave the beds to someone else and now the hostel is full. They have no beds whatsoever due to the festival."

"So sorry, *mademoiselle*. But the clock…" She pointed at the utilitarian round black-and-white timepiece on the wall.

"Geez, where should we stay? Out in the park?" She didn't want to sleep out in the open but with Jack for company, it might be safe.

He conferred with the hostel manager again, who made a telephone call. "She's going to call one of the local women who has rooms for rent. Maybe she has something for us."

"Okay."

The hostel manager hung up the phone with a grin. "Ah, good luck *pour vous*. One chamber."

"Great!"

Jack got directions and they headed off. "It won't cost too much more than the hostel, and they might have breakfast for us."

"Really, I don't mind," she assured him. A pair of twin beds would be fine.

7

"OH." Their impossible-to-find, last-one-available-in-the-whole-village room did not have twin beds, like every other European hotel room she'd ever heard of.

It had one single-and-a-half bed, because for sure that mattress was not a standard American double. Even that shrimp Napoleon and his wife would have barely fit in that sucker.

The rest of the room was pleasant enough with white walls and a small balcony overlooking the lavender fields.

Jack was chatting with the wizened madame who owned the house, who melted under his charms like a hot stick of butter. He turned back to Lily. "This is it, Lily. Can you make do?"

"Of course," she said brightly. "It looks…cozy."

He gave her a look that said he knew what she was thinking but made arrangements with the lady of the house.

Glad to be off the street for the night, Lily set her backpack on the floor and rolled her neck.

Lily couldn't help glancing at the bed. There was hardly anything else in the room. She suspected this had been either a poor relation's room or the maid's quarters once upon a time.

Jack cleared his throat and went to his backpack. "I'm going to take a shower. The bathroom is down the hall." He selected clean clothes and a towel and slipped into a pair of rubber flip-flops.

"Okay." Once he left Lily set up her laptop at the small desk and plugged in the round-pronged French electric adaptor. She selected several photos to upload from her camera to her blog and wrote several paragraphs about their arrival in Provence.

She stopped and realized that Jack featured prominently in her entry—what he'd eaten for lunch, what he'd liked best, how they'd found the last room in town…that had the smallest bed in France.

She dragged her eyes away from the bed and ruthlessly edited her rough draft. Readers didn't need to know every-thing. Jack was still "Pierre," a friendly Provençal local who had offered to show her around the perfume festival. She did add several of his insights on how the climate and weather was perfect for growing so many fragrant ingre-dients for the local perfumeries.

Her photos of the cut lavender in buckets looked great, and the elaborate glass perfume bottles from the antique store sparkled in the sun. If only the internet had smell-o-vision. But no shots of Jack's face online due to his re-quest for safety reasons. She'd never asked his permission to post his photo and name.

She hit Post, and Jack was still safely anonymous.

And by the way, where was he? Surely done with his shower. A shower sounded like a good idea after hiking around the dry, dusty town, so Lily gathered her supplies and set off down the hall.

He wasn't in the bathroom, which was shoehorned into

a former broom closet by the looks of it. She'd take a picture later for her blog. No need for a wide-angle lens, that was for sure.

She took a quick shower to get the dust and sweat off and returned to their room. Still no Jack. Was he hiding until she was safely asleep? It was well past ten, but she wasn't tired at all.

Lily hadn't come to Provence to sit alone in her room. She went down the stairs and heard laughter coming from the patio. She poked her head outside and Jack was sitting in a comfortable looking wicker love seat, chatting with the plump lady of the household and her mustachioed, equally round husband.

Jack looked relaxed and cheerful, his hair slicked back from his shower and his towel and clothing folded neatly on the side table.

The older couple spotted her and beckoned her to join them. "Ah, *mademoiselle!*" the man exclaimed expansively, his mood no doubt helped by his big glass of wine. He struggled to his feet and eagerly shook her hand, planting a juicy smooch on each cheek. She was discovering that the people of Provence were avid hand-shakers in addition to cheek-kissers. One man in the flower market, his arms full of blooms, had offered his friend an elbow to shake.

Jack stood as well and greeted her a bit more coolly, still feeling the awkward vibe of too much bodyspace and not enough bedspace. He introduced Monsieur Roussel, the husband of the lady who was charging them an arm and a leg for the night.

Their hostess stood, as well. "Sit, sit." She pointed to the seat next to Jack and Lily sat. "Our wine." She poured Lily a big glass and went to a large stone table behind them, reappearing with two plates full of goodies.

"Oh, wow." Lily didn't normally eat so late at night, but when in France…

Madame Roussel spoke in an emphatic manner, waggling her finger at Jack several times.

"Is she chewing you out?"

"Yeah, Madame was horrified that we had granola bars for dinner and she thinks I am much too thin to be a proper Provençal—that's a man from Provence. The common physique is that of Monsieur Roussel."

"Ah." Lily nodded. Round, to be sure, but a more packed, prosperous fat, rather than flabby.

"Eat." Madame glared down at them.

Actually, Lily was hungry. The heat of the day had lowered her appetite, but now that the sun had set, she was getting it back.

She picked up a baby carrot pickled in vinegar and spices. The flavor was sour and fresh, crispy but mellowed around the edges by the vinegar. "Delicious."

Madame understood and beamed. *"Mangez, mangez."* She made a flapping gesture at the rest of the food.

"Eat up, Lily, we don't want to offend our good hosts."

"Of course not."

Madame pointed at Lily and said, "Tart."

Lily flinched. Was Madame some Provençal version of a gypsy mind reader?

Jack muffled a laugh. "It's a tomato tart. She's not making a comment on us sharing a bedroom. It would seem odd if we weren't."

"Oh." Now that she wasn't being scolded for wayward thoughts, Lily picked up a slice of tomato tart. It resembled a thin pizza with overlapping tomato slices. She bit into it and moaned in satisfaction. The pastry was crispy, almost like a puff pastry, and there was a hidden layer of soft, white cheese spread under the tomatoes. But the tomatoes were the star of the dish, thinly sliced and baked until chewy and almost caramelized around the edges.

Pure summer burst on her tongue, sweet and savory. "Oh my gosh, Jack, you have to try this. It is sooo good."

She shoved the tart between his lips and he opened his mouth in pure instinct. "Mmmph." He chewed and nodded in approval. Madame watched them both in satisfaction.

"Where does she get the tomatoes?"

Jack translated and their hostess laughed and gestured beyond the patio wall. "Her own garden, of course. The weather is perfect for vegetables of all kinds."

Lily cut another slice and handed it to Jack. "Eat." She sounded suspiciously like Madame.

"Bossy." But he took the tart and nibbled at it.

She finished hers quickly and moved onto a soft goat cheese spread onto a thin toasted slice of French bread. "Is this their own goat's milk, too?"

He asked and smiled. "No, the goats belong to Madame's brother."

"What a talented family."

Madame passed her a dish of what looked like olive spread. Lily spread it on another slice of bread and passed it to Jack.

"Trying to fatten me up?"

"Like a goose for *foie gras*," she teased him.

Madame perked up. "Ah, *foie gras!* You like?"

Lily's mouth watered. "Oh, I love it, but I haven't had it in years." Mrs. Wyndham had served it at her parties, and Lily and the other staff snuck crackers full of it when they ducked back into the kitchen.

He looked at her in surprise. "You like *foie gras,* eh?"

"We have it in America, too." Especially if you'd grown up in the richest neighborhood in Philadelphia.

Madame disappeared into the house and emerged a

couple minutes later, triumphantly bearing a glass jar. She set it on the low table in front of them and unscrewed the lid with a flourish.

Lily leaned forward and gasped. Surely that huge jar wasn't what she thought.

"Pâté de foie gras!" their hostess announced.

"Holy cow, Jack, do you know how much a small jar of that stuff costs?"

He shook his head. "Homemade, probably from the geese of Madame's brother, along with the goat cheese." He listened to the older lady's explanation. "Ah. The geese belonged to her sister, and they were the plumpest, fattest geese in Provence."

"Mais oui. Très bon." That was the best French compliment she could manage, but it earned a wide smile.

And of course, after she had brought out the *foie gras* with as much pride as an American cook bringing out the Thanksgiving turkey, Lily couldn't refuse a hefty sample, along with another glass of rosé wine. Jack accepted a much smaller portion, and murmured, "That stuff packs a kick, Lily."

"What, the wine?"

"All of it."

She nodded, realizing her bare-bones, rolls-and-coffee Parisian diet was light years away from the food bonanza exploding in front of her. He was wise to eat in moderation, but her, she was perfectly healthy.

If the tomato tart was pure summer sunshine, the *foie gras* was pure autumn, earthy and dark. She'd never eaten it on a toasted baguette before, but it was the perfect combination.

Jack chatted with Monsieur and Madame Roussel as she sipped her wine and nibbled at the *foie gras*. Such a delicacy couldn't be gobbled.

He was careful to include her in their conversation, translating their recommendations for the tourist sites in the area and explaining the frequent bursts of laughter. Apparently the Provençaux were very fond of jokes.

She yawned. What a busy day. Closing her eyes, she leaned onto Jack's shoulder. He hesitated for a second but put his arm around her.

Did he smell good, his cologne a woodsy blend that fit this country setting perfectly. She snuggled into him, content to doze to the murmur of French voices and the drone of the cicadas in the trees.

She couldn't remember the last time she'd been so relaxed—replete with good food, good company and a good man. Jack was the best part, even better than homemade *foie gras.*

JACK RELAXED FOR the first time in a long time. He was finally home. He'd never met their hosts before, but they were still familiar to him, warm and hospitable and generous to a fault with the food.

That late-night snack had been more than enough to put anybody to sleep, but combined with heavy *pâté* and young wine that always had a higher alcohol content, it was a wonder Lily was still conscious.

And unless he wanted to carry her upstairs, he'd better get her to bed *immédiatement.*

Lily in his bed, warm and willing instead of stuffed and sleepy. The image was instant and powerful. He knew she would approach lovemaking with the same enthusiasm she approached life.

Ah, well, he'd given his word to be a gentleman, and gentlemen did not pour girls into bed and then crawl in after them for some nighttime sport.

He made his excuses and gave his thanks to the friendly couple. "Up we go, Lily."

She blinked at him with her big green eyes and extended a hand for him to pull her off the sofa. "Bedtime, Jack."

"Indeed." She wasn't intoxicated, just well-fed and slightly tipsy. He helped her up the stairs to their room and flipped on the light. The room was cozy and golden, the cream-colored embroidered quilt especially inviting.

He needed to decline that invitation. "Lily, you can have the bed. I'll sleep on the floor."

"What?" She wrinkled her nose. "Don't be silly. We can share the bed. I trust you."

He sighed. He didn't trust himself. "No, no, there are extra quilts and a pillow for me to use."

But Lily wouldn't take no for an answer. "You've had the same long day as I had, and you have even less padding for the floor. Don't be silly." She grabbed her toothbrush and left for the bathroom.

He stood in the middle of the room, at a loss. He'd thought he'd fallen into hell at his mother's party, but that was nothing compared to the hell of platonically sleeping with the sexiest woman he'd ever met.

Lily returned and crawled into bed, taking the side closest to the wall. "Don't be silly, Jack." She yawned. "Come to bed."

"I, uh, need to brush my teeth," he stammered.

"Hurry up. I'm beat."

He knew he was beaten too and shuffled to the bathroom. Staring grimly into the small mirror, he brushed the wine and *pâté* off his teeth.

God must be laughing at Dr. Jacques Montford, Comte de Brissard. He'd been arrogant enough to think he knew what was going to happen in his life, and boom! Illness hit.

He knew that happened, of course, but not to him. He was invincible. He fought illness for other people, not himself.

He sighed and spit into the sink. Ah, well. Like Lily had said, he was alive and it must be fate.

Walking down the hall, he considered the vagaries of fate. It was fate that he had literally bumped into her. And maybe it wouldn't be so bad trying to keep his hands off her.

He entered their room and stopped short. Lily lay sleeping on her back, the small bedside lamp gilding her hair and skin.

She was a golden angel, her plump lips slightly parted as her breasts rose and fell, the nipples poking against her thin cotton shirt.

With an effort, Jack dragged his gaze away and turned off the light. Crawling into bed, he perched himself on the far edge of the mattress and determinedly turned his back to Lily.

He'd promised to behave himself, even if it meant a long night for him. A long, hard night.

8

LILY DIDN'T WANT to wake up from her incredibly erotic dream. She'd never dreamed like this before, never dreamed of a man pushing his, well, erection against her bottom as he palmed her breast in his hot, rough hand.

She couldn't help herself and wiggled against her dream man, who was tall and lean with chestnut-brown hair. He responded by thumbing her nipple and kissing the back of her neck, his breath damp on her skin. She sighed at the wonderful sensations shooting between her legs. "Oh, Jack."

His hand tightened reflexively on her breast and her eyes flew open.

It wasn't a dream after all. It was Jack's hand on her breast and Jack's erection pressed between her cheeks. But only for a second.

He jumped out of bed like a horde of bedbugs had attacked him. "Ah, *merde,* Lily, I am so sorry." His distress showed up in his very French pronunciation of her name— *Lee-Lee*—with the emphasized second syllable.

Lily sat up and stared at the front of his short black boxer briefs. He was impressively aroused, the fabric doing little to contain his desire. But some guys got that way during the night. Maybe it didn't have anything to do with her. But he got larger as she watched. Maybe it *was* her?

He followed the path of her gaze and grabbed a pillow to cover himself. "Again, I am sorry. I should have taken the floor as we had discussed." He turned away and fumbled in his bag. "I have an extra sleeping bag liner. I will be fine."

"Jack." Her voice came out louder than she intended. He looked over his shoulder, startled.

She took a deep breath. "Do you want me?"

"I, uh…" He licked his lips, his breath speeding up.

That was enough answer for her. She slowly pulled her T-shirt over her head so she sat in bed wearing nothing but her boxer shorts. "Do you want me?" she repeated, growing in confidence.

"Yes…" The word was dragged from him, almost unwillingly. "God, yes…but—"

"What, Jack?" She got up on her knees to face him.

"I shouldn't, all right? You're a very sweet girl and I don't want to take advantage of you. Your first trip to France, and here we are thrown together in a small hotel room with the heat and the flowers and the feel of your skin…" He stopped suddenly, and that was when she knew she could have him.

And she wanted him.

She stood up and padded over to him. "What does my skin feel like?"

He stood there tongue-tied.

"Maybe you need to check it again." She shoved her boxers down and kicked them away so she was naked in front of him.

His hands twitched at his sides. She picked up his wrist and brought his hand to her hip. "How does my skin feel?" she repeated.

"Wonderful," he said hoarsely, his fingers tightening into her butt.

"More specific," she chided him, picking up his right hand. "How about up here?" This time she placed it on her breast.

"Like satin. Like silk. Like *crème*." He cupped her breast and stroked it gently.

"Like cream?" She was starting to breathe harder, his hands straying from their original positions. He kneaded her butt and he thumbed her nipple like he had while they were sleeping.

Only this time they were wide awake.

"I'll have to check to see if you taste like cream." He bent forward and nuzzled her neck. Lily clutched his shoulders as his tongue lapped at her skin.

"Well?" she managed to say.

"Better than cream. Cream with raspberries. Cream with honey." He stopped talking and did little swirls with the tip of his tongue.

"Ohhh." Her knees started shaking. "Jack, please."

"Please, what?" He laughed, his breath hot on her. It was a sound she hadn't heard from him before, pleased with himself and self-confident.

"You know." Heat climbed into her face, a mix of arousal and embarrassment.

"Tell me." He sank to his knees, sliding his mouth down her breast. He captured the peak between his lips, sucking it to aching fullness.

She gasped and ran her fingers through his thick, wavy hair. "Jack…"

"Mmm." The hum buzzed her nipple and she fought for balance, widening her stance. He cupped her butt in one hand, his other hand toying with the damp curls between her legs.

She fought for breath as he slipped his finger there, finding her moisture and spreading it up to her clit. A cry escaped her as he lingered there, massaging and rubbing the little nub. It had throbbed since he'd touched her in her sleep, creating that erotic dream that she had never wanted to end. "But it's not a dream anymore," she murmured.

He released her breast and rubbed his thumb over her slick nipple. "A dream come true."

She blinked hard at the sudden rush of emotion. He was right—she had never considered the possibility of finding someone like Jack, someone who could be her companion during the day and a powerful lover at night.

"Tell me what you like, *ma belle*," he continued conversationally, as if he were asking her how she took her coffee. "Do you like it slow and sweet?" He slowed his pace at her clit, dragging each caress out into a torturous pace. "Or do you like it hard and fast?" He flicked her until she fell back on the bed, her legs too weak to hold her up.

"I like it all. Any way you want."

"Good, because I have many, many ideas for you." He stretched out next to her. "Beautiful Lily. Such a beautiful woman. I fought to keep my hands off you, but sleeping next to you was too much temptation." He stroked her breasts and she arched into his touch.

"I knew it was you in my dream."

"Did you?" He toyed with her nipple, first one and then the other. "Have you been thinking of me that way?"

"I thought you were cute when we first met, but after you lost that shaggy look, you were gorgeous."

He puffed out a disbelieving breath. "I am not gorgeous."

"I am the only one in this room who is an expert on handsome men, so there. Unless you're putting on a phenomenal act…" she teased him.

"No act," he promised. "I have never been more sincere in my admiration."

She ran her fingers through the short chestnut hair on the nape of his neck and tugged his face down to her breast. "I'm in a mood to be admired, so keep going."

"Oh, you are a bold one." He kissed her breast but quickly moved right below her belly button.

Lily crimsoned in shock because she'd meant for him to keep going at her breast, not keep going down her body.

But he gently opened her folds, and at the first stroke of his finger all her protests dropped away. "Oh, Jack."

"Lily," he murmured. "Relax. Let me give you this pleasure." He guided her to sit on the edge of the bed and nestled between her thighs.

At the first gentle touch of his tongue, she cried out and he smiled against her. Her surrender spurred him on, as he slowly flicked her clit, then faster and faster until she fell back onto the bed.

Jack only stopped to hook her knees over his shoulders. In that wide-open, vulnerable position, Lily felt a moment of anxiety and closed her thighs around him.

He lifted his head immediately. "Are you all right, my Lily?"

His Lily. She liked the sound of that. And she liked how he made her feel—loved it, to tell the truth. She relaxed onto the tiny bed. "I feel wonderful."

"All right." He eased down again and in an instant she was lost in his touch. His mouth, his hands as they cupped her bottom, his cheeks as they brushed the sensitive inner skin of her thighs.

Her excitement started spiraling up into her belly and breasts, down her arms and legs. She tried pulling away again because it was too intense, but he held her close and refused to let her escape.

He seemed to know she couldn't take any more teasing and slipped a finger in and out of her slick, hot passage. She muffled a scream with her arm as he licked and stroked her. Her face burned and she could hardly breathe until he stopped and sucked her clit hard. She arched her back and climaxed hard, shaking with heat but shivering as if she had the chills.

Jack pushed her and pushed her until she couldn't tell where one climax ended and the next began. Finally she lay spent and limp under him and he stopped the exquisite torment, straightening to lie next to her.

He stroked her sweaty hair off her forehead.

"Wow. Oh, wow." She knew she had to look as if she'd run ten miles, but he didn't seem to mind. She smiled in an effort to stop panting.

He smiled back. "You liked that?" he asked eagerly.

"Very much." She caressed his cheek. "But what about you?" She tugged at his shoulders, encouraging him to move over her.

"Oh, Lily, Lily, I don't know how long I can last. It has been so long for me."

"How long?"

"Many months. Since long before I left for the typhoon and not since." He gave a quick grin. "Too ill to even consider it."

"You don't feel ill now." She ran her hand down his side, reveling in his lean masculinity.

"I've never been better." He grabbed her hand and pushed it aside. "But you have to let me prove it to you."

"Go ahead." She hooked her thumbs in his waistband and tugged. He twisted from side to side as they both stripped him naked, laughing as his underwear hit the floor.

She immediately grabbed his cock and he moaned. He

was long and thick, his silky skin covering a hot shaft. She brushed his fat tip with her thumb to spread his juices around.

"Ah!" He pulled away. "Not yet." He fumbled in his backpack and came out with a foil packet, quickly rolling on a condom.

Lily was disappointed because she hadn't gotten a good look at him in the dim light, but there would be many more chances to explore his body if she had her way. And it was time to have her way with him. She eased her thighs apart. "Come to me, Jack."

He moved between her knees and gently brushed her with his tip, wetting himself with her. He slowly slid inside as Lily consciously relaxed her internal muscles—it had been a long time for her, as well.

Finally he was locked deep within her and they both sighed in satisfaction. He felt wonderful, sure, but it seemed more than that. More as if he had claimed her, had taken her and said with his body, *She is mine.*

She blinked hard at her surprising sentimentality. He was a nice, sweet sexy guy, she was on summer vacation— the right mix for a fun holiday affair—no point in making it anything more.

"Lily?" he questioned gently, staring down at her. He could read her moods almost frighteningly well.

"Nothing." A rush of honesty prompted her to say, "I wasn't expecting this."

He smiled, shrugging as best as he could while bearing all of his weight on his arms. "I wasn't, either. But as you told me yesterday, I should look more to fate than to logic."

"Fate," she repeated. "But that means I'm not in control." And she hated that.

"Control is an illusion, a chimera. Life is a typhoon that

bears you where it will." He winked at her. "You will have much more fun if you lose control, especially tonight. I guarantee that."

She giggled. No more navel-gazing, especially since if she were to look down at her navel, she would see something infinitely more interesting than belly-button lint.

He started to thrust into her, and her giggles quickly turned to moans. She hooked her calves around his thighs, gripping his cock even tighter as she squeezed down on him.

Faster and faster he went, his butt and thigh muscles flexing. He dropped to his elbows, his chest hair catching and rubbing her nipples. She buried her face in the crook between his neck and shoulder, tasting his sweat. She had the most primitive urge to nip his skin—so she did.

He reared back in surprise.

"Did I hurt you?" How embarrassing.

A devilish grin spread over his angelic face. "My little cat has marked me. Did I taste good?"

She wiggled her eyebrows. "That part did. I'll let you know when I taste the rest of you."

His laugh turned into a groan and he lowered his head, slamming into her. "*Mon dieu,* the thought of your pink lips on me has tormented me all day."

Lily had a sudden fantasy of kneeling in front of him like he had kneeled to pleasure her. Sucking and caressing him with her lips and tongue until he exploded…she groaned and shivered.

"*Oui,* you want that, too. You are shaking around me." He leaned slightly to the side and slipped his fingers between them. "I'll make you shake even more."

He stroked her already swollen clit as he ground into her, his belly sliding over hers. His gaze burned dark and mysterious in the dim light. Heat built in her again, as if he'd never touched her before, never licked her to so many climaxes they all melted together.

But here it was again. He pinned her to the bed, claiming her. She wrapped her arms around his ribs and held tight. Her hips moved of their own accord, falling into pace with his rapid, almost frantic rhythm.

"Jack…" she gasped, desire boiling over. "I think I'm going to…" She gave up speaking and arched her back as an even more powerful orgasm hit, zinging up from where they joined into her whole body.

"Oh, Lily." He gritted his teeth and threw his head back, his neck pulling into cords. She held him tight as he jolted into her. Calling her name, he exploded, his cock jerking and pulsing deep inside her.

Slowly, he came down from his peak, panting as if he'd run all the way from Paris. He groaned and forced his gaze to focus on her. "Lily, are you all right?"

"Never better." She hugged him again and he sighed in satisfaction.

"Good. That is good." He slowly pulled out of her and looked around blearily. "Eh, this would be a good time to have a private bath."

She giggled. "You were the one who said Madame Roussel was much too sophisticated to shock."

He shook his head. "I am not worrying about shocking her—I am worried about being scolded for making a mess."

"How embarrassing."

He made do with several tissues and they tossed on some clothing. After they took turns sneaking down the hall to the bathroom, Jack urged her into bed. "You had your wicked way with me—now it's time for sleep."

"You were the one putting his hands all over me," she pointed out, taking off her T-shirt again. She wanted to feel his skin on hers, even if they were only sleeping. She slipped under the sheets, the cotton slightly more rumpled than before.

Jack shucked off his underwear. "You have a body made for pleasure. Soft and creamy-white in the moonlight, but with your skin you would be a golden goddess in the sunlight." He slid into bed next to her.

A delicious shiver rippled through her. "I've never been naked outdoors."

"Not even to sunbathe?"

She shook her head.

"Then not for sex."

"Nope again."

"We'll have to fix that."

"Outdoor sunbathing or outdoor sex?"

"Both." He swallowed hard. "And if that gives you erotic dreams again, please feel free to do to me whatever you'd like. I won't complain."

She yawned, utterly wrung out by their shockingly hot sexual romp. "Good. But let me catch up on a few hours' sleep first. By the way, how many condoms do you still have?"

He laughed and kissed the back of her neck. "Enough to last until the pharmacies open tomorrow." He wrapped his arm around her waist and she snuggled back against his warm, muscular chest. "Time to sleep, *chérie*. Tomorrow is a big day."

Oh, yes, it would be. Lily had big plans for hitting the sights—the sights of Jack, not the tourist kind.

9

LILY HAD SLEPT only until dawn. Jack was apparently an early riser in more ways than one. But she wasn't sleepy at all, thanks to the major endorphin buzz running through her veins. She and Jack making love…well, it was magical.

He came into their room as she was attempting to fix the nightmarish tangle of sheets that had once been neat and flat. They looked beyond hope. "Madame Roussel says our room is reserved for tonight and we need to find something else."

Lily straightened and nodded. The B and B room had been cozy but cramped, and the lack of connected bathroom was no fun. "You're the expert. Where's a good place to stay?"

He thought for a second. "There is a lavender farm up in the hills. My friend is the farm manager and I have stayed in the guesthouse before."

"Really? A lavender farm?" That sounded impossibly romantic.

"They are beginning the harvest, so it is a busy time, but Jean-Claude would not mind. What do you think?"

"It sounds wonderful, but I don't want to impose."

He waved a hand. "No imposition. Jean-Claude will be glad to see us."

"Well, okay." Lily began gathering her scattered belongings. "How far is it?"

"An hour or so, depending on traffic." Jack was much neater than she was and started rolling his clothing into tight rolls. "There is a nice pool and terrace with views of the fields. And a washing machine and dryer."

"Ooh, a washing machine?" That settled it. The bohemian life was fun, but dirty socks weren't part of the fun.

"Always practical, Lily?"

"Not always." She wiggled her eyebrows at him. "Flying to France alone and letting a sexy Frenchman sweet-talk me into his bed should qualify as extremely impractical."

"For the French, affairs of the heart are always practical," he informed her.

"Affairs of the heart—I like the sound of that. How do you say it in French?" She walked her fingers up his chest and curled them around the curve of his ear.

"Les affaires de coeur." He turned his face to nibble at her fingertips.

She leaned into his chest and cooed up at him. "Ooh la la."

He lowered his face to hers and captured her lips. She eagerly accepted his kiss, warm and affectionate, but playful and sweet.

A throat clearing from the hallway startled them apart. Madame Roussel eyed them knowingly and told Jack something.

His cheeks flushed. "She needs us to check out so she can clean the room." He bent to whisper, "And change the bedding."

Now it was Lily's turn to blush. She faced their hostess. *"Merci beaucoup,* Madame."

She waved a dismissive hand. *"Pas du tout, pas du tout."*

"Is that the same as *de rien?*" Lily asked Jack. He nodded. See, she was learning more French every day, although she'd bet several euros that several of the phrases he'd taught her last night were for bedroom use only.

JACK RELAXED KILOMETER by kilometer as they climbed into the rocky hills. Lily dozed in the seat next to him. He thought about pointing out some of the sights but decided there would be enough time for them to explore the outdoors later.

He glanced down at her. She was so beautiful lying next to him. He hadn't had the opportunity to watch her, except surreptitiously. He'd been right—she was a golden goddess in the pure sunlight, her honey-blond hair shining and her tanned skin glowing with good health.

The guesthouse he'd mentioned had actually been his uncle Pierre's house, an old farmhouse on the property. His uncle had decided to fix it up because it was far enough away from the main villa for privacy but close enough for the housekeeper to bring meals without the food getting cold. *Oncle* Pierre had been eminently practical.

The house had had the perfect setup for whatever sexual exploration he and Lily wanted—pool, hot tub, tiled terraces and a nice high wall around most of it to keep out prying eyes.

He knew she wouldn't be tanned all over thanks to her admitting she'd never sunbathed nude, but he was hoping he could convince her to try it with him.

He shifted in his seat as his cock hardened. Spreading coconut oil to slick her nipples and ass, their hot flesh sliding together as the sun beat down on them. He groaned and adjusted himself, but to little avail. The only thing better would be to take her without any barrier between them, his bare cock dipping into her tight wet depths. She would squeeze him, milk him dry as their juices mingled.

It was such a potent fantasy for him, the doctor who had never once in his disease-fearing life had unprotected sex. Dangerous, dirty and raunchy, but oh, so tempting.

He groaned again and forced himself to concentrate on his driving.

Lily opened her eyes sleepily and moved her seat upright. "You shouldn't let me sleep when I want to see the sights," she complained, rubbing her eyes. To his chagrin, her gaze fell on Jack's lap. "My, that is a sight." Her lips pulled back in a sly grin. "How long have you been driving around like *that?*"

"Not very long," he muttered. "Oh, look at that old barn." He was trying to distract her with the ancient building. It had been abandoned for years, and the scrub bush was starting to overtake it.

Lily glanced out the window. "Interesting. Can we see it up close?"

"We're almost to the lavender farm, and that is much more interesting." He needed to get her naked in that big four-poster bed in the master bedroom.

"No, no. This looks great. I want to take some pictures."

He'd distracted her too well. He sighed and pulled off the road, circling the bumpy road to the back of the barn. It was the typical creamy limestone found in almost every building. He cut the engine and undid his seat belt, but before he could get out, Lily's hand was on his lap.

He looked at her, startled. She smiled at him. "I think I found something more interesting than an old barn." She slowly undid his belt and zipper, and he bulged through the new opening.

She stroked the tight fabric over his erection as he stared

dumbly at her. "What were you thinking as you were driving?"

"What?" He couldn't remember what he'd been thinking as her fingers traced his shaft.

"Driving. Erection. You. And me, I hope."

"Of course. You, naked and slick in the sun."

"Mmm," she hummed approvingly. "What else?"

He shook his head. He didn't want to frighten her or make her distrust him with his fantasy of unprotected sex.

"Must be something really naughty." She shook her head. "You'll tell me sooner or later. Lean your seat back."

"No, Lily," he protested, but she pulled his briefs down and he jutted into the narrow space between his belly and steering wheel.

She traced a finger over his tip. "Now, how am I supposed to suck on you when I can't even reach you?"

He groaned and reclined the seat, a flush of needy embarrassment climbing his face.

She laughed softly. "Oh, Jack, so shy?"

"No," he choked out.

"Good." She gently kissed his tip. "I've wanted to do this since last night. I didn't get a good look at you."

"And what do you think?"

"Very nice." She cupped his shaft and played with the head. "You really want me, don't you?"

He brushed his thumb over her cheek. "What gave you that idea?"

"I'm a good guesser," she teased him.

"No guessing needed. You ask me and I'll tell you the truth." At least part of it.

She smiled and gently blew on him.

"Ah, Lily." He threaded his fingers down to her scalp, pulling out the band holding her hair back. The golden brown mass fell over her rosy cheeks and brushed his groin.

She enveloped him with her mouth and he clenched her hair. She was wet and warm around him, like last night. He thrust up between her lips.

It was heavenly. Lily was heavenly. She sucked deeply on him, jolting his nerves from head to toe. He dug his heels into the floormat, her hair wrapping around his hand.

She gave an utterly feminine hum of satisfaction, the vibration buzzing his shaft. Sweat beaded on his forehead and dampened his shirt. She swirled her tongue around the head of his cock and then licked him from the base to the tip as if he were an ice-cream cone.

His balls tightened and he gasped in pleasure. He'd never been so decadent, so intoxicated with lust, the southern sun burning him from the outside as Lily burned him from within. The cicadas buzzed and blood pounded in his ears. "Ah, Lily," he moaned. "Stop, stop. I'm losing control."

She laughed and lifted her mouth for a second. "Good, that's the idea." She resumed her tender caresses and sucked him deep.

He couldn't hold back any longer and exploded, Lily draining him dry until he stopped bucking and jerking under her.

She finally lifted her head and smiled at him. "Jack."

He stroked her silky hair down to the nape of her neck, amazed at her sexiness and sheer generosity. "Lily, you didn't have to do that—I never expected you—"

"I know." She smiled mischievously at him. "I'm learning to expect the unexpected this whole trip. But it was all my idea and I really wanted to pleasure you like you did for me last night."

"Thank you, Lily." He pulled her into his arms and hugged her.

She shook her head. "No thanking allowed. Unless you want me to start thanking you for everything you've done."

"No." He didn't want gratitude from her. "I want your warmth, your passion and the pleasure of your company. Gratitude is not on that list."

"That sounds lovely. You're lovely." She smiled at him and his heart flipped.

"Don't be silly," he said gruffly, trying to cover up his unruly emotions. "Men aren't lovely."

"You are." She kissed him on the cheek. "Can you show me around the barn?"

Jack laughed and fixed his clothes. "Back to work, eh?"

"A freelancer is never off the job." She started to blush. "Except for certain occasions."

"Exactly." She charmed him with her mix of boldness and shyness. He hopped out of the car and helped her out of the other side, where she oohed and aahed over the typically Provençal building.

Jack smiled to himself. If she liked this old wreck, she'd fall in love with the estate's guesthouse. And he'd love seeing her there.

FORTUNATELY FOR LILY, there was plenty on the drive to distract her from memories of her boldness. She'd never imagined she'd do *that* to a man in a parked car, but she couldn't help herself. Seducing Jack was as intoxicating as the local wine, and much more fun.

It was so flattering to know that watching her sleep aroused him to a fever pitch. And to feel him under her mouth—wow. It had been incredibly arousing and she couldn't stop thinking about the next time they would make love.

She knew it was just a vacation fling, but sex with Jack was more than scratching an itch—she was glad to be with him and get to know him in and out of bed.

Did the house he had mentioned have a nice bed? Anything would be better than the tiny one they'd shared last night, but they had managed just fine.

"Almost there." Jack turned down a narrow unpaved lane saved only from tedium by a row of trees on each side. Their trunks were silvery-white and mottled, almost as if some avant-garde artist had sculpted them out of concrete and then sandblasted them to make them look old. The branches grew straight up with glossy green leaves.

"What kind of trees are these?"

He slowed the car to avoid kicking up dust. "Ah, plane trees—from what you call the sycamore family. These are very old and have been trained over the years to grow upward, unlike the ones in the village that grow horizontally."

"Mmm." Lily pointed her camera out the window and took several shots. It was like driving in a green, leafy tunnel, much nicer than the New York underground version. Then the tunnel opened up on a stunning view of a gigantic stone manor house with a fence surrounding it. Lavender fields grew in the distance, their purple rows stunning alongside the low-growing orange spelt crop. "Holy cow, Jack. Whose house is that?"

He smiled at the building. "Isn't it beautiful? It's been here several hundred years and the owners have enlarged it over the centuries."

"This is your friend's house, then. What's their name?"

"The de Brissard family owns it." He shifted in the seat. "The guesthouse is another couple kilometers down the road and past that are the lavender fields and the farm buildings. There is even an old lavender press dating from the early Middle Ages. The farm, however, now uses a more modern facility in a nearby town."

"Hygiene and regulations suck the romance out of everything." She shook her head. "And I suppose you can't have the peasants crush grapes with their feet anymore, either."

He laughed. "Not unless you want to make the bureaucrats faint from horror."

They passed the main house and Lily craned her neck. "Can I have a tour of the mansion sometime? I'd love to see the inside."

"The housekeeper would love to give you one. They are very busy this time of year with the beginning of the lavender harvest. Many migrant workers come and Marthe-Louise and her staff make sure they all have enough to eat and drink. We keep the best workers that way."

"Oh. But if they're so busy, they might not want us borrowing the guesthouse."

"No, nobody is using it now and we are well out of the way of their work."

"If you're sure…"

"I am positive," he said firmly. "Please do not worry that you are imposing because that is not the case. I would never put you into an awkward situation where you are not welcome."

"Thank you, Jack." She couldn't reach him to kiss his cheek, so she patted his knee.

He smiled at her, his warm, relaxed smile that was appearing more and more frequently as they settled into Provence. "You are most welcome." He covered her hand with his and steered around a corner with his left hand. "And here we are."

Lily gaped at the guesthouse. It was smaller than the

main house but no less impressive. Jack parked the car in the circular gravel driveway next to a limestone fountain. She hopped out to admire the two-story stucco building. It was a lovely weathered peach blush color with pale blue shutters and white trimmed doors. The roof was Spanish-style red clay rounded tiles. She guessed it was too dry to grow a traditional American lawn since the grounds were landscaped in beds of carpet-type junipers, silvery hedges and tall evergreens pruned into perfect slim columns.

"This is called *la petite maison*—the little house."

"Little? How many bedrooms?" Her shoes crunched on the pure white gravel as she approached the fountain.

He hopped out of the driver's seat and looked up at the house. "Four, five if you consider the den has a sofa with a pullout bed."

"Oh, only five bedrooms—a real hovel." She twisted her camera strap. "Jack, this is too much. We can't just show up, even if they are your good friends."

He caught her shoulders and kissed her forehead. "Would it make you feel better if I called the farm manager and talked with him first?"

"Yes." She smiled in relief. She had no desire to do firsthand research on what the local French police did to trespassers. Not exactly good blog material.

"Good." He reached into the backseat and pulled out a water bottle. "Here, have a drink while I call Jean-Claude. I'm going to walk down toward the main house where the signal is better."

Lily nodded and unscrewed the bottle. Jack flipped open his phone and gave her a reassuring smile as he walked down the driveway.

She turned to look up at the guesthouse—the "little house." It would be wonderful to stay there, a luxurious hideaway of all the best of Provence.

Undoubtedly there was a beautiful garden in the back and killer views. But the best part would be spending time with Jack, to explore its four bedrooms with him. Five, if they considered the den, but Lily didn't expect a sleeper couch mattress would be all that comfortable.

She sighed. Maybe she was getting in over her head. Anybody would be. A chance meeting two days ago with a sexy Frenchman, a trip to Provence, unexpected passion last night and the prospect of even more in idyllic settings would turn any red-blooded American woman's head.

Lily would have to be careful to keep a good head on her shoulders. She was a writer in search of interesting stories, not a sappy tourist who, disillusioned with American men, had come to Europe in search of "true love."

And was it possible to be disillusioned if you had few illusions in the first place?

10

JACK WAITED UNTIL he was out of Lily's hearing and called Jean-Claude, his estate manager. Jean-Claude was not merely an employee, but more like an uncle. He had taken Jack under his wing after Jack's father died. Jack's mother was a sweet lady—too sweet-natured to deal with the precocious, obnoxious boy he'd been. Fortunately for Jack, Jean-Claude and Madame Finch were not sweet-natured in the least.

"Allô?"

Jack couldn't help but smile at the familiar sound of his old friend's heavy Provençal accent. "Jean-Claude, *c'est moi*—Jacques."

"Jacques? Where the hell are you?"

"Shhh. Meet me in down by the old oak tree near the fence line."

"You're here?" he bellowed.

"Calme-toi, mon ami. I will tell you everything as soon as you get here."

Jean-Claude grunted and hung up. Ten minutes later the sturdy man was standing on his toes so he could shake his finger in Jack's face. "And you are back in Provence after nearly dying in whatever jungle hellhole you ran off to, and you expect me to come running? We happen to be in the middle of the lavender harvest, in case you've forgotten. Lavender that I am harvesting for you, *M'sieu le Comte.*" He pursed his lips and then grabbed Jack for an emotional embrace. Jack got kissed on both cheeks and then once more for good measure.

Jack patted Jean-Claude's back, accepting the traditional French greeting. His estate manager had probably received a hysterical phone call from Jack's mother describing his admittedly nasty case of dysentery as a cross between the bubonic plague and Ebola hemorrhagic fever. "Eh, *mon vieux,* as you can see, I am here and healthy."

"*Bien oui,* you are too skinny." Jean-Claude released him, the corners of his sun-creased brown eyes crinkling as he gave him a hard stare.

Jack shrugged. "A few kilos, that's all."

"More like ten." Jean-Claude sniffed. "And now that you are here, you will stay with us and Marthe-Louise will cook for you all your favorites." Marthe-Louise was the family cook and also Jean-Claude's wife.

"Actually I'm not staying at the big house." He braced himself for the explosion, which erupted right on schedule.

"You come here sick and skinny and then you tell me you will go?" Jean-Claude gestured voluminously. "Go where? Go fall down in the lavender field and die? Eh, we could use goat shit for fertilizer—you do not need to volunteer!"

"Jean-Claude, *s'il te plaît,*" Jack soothed. "I called you because I can trust you." He lowered his voice and looked around the empty courtyard like a bad dinner-theatre actor. "It involves a woman. A special woman."

"Ah!" His old friend burst into laughter. All was forgiven if women and sex were involved. "Why didn't you say so?" He dug his elbow in Jack's side with less force than usual. "And this woman, where is she?"

"Waiting at the little house."

"*La petite maison?* Why?"

Jack knew this next part would be the trickiest. "She doesn't know I own all this. I don't think she likes rich guys."

Now Jean-Claude was really laughing. "Pull the other leg, Jacques. What woman doesn't like rich men? Or is she not very bright?"

Jack made a chopping gesture with his hand. "Enough." Jean-Claude raised his bushy eyebrows. Jack hardly ever used his aristocratic mien. He continued, "We will be staying at the *petite maison* and I do not want her to know the extent of my holdings. She is an independent American girl and very much believes our French concept of *liberté, fraternité* and *egalité.*"

Jean-Claude gave a loud snort. He knew himself the equal of any man in France, but knew the class system had well survived the Revolution. "If you say so, milord."

Jack rolled his eyes. "If you're going to act the role of a peasant, at least give a little bow or avert your eyes as you talk to me. Now as you know, Princess Stefania will be setting her wedding date soon, and she needs lavender oil for a special perfume. She is planning to sell it for the benefit of her children's charity. Do we have enough high-quality lavender to supply her needs?"

Jean-Claude drew himself up in affront, as if explaining their business to a particularly dim-witted farmhand. "*M'sieu le Comte,* all our fields are, *as always,* Haute-Provence Lavender, designated by the government as AOC, Controlled Destination of Origin. We *never* have low-quality lavender." His lips curled at the very thought, and he spit on the dry ground.

"Very good." He wrapped his arm around his friend's shoulders. "Where would I be without you, *mon vieux?*"

Jean-Claude puffed out his lips. "Taking care of your own land and your own lavender."

"I know, I know." Jack raised his hands in surrender. "But I am still grateful. And Princess Stefania will be, too."

"A wedding for her. I remember when she came for the summer when she was what, twelve? Thirteen?"

Jack nodded.

"Marthe-Louise taught her how to cook, how to garden, how to sew. My poor wife, she cried for weeks when Stefania left to go back to school."

"I'm sure Stefania will want to invite both of you to her wedding."

Jean-Claude shuffled his feet and looked at the ground. "Eh, why would she want two old Provençal peasants at her fancy wedding? Us rubbing elbows with all the aristos and royalty in Europe."

"Marthe-Louise would chase you with her carving knife if you declined the invitation and you know it."

"*Eh, bien,* you are right, Jacques." He heaved a theatrical sigh. "If we are invited, I suppose I must buy Marthe-Louise a new dress."

"Probably two or three," Jack pointed out. "And a new suit for yourself." He happened to know that Jean-Claude's good suit was a relic from Jack's parents' own wedding, more than thirty years ago. The lapels were wide enough for Jean-Claude to hang glide off the mountains of the nearby Haute-Alpes.

The older man winced. "Well, for Stefania, I will do it."

"Good man." Jack clapped him on the back. "I am not sure how long Lily and I will be staying, but if Marthe-

Louise wouldn't mind cooking an occasional meal for us…"

"She is away in Nice with our daughter who had a baby but will be back in a couple days. And what did you say? This girl's name is Lily?"

"Yes, why?" he asked, unsure why Jean-Claude was fighting a smile.

"Ah, ah, ah." Jean-Claude wiggled his gnarled finger at Jack. "You be careful, *mon ami*. This girl is already part of your life."

"What? Why do you say that?"

He lifted his hand in mock innocence. "Because of the de Brissard coat of arms, of course. A triple *fleur-de-lis* on a red background—three lily flowers. *C'est parfait*— it's perfect!" He doubled over in laughter as Jack realized his friend was correct.

For the past thousand years, the family's coat of arms had been golden lilies on a red shield. He'd grown up seeing them every day but had never thought much about them.

Now he had his own Golden Lily. But how could she be a part of his life? And did she even want to be?

LILY WANDERED AROUND the courtyard, wondering what the fountain looked like with the water turned on. It made sense that it had been shut down if there was no one staying there. A working farm had priorities for water elsewhere, especially if they were irrigating vegetables or flower crops.

She sat on a bench in front of the house and wondered if the house's blue shutters were decorative or functional. Probably both, considering what she'd read about the wild mistral winds that funneled south from the mountains.

Fruit trees lined the courtyard—always practical, those

Provence farmers. Almond, apple, cherry and dark plum. Ooh, and a fig tree. You didn't see those outdoors in Philly, and this was a big fig, its grayish trunk a mass of columns as if it were many tree trunks woven and grown together.

The still, warm air buzzed with the sound of cicadas. It was as if she had fallen back one century, even two, as she sat in the quiet courtyard.

And this was Jack's country. No wonder he had looked ill at ease in noisy, gray Paris. He thrived on warmth. Warm sun, warm people and warm colors.

She was flowering as well in Provence, enjoying the beautiful scenery and kind people. But Jack was the biggest reason she was enjoying herself.

Lily leaned her head back against the thick plastered wall and closed her eyes. Yep, she could get to like this too much. She must have dozed off because the next thing she realized, Jack slid next to her on the bench and kissed her awake.

"Hello, Sleeping Beauty."

"I'm no beauty."

He laughed and then grew serious when she lifted an eyebrow at him. "And you think you are not?"

She shrugged, uncomfortable at this serious turn of conversation. "I'm not particularly blonde, particularly tall or particularly, um, well-built."

"You have hair like honey." He cupped her jaw and lifted several strands. "It shines golden-brown in the sun. You are the right height to fit against me. And if you were any more shapely, I would be an even bigger gibbering idiot when you are near me."

"You don't seem like an idiot now."

"I hide it well." He brushed her hair to the side and kissed her cheek. "All I want to do is stare at you—and try not to drool down my chin."

She gave a startled laugh at the image of sophisticated, urbane Jack with drool down his chin because of her.

"And you are even more beautiful when you laugh."

"Really?"

"Really. Now come see the house. I talked with Jean-Claude and he was happy to let us stay here."

"If you're sure."

"Positive." He selected a key from his ring and unlocked the front door. "Come see. I think you will like it."

Jack pushed open the door and ushered her in. She stood there enjoying the sunny, two-story entryway while he carried in their bags. "*Voilà,* the foyer." It was a wide, modern-size space with a sweeping staircase going up into the second floor, but the bones of the house were definitely not modern. The exposed walls were old limestone like the outside, and the ceiling was white plaster with dark timbered crossbeams that were obviously not only decorative but still structural.

"How old is this place?" It looked even older than Mrs. Wyndham's house, and Ben Franklin had actually dined there with a Wyndham ancestor.

"It was an ancient farmhouse that *Oncle* Pierre renovated, adding all the modern comforts, of course. This main level used to be the stable, and the heat of the animals would rise to the rather meager living quarters upstairs. It is of course several times larger than it used to be."

"*Oncle* Pierre?"

"Yes, he was the younger brother of the family. Wanted his privacy." Jack shrugged matter-of-factly. "His mistress was not only a very famous actress, but a married one, no less. They needed much privacy for their rendezvous."

Lily pursed her lips and Jack laughed. "Do not worry about that lady's husband, *chérie.* He had a boyfriend of his own. Everyone was very civilized, and I believe they used to exchange Christmas presents."

"Hmmph."

"Ah." He carried their luggage up the front staircase, framed by an elegant wrought iron railing decorated with bronze medallions of bundles of lavender.

"What do you mean, 'ah'?" Lily narrowed her eyes at his back.

He pushed open the door to a wide, airy bedroom. It had a large bed with four dark wooden posts rising to a canopy frame. Gauzy white fabric draped artfully from one side to the next. "You are worried that I am very civilized, that I have a wife or mistress—or both, and they are all very French and unconcerned about my doings. Is that right?"

"Madame Finch said you didn't," she muttered.

"Madame Finch?" His eyebrows shot up. "When did you ask her about my sex life?"

"I called her after you kissed me in the car. She says you are single."

"And did she ask why you wanted to know?"

"I told her you'd just stuck your tongue in my mouth and I needed to decide whether or not to have sex with you."

He made a small choking sound.

"Because I really, really wanted to have sex with you, but I wouldn't if you were involved with someone else. She gave me the all-clear and said to have my wicked way with you."

"That does sound like something she would say," he replied dryly.

She couldn't keep up the joke any longer and giggled. "Oh, Jacky, don't be silly. I asked her about the being single part. We were very civilized, as you say."

He set down their backpacks on the wide wooden planks

of the floor. "I can tell you I have no wife, no fiancée and no mistress. I am normally a very orderly, very civilized man, but I have found over the past day that that veneer of civilization is paper-thin and peeling off me as we speak." He yanked off his T-shirt and tossed it away. He unlaced his boots and kicked them and his socks free. "And I like it very much when you call me 'Jacky.' Maybe you can call me that when I am pounding inside you."

Lily's jaw dropped as Jack dropped his shorts and briefs and stood entirely naked in front of her. "You don't look civilized at all."

"Good. Now take off those clothes before I rip them off you." His eyes glittered, and she knew he meant it.

He looked primitive and aroused, his cock jutting up into his belly, huge and dark with blood, a drop of silvery moisture slicking his tip. His heavy sac rested on a nest of dark brown hair and a vein pulsed along the side of his shaft. An answering throbbing started between her thighs. She had never seen him totally naked in the daylight, and he was impressively built. A little thin, but still muscled, his shoulders broad and tapering into a narrow waist and strong thighs.

He pulled a foil packet out of his backpack and covered himself. No pretending with this man. He knew she wanted him, and he wanted her, too.

Of all the stylish, sophisticated women in France, he had chosen her. And she had chosen him. She slowly pulled her shirt over her head and ditched the rest of her clothing until she stood in front of him in her plain cotton bra and matching panties.

"Take it all off." A command, not a suggestion.

Her underwear joined the rest of her clothing. She shivered under his hungry gaze.

"And you say you are not beautiful?" He shook his head.

"Mon dieu." He stalked toward her, his cock bobbing with each step. Lily waited in anticipation for him.

Jack scooped his hands into her hair and crushed her mouth to his. She gasped and he took advantage of it to plunge his tongue inside. He stroked her tongue with his, sucking on her and letting her suck on him.

Her breathing came fast and hard, and she clutched his wrists. Jack was right—he was being totally uncivilized and savage, and she loved it. He moved her backwards so the edge of the bed clipped her legs and they sprawled onto the bed in a tangle of limbs.

His thigh had come to rest between hers, muscled and hot on her clit. She automatically moved against him, and he smiled, slowly rubbing up and down so the hair rasped her tender folds. "You like this, eh?" He lowered his head and nibbled her neck.

Lily arched her back as his mouth traveled leisurely across her skin, licking and sucking her tender earlobe, down to her collarbone.

"Lovely Lily," Jack murmured. "You turn me into a savage. I want to suck on your golden skin, give you a love bite."

She shivered at his sultry tone. "Why would you do that?"

"To stake my claim on you. So every man who sees you knows that you are taken. Possessed. Mine."

"And what should I do so other women know you're taken?"

"Nothing. I do not even see other women since you have dazzled me so."

"Oh, Jack." She grabbed the sides of his head and brought his mouth up to hers.

He kissed her eagerly. "It's true, I swear," he explained between planting kisses on her cheeks and lips. "You may think we Frenchmen are casual about *l'amour,* but I am not. I never have been."

"Me, neither." Lily gasped as he moved down to her breasts. "Oh, Jack, that feels so good."

His only reply was a muffled hum as he sucked on her nipple, rubbing his thigh between hers. His cock swelled even more, rising to her belly.

She wrapped her hand around him and shifted so he was brushing her opening. "Come inside me, Jack."

He shook his head. "No, you need more."

She guided his hand between them. "Does this feel like I need more?" She was dripping wet and throbbing.

He gave her a slow smile. "Why, yes, it does. More of this." He slid a finger into her tight passage and she squeezed down on him. "More of this." He moved his finger in and out, rotating it around like a naughty little sex toy. He brushed a particular spot and she squealed in surprised pleasure. He immediately returned there. "Oh, yes, the G-spot. And yours is so sensitive. You must like coming from this."

She shook her head.

"You don't?" he asked in surprise. "Do you want me to stop?"

"No! I never have before."

His smile grew positively wicked. "Then allow me to be the first." He circled her G-spot and alternated light and firm pressure across it.

She gasped as he devoted his entire attention to those few centimeters of tender flesh, murmuring in French as he touched her. She almost came from listening to his dark, sexy accent. He could have been reciting French nursery rhymes for all she cared.

Then he switched into English. "Beautiful Lily, I love to see your naked breasts pointing up, waiting for me to suck on the hard tips. I love to see your smooth skin bead with sweat so I can lick it off. And I love stroking you inside, so wet and hot and tight that I wish it were my cock inside you instead of my finger."

Her nipples tightened even further at his raunchy sex talk and she grabbed at him to put his money where his finger was, so to speak.

"Not yet. I'll take you when I say so." He easily fended her off with an increase in speed that left her gasping.

It was a pleasure that spiraled upward, burrowing deep into her very center, a pleasure that skirted the edge of pain from its intensity. A pleasure that made her dig her heels into the soft bedding and arch her back off the bed as if she were a bow drawn taut and he was a master archer.

"That's it, Lily, beautiful Lily," he coaxed her. "Surrender to yourself. Surrender to *me*."

"No." She whipped her head back and forth. She wouldn't surrender to him or anyone.

"You want to," he whispered. "You want me to possess you. Like you possessed me with your wicked mouth in the car. Mindless, physical passion."

She groaned. She'd always been careful to have her mind rule her body, but Jack was turning everything upside down with a wiggle of his finger.

"Do it, Lily. Lust. Sex. All you have to do is feel."

Suddenly she was tired of thinking. That could come later. She wanted to come *now.* She sighed and relaxed into the bed, and he chuckled. "That's it." He flicked her with his fingertip and then suddenly pressed hard.

She screamed his name and arched off the bed again, twisting the sheets into wrinkled handfuls. Her orgasm blasted through her like a shock wave, the epicenter at his fingertip and radiating out to the far reaches of her body. She quivered and clutched at Jack, her only anchor in the most powerful climax of her life. He held her close and murmured to her in French again as she fought the pleasure and then finally surrendered to it. Surrendered to him. The shock wave became a soothing rocking and finally a ripple.

She opened her eyes and swallowed hard, her mouth dry. Jack stared down at her, his eyes wide. "What?" she asked.

He shook his head. "Only that that was the most beautiful thing I have ever seen. And that you would share it with me."

"Really?" She was sweaty and probably red as a beet, but he was looking at her as if she were the last truffle in France.

"Really."

She preened a bit. "I'm not done sharing with you, if you know what I mean." She reached down and cupped his cock, still stiff as a board after all that foreplay. Poor man, he was so patient. And so virile. She pulled him on top of her so he rested between her legs.

He groaned and thrust against her as she squeezed her thighs around his erection. "Oh, Lily."

"You like that?"

"I like everything you do to me." He nudged her legs wide open. "But I *love* being inside you." He plunged forward and sank deep into her.

His thick cock filled her sensitized center and she let out a short scream. He stopped for a brief second, but she smiled at him and he started to move inside her.

And like that, Lily was back in the realm of mindless lust, where her only thought was how soon she could come again. His flesh slapped into hers and pulled out, making her whimper until he filled her again. She hooked her legs around his waist to keep him locked inside but he couldn't keep still, his body in control and driving toward his own orgasm.

His body rubbed hers and she responded, tightening around him. His chest hair caught on her nipples, rasping their swollen peaks. He bent down and licked the top curve of her breast and then sucked hard on her nipple, sending exquisite jolts down to her clit.

She dug her fingers into his shoulders and moaned, "Jacky."

"That's it, Lily. Show me how much you want me," he commanded. He moved to her other nipple, leaving the first glistening and pink like a ripe berry.

Before she could stop herself, she nipped at his shoulder.

Jack grinned and lifted his head. "The little cat has claws and teeth. Maybe I can make you purr."

After that, Lily didn't purr as much as moan, pant and scream as he slammed into her, moving them across the bed until she was against the headboard. He hooked his hands under her shoulders and pulled her down under him, their sweaty skin clinging and releasing as his cock slapped wetly in and out of her pussy.

He stopped for a second and reached between their bodies to unerringly find her clit. A couple strokes and she clutched wildly as she spasmed around him. He thrust long enough to make sure she'd hit the highest peak and then let go of himself.

He tossed back his head, his eyes dark and blind to anything but the powerful spasms of his climax. His lips drew into a snarl as he roared his release like a lion who had claimed his mate.

It was the first time she'd been able to see his face at his peak and she was entranced. His easygoing, suave exterior was entirely gone, his primitive sexuality on display for only her to see. She held on tight to him as he gasped and collapsed. She welcomed his heavy weight pressing her into the bedding and inhaled the scent of their lovemaking rising from their skin.

"Ah, *ma belle* Lily." He was still breathing hard. "How can it be like this?"

She shook her head, enjoying how his chest rasped along her cheek, his heart thumping sturdily inside his ribs. "I don't know, but I'm not looking a gift horse in the mouth."

He laughed and rolled them to their sides. "I hope that I am not the gift horse, *non?*"

"No, you're the *stallion*." She wiggled her eyebrows lasciviously, making him laugh even harder. "How do you say that in French?"

"Oh, no, no." He shook his head. "I'll teach you any other French words you want, but not that."

"Okay, I'll ask the next Frenchwoman I meet. And if she asks why I want to know, I'll look at you and smile."

He groaned. "Ah, my reputation will never recover if you do that. *Stallion* is *étalon.*"

"Ay-tal-ohn," she mimicked. "My stallion."

"Ah, *mon dieu,* Lily." He laughed. "I never know what to expect from you."

"Is that a bad thing?"

"Not at all." Jack kissed her mouth and extricated himself from the rumpled bedding. "I'll be right back." He pulled on his briefs and disappeared downstairs, quickly returning with a pair of champagne flutes and a bottle of champagne. "I was going to do this first. Show you the house, offer you champagne, feed you and then…" He gave a shrug and laughed, setting down the glasses to open the bottle.

"Then this?" She pointed at her naked body. Somehow she wasn't shy around him.

"Only if you wanted." He poured the pale bubbly into the tall narrow glasses, designed especially so the bubbles would not immediately evaporate and flatten the wine.

"I did want."

"Good. So did I." He offered her a full champagne flute. "To this. To us."

They delicately touched the rims of what had to be fine crystal and Lily sipped, her eyes widening in shock. "No. This isn't—"

He gave her a sidelong glance. "Isn't what?"

"Did you open a bottle of Bollinger Blanc?"

"You have an excellent palate. That's exactly what it is. 1995, to be exact."

She sat bolt upright. "Jack! We can't accept their hospitality and then drink all the expensive wine. How tacky is that?"

"Not tacky at all. I bought it myself the last time I visited and we didn't get around to drinking it, that's all."

"Oh." She relaxed a bit. "But you really should replace it before we go, don't you think?"

"Of course. There is an excellent wine store in a nearby town. I'll order another bottle."

"Okay, but you have to let me help pay for it. You're not the only one drinking it, you know." She took another sip. It was the best champagne she'd ever tasted, and this time she had a whole glass of it, not just a stolen sip from an untouched party glass.

A whole glass…she dribbled some down her belly so it pooled in her navel. "Have a drink, Jack. Nice and wet, the way you like it."

His nostrils flared and he dipped his tongue in her belly button. "I like it all. I like you, nice and wet." He inhaled greedily. "I can smell myself on you, smell your arousal."

He drew lazy circles on her belly with his tongue and then stopped suddenly.

She nudged him to get him going again but he sat back on his haunches and gestured at her glass. "Have some more champagne."

"You don't have to get me drunk to have your wicked way with me. I'm perfectly willing." But she wasn't willing to let her champagne go flat, so she drank more.

"Bah," he puffed in disgust. "Real men do not need to get women drunk to make love. That is why we only went to sleep first our first night in Provence—you were tired and had much wine in addition. I would not take advantage of that."

"Good thing I sobered up in my sleep." She deliberately stretched and yawned, making sure her breasts pointed up invitingly.

He took a large mouthful of champagne and before she realized what he was doing, fastened his mouth on her nipple. She shrieked at first from the cold and then the bubbles popping against her tender skin. A chuckle rumbled through him, but he sucked at her with the sparkling wine.

He finally let go and swallowed. "Ah, what could be better?"

"Doing the same to my other nipple?" she suggested.

"Excellent." He complied with her request until both peaks were tingling. He refilled her glass and she spilled champagne onto his belly and licked it off. He was rock-hard again and inches from her lips, his head ripe and purple like a juicy sweet plum. And she knew just how to eat it.

She sat up and gave him a wicked smile before filling her mouth with champagne. His eyes widened. "Oh, no, Lily."

She smirked and closed her mouth around his plump flesh and it was his turn to arch off the bed in a howl of pure sensation. The bubbles buzzed him as she sucked on him. Champagne dribbled down his shaft as she took him deeper between her lips. He fisted his fingers through her hair, tiny pinpricks of pleasure and pain tingling her scalp.

"Enough," he growled, lifting her head so she released him.

"Don't you like that?" He'd sure seemed to enjoy it so far.

"Too much. I want to be inside you, want us to explode together." He pushed her onto her hands and knees and she heard a packet rip open. "Have you ever seen a stallion take a mare, Lily?"

She shook her head, quivering in anticipation as he moved behind her. He quickly found her clit, still throbbing and swollen from their previous loveplay. She tossed her hair back and he nudged her legs apart.

Jack covered her body with his, his chest on her back, his strong hands braced on the bed next to her smaller, more delicate ones. She expected to feel confined, intimidated, even frightened since he had the position of power and she couldn't see what he was doing. But there was no coercion in his actions, only security and shelter in his arms. "Take me like that, Jack."

"Yes…" he hissed and pushed inside her. Lily gave a little scream as he nipped at her neck. She bowed her head and saw her hard-tipped breasts swaying in time to his thrusts—the nipples he'd sucked on. Saw his thick erection moving in and out of her—the erection she'd sucked on. Their raw animal passion shocked her and aroused her to a fever pitch.

"You like it like this, don't you." It wasn't a question.

He could obviously feel how her body melted around him, wet and creamy.

"I want to feel you inside me."

"I am, *bébé,* I am." He shoved himself to the hilt to let her feel his power, his heft.

She shook her head, not daring to say what she wanted.

"What?" he soothed her. "Tell me what you want. I'll do anything you want."

She allowed her imagination to run wild for an instant, wanting the most impossible thing. "Inside me without the condom," she gasped. "Skin on skin. Feeling you shoot inside me when you come, hot and sticky."

"Oh, *merde.*" His reply was anguished and his whole body shook. "You'll make me come just by saying that. I want that too, but…" His cock pulsed inside her, as if readying to fire.

"Yeah, I know." Better to be safe than sorry. But it would be so intense for both of them.

"Lily, that would be my biggest fantasy." He moved inside her again, in and out. "When we were driving here today, I was thinking of how powerful that would be."

"Ohhh…" That was the cause of his arousal while driving. "No wonder you were so turned on."

He grunted, whether in passion or embarrassment, she didn't know. Or care, since he had seized her hips and was thrusting into her, hitting all the right spots. And then he reached around her and found her clit, and she screamed, coming really hard.

He followed her, his cock tensing and flexing inside her as he roared his release. He pulled out of her and eased them down to the bed.

Lily pried her eyes open and kissed his shoulder, the nearest body part she could reach without moving too much. Her eyes widened. "Geez, did I do that?"

"What?" He looked down at where she pointed to his chest. "A love bite." A smug smile spread over his face at the idea that she had bitten him in a fit of passion. Her own face flushed.

He laughed, a rich and hearty sound. "Why, Lily, you little savage." He sat up and turned his back to her. "Do I carry your claw marks, too?"

In fact, he did—eight red lines on his shoulders from where she clutched at him. He looked over his shoulder at her and lifted an eyebrow at her guilty expression. "Those, too, eh?"

"Oh, my God." She buried her face in her hands and rolled onto her stomach. How embarrassing to mangle the poor guy when all he was doing was helping her enjoy herself.

"Uh-uh." He rolled her back, his eyes warm and crinkling at the corners. "I knew the risks going in, but I will always be willing to sacrifice a few centimeters of epidermis for your pleasure."

She flicked her fingers against his upper arm. "Your pleasure, too, as if you didn't notice."

"I have rather delicate skin, you know." He scooped her into his arms, forestalling any of her attempts at retaliation. "All I ask is that you do not leave any permanent marks."

"Oh, Jack." She buried her face in his chest, his chuckle rumbling under her ear. She may have marked him physically, but he had marked her emotionally with his tenderness, his kindness and his care—and this was only after a few days. Once they parted, she would carry a mark more painful than any bruise or scratch.

11

LILY PADDED DOWNSTAIRS in her chocolate-brown shorts and white tank top after waking up alone in the pleasantly mussed big bed. After a couple peeks into a formal dining room, family room and study, she found him in the kitchen. "There you are, Jack." He sat at the big island in the middle of the room reading a newspaper.

"Have a good nap, Lily?" He set down the paper and swiveled to face her.

She nodded and yawned, her muscles pleasantly loose and relaxed from their romp upstairs and the nap that had followed it. She wrapped her arms around his waist and nuzzled his cheek. He was clean-shaven and smelled sunny, like lemons and green herbs. He must have showered while she was sleeping. "I've been asleep for a couple hours—you should have woken me up."

"You needed the rest." He kissed her neck and she half-heartedly pushed at him.

"Stop, Jack, I need to shower."

"Mmm, you smell great." He slipped his hand up her tank top, his long fingers unerringly finding her breast. "No bra, either."

Lily relaxed into his embrace and was beginning to

wonder if the granite countertop would feel terribly cold and hard on her back when her stomach growled. Not once, but three times.

Jack laughed and withdrew his hand, kissing her on the tip of her nose. "I am a poor host. We have been here for hours and the only thing we've had is some champagne."

She wiggled her eyebrows. "We've had a bit more than that."

He laughed and stood up. "Food for now. The pantry is usually well-stocked, and we can drive to town later for fresh bread, fruits and vegetables."

"And cheese, Jack. Ever since we had that wonderful late-night snack at the bed-and-breakfast, I've had a taste for goat cheese."

"Layered with fresh tomato and basil, drizzled with fine olive oil and cracked black pepper," Jack teased, making her mouth water.

"All right, you better get cooking." She shook her finger at him and he laughed.

"This is a beautiful kitchen, Jack." The big kitchen was bright and sunny, like everything in Provence. The walls were plastered in a creamy yellow, and the exposed ceiling beams were dark and weathered, as if they had been exposed to centuries of cooking smoke.

"I am glad you like it." He dug through the large fridge. "Hmm. Not a lot of fresh ingredients, but I can make some pasta. How does that sound?"

"Lovely." Lily hopped up onto the stool he'd vacated. The island's base was cream weathered oak cabinetry to match the rest of the kitchen.

"Good." Jack pulled out a large stockpot and filled it with water, setting it to boil. He went to the pantry and pulled out some cans and jars.

Lily was glad to have him cook but reminded herself to

take some pictures for her blog. She scanned the room—a big brick fireplace and a seating area with a leather couch made the area cozy. "But why the fireplace? It doesn't get terribly cold, does it?"

He nodded. "The fierce mistral wind can drop the temperature within minutes, and winter can be very damp and cold. We are thin-blooded here and not used to the low temperatures."

She had a flash of her and Jack sitting on the leather couch in front of a lit fire. He would hand her a glass of rich red wine (that always seemed more like a winter beverage) and they would toast each other before snuggling together.

She shook her head. Winter was months away. She was returning to New York, and Jack was returning to the next dangerous disaster area that came along—not exactly good for a relationship.

Lily hopped up and paced toward the wide picture windows overlooking the back garden. She opened the French doors and stepped onto the flagstone patio. Big terra-cotta pots of herbs dotted the edges. Basil, thyme and tarragon. The warm, dry weather here was perfect for growing herbs. There was even a row of rosemary bushes near a bench. "Parsley, sage, rosemary and thyme," she sang to herself.

"You have a lovely voice." Jack was leaning against the door frame, a small stainless-steel colander in one hand.

"No, I don't." She waved her hand dismissively. "The choir director at my school told me I'd never improve unless I had private lessons."

"And you didn't get to have lessons?" he guessed, coming onto the patio.

She shrugged. "It was only my mom and me growing

up, so it was hard for her to come up with the money for lessons."

"The two of you? And your mother never remarried?"

Lily had to smile. "She finally did after I was grown. At least Stan is good around the house." She burst out laughing.

"What?" Jack looked puzzled.

"Hmm." She stopped laughing and gave him a steady look. He'd been nothing but open and honest with her, and she'd been holding back from him. "Let's pick some herbs for the pasta."

He nodded, and they quickly selected some thyme, tarragon and a touch of savory. Lily rinsed the herbs off in the sink while Jack broke spaghetti noodles into the pasta pot and heated a sauté pan on the stove with a splash of olive oil and chopped garlic.

With his back to her, it was easier to tell her story. "I grew up in a house like that big manor house we passed on the way in."

He whipped around to look at her, a puzzled look on his face. Obviously she was not some rich girl out for a lark in Europe.

"My mother was the housekeeper," she clarified.

"Oh." He nodded. "Hence your taste for truffles and *foie gras*. You have a very sophisticated palate."

"Oui." She wrinkled her nose in amusement. "As the American phrase goes, I have champagne tastes with a beer budget."

"Another fascinating colloquialism. I am improving my English thanks to you every day."

She rolled her eyes in bemusement. He spoke better English than many native speakers.

"And you know I am more than happy to supply you champagne whenever you desire." The smoky look he shot her sent shivers down her spine. "But did the family you worked for treat you well?"

"Mrs. Wyndham isn't the warm and cuddly type, but she's always been fair with my mother and me," she allowed. "My father was killed in a car accident when I was a baby and my mother started working as an assistant to the housekeeper. When she retired, Mom took her job and we moved into the carriage house over the garage. It was bigger than the tiny Philly apartment we'd been living in and the countrylike atmosphere of the upscale Main Line suburb seemed like paradise."

Jack nodded as he sliced a narrow, pepperoni-like sausage into slices. "Rip up those herbs and tell me more."

Lily busied herself with pulling the fresh leaves from their stems, the spicy green scent a kind of aromatherapy. "You know, I never like talking about this."

He paused slicing and raised his head. "Why not? Are you ashamed of the work your mother did? That she was a servant?"

"Don't call her that!" Lily snapped without thinking.

He gazed at her steadily. "To serve is not a shameful thing. A widow with a small child would have had limited choices in careers—that is, if she wanted to keep you with her instead of giving you up to relatives or foster care."

Lily bit her lip.

"I am a servant, too," he continued. "I serve the poor and the needy instead of the rich. Does that make my work of even less value?"

"No." She struggled with a particularly tough stem but her hands were shaking with emotion. "That's different. That's charity—altruism for the less fortunate."

He set down the knife. "Charity begins at home. I know that American saying. But your mother did her work out of love for you, an even more powerful motivation."

Lily stared down at the green mess in her bowl. Jack dumped the cooked pasta into a colander in the sink and shut off the burner under the sauté pan.

He came around the island and gathered her into his arms. "I am sorry. This is a tender subject for you and you are hungry and tired."

She shook her head. "You're right. I guess I resent it sometimes. Being the poorest kid in a school full of rich ones wasn't the best situation."

"Oh, Lily." He started to say something and then stopped, kissing the top of her head.

She wrapped her arms around his waist and settled into his embrace. Had she ever really discussed her childhood with anyone but Sarah? She doubted it. "You make me think about things I don't usually think about."

"Then don't. Madame Finch would whack me with a ruler for treating you so poorly. We are here to relax and get to know each other, that's all."

How could she let him get to know her when she didn't know herself? For a writer, she was singularly not interested in self-reflection. Maybe that was why she wrote how-to and travel articles instead of weepy book-club memoirs. And really, what did she have to complain about? She sighed. Maybe it was time to look at her unusually overprivileged underprivileged childhood.

Jack pulled back so he could see her face. "Still want to eat?"

"Still want to feed me?" she parroted back.

"Of course." He planted a quick kiss on her lips and then rinsed the mass of pasta before tossing the sausage into the sauté pan. He pulled a jar of sun-dried tomatoes from the fridge and chopped them before adding them and the herbs to the pan. Once everything was heated through, he shook out the excess pasta water and dumped the noodles into the olive oil mix, stirring to coat them.

Lily found a couple plates and he served them heaping helpings with a generous grating of Parmesan cheese on top. While it cooled for a minute, he poured a ruby-red wine into what had to be Irish lead crystal—the real, handcut kind. *"Bon appétit."*

It was beautiful, had taken ten minutes and was straight from jars and boxes. A perfect recipe for her blog. "Wait a second." She sprinted upstairs and brought back her camera, taking several shots of the food and wine.

"All right, all right, enough with the photos," he finally said after a few minutes. "The pasta is getting cold and you need to eat."

She grumbled a bit but was secretly pleased at his concern for her well-being.

He raised his glass in a toast. "To Lily. I am so lucky we met."

"To Jack." She raised hers, as well. "For showing me the real France—and a lot of a certain real Frenchman."

He laughed and sipped his wine. "Eat, eat."

The food was exquisite, as good as any restaurant meal she'd had. "You're almost as good in the kitchen as my mother's new husband, Stan."

"Ah, you did mention he was skilled around the house—he can cook, as well?"

Lily couldn't help giggling. "I should hope so. He's the Wyndham family chef."

"Lovely!" Jack started to laugh. "The housekeeper finds happiness with the family chef."

"Their new house is spotless and they eat like kings. What more could you ask for?"

"Love." He said it so matter-of-factly that she knew he meant it. "If they have love, then nothing else matters."

"Nothing? Not money or age or different backgrounds?"

He was already shaking his head. "Nothing. Everything else can be dealt with, but love is the one thing that should never be compromised."

"They do love each other," Lily whispered. Sometimes it made her feel left out since it had been just Mom and her for so many years. But she was a woman now, and it was time to let her mother be a woman in her own right, as well. "Have you ever loved like that?" she blurted and then immediately blushed. If she were going to drink wine like a Frenchwoman, she needed to get better control of her tongue.

He stared steadily at her and she raised her glass to block the mortified expression on her face. He waited to answer her until she had set down her glass. She couldn't spend the entire meal hiding behind it, despite her cheeks that felt as red as the wine. "I thought I did once, but I was wrong. And you?"

Turnabout was fair play and she answered him as bluntly. "No, never. Not even close."

He nodded. "I know we are not in love, Lily, but I am glad we are lovers."

"Lovers." She tested the word on her lips, remembering the first time she had used it with the Frenchwoman on the train. Then, it had been awkward and embarrassing. But now that she and Jack truly were lovers, it was natural and freeing to say the word, at least with him. "Yes, I am glad, too."

Not that she would go around introducing him like that, as in, *Have you met my lover, Jack?* Really, a woman had to draw the line somewhere in maintaining some mystery.

"However long you want me—you want *us,* Lily," he promised solemnly.

That was what she wanted, too—but what if she wanted

him forever? The thought stunned her, and she used her jaw dropping as an excuse to shovel in a mouthful of pasta. *Lovers* did not equal *forever;* it was a live-in-the-moment kind of thing.

He watched her eat for a minute, satisfied that she was replenishing her body, and then settled down to his meal. They chatted as they ate, finding common interests in music, art and movies. They of course had different perspectives, but that made it more interesting to debate the fine points. He was witty and well-read, intelligent and amusing.

Lily paused for a second and looked at Jack and looked at their amazing meal. Their relationship was like the pasta—hot and fresh, but after a certain point would get cold and lumpy, not ever quite living up to its original flavor. But for now, oh, was it delicious.

THE NEXT DAY, Jack left Lily chatting with her cousin via webcam and headed out to meet Jean-Claude to talk about estate business. This was the first summer in many years that Jack had been in Provence for the lavender harvest, and Jean-Claude was eager to involve him. Probably so Jack wouldn't stay away so long again. Halfway up the hill to the field, his own phone rang.

He smiled at the display and answered it. *"Bonjour, chérie."*

"Oh, Jack, I'm so glad to talk to you. I was worried to death when George told me you were sick." It was Stevie, his little sister in all but DNA. Even though Princess Stefania was a beautiful grown-up lady, he couldn't help remembering her as the inconsolable twelve-year-old who had come to live with them after the death of her parents. George had been a sophomore at the university living off-campus with Jack and Frank, but had quickly hired a housekeeper to care for Stefania and make sure their flat wasn't condemned by the New York Board of Health.

"George tells me you are in Provence now. Good for you. I never liked Paris that much anyway."

He grinned. Translation: Stevie never liked his mother that much anyway, and had absolutely detested Nadine. "How else can I make sure your lavender will be ready for the *parfumerie?*"

"I know, and I'm absolutely thrilled you're doing this. I want to sell the perfume and give all the proceeds to my charity—you know, the obnoxiously named Princess Stefania of Vinciguerra Foundation for Women and Children?"

"Why is that obnoxious?"

"Because, dummy, my grandmother set it up when I was too young to know any better and named it after me, as if I wanted to blow my own horn. On the other hand, that self-servingly-named foundation is going to pay for several new schools in poor countries and is rescuing girls from sex slavery in Western Europe as we speak. But don't tell anyone about that last part, because I fund them under the table. Dangerous work, prying girls away from their pimps."

Jack's eyebrows shot up. "Am I to assume you've gone on these missions yourself?"

"Assume whatever you like," she said airily. "I will categorically deny we've ever had this conversation if necessary."

He shook his head. "Stevie, are you working for the CIA now?"

She laughed. "And if I did, would I tell you? Besides, I am a loyal subject of my brother and our principality."

Which wasn't much of an answer, but she had always been maddening in her own lovable way.

"Don't work too hard on the lavender harvest. Jean-Claude can handle it," she informed him.

"Stevie, I am not some ancient invalid. I have been quite active the past several days and have no ill effects." He smiled at the memory of several of his activities.

"What have you been up to?" Her tone was suspicious.

"What?" She caught him off guard. Maybe she did work for the CIA.

"What kind of activities?" she repeated and then paused. "You have a woman there with you, don't you?"

"I don't know what you mean," he replied with some dignity.

"Mmm-hmm. What's her name?"

"A gentleman never kisses and tells." And he wasn't going to talk about his sex life with Stevie.

"So you do have someone!" She sounded delighted. "Have Jean-Claude and Marthe-Louise met her yet?"

A reluctant laugh was dragged from him. "Stefania…"

"Uh-oh, you only call me that when you are trying to be stern and paternal. Tell me her name."

"Lily." It slipped out. But once he did, he couldn't stop grinning. He'd been hugging the secret of his new relationship to his chest like a teenager with a photo of a movie star, and Stefania was the first of his friends to learn about Lily. Next thing he knew, he'd be skipping through the lavender fields, sniffing a sprig and mooning over Lily. At least the field workers would get a hearty laugh.

"Really? I was just guessing, you know. Is she French?"

"American. But we met in Paris."

"An American in Paris." Stevie hummed a few bars of the Gershwin ballet. "Did you dance around the fountain with her?"

"I am no Gene Kelly." Jack smirked. Thanks to ten years of dance class, Stevie was extremely knowledgeable about ballet. Good thing she couldn't see him tap dancing around her inquisitive nature. "But we went to the Parc Buttes-Chaumont."

"How dreamy," she sighed. "You met, swept her off her feet and then whisked her off to your ancestral home in Provence. Jack, sweetie pie, you are becoming quite the romantic. You sound like those novels I love to read."

"Enough, enough." His cheeks were heating.

"Well, whoever Lily is, she can't be any worse than Nadine. Ugh."

"Stefania…" he said in warning.

She grinned. "Again with the stern authoritarian tone. But I also wanted to let you know Dieter and I have set our wedding date. We met with the bishop and chose a date next June because I want all the roses blooming for me. That's only eleven months away! And I want to give you enough time to make my perfume, right?"

"Of course. We will press the oil right after harvest and then you and the perfumer can create a blend and choose a bottle and packaging."

"Great, Jack." She blew kisses into the phone. "Take care of yourself," she reminded him. "No more parasitic infections for you. You and Frank are ushers at my wedding, so I want you to look good in your tux."

"It would be an honor."

"Maybe you can come see me in New York when you feel better?"

"Of course." They said their goodbyes and Jack hung up, staring thoughtfully across the purple valley of his farm.

Traveling to New York in a few weeks? Lily lived in New Jersey, a quick train ride from Manhattan. But did she want him to come visit her? He blew out a sigh of frustration. He hated uncertainty. As the old American saying went, failure to plan meant planning to fail.

What was his plan with Lily? He knew one thing, though—he didn't want her to leave. Was that a plan? To keep her with him indefinitely. Or forever?

12

LILY LOOKED UP from her computer screen and rolled her neck to loosen the kinks. She would much rather be smooching with Jack in the big bed upstairs, but she'd already neglected her blog for the past couple days to do just that.

Traffic was increasing. Sarah, although pretty much confined to her recliner at home, was doing a champion job of cross-posting her blog to various travel sites, sites aimed at young single women and foodie websites. Lily hadn't intended to be so food-oriented, but her photos of the Provence markets and descriptions of Madame Roussel's late-night hors d'oeuvres proved popular, according to her blog traffic stats.

Lily had mentioned "Pierre" a few times in her blog posts. Not the sex parts, obviously, because it wasn't that kind of a blog. Sarah was already anxious about Lily traveling with Jack. She didn't need to get all the lurid details. Lily might tell her at some later date, but only when Lily was safely back home.

At this point, Lily would take all the traffic she could get. She got up and walked around the desk. Jack had set her up in the guesthouse study, which was a far cry from her makeshift "office" at her breakfast bar at home.

A wall of books stood behind the desk, which was a rustic-looking wooden plank several inches thick varnished and fastened to four heavy square legs. It matched the exposed beams in the ceiling and was big enough to spread out several reference books on Provence—cookbooks with mouth-watering recipes, coffee-table photo books of breath-taking photography and of course an assortment of memoirs and travelogues describing falling-down farmhouses, weed-choked olive groves and robust peasant neighbors.

But all Lily had to do was look out the floor-to-ceiling picture windows to see Provence for herself. The study was tucked into the corner of the house where she could see the lavender fields and upright, skinny evergreens, and nary a weed or crumbling building in sight. Jack's friends certainly had pride in their property.

Pride and lots of money. She'd grown up around it and could smell it, like a new dollar bill fresh from the mint.

Lily's email program dinged and she found a new message. Ooh, from Margo, an editor at *Fashionista Magazine*. But why would she want to email her? She wasn't writing about clothes, and her own fashion style on this trip had consisted of either hiking outfits or being buck naked.

She clicked on the icon and read the screen, stunned. The editor was interested in her blog and wanted her to write an online column on traveling in France from the point of view of a hip, single woman. Lily rolled her eyes. She didn't know how hip she was, but, hey, she could fake it.

She read on. Oh. They wanted her to write about Frenchmen in general, "Pierre" in particular. She'd never shown Jack's face in any photos she'd posted, but perhaps the element of mystery had intrigued the editor, who had left her number with an invitation to call her for more details.

Ten minutes later after calling New York, Lily had agreed to posts every other day, which would be linked on the magazine site's home page. And Margo had hinted there would be more work for her, maybe even feature articles in the print version of the magazine. Lily didn't know exactly what her topics might be, since she wasn't going to travel around Europe dating more men just so she could write about them. Professional dating was not to her liking.

She and Margo had agreed on some boundaries for her blogs. The editor, of course, was interested in as much juicy detail as Lily would offer, but Jack had a vested interest in not becoming the latest internet heartthrob.

She'd have to double-check with him about being a semifictional character in her blog—names and details changed to protect the innocent, as they said on TV.

Jack came into the study. *"Bonjour, chérie."* He leaned over the desk and kissed her.

"Guess what, Jack?" She told him about her new writing job.

"I am not surprised at your success, Lily. Your sincere interest in my country comes through in your work."

She took a deep breath. "The editor wants me to write about you, as well."

"Me?" His eyebrows shot up. "But you have hardly mentioned me and you aren't even using my real name."

"She says American women are fascinated by Frenchmen and wants more detail about dating and romance in France. But I don't want to put any of our own personal situation online," she added hastily.

He rubbed his chin. "Dating and romance in France is

much the same as anywhere else, but I'm sure you and I can think of something that editor might like. But again, I have to ask you not to post any photos that show my face."

"I won't," she promised.

"What would you like to do this afternoon? Research French romance?"

Lily pressed her lips together and thought. The view out the window caught her eye again. "Get a tour of the manor house."

He blinked in surprise.

"That is, if your friends don't mind," she amended, not wanting to be a bad guest.

"Hmm." He rubbed his chin thoughtfully. "Marthe-Louise would be delighted to show us around."

"Great." Lily shut down her computer and grabbed her camera. "Let's go."

DELIGHTED WAS AN understatement—the plump woman in her fifties was ecstatic to see Jack. If she'd been any younger, Lily would have been jealous.

"Jacques, oh, *mon petit* Jacques!" She spotted them at the kitchen door and wiped her hands on her apron before dragging Jack inside.

"Marthe-Louise is the housekeeper here," he called, as the older woman plastered his cheeks in teary kisses.

"She certainly remembers you fondly."

He grinned ruefully and said something soothing to Marthe-Louise, patting her shoulder. "Okay, Marthe-Louise, this is Lily. Lily, this is Marthe-Louise."

"Lee-Lee!" Marthe-Louise released Jack and seized Lily, kissing her vigorously twice on each cheek. She unleashed a torrent of excited French. "Ah, *belle, belle, si belle!*"

"She says you are very beautiful."

Lily blushed and Marthe-Louise cooed and pinched her reddening cheek before asking Jack a question.

He nodded and replied at length. The housekeeper gave him an exasperated look but finally nodded her head.

"Merci." Jack blew the older woman a kiss and she giggled. "She will give us a tour of the house but needs to straighten up a bit first."

"Oh, okay." The house looked immaculate, but there was probably a pile of mail here and a newspaper there that would take away from the manorial splendor.

The housekeeper darted out and returned in a couple minutes.

The house was impressive, with a huge salon and dining area for hosting large soirées, several sitting rooms, a giant library filled with books that Lily itched to read and a glass-enclosed conservatory, or *orangerie,* where they grew potted orange and lemon trees for fresh fruit during the winter.

It was a massive building, but with few personal touches and no family portraits. Probably those were upstairs in the living quarters, which weren't part of the tour.

They returned to the kitchen, easily twice the size of the kitchen at the guesthouse. *"Ongree?"* Marthe-Louise asked.

"What?" Lily asked politely.

"You *ongree?*" she asked her.

"Oh, hungry." Her stomach growled and they all laughed. "Yes, I am hungry."

The housekeeper flew into action and quickly had a platter of crusty sliced bread with a variety of spreads in little ceramic pots.

Jack pointed to one pot and then the next. "Olive and dried figs for a sweet-and-salty mix, fresh tuna and olive, and chickpeas with cumin—a variation on hummus."

"And pasta," Marthe-Louise added. "Jack, he no tell *moi* he come. Bad, bad boy." She retaliated by smacking his arm. "I cook now."

Jack opened a cabinet and got out three wineglasses. He opened the under-counter wine refrigerator and pulled out a couple different bottles before settling on a white wine. He certainly was making himself at home in the manor house kitchen, and Lily glanced nervously at Marthe-Louise to make sure she didn't think it was presumptuous.

Jack set the full glass next to the housekeeper's elbow, and she thanked him, so it wasn't a problem for her. Lily relaxed a bit, especially when he lifted his glass in a toast. "*A votre santé.* To your health."

"And to yours." He had lost the gaunt, pale look in his cheeks and this giant lunch would help fill out the rest of him. *"Bon appétit."* He and Marthe-Louise smiled approvingly at her French.

Lily didn't know if *gorged* was quite the right word to describe what she and Jack did to the little slices of breads and savory toppings, but once she took artsy, foodie photos of the Provence-made yellow ceramic dish with its black fig spread and the red ceramic dish with the creamy tan chickpea spread, *gorged* came close. Good thing tuna spread wiped off her phone, which she used to make notes for her next blog.

Marthe-Louise was pouring a green sauce into her top-of-the-line food processor to blend with several cloves of garlic and a couple egg yolks while a pasta pot bubbled on the stove. She stopped to shake a spoon at Jack and scold him.

"Okay, okay." He laughed. "We should save some room for her spaghetti."

Lily obediently put down her last crust of bread. She really needed to get some physical exercise in or else she would need to buy a second seat for her plane ride back to New York. Her plane ride scheduled four days from now. Well.

Marthe-Louise drained the spaghetti and poured in the rich green sauce, letting it sit.

Lily elbowed Jack. "Those are raw egg yolks. Haven't you had enough digestive problems?"

He whispered back, "Those are from her very own chickens and the heat of the pasta cooks them. No bad eggs allowed. Except for me, of course."

She giggled. Jack was about as far from a bad egg as you could find in a man. "You're a good egg." She rested her hand on his knee and aimed a kiss for his cheek.

He turned his head and her kiss landed on his mouth. He deepened the kiss and Lily opened her lips under him. He tasted spicy and warm, and she promptly forgot they weren't alone until he broke the kiss and smiled at her.

"Ah, l'amour, c'est grand!" Marthe-Louise was smiling too, and Lily blushed at the housekeeper's mention of love. The older woman gave Jack a doting glance as she dished green pasta. "Eat, eat. Then go sleep."

"How about it? Do you feel like an afternoon nap?" Jack murmured.

"Do we have to sleep?" she replied, and he laughed again, a hearty, baritone sound.

"Not unless you want to." He twirled a forkful of noodles and popped it into her mouth.

"Oh, yum." The garlic and basil mixed with the creamy egg yolks slid perfectly over the firm spaghetti.

Jack took a bite and hummed in pleasure, calling compliments to Marthe-Louise, who modestly waved a spoon at him.

They nibbled away at the pasta until Lily really did feel tired. "Jack, about that nap…"

He pushed away his bowl as well and glanced at the old ceramic clock on the countertop. "It is siesta time, and I have had enough carbohydrates to knock me unconscious."

"Let's be unconscious together." Lily hopped off the stool and wavered slightly. Jack steadied her.

"*Au revoir,* Marthe-Louise." He kissed her three times and pinched her cheek. She put one arm around him and scolded him affectionately, waggling her finger in his face. He protested tolerantly, gesturing nearly as much as she did. "She says to stop by anytime and she will cook us anything we want. She won't be happy until I am round and portly like her husband, Jean-Claude. He has never been sick a day in his life thanks to her cooking."

The housekeeper nodded emphatically, pushing a platter of pastries and a second bottle of wine into their hands.

"An afternoon snack?" Lily asked.

"For later. I may burst at any minute." He blew Marthe-Louise a kiss, leading Lily out of the kitchen to the gravel driveway leading to their guesthouse.

"She certainly takes good care of you. She knew you were sick?"

"Yes, but really, she's usually like that anyway. Eat, eat, eat. It's a good thing the men around here have physical jobs to burn off all the good cooking. And me, who practically has a doctor's prescription to do nothing but gain weight? A dream come true."

He was, but not necessarily in the culinary arena. Marthe-Louise obviously loved Jack like a son. She'd seen her own mother make sure Mrs. Wyndham was well-fed and living in clean surroundings, but her mother had never evinced this degree of maternal affection toward a guest of the family—she'd saved all that for Lily. She blurted, "I should call my mother."

"Of course," he said easily. "Feel free to use the phone

at the guesthouse." He shifted the wine bottle under his opposite arm and offered her his elbow. The gravel crunched under their feet as they strolled uphill. The air was hot and still, the buzz of the cicadas crescendoing with the rising afternoon temperature.

"I have an international plan on my cellphone." It would be almost cheaper to fly home to talk with her mother in person if they spent much time on the phone.

"Unnecessary," he said promptly. "Marthe-Louise would have my head if I let you do that."

"Hmmph." She'd leave some money on the counter to pay for her bill.

Jack showed her how to dial internationally and kissed her forehead. She stared dreamily after him and then snapped to attention as her mother's voice came on the line.

"Hello?"

"Mother? It's Lily."

"Lily. Are you well?" Her mother sounded pleased to hear from her.

"Yes, I'm fine. How are you?" For someone who attempted to make a living with her words, she was certainly falling short.

"Very good. I read your blog about how you're in Provence now."

Lily winced. She should have called her mother about her change in plans, but she'd sent her an email and was too used to doing things on her own. "Yes, and it's beautiful here. I'm in the middle of the lavender harvest and got some great photos that I'll post later as soon as I get the blog post written."

"Sarah told me how to subscribe to your blog, so I've been reading all your posts. You met a man named Pierre in Paris?"

"Yes, well, that's not his real name. I don't mind the publicity, but he works for a government agency and doesn't want his name splashed around the internet."

"Oh, my." Mother sounded amused. "Is he a French secret agent?"

Lily laughed. "No, he does relief work overseas and they go into dangerous regions sometimes. Publicity would put them at risk."

"Well, as long as you know his real name. I assume he is with you in Provence?"

Lily squirmed. Her mother didn't need to know all the details of her traveling—and sleeping—arrangements, so she settled for a bare-bones outline. "He comes from here, so we're staying at a guesthouse that belongs to his friends. The housekeeper fixed us several kinds of spreads and crackers and then we had this Provençal version of pesto sauce and spaghetti."

"Be sure to write down the recipes," Mother reminded her. "Although the ingredients somehow taste different when they are grown somewhere else. Much like the home-made *foie gras*—I enjoyed your post about that."

"Holy cow, was that good."

"I think you mean 'holy goose,'" her mother teased.

Lily was taken aback for a second but then joined in the laughter. Mother had never laughed or shown much of a sense of humor in years past. Stan the Chef (Stan her Stepdad, she reminded herself) was a jolly guy, and maybe he was helping her mother lighten up. "And how is Stan?" she asked.

"Fine, thank you for asking." Her mother sounded pleased at her interest. "He's at the market right now shopping for a dinner party tonight. Mrs. Wyndham is hosting one of the U.S. senators—he's up for reelection next year and is working on his fundraising."

Lily made a terrible grimace. "Good grief, Mother, those dinners are even more deadly than her usual parties."

"That's right, dear, you never did like that part of the job."

"But, Mother, how can you stand doing that stuff after all these years?" Lily burst out. "Don't you want to do something else before—?" she broke off her sentence.

"Before I get too old and feeble to work?" her mother replied. Fortunately she seemed more amused than offended. "Unfortunately I'm not even fifty yet, so retirement is a bit away."

Lily winced. She always forgot how young her mother was, only twenty when Lily was born.

"Besides, I'm not like you, Lily. I don't get bored easily and I enjoy routines and organization. For me, life is better when I know what's happening next."

"Gee, you sound like Jack. He's very organized and a real homebody, too."

"So your mystery Frenchman is named Jack?"

"Jacques, actually."

"I assume he's treating you well?" Mother's voice took on a steely tone she reserved for rich, drunken letches and lazy housemaids.

"Very well, Mother. I wouldn't be here otherwise."

"Good." Her tone softened. "I wish I had seen things differently when you were younger. I didn't understand your situation at school."

"Well, rich guys are pigs."

"Lily!" her mother scolded her. "Those particular young men were pigs, but don't be a reverse snob."

She shifted on the desk chair, remembering how she had accused Jack of snobbery, and that had proven so untrue as to be laughable. "Sorry." But he was just a regular guy anyway.

Mother was never one to harp on an admonishment. "When do you come back, dear?"

"My ticket is up in four days." Unless she extended her stay. Maybe there would be a general strike and they'd close the airports. That grim thought cheered her up.

"Please call when you get back. And come see us here in Philly. We've finished remodeling the carriage house kitchen and it's Stan's pride and joy."

"He cooks at home?" Why would he want to, after a long day in the kitchen at the main house?

Mother giggled like a teenager. Lily's jaw fell open— she'd never heard that sound before. "Sure, he does. He takes good care of me." That simple statement, filled with pride and love, made Lily's heart flip and her eyes tear.

"He'd better," she blustered, sniffing discreetly. "Or else I'll hide his favorite knives and sharpening stone." She'd grown up in a kitchen and knew how to punish a chef.

"Oh, my, how fierce." Her mother laughed again but cleared her throat. "And Lily, be careful with this man. I would hate to see you hurt."

"Mother, he's very nice."

"A nice man can break your heart as easily as a bad man. Sometimes worse, because you're not expecting it." Her tone had the ring of past experience.

Lily hesitated, but didn't know how to reply. "I understand," she finally said.

"I hope you won't have to," she said simply. "But keep up the good work and get those recipes for Stan and me," she emphasized with a chuckle.

Lily agreed and blew a kiss into her phone before hanging up.

Mother had found happiness after heartbreak and many long, hard years alone. Lily knew she wasn't ready to settle down herself, but couldn't help wondering what the future would bring.

Hopefully not heartbreak, but like Mother had said, it was unexpected. Lily just hoped Jack wouldn't be the one to bring it.

13

LILY SAT CROSS-LEGGED on the stone patio behind the guest-house kitchen, her camera aimed at an industrious bee buzzing around a purple sage plant. Not being a fan of bee stings, she moved slowly to frame her shots. One set had the golden-and-black insect in front of a solid wall of purple blooms, and for the second set, she lay down on her back and aimed upward. That angle showed the bee more in profile against the blue, blue sky.

She took a few pictures of the sky to capture the color. No wonder painting legends like Cézanne and Van Gogh, Picasso and Matisse had immortalized Provence in their art. She only wished she had the talent to do the same.

Ah, well. Her talent was with words, and maybe her photos would illustrate the land in some small way.

A shadow fell over her and, still looking through the viewfinder, she rotated to see Jack looking down at her. She fired off a couple shots of him silhouetted against the sky.

He looked startled. "That's an odd angle for a photo. Wouldn't you like my regal profile instead?" He turned his head to the right and put his finger under his chin, staring haughtily into the distance.

"I'm aiming for the artsy look. Don't worry, I won't put that one on my blog. But you do have that snooty expression just right."

He chuckled and extended a hand to her, the bee buzzing around him for a second until it decided to find greener pastures.

"You must not be scared of bees," she told him, standing and shutting down her camera.

He grinned. "Working on a flower farm knocks that out of you pretty fast. I don't *bug* them and they don't *bug* me."

She groaned at his pun.

"Bee-sides," he continued, "you have probably never had lavender honey. It is a local delicacy and Marthe-Louise has a wonderful recipe of duck glazed with lavender honey."

"Oh, yum. Do you think she would give me the recipe?"

He shrugged. "Sure, but she'll cook it for us if we ask."

"We could bring her the ingredients."

Jack rubbed his chin. "Let me talk with her and see what she would prefer. I know she has a little understanding with the butcher and likes to pick out her own fowl."

"The sign of a true artist," she told him. "Stan would never let anyone else pick the giant beef roasts that Mrs. Wyndham likes to serve at her dinner parties."

"Fortunately for us today, we will benefit from Marthe-Louise's culinary generosity. You can't come to Provence in the summer and not have a picnic. She fixed us a basket full of food and we're going up into the hills for the afternoon."

"Great." Lily tightened the laces on her sturdy hiking boots and socks. Bees and bare feet were a bad combination. "We've been staying close to home for the past several days."

"I haven't heard any complaints." He nuzzled her neck. "On the other hand, we could eat here. Later." She shivered as he nibbled her ear. "Much later."

"Oh, no, you don't." She pushed him away, though gently.

"Rejected." He pressed a hand to his heart.

"Hardly." Jack laughed and Lily realized her unintended pun. "Oh, you." She started to blush and his grin widened.

"Yes, me indeed. But alas, it is picnic time." He locked the back door of the guesthouse and they went around to the driveway. The picnic basket was already waiting in the car's backseat, and they drove up a dusty road deeper in the hills.

They stopped at a field full of workers. "Would you like to see how they harvest the lavender?"

"Absolutely."

A couple dozen harvesters, mostly young men and a few women, straightened as they approached. An older man started to chastise them for pausing but caught sight of Jack. He shouted a greeting. "Eh, M'sieu le…Jacques!"

He rapidly picked his way across the lavender field like a plump but nimble ballerina, not trampling or bruising a single plant. He wore a button-down shirt that had seen better days, a vest with several pockets, work boots and a round, flat-topped hat that she had seen on several of the older men. His face was round as well, bisected by a luxurious black mustache. "Jacques, *mon brave*." He slapped Jack on the back. "And who is this?" he asked in heavily accented English.

"Lily, this is Monsieur Jean-Claude Chailan, husband of Marthe-Louise. Jean-Claude, this is Mademoiselle Lily Adams from America."

"Pleased to meet you." Lily extended her hand.

"Ah, Mademoiselle Lily, I am sorry we have not met

before. I have been supervising the farm workers and Jacques has been keeping you all to himself." Jean-Claude swept off his hat and actually bowed to her. He replaced his hat and clasped both of her hands, gazing at her with such a fond expression that she was momentarily taken aback. She saw the cheek-kiss routine coming, though and was prepared for it, although the third and fourth kisses were a surprise. Jack had told her that a fourth kiss was basically reserved for special occasions.

Jean-Claude drew back, still holding her hands in his work-hardened ones. "Ah, Mademoiselle, my good wife said you were beautiful, and I can see she was not exaggerating."

Lily reddened and Jean-Claude shook his head. "Ah, the touch of the rose on your cheeks. Jacques, you old dog, what did you ever do to deserve such a pretty girl?"

"Nothing, *mon ami,* nothing."

"Too true." The older man barked out a loud laugh. "Eh, but I should not tell all of your secrets today, no?"

"No," Jack said firmly.

"Oh, you've known each other a long time, then?" Lily asked.

"A lifetime, *chérie,*" Jack answered. "Jean-Claude came to Provence with the Roman legions and liked it so much he stayed."

Jean-Claude gave him a narrow stare. "Are you calling me an old man?"

"Just joking," Jack said hastily. "You are a man of experience, seasoned like an expensive red wine."

"That is better, you young punk." Jean-Claude let go of Lily's hands and slapped Jack on the back again. He bent and broke off a lavender sprig. "*Voilà,* Mademoiselle. This is the best lavender in France." He offered it to her.

Lily inhaled deeply. The perfume spiraled up into her nose, making her almost dizzy with the ripe scent.

Jack steadied her. She smiled at the men. "Powerful. But it doesn't smell like what I'm used to."

"You are used to the scent of the lavandin plant, a sterile hybrid that has more of a woodsy, camphor smell," Jack told her.

"Good for soap and clothes washing, but perfume— bah!" Jean-Claude waved his hands dismissively. "No good unless you want to smell like laundry." He puffed out his chest. "In fact, we are providing the lavender oil for an up-coming royal wedding. The bride is creating a perfume to be sold for her children's charity."

"Fascinating." Lily turned to Jack. "Did you know about this?"

"Many of the details are hush-hush, right, Jean-Claude?"

The older man put a finger to his mustache in a shush-ing gesture. "But of course."

Lily was disappointed not to have a big scoop like this but she wasn't some tabloid journalist to snoop around. "Tell me all the details as soon as you can."

Jean-Claude spread his hands wide. "I promise, you will be the first to know." His stomach growled loudly. "Lunch!" he called to the crew, who cheered and straight-ened. "I would invite you to eat with us, but Marthe-Louise told me you are going on a picnic."

"I thought we'd go to the northeast field. It has a great view and some shade."

"Ah, *oui,* that field will be ready for harvest next week. But not yet—there will be no one around." Jean-Claude didn't quite wink or waggle his eyebrows, but Lily got the gist of it.

"*Merci,* Jean-Claude. We'll see you later." Jack put his

arm around Lily's shoulders and they strolled back to the car.

The northeast field was as beautiful as the lower field, overlooking the valley. A large oak tree stood nearby, and Jack spread out their picnic blanket underneath it.

"What did Marthe-Louise pack for lunch?" Lily asked eagerly.

He opened the big cooler and handed her a plate from the smaller bag of supplies. "Cold roasted chicken, ham on baguettes, a wheel of goat cheese, crackers, fruit and her special potato–green bean salad with an oil-and-vinegar dressing."

Lily's mouth watered as he served her a heaping plateful. "Any dessert?"

"But of course." He grinned at her, lifting a container. "Cherry tarts, made fresh from our own trees."

She moaned in anticipation, and he laughed. "I've heard you make that sound before."

She swatted at him with her fork. "I enjoy the basics of life."

"And that is why you fit in so well here." He gestured to the beautiful farmland and perfect weather. "The basics of life are the best things in life." He pulled out a bottle of white wine and deftly decanted it into two goblets. Marthe-Louise had thought of everything.

Lily raised hers. "A toast to the most beautiful day in the most beautiful place on earth."

"To the most beautiful woman on earth." He raised his in return.

"Where?" Lily looked around, half in jest, but subsided when he gave her a stern look. "Well, um, thank you."

"To the most beautiful woman on earth," he repeated, and they touched rims.

"A votre santé." She remembered the traditional French toast to his health.

Jack smiled approvingly. "Very good." They drank some wine and did their best to do justice to Marthe-Louise's picnic.

Between the wine, the sun and the hypnotic buzzing of the cicadas, Lily's eyes started to droop by the end of the meal.

"Come lie down, *chérie,* we will have dessert later." He cleared the remnants of their meal and beckoned to her.

"Only for a little," she insisted. He nodded and she rested her head on his shoulder, closing her eyes.

It seemed like only a few minutes later, but the angle of the sun had dropped when she opened her eyes to find Jack watching her, an indescribable expression of tenderness on his face.

Without saying a word, she reached for him. Their clothes quickly disappeared and he was inside her, their gazes still locked. She didn't close her eyes until her senses were overwhelmed with the touch of his body, the scent of the lavender, the heat of the day and the blue of the sky.

They came simultaneously, and stayed in each other's arms for another eternity. Lily wondered at the perfection of it all, knowing she was at least half in love with Jack, if not totally. And remembering the expression on his face as she'd awoken, she thought he might feel the same way.

LILY SHUT DOWN her laptop after webchatting with Sarah. Her cousin was predictably over the moon with her pregnancy, which was continuing well, but not so engrossed that she forgot to warn Lily about the dangers of strange men, particularly strange Frenchmen.

Sarah had lowered her voice, presumably not to have her husband, Carl, overhear, and said, "Lily, believe me,

I spent a whole year and several summers there. I know how sexy and charming they can be. There was this one chef in Lyon who could do the most amazing things with chocolate…" Her voice trailed off and her eyes got dreamy for a second as Lily watched in amusement. "But that's not the point."

"The point is that I am being careful and having as much fun with Jack as you did with your pastry chef."

"That much, huh?" Sarah had sighed in nostalgia. "Oh, well, all of that is off my plate, so to speak, until I hear the all-clear from the doc. I'll get the details from you at some point, but not now."

Lily smiled as she remembered all the so-called details of last night. She stretched and stood up from the desk. Jack was up in the lavender fields with Marthe-Louise's husband Jean-Claude. Lily worried about him overexerting himself, but Jean-Claude seemed to look after Jack like a kindly old uncle.

The morning sun and sky were too nice to waste indoors. She ran upstairs and pulled on her swimsuit, a lime-green string bikini. Only old ladies wore one-piece suits in France. Even then, they rolled down the top and went topless like everyone else at the beach.

No issues like that at their private pool, however. Thanks to *Oncle* Pierre's privacy issues, a high limestone wall surrounded the pool area.

She went downstairs with a towel and grabbed a bottle of sparking water and a bowl of plump red grapes.

She carried her snack outside and decided to get some color, lying down on the large chaise lounge. With her round-framed sunglasses and pricey French water, she felt positively decadent. All she needed was a pool boy.

She closed her eyes and tipped her face up to the

sun. She drifted in and out of sleep, enjoying the lavender-and-rosemary scented breeze.

"A good idea on such a hot afternoon."

Ah, there was the pool boy. She opened her eyes to see Jack wearing a tiny competitive-swimmer type suit.

"Ack, what is that?" She still wasn't used to European-style men's swimsuits.

"Oh, is this the clothing-optional pool? I should have realized." He hooked his thumbs in the waistband and calmly pulled them off, kicking them away.

"Jack!" Sure, she'd been naked with him, and in daylight, too, but that time in the lavender field had seemed like a dream.

"Come on, sunbathe topless. You're in France, you know."

"Oh, fine." She rolled onto her stomach, untying the bottom string so her back was bare. She rested her face on her arms, ignoring his laughter. "If you want to get sunburned on your…well, that's up to you."

He laughed even harder and sat next to her. "Maybe you could put some sun lotion on my…well…"

Lily rolled onto her side. "Oh, yeah? And why should I do that?"

"I'd do the same for you." He wiggled his eyebrows suggestively.

She looked down and saw her top had shifted to the side, baring her breasts. "Hmmph." She unknotted the tie at her neck and tossed the two triangles aside.

"Ah, that's better," he said in appreciation. "We'll make a Frenchwoman out of you yet."

She sniffed. "Somehow I can't imagine your Provence ladies wanting to sunbathe topless." The image of Marthe-Louise getting a lineless tan was a bit much to imagine.

"You'd be surprised." His deadpan expression amused her. Who knew what these staid matrons got up to?

Jack was not tan all over, either. Working shirtless with Jean-Claude had browned up his torso, but he had a definite tan line at his waistband. Somehow, though, she didn't think he'd come out to even up his color, considering how hard and aroused he was growing under her gaze. "Good thing you took off your suit. You might have hurt yourself trying to fit all that inside."

He crawled up the lounge and positioned himself between her thighs. "But I like fitting myself inside…you, that is." The tip of his erection prodded the thin green fabric of her bikini bottom.

He was so big and hard and hot on top of her, a summer god come to life and wanting to have his way with her. Her nipples tightened in anticipation.

"Chilly?" He lifted an amused eyebrow. It was at least eighty-five degrees outside. She pursed her lips and he laughed. "Mmm, let me warm you up." He lowered his mouth to one tight pink peak and drew it into his mouth.

Lily was burning up. Jack licked her gently, first back and forth, then with round swirling strokes around her whole areola. Then a hard suck and a little nip. She gasped in a mix of shock and pleasure, and then he soothed her with his tongue. He lifted his head to admire his work. Her nipple was like a berry, firm and reddish pink, glossy and ripe.

"Oh, Lily, I could suck on your pretty tits for hours." He blew a cool stream of air over her wet flesh and she bit back a scream. He shook his head disapprovingly. "Don't you want to scream for me?"

"Well…"

"Don't be so shy. No one is around."

"Are you sure?" she whispered.

He laughed. "Jean-Claude is a stern taskmaster. Everyone is in the upper fields to harvest the prime lavender crop. Where we were the other day."

"Why aren't you?"

"There are benefits to being the…guest. Enough of that business. You are my business now." He moved to her other nipple and gave it his full attention.

The first wasn't neglected, though. His long, clever fingers caught it and gave it several gentle tugs. The double attention was more intense than anything, making her hips start to writhe under him.

He angled his erection so she rubbed up and down his length. He moaned against her breast and then his fingers were undoing the side ties of her bikini.

The fabric easily fell away and he was pressing on her, almost into her. He was so hard, and she was so wet. She shifted slightly so his tip entered her.

His eyes flew open. "Lily, the protection." They were both gasping at the new, erotic sensation. "Let me go get a condom."

"Why not like this? I'm on the Pill and healthy. Aren't you?"

"Not on the Pill." He gave a choked laugh. "But healthy. I've been tested for every infectious disease known to man."

Jack was wavering, she could tell. But it was his decision.

He surrendered with a groan and slid all the way into her to his hilt. She automatically locked her legs around him and they both stared at each other.

"I've never done this before," she confessed.

"Me, neither." He closed his eyes and shuddered. "Oh, Lily, it's beyond words."

"Tell me," she coaxed.

"You're burning me up, my sweet. Your heat, your creamy juices on my skin." He started moving inside her. "You make me crazy for you."

She tipped her head back. Every part of him touched her, unblunted by any barrier. His juices mixed with hers, making his thrusts even more slippery and delicious. Her plump, swollen nipples caught in his russet chest hair and she cooed in pleasure at the rough texture.

"Ah, you like, eh?" He picked up his pace, slamming inside her as she moaned with every jolt. "You're such a bad girl, Lily. I shouldn't do this, but I can't help myself. Sexy girl. Naughty girl."

Lily had never thought of herself as bad, sexy or naughty, but it sounded fun.

Suddenly, he raised his head. "Uh-oh."

"What?" She looked around but Jack kept thrusting into her.

"I think someone's there."

"What? Who?" She stopped moving but her body was drawing her on, not letting her matching thrusts stop.

His brown eyes were mischievous. "Someone who might hear how much you like this."

She moaned, sinking into the lounge, letting his fantasy take her away.

"Someone who wonders how wild you get with a bare cock inside you." He moved his hand between their bodies. "How wild you get with a finger on your clit." He touched her and she screamed. "Like that."

"Jacky…" she moaned.

"I love it when you call me that. Only you, *mon coeur* Lily."

She swallowed hard in a wave of sudden emotion. He called her "his heart." She threw her arms around him and kissed his neck, his chest, wherever she could reach.

He responded by renewing his touches and caresses, worshiping her body with his as they moved together as one.

She dug her fingers into his back and tightened around him. He caught her earlobe between his teeth and flicked it with his tongue. She arched into him and broke apart, her climax pitching her up fast and strong. "Oh, Jacky, Jacky…"

He pushed with one last strong thrust and groaned, his head tossed back with all the cords in his neck pulling taut.

He flooded into her and she climaxed again, even harder. He called her name over and over again and she loved how his French accent got thicker during passion. She clung to him, almost desperately as they gasped for air.

He slumped on top of her, resting his head next to hers against the lounge cushion. She kissed his cheek and he turned his face to softly kiss her lips.

"You are wonderful, Lily. So much fire when we make love."

Love.

A ray of sun lit up his hair as she twisted her fingers around a strand of burnished copper. He was heat and fire and tenderness and…love?

He lifted his head and smiled sweetly at her. "What is it?"

"Nothing." She hadn't meant for him to notice. But to her horror, her eyes started to prickle. Why would that happen? She quickly closed her eyes so he couldn't see them fill.

"Look at me, Lily."

Rats. There they were naked on a huge chaise lounge with the sun shining on them and she was starting to cry. She opened her eyes and gave him a wide smile. "Yes?"

His brown gaze didn't miss a thing. She wondered if they trained him for that in foreign-aid school. "Do you have any regrets, Lily? I know this is a very sudden relationship, and neither of us has ever been with anyone else…like this."

She didn't answer, didn't know what to say, and his face tightened in concern. His muscles tensed as if he was about to get up.

"Wait!"

He rolled next to her, brushing her hair off her face.

"I, um…" she started. "It's not what you think. I was looking at you, and the sun was shining on you, and I thought how, um, wonderful it was to be here at this perfect time and perfect place." Geez, for a writer she was incredibly incoherent. Maybe because she preferred describing other people and their activities rather than open up her own emotions for scrutiny.

"Oh." Relief spread across his face. "As we talked about before—the moment where everything is exactly as it should be. The poet Baudelaire said to 'dream of sweetness,' where everything is rich, peaceful and sensual."

"That's it, exactly. I've never experienced that with a man." She fought back a blush at being so open, but, hey, she was already physically naked. A little bit of emotional nakedness wouldn't be out of place.

His eyes widened. "And you feel that with me?"

"Well, yes."

"And I have felt that with you—from the first time you bumped into me at the hostel."

"No." She narrowed her eyes at him. "You thought I had a terrible accent and was an obnoxious summer tourist."

"I did not. I thought you were a beautiful, cheerful American woman who took pity on a scruffy, rude backpacker and bought him breakfast."

"And look how well you cleaned up," she joked. "All for the price of a cup of coffee and a croissant."

"Did you call me cheap?" He placed his hand on his chest in mock dismay. "Cruel woman."

"Cruel man." He was the furthest thing from cruel, but he knew she was teasing him.

"What? And considering how hard I work to please you?"

"How can I ever make it up to you?" she purred, running her hand down his belly to cup his growing erection.

He thrust into her hand. "Surprise me."

She pushed him onto his back. "You're on." She swung her leg over his waist and straddled him.

"Ah, Lily." He grabbed her hips and helped her settle on him, his cock pushing inside her again. He cupped her breasts and played with her sensitized nipples, his big hands brown against her paler skin.

"My favorite bikini top." She smiled down at him.

He grinned. "If you have to wear anything, wear me."

"You wear me out." Her legs were starting to burn from moving up and down on him but she didn't care. "But in a good way."

"Poor Lily." His chest glistened with sweat and his hair was falling into ringlets at the edges. "I'll make it up to you, I promise." He caressed her clit and she leaned forward, bracing her hands on his shoulders.

His free hand cupped her bottom running up her back to the nape of her neck. "Kiss me, *ma belle* Lily."

She eagerly complied, opening her mouth to him as his tongue possessed her as thoroughly as his cock. She moaned and squirmed, her climax building. He slid his hand down to her bottom and massaged there. The double sensation of his hands in front and back was overwhelming and she bucked sharply on top of him.

He hummed low in his throat and kept it up until she arched and clutched at him. He quickly followed her over the edge and she collapsed onto him.

Jack rolled her onto the chaise and they kissed naked in the sun. "Not so shy anymore, eh, Lily?"

"Only with you." She nuzzled his neck.

"But of course." He gathered her into his arms. "And despite what you may think, I am only clothing-optional with you."

She laughed and pinched his firm buttock. "I know that—you have tan lines."

"And we are going to get burn lines if we don't get out of the sun." He stood and scooped her up as she squealed in surprise.

"Don't hurt yourself."

He scoffed and walked toward the house. "You are much lighter than some of the equipment Jean-Claude has me tote around."

"Don't let him work you too hard," she fretted.

He pinched her bottom and she yelped. "Oh, I work hard. A strong woman like you needs a strong man."

"You think I'm strong?" Lily hugged him closer.

He shook his head in mock dismay. "But if only you could be a little more docile instead of quizzing everything I say."

"Yes, milord." She fluttered her eyelashes.

"What?" He looked shocked at her joking acquiescence.

"Isn't that what all the French peasant girls say to the local nobleman who's offered to ravish them?"

He tipped back his head and roared with laughter. "And I am the local nobleman who has the right to ravish the peasant girls!" He nudged open the patio door with his foot. "I am luring you to my noble lair to have my way with you. How do you feel about a noble attempt at a bath in a hot tub?"

"Milord, lead the way."

14

LILY CAME DOWN to the kitchen early the next morning and found a note from Jack. "Lily, meet me at the lavender field up the hill. Bring coffee. Yours, Jack."

She smiled and set to brewing the milky *café au lait* she was coming to prefer. Once that was perking, she picked up his note and reread it. *Yours, Jack.* That was nice. Lily put great stock in words. She knew not everybody did, but Jack was a methodical, precise man and meant exactly what he said—and wrote.

She didn't expect him to sign it *Love, Jack* or *All my love, Jack,* so that word of affection was a pleasant surprise.

Once the coffee was done and poured into a battered steel thermos, she slung her camera around her neck and headed up the hill to the lavender field, her calves burning in a pleasant way as the gravel road crunched under her hiking boots.

The first field she came to was empty of blooms and workers. That made sense, since it had probably ripened first, being at a slightly lower and warmer elevation. Another quarter mile or so brought her to the field under harvest.

Lily stood at the edge, her gaze immediately drawn to Jack's chestnut head—and his bare torso. Her lips pursed. He was going to get sunburned if he wasn't careful. But he was a grown man and had worked in tropical areas with much more intense sun than France.

His muscles bunched under his skin as he stooped and clipped the wiry stems, setting them aside. He moved down the row and stopped at the end, straightening to stretch his back. Jean-Claude yelled at him, gesturing for Jack to get back to work. Jack replied in kind, causing the older man to bellow with laughter.

The other harvesters glanced up from their own rows and grinned, obviously used to the byplay between the two men. The farmworkers were a diverse lot, men and women both, young and old.

Lily set down the thermos and took several photos, the tableau reminding her of the popular bucolic nineteenth-century paintings of peasants gathering harvest.

But her lens kept swiveling back to Jack. Instead of the sleepy shepherd lad he'd resembled on the train, he looked like a pagan harvest god, powerful and fertile, ripening crops with his touch.

He had joined Jean-Claude on the side of the field and the two men had an intense discussion, pointing at the current field and then up the hill at what was probably the next one on the list. Jack was insisting on something and finally Jean-Claude tossed his hands up in the air and slapped him on the back.

Almost as if Jack were in charge...but he did know about lavender from his family's own farm. Then he spotted her and strode toward her, leaping the low stone fence surrounding the field with an easy jump.

"Good morning, *chérie*." Jack lifted the camera over her head, bent her over his arm and kissed her. His skin was hot velvet, warmed by the sun. She clutched his shoulders as he leisurely moved his mouth over hers.

She dimly became aware of the cheers and catcalls from the harvesters, and Jack planted a kiss on the tip of her nose. "Sorry, Lily. Farmwork brings out my earthy side," he murmured suggestively.

She blinked a couple of times. His "earthy side" had popped up in the bedroom, of course, but this public display of affection was new. She didn't mind, and in fact found it fascinating how life in Provence was healing him from the thin, tired man she'd first met in Paris.

The harvesters had returned to work after Jean-Claude's good-natured shout. Jack pulled on a T-shirt he'd tossed on the wall and took her hand.

"I have a surprise planned for this morning."

"Really?" More of a surprise than a kiss. "What kind of surprise?"

His eyes fell to the scoop-neck blouse showing the top curves of her breasts. "I forget."

Lily huffed in pretend exasperation. "Start remembering."

"Cruel woman." His brown puppy-dog eyes were almost enough to make her relent, but her natural curiosity won out.

"Jack…"

"All right, all right. Remember the perfume lab at the factory? You have an appointment with the 'nose,' the master perfumer, to make your own signature fragrance."

"Really?" She flung her arms around his neck and kissed his cheek. "I read about that online but didn't think I'd have the chance to do that. It doesn't cost too much, does it?"

He hugged her back. "Not at all. It is a popular tourist

outing and no trouble to arrange. We have time for coffee but not anything else," he said regretfully.

She handed him the thermos. "Drink up. I'll model my new perfume for you later."

"Your perfume and nothing else."

She giggled and soon they were in the little white car heading toward the village.

Jack parked near the perfume factory and they quickly found the perfume master, an elegant woman in her fifties with a gray-streaked blond bob and skin that would have looked great on a woman half her age. Probably kept out of the sun and had an inside track on wonderful botanical products.

Jack introduced them. "Simone Laurent is the best nose in the business. The House of Laurent is built on her skill."

"I'm so excited," Lily told her. "The world of perfume is fascinating, especially when you grow so many of your own ingredients right here in Provence."

Simone smiled. "We are indeed fortunate to have such a perfect climate for the flowers and plants—our own corner of paradise."

"I love it here." Lily squeezed Jack's hand. "The sun, the blue skies and hot, dry air. I'm from Philadelphia, and it's very humid there. Much of the city was built on a swamp. They even had the largest yellow-fever outbreak in American history."

Jack smiled. "Fortunately I've had my shots for that, so I will be safe."

Did that mean that he was coming to visit her there? Her heart gave a funny thump, and she smiled up at him. "The Liberty Bell is always a fun sight."

Simone was already leading them down the hall. "Come, come, we have work to do." She ushered them into a laboratory-type space with a large white desk and several dark brown glass bottles on shelves lining the walls. "This is the perfume laboratory. Nothing but the highest quality oils and essences for the House of Laurent." Simone pulled out a clipboard and paper. "We will write down your final choice and keep it on file. Whenever you need a new bottle, you can call us and we will mix it to order. Now tell me which fragrances you like and which you dislike."

Lily thought for a second. "Not roses." Mrs. Wyndham loved fresh roses in the house and she always associated that scent with her.

"Good." Simone made a note. "What else?"

"I like vanilla." The elderly pastry chef who'd preceded Stan had always made sugar cookies for Lily.

"A good, warm base."

"And in honor of my trip to Provence, I thought I could have some lavender in the blend."

"Lavender?" Simone smiled. "Excellent. We have the best lavender oil in the world here in Provence. And the best of the best comes from the de Brissard estate."

"Really?" She turned to Jack in excitement. "You're helping harvest the best lavender in the world. Doesn't that make you proud?"

"Hot and sweaty more than anything," he quipped. "But yes, we are undeniably proud of that lavender."

Simone grinned widely. "Family-owned since 1323. Isn't that correct, Jacques?"

Lily gasped in amazement. "That long. What a sense of history. Jack, maybe I should do a blog post on the de Brissard family."

He shifted from foot to foot. "I wouldn't bother. They have always been an extremely boring lot. But a blog post about Simone and the factory would be very interesting."

Simone smiled. "We are always looking for good publicity, especially to introduce our name and creations to North American buyers."

"I'm writing for *Fashionista Magazine*." It still sent a thrill through her to say that.

"Congratulations. My daughter enjoys that magazine. Me, I cannot read fashion magazines because of all the perfume samples mixing together. Overwhelming for a woman like me." She laughed and reached for a plain brown bottle. "But here we have the de Brissard lavender." She uncapped the bottle and dropped a couple drops of the oil on a paper strip about six inches long. She let it dry for a few seconds and handed it to Lily.

Lily took a cautious sniff and her head almost spun from the concentrated essence. She was immediately thrown back in time to their afternoon in the lavender field, the heat and sun and buzz of cicadas almost loud enough to drown the pounding of the blood in her ears. "Jack, it smells like those fields where we…toured the plants," she finished.

Simone gave her a knowing smile. "That is the power of scent. One wears it outwardly to communicate with others but it conjures the most personal and private memories to the wearer."

"Almost like a secret—I know something that you don't know."

Jack brushed her hair back over her shoulder, his fingers lingering on her collarbone. "The mystery of a woman. Inviting and intriguing to us poor men as we strive to discover the hidden depths."

Lily covered his hand with hers. "You men can be pretty mysterious yourselves."

Simone interjected, "Ah, but that is the wonder of life, eh?" She clapped her hands together. "Enough philosophy. Let's get to work."

For the next hour or so, Lily sniffed test strips until they all started to blend in her poor, untrained mind. She stepped outside a couple times to clear her head, but even the town smelled of flowers, so that didn't help much.

Finally, though, she and Simone had put something together that was floral but woodsy, sweet but exotic. "It's not quite there," she said in disappointment. "The lavender and vanilla are wonderful together along with the base of cedar, but it's missing something."

Simone smiled and dipped a paper tester strip into a bottle, adding it to the wand of papers. Lily cautiously sniffed and her cheeks pulled into a wide grin. "That's it!"

Jack leaned in for a sniff and nodded in approval. "Wonderful. Whatever did you add?"

The perfumer spread her hands wide. "Lily, of course. One cannot make perfume for Lily without any lilies."

They burst out laughing. Jack bent down and kissed Simone on the cheek. "Ah, Simone. The 'nose' knows, as they say."

"Always. Now, Jacques, we still have your cologne formula if you need a new bottle of it."

"You've done this before?" Lily didn't know why that would surprise her since he and Simone were obviously old friends.

"A long time ago, but no, Simone, I don't need any more fragrance."

The perfumer shook her head. "But, Jacques, you know that the oils start breaking down after about a year and quality suffers. Certainly you will not wear your old supply anymore?"

"Well…"

She scoffed. "If you do, don't you dare mention where you got it. I will not have people wondering why Jacques

Montford is wearing something of ours that smells like a Marseilles alley."

He sighed in exasperation and threw up his hands. "I promise to throw away that bottle if you will make me another."

"Bon." Simone smiled like the cat with the canary. "You know, Jacques, we should go into partnership. Put your fragrance into mass production and split the proceeds. We could call it—"

"Merci, but no."

Lily thought it sounded like a great idea. "But you could use the money, Jack. Especially since you've been ill and aren't working right now."

"What?" Simone eyed him from head to toe. "You've been sick?"

"I caught a bug overseas but I am much better now. And I *am* working—working for Jean-Claude."

"Well, that is certainly a switch. I hope you've been kind to him."

"Always." Jack smiled. "And Lily is getting all of Marthe-Louise's recipes."

"I wish—she probably knows several thousand." At the mention of food, Lily's stomach rumbled.

He pulled her to her feet. "Lunchtime, eh? Would you care to join us, Simone?"

"No, no." She waved her hand dismissively. "I must mix both bottles for you and besides, I would not want to intrude on your *tête-à-tête.*" She stood and kissed Lily first on both cheeks, then Jack. She clasped his hand for a second. "Please take care of yourself, Jacques. You are very important to all of us."

"As are you, Madame Simone." He gave a quick bow and kissed the back of her hand. "Mmm, you smell wonderful."

"Ah, Jacques, be gone." She waved him away, laughing. "Come back later for your *parfum*."

Jack took Lily's hand and guided her out of the perfume lab. "Anything you want for lunch, it is yours."

She looked up at him in worry. "Jack, we have to stop this crazy spending. Custom perfume and fancy lunches must be cutting into your budget. At least let me help. Since we're staying at the guesthouse, I haven't used the money I planned for the hostels."

He wrapped his arm around her shoulder and guided her down the crowded sidewalk. "You are a generous woman, *chérie*. But don't worry about the money. I do still get my salary from the relief agency. I am on a medical leave, not unemployed. As you said, the guesthouse is free and I believe Marthe-Louise would slap me with a spoon if I offered her money for the meals she has been cooking for us."

"True." The housekeeper would be vastly insulted, even if they meant well.

"Now what would you like for lunch?"

"I would like…fresh mussels in a white wine sauce tossed with fresh pasta." Her stomach growled again. "Also a crusty loaf of bread to dip in the leftover sauce."

"Wonderful. There is this nearby café that gets shellfish fresh from the sea. The owner's nephew has a fishing boat and then sends the best to his uncle."

"Jack, you know the most fantastic places around here." She snuggled into his side. "And after lunch, we'll pick up the perfume and model it for each other later."

"Sounds delightful."

Lily smiled in satisfaction. Perfume, pasta and Jack—but definitely not in that order. Life couldn't get any better.

JACK LEFT A sleeping Lily, the fragrance of their mingled cologne and perfume still scenting the air of their bedroom.

He was still dishonest with Lily. His stomach churned, and he couldn't even blame the shellfish.

He was a forthright man—why had he started this deception? Had his experience with Nadine so jaded him that he thought every woman was out to snag a rich man, a titled man?

His only title should have been "Loser." Lily was nothing like Nadine—and that was good. But he needed advice, so he pulled on a pair of shorts and picked up his phone. He stopped in the kitchen for a bottle of water and walked out to the pool.

Jack sat heavily into a cushioned chair and turned on his phone. It immediately signaled a new text message from the coordinator at the relief agency, asking how he was feeling. Apparently there was a volcanic eruption in Malaysia and they needed a doctor. Not for anything long-term, she assured him. Just long enough to set up a clinic in the refugee camps and take care of immediate needs.

He touched the reply screen. He should go—they needed him. But then he stopped. Maybe he should get some advice.

He dialed another number instead. "Hi, Frank, it's Jack."

"Jack!" Frank sounded delighted. "How are you? Enjoying the sun?"

He stretched his legs out in the sun. Still rather skinny and pale. "The weather here is wonderful."

"Ah yes, I remember from that one summer we worked the lavender harvest," Frank reminisced. "And those beautiful French girls sure enjoyed how nice we smelled, didn't they?"

Jack grunted in agreement. One particular woman and her perfume were what had put him into this strange mood.

"You find anyone to share the sun and lavender with you?"

Jack sighed heavily. "Yes. And I think I may have royally screwed up."

There was a moment of silence. "Uh-oh. We'd better call George for this one."

In a minute, George was on the line.

Frank minced no words. "George, Jack is in trouble."

"What's wrong, Jack? Are you still sick?" George asked in alarm.

"No, I feel much better. It's just—" He broke off his sentence, not knowing what he was trying to say.

"Go ahead and tell us the details. It's about a *woman*," he stage-whispered to George. He had always been Mr. Fix-It, leaping in to help whenever he could.

"Let the man think, Frank." George sounded amused. He well could afford to be, having gone through his own struggles with the female sex earlier in the spring.

"I *can't* think, that's the problem. I can only think about—about Lily, this woman I just met last week. I can't sleep unless I'm next to her. I can't be away from her without wondering where she is, if she's enjoying herself, if people are being kind to her…" he wound down, verbally if not mentally.

"Jack, Jack," George soothed. "It's okay. You've had a rough few months stuck off in Asia. No wonder you're attracted to the first pretty face that came along."

"Pretty face?" For the first time in his life, Jack wished he could hit George. "Lily is smart, beautiful, talented, witty—not just a pretty face," he spit out.

After a few seconds of tense silence, Frank cleared his throat. "George didn't mean it that way, Jack. She sounds great, she really does."

"Well, she is."

"I am sorry, Jack. I didn't know you felt that way about her," George apologized.

"What way?" he demanded. Another awkward silence. Jack realized he was totally losing his grip. Chewing out his best friends, for crying out loud, letting a woman come between them?

Frank jumped in again, hating to see them argue. "George and I are glad you met somebody nice. Does she like Provence?"

Glad for a more neutral topic, Jack readily said, "Oh, she can't get enough of the landscape and the food, but it's really the people that fascinate her. I spend hours translating for her with all her questions about how they grow lavender, what their mangy hunting dogs are named, how many children they have, anything at all."

"Well, that sounds promising," George said. "You're tied to the land, like we are. Any woman you are serious about would have to understand the pros and cons of you being the Comte de Brissard."

"That's my problem. I haven't told her who I am."

There was another second of silence. "She doesn't know?" Frank asked in amazement. "But you're staying at your own home, harvesting your own lavender and roaming your own estate. She must think you're the biggest moocher in France—the houseguest from hell."

"Really, Frank," George chided him. "I'm sure Jack had his reasons for portraying himself as a simple disaster-relief physician."

"She doesn't know I'm a doctor, either," he mumbled.

Frank guffawed. "You've really stepped in the cow patties now." Frank had always loved American farming colloquialisms. "Your only hope is to tell her the truth—and pronto, before someone else does."

"I have to agree with him, Jack. It sounds as if you've been less than forthcoming. And especially if you like her, and she likes you. It sounds as if you have much in common—both the adventurous types and you both like Provence."

"Like? Aside from the language, it's as if she were a native. Lily loves it here."

The L-word hung significantly over them. Lily loved his homeland. What else did Lily love? She couldn't love… him, could she?

No, of course not. Why would she love him? He was a skinny, pasty Frenchman who knew too much about dying and not enough about living. "Another thing just came up. The agency wants me to go to Malaysia. Just short-term," he hastily added. "I haven't told them my answer yet."

The air of disapproval was palpable. "I know what you can tell them," Frank announced. "You can tell them you almost died earlier in the year and they can go to hell."

George cleared his throat. "I have to agree with Frank, though not quite as bluntly. What would you say to a patient who wanted to do the same thing? You'd keep them home for much longer, wouldn't you?"

"Yes, but they need me."

"So do we, Jack," said George.

"You guys are fine. This farm runs well without me. My mother is tied up in her social events. I'd be at loose ends if I didn't have someone to help."

Frank made a sound of exasperation. "We all need to be needed. You don't have to become a martyr for it."

It was as if someone had chopped him in the gut. Nadine had said almost the same thing to him at his disastrous homecoming party. Had called him St. Jacques and told him he wanted a statue to himself. "Guys, I have to go."

"Oh. Right," Frank said hesitantly. "Take care of yourself, okay?"

"Yes, please do," echoed George. "And again, accept

my apologies in casting aspersions on your ladyfriend. I misspoke."

Jack accepted, of course, feeling grumpy and irritable and generally pissed off—at himself, not George.

Jack hung up. He could go to Malaysia without having some kind of martyr-complex. His friends just didn't understand the shortage of willing doctors. Jack should know better than to get all worked up over trivialities. After all, he was the cool, collected Dr. Montford, trained physician, award-winning philanthropist—and all-around jerk to his friends.

"DID HE HANG up, George?"

"I believe so, Frank."

"He's a goner for this girl, George."

"I think you're right, Frank."

"I usually am."

"Ha."

"Ha, yourself. Go give Renata a kiss for me."

"*Ciao,* Frank."

"*Ciao,* George."

15

LILY FINISHED HER blogpost for *Fashionista Magazine* and checked the clock again. Jack had been working outdoors for several hours and she hoped he wasn't overdoing it. Maybe he was back at the manor house with Marthe-Louise. Her stomach growled. And if not, maybe there was something to eat there.

Lily wandered down to the kitchen garden. Tomatoes, herbs and various squash overflowed the beds. Mrs. Wyndham's gardener would be pea-green with envy. He fought humid weather and various related plant ailments all summer. Marthe-Louise was stooping over to clip some chives. "Ah, *bonjour,* Lily. You desire Jacques?"

Heck yes, she desired him, but probably not what Marthe-Louise meant since even Lily knew the French verb to want in a generic sense was *désirer*. Her cheeks heated. "*Oui*. Where is he?" She mimicked searching for him and Marthe-Louise laughed.

"The lavender, it is ready. Men working together in field."

Ooh la la. The memory of Jack, a sweaty field hand, stripped to the waist was hot. Maybe she could see him from the side of the house that had a view of the hills. "Can

I…" She gestured at the doorway leading to the formal living area of the manor.

Marthe-Louise waved her on. "Go. I cook nice dinner, eh?"

"Good." She smiled at the older woman. She and Jack would have to get her a fancy gift before they left. Cooking for them all the time was above and beyond what she had expected.

Lily had asked Jack when the de Brissard family would return, but he said the lady of the house preferred Paris and probably wouldn't be back this summer. Lily had no idea why not. She'd enjoyed Paris but loved Provence.

Lily walked down the hallway past the dining room and turned into the formal living room, or salon. Undoubtedly this was used for parties and maybe even weddings, being able to hold over a hundred people by her calculations.

She peered out the large French doors leading to the stone terrace, but no sight of Jack in the lavender fields. Maybe they were farther up the hill. She turned and caught sight of a large framed photograph hung on the wall that hadn't been there during her tour. She would have remembered it because Jack was the subject.

Her eyebrows shot up as she peered closely at it. Jack in some fancy tux and tails, with a red sash across his chest, complete with a large gold sunburst medal pinned to it. And there was a woman in the photo. Unless Jack had a thing for older women with hair the same shade of auburn as him, she was his mom.

Lily looked closer and found several similarities in their high cheekbones, strong jaw and wavy hair. His mom was dressed just as fancily in a copper silk dress with a full skirt, and she was seated on an elaborate French-style chair upholstered in white and trimmed in gold. Jack stood behind her, his hand on her shoulder.

Pieces of the puzzle were starting to fit together, and she had the feeling it wouldn't be a cute puppy puzzle or panoramic lavender field jigsaw.

Lily went back into the kitchen. "Marthe-Louise?" she called.

"Oui?" The housekeeper came out from the butler's pantry, wiping her hands on a white towel.

"Photo." Lily jerked her thumb backward at the salon. *"Grand* photo."

The guilty look on Marthe-Louise's face confirmed her suspicion. When Jack had brought her for the tour, he'd sent Marthe-Louise in there first to take down the evidence that he *owned* all of this.

Not only was he probably ten times richer than Mrs. Wyndham back in Philly, but he owned a huge chunk of France, the farm, this giant house plus the guesthouse. Where he had pretended to be a guest.

"Marthe-Louise." Her tone was harsher than she had planned and Marthe-Louise shrank back. Lily took a breath. "What is Jack's real name?"

The older woman frowned. "Jacques Charles Olivier Fortanier Montford. Comte de Brissard."

De Brissard. The lavender family. *"Comte?"* She'd never heard that name before.

"In English, *count*. His mother is the Dowager Countess de Brissard."

Lily made a choking noise. "Royalty?" That jerk. He had said the de Brissards were a dull lot, and not to bother writing about them. No wonder.

"Oh, no." The older lady chuckled, relieved to give Lily some good news for once. "Nobility."

"Oh, is that all?" Lily gave an appalled laugh. "Good grief. I should have been curtsying before getting into bed with him."

Marthe-Louise had caught the gist of Lily's statement and pulled her wide cheeks back in a nervous grin. "Ah, the food—it burns." She scurried away before Lily could say that it didn't smell like anything was even cooking.

The mythical food wasn't the only thing burning—so was Lily's temper. She glared at the photo of the lying Comte de Brissard and stalked through the kitchen and out the back door.

She hit the stone pathway leading from the kitchen garden to the guesthouse.

Jack was walking shirtless down the hill from the lavender fields, wiping his face with a cloth, bits of lavender blossom and twigs stuck to his chest and back. "Ah, *chérie,* there you are. Did you get a lot accomplished this afternoon? I hope so, because I have plans for *you* this evening."

He smelled of lavender and sun and heat. Yummy. She tamped down any wayward twinges of desire. She was mad at him and had to remember that. "Hello, Your Royal Highness."

"Oh." He stopped. "Lily, I was going to tell you, but the time was never right and then…" He tried to hug her but she pushed him away.

"Forget it! You can go be a sweaty field hand for all I care. I never thought it was such a hot look anyway."

"What?" He raised his eyebrows. "It *is* hot outside."

"Never mind!" Lily tapped her foot. "Any other secrets I should know about?"

He looked away guiltily.

"Oh, *milord,* now what? Are you next in line for the French throne?"

"I wouldn't take that job for a million euros. Look what happened to Louis the Sixteenth." He laughed but quickly became serious at her cold gaze. "Nothing so glamorous.

My training for disaster-relief work is in medicine. I'm a physician. They want me to go to Malaysia, but I told them no this morning. I'm staying in Provence."

Lily exhaled a long breath and slowly circled him.

He stared at her warily, craning his head over his shoulders. "What is it?"

"Looking for either a halo or a superhero cape."

"Lily…" He held out his hands to her.

"No wonder you knew the names of all those tropical diseases. You probably teach a course in that stuff."

"Some seminars at the tropical medicine institute in Paris," he admitted.

"A professor, as well. And yet you have time to chat with the rest of us mere mortals. How ever do you do it?"

He set his jaw. "And you wonder why I don't tell everyone about my background?"

"I am *everyone*. That's really nice."

"You know what I mean. You're more than that."

"So you should have told me. Madame Finch should have told me."

"I asked her not to. I wanted you to get to know the real me, and I wasn't sure if you'd be thrilled or repulsed at my circumstances."

"Lots of gold diggers?"

"Another entirely appropriate American saying." He took her hand, but she let her arm dangle loosely. "But I knew from the beginning that you weren't like that. In fact, from what you said, you didn't care for rich men anyway. I was afraid you would lump me in with them and not see me for myself."

"I would have seen you for yourself," she protested.

He shook his head. "What if I had said, 'I am the Comte de Brissard, physician and nobleman. Come to my luxurious villa in Provence where I can woo you with my worldly riches'?"

Lily automatically made a face and he pounced. "You see? That would have been your honest reaction and that would have been the end of any possibilities between us."

She considered her gut reaction and admitted he was probably right. "But that doesn't mean you should have waited until I found out. You could have told me you were a doctor when we talked about infectious diseases. And you could have told me you owned this whole place when we first came here."

"I know, *mon coeur,* and I am so sorry. My only excuse is selfishness. I did not want to risk having you leave me before we got to know each other, but I should have been up-front and honest with you as soon as possible."

"Yes, you should have." But she wasn't so angry anymore. "And I'm actually more impressed with your education. You had to earn that, not inherit it."

"Exactly." He smiled in relief. "I am not ashamed of my heritage, but the title of Comte de Brissard would have fallen to me if I were the biggest idiot in France. But being a physician, that is my real accomplishment." He tugged her closer. "And that is why I appreciate your hard work, as well. You are a writer, an entrepreneur. You are not relying on any family wealth or connections to succeed."

"Oh, Jack." She blushed a bit but rallied. "No more secrets." She started to shake her finger at him but instead started picking lavender bits off his firm, sweaty chest.

"I promise." He leaned down to kiss her but she turned away at a sudden loud engine noise. "What is that?"

Jack's eyes bugged out. "Oh, no."

"What?"

"Look, promise me you'll take the next ten minutes with a grain of salt."

"Oh, come on, are we in a soap opera? If you have an evil twin or are getting over amnesia, I swear I'm leaving right now. I knew I should have looked you up on Google, but you said you kept yourself off the internet."

"As much as possible, but you would have gotten several hits." The engine got louder, traveling along in a cloud of dust so Lily couldn't see what was coming.

"Grrr." Lily felt like kicking herself. Crack Reporter-Girl had fallen down on the job.

A big silver Rolls-Royce pulled up in the driveway, looking exactly like the old TV ad. The window rolled down, but instead of a distinguished gray-haired gent asking for American-made French-style mustard, the middle-aged, *very* well-preserved Frenchwoman whom she'd seen in the family photo gave them a startled look before stepping out of the car. Lily dropped his hand.

She kissed him on both cheeks, skillfully avoiding his damp skin, then scolding him. "Oh, Jacques."

"Oh, *Maman*," he groaned. Lily was so shocked by everything that was happening that she almost missed the fashionable blonde sliding out from the backseat.

Almost. "If that's Jack's mother, then who are you?" Lily asked. "His sister?"

The blonde gave what might be called a tinkling laugh by writers more twee and fanciful than Lily, and Lily disliked her immediately. "Don't be ridiculous. I'm Nadine, his fiancée."

Lily's dislike for the blonde turned to hate. And Jack the Count wasn't far behind.

"WAIT!" JACK BELLOWED, seeing Lily sprint up the hill toward the guesthouse. His mother deftly blocked him as if she were some kind of American football linesman and he had to stutter-step past her. "*Maman,* please get out of my way."

"Jacques, we just got here. Nadine found your photo online on *Fashionista Magazine* and we recognized the birthmark on the back of your neck right away. Whoever that girl is who is calling you Pierre in her blog, she certainly is temperamental. Standing here shouting at you and then running away. Not very dignified, if I may say so."

"Forget about dignified, *Maman.* What are you doing here? What is Nadine doing here?"

"Making sure you're all right." She lowered her voice. "Nadine says the dysentery can affect your brain." The last word came out in a horrified whisper.

Damn Nadine for scaring his mother. "Dysentery affects your guts, not your brain, and besides, where did Nadine go to medical school anyway?"

"You know I'm concerned about you, Jacques." She made as if to embrace him but realized he had dead plant matter all over his sticky skin. Lily would have hugged him anyway if she'd thought he had a brain disease. Nadine would probably welcome a bit of brain damage in him, preferably in his frontal lobe to destroy his long-term memory of all the crappy things she'd done to him.

He gave her a hard look and ran after Lily. She was moving at a good clip, but he caught up to her when she slowed for a corner. "Lily, wait!"

She spun to face him. "Another woman, and you didn't think to mention this, either." She gave him a disappointed stare. "What did I do to you to deserve this?" She gestured at the house. "Not trusting me to tell me who you actually are. And after I was so careful to keep you anonymous in my blog. Apparently I could have made much more money by revealing your true identity to one of the tabloids and giving them all the inside gossip."

"I wanted you to like me for myself. And we're not engaged anymore."

"Right. I bet if I went on Google, I could find your engagement announcement."

"Yes, but—"

"Weak, weak, weak!" she blurted.

"It's the truth."

"And," she continued as if she hadn't heard him, "not only do you have a fiancée, but she's an upperclass blonde bitch. Well, at least she was pretty bitchy to me, but then again, I'd be bitchy to a woman who I was pretty sure was sleeping with my husband-to-be."

She turned her back to him and stalked in the door of the guesthouse.

"She's not my—!" Jack was distracted suddenly by the Rolls rolling up the driveway. The blonde bitch popped out. "Go away, Nadine."

"This heat is bothering your mother. She was feeling faint, so I left her on that cute bench in front of the house."

"What? Did you at least get her a glass of water? Is she going to pass out and hit her head on the stone?"

Nadine widened her eyes as if she'd never considered any consequences to her actions, which she probably hadn't. "My goodness, Jacques, maybe we should get back down to her. Marthe-Louise won't know what to do if your mother goes into heat shock."

"Heat stroke," he corrected automatically. "I'll have Marthe-Louise mix her some homemade rehydration solution." But Lily was in the guesthouse, upset and hurting. He ran in the door and shouted her name.

"Go away, Jack!" she shouted. It sounded like she was upstairs.

"Lily, my mother needs me—wait for me." Nadine was

tugging on his arm so he left, casting an anguished look upstairs.

"Here, take the Rolls," Nadine told him. "I'll walk down in a minute." His ex bundled him into the car and he directed the chauffeur to take him to the manor house.

He'd fix up his mother and then he'd fix up his mess with Lily.

"LILY?" A FEMALE French voice called her name.

Lily came out from the bedroom and peered over the railing. Nadine stood in the foyer staring up at her with a pitying glance. If there was anything Lily hated in the world more than humiliation, it was pity. She took the offensive. "So you're Jack's fiancée."

"Jack?" She gave that nerve-grating laugh again. "Ah, Jacques and that American phase he went through."

Lily squeezed the railing hard, not liking the idea that she was a continuation of his "American phase," whatever that had been. "He never mentioned you." That was the closest she could come to apologizing for inadvertently committing premarital adultery.

Nadine shrugged and climbed the stairs, Lily's stomach falling with every step. "Jacques and I have a different relationship than you are accustomed to." She reached the top landing and stood eye to eye with Lily.

Next to the Frenchwoman's perfectly tailored cream-colored linen pants, white T-shirt and French designer silk scarf knotted chicly around her neck, Lily's own outfit fell sadly short—cutoff khaki shorts and pink tourist T-shirt with a big black camera and strap silk-screened on it that she'd bought for herself as a gag gift.

But she tried to rally. She was not the high school's token poor girl anymore. "What kind of relationship *do* you have?"

Nadine smiled gently. "Jacques was not himself when he came back from Borneo."

"Burma," Lily corrected. Geez, didn't she know what country in which he'd been deathly ill? "And you didn't fly out to be with him when he was so sick?"

Shock and disgust flared in her crystal-blue eyes but she quickly dampened it. "I didn't have all my immunizations, and I knew Jacques wouldn't want me to become ill, as well."

"Hmmph." Lily would have risked it.

"He needed space and a way to, how to say it? Blow off steam." She gave Lily a meaningful look. "I knew very well what he might do once out here in the country. He gets the physical appetites of a peasant."

Ah, and Lily was the peasant pressure release valve. Did Nadine *not* like "blowing off steam" with Jack? Was she nuts? Or as cold in bed as she seemed outside of it? "Look, I don't know how the French nobility does things, but you don't seem very upset that he has cheated on you."

"Men do what they must." Catching the doubt in Lily's eyes, she raised her eyebrows. "But perhaps you doubt me? I *am* here with his mother, after all."

Lily pursed her lips.

"You would like proof we are engaged? You of course may ask Jacques himself, if you are inclined to a messy and upsetting conversation." She pulled her phone out of her purse and pressed it a few times. "Here is our engagement photo."

Lily unwillingly looked at the small digital display. Yes, it was Jacques in that formal tux-and-tails outfit, complete with sash across his chest, tastefully embracing Nadine, dressed in an ice-blue satin ballgown.

"And here is the notice of our engagement in the Paris newspaper." She typed for a minute and brought up a newspaper webpage written in French, of course, but their names and the words *fiancé, fiancée* and *le mariage* were mentioned several times.

There it was in black-and-white on the web. She cleared her throat. "And you still want to marry him despite the fact he cheated on you?" This didn't make sense. Jack was scrupulously honest.

Except that he had lied about what he did for a living, lied about his real name and lied about his family owning a good chunk of Provence.

So much for scrupulously honest. She shook her head. Had she ever really known him?

Nadine waved her nicely manicured hand—French-manicured, of course. "We will, naturally, have much to discuss. But I am a forgiving woman. Jacques already told me about you. He said you are trying to be a writer."

"I try." Nadine needed to leave before Lily biffed her.

"Jacques says someday if you get lucky, you may be able to get a real writing job."

"He said that?" That really stung. Her blog and the articles for the *Fashionista Magazine* website wouldn't earn the Nobel Prize for Literature, but, dammit, she wrote carefully and put a lot of effort into them.

"Although every tourist who comes to France dabbles in travel writing, you were luckier than most and found your own personal tour guide."

"Right. But I think my tour is over."

"Good, I had hoped you will understand that he and I need some time together." Nadine gazed meaningfully at the open bedroom door, which showed Lily's clothes tossed on a chair.

"I understand." Lily headed into the bedroom, blinking hard.

Nadine followed her. Why didn't she back off and leave

Lily alone? She'd go as soon as she could pack. But how would she leave? They were in the country, several miles from the nearest train station. "I'll have to get a ride to the train." Not that she wanted to run into Jack, rather *Jacques,* again.

"The driver will take you," Nadine quickly offered. "You can ride in the Rolls-Royce. You will like it, your first ride in a Rolls."

Lily didn't bother to tell her she used to ride in one to school if Mrs. Wyndham was out of town. "Fine. Now, if you don't mind…"

Nadine made a graceful gesture and wafted out of the room, her heels clicking on the steps.

Lily chucked her clothes into her suitcase and grabbed her toiletries. She spotted the lavender perfume from the Count de Brissard's special AOC fields and dropped the bottle into the wastebasket. That kind of souvenir she didn't need.

Her shredded heart was enough.

16

JACK'S MOTHER WAS nowhere in sight as the Rolls dropped him off. He ran into the manor-house kitchen. "Marthe-Louise, where is my mother?"

She looked up from her pots and pans, startled. "What?"

"My mother. Where is she?"

Marthe-Louise gestured upstairs. "In her rooms. She said she was feeling the heat…."

Jack headed upstairs two at a time. "*Maman, Maman,* are you ill?"

There was no answer at her door, so he opened it. His mother was stretched out on her bed with a wet washcloth on her forehead. He crossed the wide room to put one hand on her forehead and the other around her wrist to check her pulse.

She lifted the cloth and stared at him. "Jacques, what are you doing?"

"Nadine said you were getting heat exhaustion."

"What?" She batted his hands away and he'd noticed she'd changed into a lightweight caftan, or muumuu, or whatever they called it. "I always get a touch of the heat when I am forced to come to the South in the middle of the summer."

Jacques decided not to point out she regularly came to the Riviera that time of year, but probably the sea breezes and glamour helped.

"Marthe-Louise gave me a cool drink and sent me upstairs to rest. But heat exhaustion?" She gave a tiny laugh, covering her eyes again. "Don't be ridiculous. And what are you doing with that American girl?" She laughed again. "Never mind, if you and Nadine have an agreement, it is none of your *maman's* business."

Jacques shook his head. "*Maman,* Nadine and I have no agreement because we are not engaged anymore."

She sat upright, the cloth falling onto her mouth. She tossed it aside impatiently. "What?"

"*Maman,* I told you we broke up before I left for Burma."

She waved her hand impatiently. "She told me that was a lovers' spat."

He shook his head. "I won't tell you all the details, but Nadine cheated on me. I caught her."

She stared at him with narrowed blue eyes. "She did?"

"*Oui.* I didn't want to tell you because…"

"Because you were terribly hurt."

Jack shrugged, lifting his hands in a helpless gesture. More relieved than hurt once the shock had worn off, but still…

"Jacques! Always when you are hurt you are crawling away to lick your wounds in private." She puffed in exasperation. "And you do not think to tell your poor *maman?* I invite that *salope* to your party. Oh, *mon dieu,* no wonder you run away. Your poor heart, it was broken, and to find the cause of it standing in your own home." She threw back her head in an anguished gesture.

"Really, I am fine now.…"

"And now that you have found *l'amour* again with the

American girl— She isn't a bimbo you picked up, is she, Jack?"

He shook his head, trying to stifle a startled snicker at Lily being called a bimbo.

"Now that you have found love," his mother continued, "your own mother brings the lying piece of trash who broke your heart back into your country home. Ah!" She clutched at the breast of her muumuu, or caftan. "How can you ever forgive me?"

"I forgive you, *Maman*," he answered truthfully. His mother may have been a drama queen, but she was sincere in her efforts.

She cast away the wet cloth and jumped out of bed. Jack followed her. "Where is that awful girl? Nadine? Nadine?" She descended the stairs, shouting for his ex. Nadine appeared from the salon with a fashion magazine, having wisely decided to stay away from the kitchen, a pissed-off Marthe-Louise and her collection of sharp utensils.

"Oh, madame, you're feeling better. Jacques and I were worried that the heat was making you sick."

"You better worry about yourself, *ma petite*." It wasn't an endearment. "How dare you lie to me—twice—about being affianced to my son? After what you did to him, with whomever you did it." His mother looked at him for more information but he shook his head.

His mother continued, obviously disappointed at the lack of details. "He is a good and brave man who deserves a decent woman, and you are not the woman for him. Get out!" She flung her arm to point to the front door.

Jack was torn between the desire to clap at her stage-worthy (but genuine) performance as Outraged Mother and the desire to get back to the guesthouse and smooth things over with Lily. Option two won. "*Maman,* you deal with her. I have to talk with Lily."

Nadine gave him a half smile. "Oh, I'm sorry. She left."

"Lily left?" He seriously considered throttling Nadine. "What did you say to her?"

"We chatted." Her half smile pulled into a smirk. "She decided she wanted to return to Paris. I suppose the slow, rural pace wasn't to her liking."

"That's not true," he snapped. "She loves it here—loves Provence, loves the lavender farm."

"Obviously not, or she would have stayed," she answered.

"And how did Lily leave?"

"The Rolls." Nadine started to get defensive as she realized how angry he was getting. "She insisted. She said she wasn't going to stick around this dusty, hot place in the middle of nowhere and wanted to hurry back to Paris. I think she wanted to shop for clothes." She wrinkled her nose. "She certainly needs some help in that area."

Now he knew she was lying. Lily hadn't bothered to shop much when she was in Paris the first time, preferring to concentrate on the people and sights. "You better hope the chauffeur unloaded your luggage because you're taking the train back to Paris, not Lily. Now do as my mother says and get out. You and I are going to the local train station."

"Jacques, wait!" his mother called.

"No, *Maman,* I've waited too long to meet someone like Lily, and I'm not going to wait any longer."

His mother gave him a sweet smile. "Nor should you, my treasure. But you need a shirt, do you not?"

"Oh." He glanced down at his bare chest, still damp with lavender florets stuck here and there. He pounded upstairs to his rarely used boyhood room. "Nadine, you better really hope she's still there, or…or…I'll think of something nasty."

He yanked open a drawer in his dressing room and

grabbed the first T-shirt he found, pulling it over his head. It was snug since he'd filled out quite a bit since he'd last worn his scouting jamboree shirt, but he didn't care.

He ran down the stairs and found his mother nose to nose with Nadine.

"My son may be nice, but I am not. If you have driven this Lily away, you can be sure that I will ruin you."

For the first time, Nadine started to look worried. His mother continued, "You may as well move to Burma because you will never get invited anywhere, you will sit behind a column at the opera house and you will never, *ever* get your photo in the society page again. What is the English term for that, Jacques?"

"Blackball?"

"Yes, how appropriate. Social *death*," Maman hissed. "And you know I will do it."

Nadine was pale and quivering by then. Jack rolled his eyes. He couldn't imagine Lily even caring about those things, as long as they were together.

"Go, go." His mother flapped her arms at them. "And you—*don't* come back," she told Nadine.

JACK GRIPPED THE steering wheel of the small rental car, Nadine's luggage stuffed to the ceiling and jammed into the trunk. Lily hadn't answered her phone, so he was racing to catch her in person.

Nadine sat next to him, her arms crossed over her chest. Their trip had been rather predictable, first filled with begging and pleading, then accusations and insults and finally a sullen silence that he welcomed.

He slowed down as he reached the village, driving as quickly as was safe over the narrow streets, which were still made of stone in parts. He stopped in front of the nineteenth-century train station and jumped out, dodging old ladies with their market baskets and tourists with maps.

"What about me?" Nadine screeched.

He pointed to the large timetable posted. "Get a ticket because you're not staying here."

He ran to the ticket office. "When did the last train leave?"

The older man inside checked the clock. "It has been two hours."

"Good." He sagged in relief. Lily had to be somewhere around here. "When does the next train leave?"

"For where, monsieur?"

"Anywhere."

"The train to Avignon leaves in ten minutes."

Jack thanked him and moved away, scanning the small crowd gathering to board. If she got to Avignon, he wouldn't be able to catch up. The high-speed train would take her to Paris in a few hours, and hundreds of flights left Paris every day.

If Lily had left France, he would follow her to Philadelphia. He would follow her to the ends of the earth—after all, he knew his way around them by now.

17

LILY STOOD ON the train platform, the French conversations buzzing around her like the cicadas in the lavender fields of the great de Brissard family. Damn Jack. Her mother's words about unexpected heartbreak from a nice man had been prophetic. It just showed that only a person you trusted could betray you so painfully.

Her backpack weighed on her shoulders as if she had bricks in it, but she knew it was the weight of her disappointment and sadness. When was that dumb train coming? If she had to stand around much longer, she'd either scream or burst into tears. Or both.

"Lily, Lily! Wait!" Jack sprinted toward her.

"Go away." Her voice quivered a bit on the last syllable.

"Lily, don't cry."

She pulled off her sunglasses to show him her dry, extremely angry eyes. "I am not crying. I haven't cried over anything but babies and puppies for years. Certainly not *men*."

"Nadine is a liar."

"Apparently she is also lazy." Lily spotted the blonde bitch standing next to the rental car, halfheartedly tugging at a small carry-on bag while she looked around for some unsuspecting male idiot to save her. Well, welcome to the real world, sister. No man was going to ride up on his white horse to make everything all right. Or drive up in a white rental car.

"I was engaged to her, it's true. But that ended abruptly right before I left for Burma when I found her with another man. In our bed."

Lily winced. Even though she was mad at Jack, it was an appalling image, even more appalling than the image in front of her. "Good grief, what on earth are you wearing?"

He looked down at himself. The red cotton looked spray-painted on, several inches of abdomen showing between his waistline and his T-shirt hem. It looked as if he had borrowed it from a thirteen-year-old. "My scout T-shirt from when I went to the big jamboree."

She peered at the silk-screened date. "Fifteen years ago?"

He shrugged. "I've filled out a bit since then. It was the first shirt I could find upstairs."

"You had plenty of shirts at the guesthouse."

His brown eyes darkened. "I couldn't waste a single minute getting to you."

Lily's traitorous heart thawed the tiniest bit but fought it. Stay strong, she told herself. "What do you want, Jack?"

"You."

She scoffed. "Well, duh. I know you want me. You couldn't keep your hands off me."

"Not just that, my Lily. I want you—all of you—forever."

"Not forever. I'm a summer fling. Nadine said so."

"You yourself said she was a liar."

Lily bit her lip. "So are you."

"Lying to you has been the biggest mistake of my life."

She narrowed her eyes, trying to judge his sincerity. But what was she thinking? She had to get away, get out of France.

Where was that freaking train?

Jack held out his hand. "Please, Lily. Come back with me. No more secrets. You can meet my mother and she can tell you every embarrassing thing that ever happened to me and every shameful mistake I've ever made."

"I can't stay until Christmas, you know." The quip slipped out before she remembered she was still furious with him.

He laughed but quickly turned serious. "You could, you know."

She shrugged. "And do what?"

"Stay with me. Marry me," he blurted.

"What?" she shrieked. He had some nerve. Her first marriage proposal was not in a fancy restaurant with a bottle of champagne and a diamond ring in a black velvet box. Instead, she was in a crowded, smelly French train station getting a throwaway desperation proposal from a man she wanted to hate, a man who lied to her, a man who wore a fifteen-year-old scout jamboree T-shirt.

He looked as shocked as she was but rallied. "Yes, yes, I mean it. Marry me, Lily."

They were drawing a crowd. No doubt thanks to Jack's local celebrity status.

Lily spotted a wooden bench tucked into an alcove and headed for it. "Get over here."

He followed, and when she spun to face him, he had a big grin on his face. "What are you smiling about?"

"You and me."

"There is no 'you and me,'" she informed him. "There is a Lily Adams and there is a Count Jacques Montford."

"You could be my countess," he said enticingly.

"Ack! And be called 'milady Lily'? It sounds like a brand of bras."

"You could start one if you wanted."

"Stop, all right? Stop trying to bribe me with noble titles, lavender farms and bra companies."

"What, then? What can I bribe you with?"

Himself. But she didn't say that out loud. Or did she? His grin disappeared.

"Myself?"

Crap.

"Isn't that what I said?" she decided to bluff.

"Yes. And actually, that is why I portrayed myself as a plain aid worker in a borrowed guesthouse. Because I am not accustomed to people looking beyond the trappings of my life and judging me for myself."

"Right. Because everyone is so shallow they can't separate you from your money."

He shrugged. "Society can be that way. You grew up in it. Didn't you know people like that?"

"Yes. But you had plenty of chances to come clean with me once you knew me—and you didn't." That was the part that upset her the most. "I told you all about my childhood."

"Not all. Why do you dislike people with property, people with some money? Was she unkind to you, the lady your mother works for?"

"Her? No." Lily looked away, not wanting to discuss it.

"Who?" he prodded.

She set her jaw. "I survived the prep school, all right? I was almost out of there but got a crush on one of the rich, good-looking guys my senior year. He invited me to prom, I was over the moon, and he saw stars when he tried to convince me forcefully to sleep with me after the dance."

Jack took a step toward her. A muscle in his cheek twitched.

"Fortunately for me, I grew up working hard and lifting heavy objects. And our gardener had studied in Japan and taught me some self-defense techniques."

The muscle finally stopped twitching. "Dare I hope he dropped you at home sadder and wiser?"

"Definitely sadder—and sorer. But I don't know about wiser." Especially since his brains were obviously in his balls, which had come out on the losing end with her pointy-toed shoes.

"Probably not. His kind rarely learn." He studied her for a minute.

She twisted her hands together. "And yes, now I know that not all rich guys are like that, but after years of low-level harassment followed up by that one incident, it was too much for me to handle."

Jack nodded. "I understand. But pretend I am not a rich man. How do you feel about me?"

She stared at him, mute with sudden panic.

"Maybe that is not a fair question until you know how I really feel about myself."

A train whistle echoed. Jack gave her a stricken look. "Lily, pass me your train ticket."

"What?"

"Stay to hear me out. Please. Then if you still want to leave, I'll take you to Avignon myself. Or Paris, or wherever you want to go."

She nodded, even though she'd spent practically all her cash on hand on the ticket. But something was telling her to stay as he had asked her. Not ordered, and had even said please. She handed him the ticket and to her surprise he ran away.

He was with Nadine and Lily almost got up then and there to leave, but instead he offered Lily's ticket to the blonde and pointed to the train that was pulling into the station.

Nadine shook her head but Jack jabbed the ticket at her and made several very French, emphatic gestures. She clutched at his T-shirt, but it was so tight she couldn't get a grip. Lily muffled a snicker. That was the type of woman who wouldn't see anything but the exterior. If Jack weren't a doctor, or count or just plain wealthy, Nadine wouldn't be caught dead with a man who wore the T-shirt equivalent of a tube top.

Lily stared at them for any signs of lingering affection and only saw disgust on his face and desperation on Nadine's. She tried to reach up to kiss him on each cheek but he backed away, a deliberate rejection in a culture where people regularly kissed casual acquaintances.

Nadine snatched the ticket from his hand and turned her back on him. The train doors opened and she climbed aboard. Jack, gentleman to the last, handed her luggage after her. Then he came back to Lily, not waiting to see the train depart.

He focused straight on her and the noise of the train and all the passengers receded. "Walk with me, Lily." He took her backpack and pulled her suitcase behind him as they left the station.

"Where are we going?"

"Turn left here." They were in the village square and he chose a seat underneath the giant plane tree. This one was much older than any New World specimens, its low, wide branches reaching fifty feet across and with gently peeling gray paper bark.

"I know how I feel about you, Lily, and this is how I feel about myself." He took a deep breath. "When I was sick in Myanmar, I lost my authority, my dignity, everything. I wasn't Dr. Jacques Montford, Count of Brissard.

I was just another body lying on a cot, unable to move to even care for myself."

"That's horrible." Lily couldn't imagine the conditions he'd been under.

He made an impatient gesture. "It was, but it humbled me. I was used to striding through the camps, stopping to help almost as if I were a Greek god descending from Mt. Olympus to help the mere mortals below."

"Hubris."

"Exactly—overweening arrogance." He shrugged sadly. "But I didn't see it in myself until my outer pretensions were stripped away. I had come to Myanmar to help the people there, but they helped me. Several of them took turns nursing me, giving me spoonfuls of clean water and rehydration salts, changing my bedding, bathing me.

"I had had everything, but I only gave crumbs of myself to them. They had nothing, but they gave everything of themselves to me." He blinked rapidly. "How could I have gone so many years and not seen what a failure I was? What a sham?"

Lily took his hand. "You were not a failure. When you are in a terrible situation trying to help people, you cannot give your whole self away. You'd break down, experience burnout, despair even. You *must* conserve yourself so you can go on to the next disaster in one piece."

"But the arrogance," he protested.

She squeezed his hand. "Stop the presses. Who ever heard of an arrogant doctor? Hey, that reminds me of a great American joke. What's the difference between God and a doctor?"

"What?" he muttered. She could tell he had a good idea of the punch line.

"God doesn't think he's a doctor." Lily raised her eyebrows. "Add to the fact you're a hereditary nobleman whose family has ruled over a large chunk of France for the past thousand years and it's a wonder you haven't tried parting the Mediterranean off the coast of Nice and walking to Corsica."

"Lily!" She'd startled a laugh from him.

"It's true." She plopped her hands on her hips. "I grew up with a lot of rich people who only thought they were nobility, but there was nothing noble about them. I can spot an arrogant phony ten miles away, and you, milord, are about the farthest from being an arrogant phony that there is."

"Then you do care for me."

She still wasn't ready to say it, but she forced herself to anyway. "I guess you could say that because I love you, Jack."

His face lit up. "You do?"

"Yes," she muttered. "That's what made this whole situation so painful. I thought you were this sweet, save-the-world kind of guy, and then you wound up having all this baggage."

Instead of being insulted, he threw back his head and laughed. "Oh, Lily, Lily, only you would call it baggage. That's what I love about you."

She lifted her eyebrow. "That didn't count. What do you love about me?"

"I love *everything* about you," he clarified. "I love how you want to know everything about everybody. I love how you love Provence—the food, the people, the land. I love your writing."

"Are you sure? Because Nadine said—"

He said a bad French word that even she knew. "Forget about her. I love your writing, and I love you."

"Me."

"Of course, you. I fell in love with you as soon as you

bumped into me and asked me about your French accent. Madame Finch knew right away. When we were web chatting with her, she said our meeting was a true *coup de foudre*. Do you remember that?"

She nodded. "What is that—a lightning bolt, or something sudden?"

"It's also slang for love at first sight," he told her, a faint blush staining his cheeks.

She wrapped her arms around his waist. "Oh, Jack, how romantic. I think I fell in love with you when you showed up clean-shaven and promised to act the gentleman with me."

He groaned. "I failed on that part."

"And I'm glad." She tilted her face up and he accepted her invitation, kissing her. Their mouths met as they clung to each other under the shady tree. It was a promise of past, present and future intertwined together.

He finally broke their kiss. "You didn't give me an answer."

"About…?" she answered hazily.

"Marrying me, *ma petite*." He traced his finger down her cheek.

"That? You were just saying that to get my attention."

"No." Jack shook his head. "I meant it then, and now that I am certain you love me, I mean it even more. We can fly back to Philadelphia and marry there so you can have your mother with you. Every bride wants her mother on her wedding day."

"But, but…" she sputtered. "People like you don't get married like that. Don't you have to have a big, fancy wedding with the local bishop and invite every nobleman in Europe?"

"If you met some of those so-called noblemen, you could see why I wouldn't invite them to a flea market.

I will invite my best friends and they will be thrilled to come. And," he added, "your cousin cannot travel for many months now and even until after her baby is born. You need her as your matron of honor."

"Sarah." Lily bit her lip. She had been Sarah's maid of honor and Sarah had vowed to return the favor. "But wait! I haven't even agreed to marry you. And you were already engaged to Nadine. What if this doesn't work out, either?"

"She was the biggest mistake of my life and I thank my lucky stars I found out in time." He dropped to one knee and took Lily's hand. "But you, you are perfect for me. You are brave, honest and true, my Golden Lily. Be my bride. My wife."

She stared down at him, her mind racing. Never in a million years had she expected to find anyone as perfect for her as Jack. "Yes, Jack, I'll marry you."

The joy that burst across his face was contagious, and she started to laugh. He jumped to his feet and pulled her into his arms. "Oh, Lily, sweetheart." He peppered her face with kisses. "I am the happiest man in the world."

"Me, too. I mean…" She laughed again, and he caught her up and twirled her around on the sidewalk.

He set her down. "Lily, would you consider living here in Provence for the next year or so? Jean-Claude and I have several new projects for the farm but he needs my help."

"Hmm." She pretended to think it over. "The south of France year-round? The fabulous food, beautiful views and great weather?"

"It does get chilly in the winter," he warned her.

"Will you keep me warm?" She kissed his neck.

"Sizzling hot," he promised.

"I'll do it." She stood on tiptoes and captured his mouth. "Oh!" She jerked her head back.

"What?" He looked as if he expected her to change her mind. Silly man. It was too late for him to back out now.

"A cookbook! Marthe-Louise and I can do a cookbook."

"Wonderful." Jack smiled down at her. *"Cooking with the Comtesse de Brissard."*

"Good grief. I'm going to be a countess? What about your mother?"

"Sorry. It's automatic when you marry a count. And my mother has been the Dowager Countess de Brissard since my father passed away, so you won't take her title away from her." He wrapped his arm around her shoulder. "I'll introduce you to my friend George's fiancée. It could be worse—she's going to be a crown princess."

"George is a prince? What's Frank, then? A baron?"

"He's a duke."

"Jack!" She elbowed him in the side. "Any more surprises?"

"Only good ones." He kissed the top of her head. "I'll show you the family jewels later."

"I thought you already did." She winked at him and he roared in laughter.

"Ah, Lily, Lily. You are so good for me."

"And you are for me." She snuggled into him. "Take me home, Jack."

"Home to our lavender farm."

"Home to our new life together."

Epilogue

JACK WAVED TO Lily, who was doing lazy laps in the back-yard pool at the manor house, and sat down in a chair with his phone.

She swam to the side and rested her elbows on the tile.

"Lily, are we still good for next Saturday?"

"Trying to back out already?" She shook her wet head, darkened to honey by the pool water.

"Never." He would never back out, never give her up.

"Then call your friends. My mother has the chapel booked, and Mrs. Wyndham is hosting the wedding dinner in her house for us."

"As long as your mother and stepfather won't be catering it. They are guests of honor."

"No, they hired their usual outside caterer." She shook her head. "Jack, I can't believe it. Are we crazy for trying to get married in under two weeks?"

He knelt at the edge of the pool and kissed her wet, silky lips. "Crazy in love."

"Good." She swam away, her lithe tan body cutting through the aqua-blue water.

He sat back cross-legged on the pool deck to admire

her for a few seconds and then dialed George first, then got Frank on the line, as well.

After the usual round of greetings and jokes, he came to the purpose of his conversation. "I want you both and Stevie to come to Philadelphia next Saturday."

"Philadelphia? Are we visiting the Liberty Bell?" George asked.

"They do have good cheesesteaks there, George. Mmm," Frank hummed in anticipation.

"Mmm, indeed. Renata, Stevie and I will be in New York, so it would be possible for us, but why should we come to Philadelphia Saturday?"

"Lily and I are getting married," Jack announced proudly.

The brief silence was broken by both his friends offering their warm congratulations. Jack thanked them. "You don't sound very surprised."

Frank laughed. "We knew you were a goner as soon as you told us about her. It was rather entertaining to hear you lose your cool like that."

"Frank," George chided him.

Frank began to hum the melody from "Another One Bites the Dust," and Jack rolled his eyes. "I'm glad my heartache was amusing for you."

"Ignore him," George commanded. "I have a feeling he'll get what's coming to him soon."

Jack laughed as Frank abruptly stopped mid-note. "Frank, come to Philly. You can meet my new countess and get a cheesesteak all in one trip."

"Forget the cheesesteaks. I can't wait to meet Lily," Frank promised. "George, I'll fly into New York and ride down with you and the ladies."

"This won't be our only celebration. Lily and I will have a small ceremony here in the lavender-farm chapel during the harvest festival this fall," Jack explained. "So we can invite all the people here in Provence whom we we care about."

George asked, "But what does your mother say, Jack? I imagine she had a huge wedding planned for one of the big Parisian cathedrals."

"She's coming to Philadelphia, and I promised her a huge reception in Paris this winter during the society season."

"And then Stevie's wedding next June. A wedding for all four seasons." Frank hummed "Here Comes the Bride."

"I'll make sure you catch the bouquet, Frank."

Frank made a choking sound and they all laughed.

"Anyway, guys, come as soon as you can. Lily plans to call Renata to see if she has any ready-to-wear dresses."

"For her, anything," George promised. "Our gift to the bride. If you love her, then she is our family, as well."

Jack swallowed hard. "Thank you."

Frank cleared his throat as if it had tightened, as well. "Give me the address and I'll ship out a case of our best sherry today. We'll drink a toast together in Philadelphia."

"Although we are in three separate countries," George said, "I propose a toast today. To Jack and his bride."

"Hear, hear," cheered Frank. "To a woman as beautiful as her namesake and as patient as a saint to put up with our brother here."

"Hey!" Jack protested halfheartedly. "Well, you're right on both counts."

Lily swam across the pool and smiled invitingly up at him.

"Guys, I have to go now. Lily wants me."

George snorted.

"Ah, the bachelor life passes away with only a whimper," Frank lamented.

Lily floated onto her back and untied her green bikini top, tossing it at his feet. Jack bobbled his phone, catching it before he dropped it into the pool. "Ha! I think married life will be much more fun."

He turned off his phone on the chair and rapidly tossed off his clothes.

She gave him a smoldering glance. "Come on in, Jacky, it's warm and wet."

"I know." He slid into the water. "And so's the pool."

She giggled. "You are so bad."

"You haven't seen anything yet." He found the ties to her bikini bottom and easily removed it.

"DID HE HANG up, George?"

"I believe so, Frank."

"He is a goner, just as I said last week."

"You were right, Frank. And you're next. Renata and I and Jack and Lily will dance at your wedding someday soon."

"Ha!"

"Ha, yourself. I have a feeling, Frank. And you know my maternal grandmother was a fortune-teller."

"Then why can't you ever pick the World Cup winner?"

"Never works for personal gain, old friend."

"Hmmph. Kiss Renata for me."

"I will. *Ciao,* Frank."

"*Ciao,* George."

* * * * *

COMING SOON!

We really hope you enjoyed reading this book. If you're looking for more romance, be sure to head to the shops when new books are available on

Thursday
14th June

To see which titles are coming soon, please visit
millsandboon.co.uk

LET'S TALK
Romance

For exclusive extracts, competitions
and special offers, find us online:

f facebook.com/millsandboon

⊙ @millsandboonuk

𝕏 @millsandboon

Or get in touch on 0844 844 1351*

For all the latest titles coming soon, visit
millsandboon.co.uk/nextmonth